Praise for The Fleur Trilogy

For *The History of My Body*

"A delicious meal you won't want to end. Sharon Heath's sense of irony is both savory and sweet, transporting us into a world where the improbable is at once real and mysterious, and where the sparkly presence of a memorable girl named Fleur will remind you that true wisdom is born of innocence."
—**Jeremiah Abrams, author of *The Dreamtime Journey* and *Meeting the Shadow***

"Oh the joys and sorrows of inhabiting a young girl's body in the swish and swirl of sex, food, death, politics. Live them all here in their riotous complexity with Fleur, our historian of the body and the body politic."
—**Carolyn Raffensperger, *Science and Environmental Health Network***

"Fleur's capacity to leap from the sublime to the ridiculous and back in a heartbeat, her resilience, her intelligence, her love for the natural world and its creatures, her strenuous efforts to keep herself amused, alive, stimulated and out of the VOID are heartening signs of what our world needs."
—**Naomi Ruth Lowinsky, *News from the Muse***

For *Tizita*

"Heath (*The History of My Body*) continues the story of fictional young Nobel laureate Fleur Robins as she pursues matters of the heart as well as her cutting-edge physics research...Heath's adroit writing makes Fleur's remarkable life consistently captivating."
—***Publishers Weekly***

"Like Frodo and Sam in *Lord of the Rings*, the most vulnerable character in Heath's artfully constructed world, Fleur herself, is our best chance for the (at least partial) salvation that comes with understanding after a struggle. We cannot help but root for Fleur as we try to root for ourselves."

—**Joey Madia**, *Literary Aficionado*

"*Tizita*, like the first novel before it in the *Fleur Trilogy*, *The History of My Body*, is as utterly original as its chief protagonist Fleur Robins, and in some of the same brilliant, moving, and laugh-out-loud hilarious ways. Imagine a coming-of-age story intricately woven, like a bower bird's nest, of gorgeous bits of Ethiopian and Indian culture, *tikkun olam*, David Austin roses, Boson particles, geeky sex, climate change, quantum entanglements, African AIDS orphans, black holes, a chimp named Lord Hanuman, and baby birds—all into a pattern deeply informed by the wisdom of a seasoned Jungian analyst: That is *Tizita*."

—**Frances Hatfield**, *Psychological Perspectives*

Return of the Butterfly

The Fleur Trilogy, Book 3

by

Sharon Heath

Return of the Butterfly
The Fleur Trilogy, Book 3
Copyright 2018 Sharon Heath

This book is a work of fiction. While some of the place names may be real, characters and incidents are the product of the author's imagination and are used fictitiously. Any resemblance to events or persons living or dead is purely coincidental.

Author photograph by Marcella Kerwin.

Cover art: Sylvia Fein. Bound Together. 2013. Egg tempera on board, 40 x 30 inches. Collection of Dr. Jamie Anderson © 2018 Sylvia Fein.

Scriptures taken from the Holy Bible, New International Version®, NIV®. Copyright © 1973, 1978, 1984, 2011 by Biblica, Inc.™ Used by permission of Zondervan. All rights reserved worldwide.www.zondervan.com The "NIV" and "New International Version" are trademarks registered in the United States Patent and Trademark Office by Biblica, Inc.™

Library of Congress Contol Number: 2018965394
1. Contemporary fiction 2. Literary fiction
ISBN 10: 0-9979517-8-8
ISBN-13: 978-0-9979517-8-3
Thomas-Jacob Publishing, LLC, Deltona, Florida USA

Contact the publisher at TJPub@thomas-jacobpublishing.com.

In memory of my mother, Ethel Karson.

These are the days that must happen to you...

Walt Whitman, "Song of the Open Road"

Chapter One

ALMOST ANYWHERE YOU looked, the news was bad.

Honeybee colonies collapsing, school children killed in mass shootings, pesticides in breast milk, plastics strangling fish and fowl. Bigotry was blasting through the collective psyche like a cosmic flu, and western democracies were hemorrhaging. Too many claimed the sponsorship of one god or another to visit catastrophes upon places of worship, hospitals, concerts, marketplaces. And too many applauded their crimes, or used them for their own agendas, with unseemly enthusiasm. If, like me, you were of a scientific mind, you trembled at the mad race to release fossil fuels into a dangerously warming atmosphere. People popped mood lifters and anxiety quellers like candy, but there was no sugarcoating the state our species was in.

Gwennie had been pointing out for ages that the people of the earth had surrendered its bodies politic to sociopaths, its minds to meds and machines. This morning's offering was a particularly vehement variation on the theme. "The whole world's been bought off with hard and soft porn and glitzy gadgetry. Who can even form a complete, let alone original, thought with all these gizmos commandeering our attention? And so-called reality TV? Give me a break! That crap drains hearts and minds by the minute. Look at all the people who are prepared to vote for that man."

It was hard to argue. Naked bodies and naked greed were everywhere, but the naked soul stayed mostly hidden, mute, secret even to the bodies it inhabited. Some of Gwennie and Stanley's generation still croaked the old anthem, "All you need is love." But real sentiment these days seemed to be swirling down a drain composed of cynicism, denial, distraction, despair.

Yet I knew it wasn't for nothing that we humans, along with everything else the eye could discern (and all that it couldn't), were made of a great dusting of stars. Well, to be precise, dead stars. It was no less than the explosion of supernovas that swirled in a hummingbird's luminescent wing by a backyard bush. The rich blend of proteins, lipids, and nucleic acids expelled by a man relieving himself into his lover's tweeter and the copper-scented blood accompanying a baby's birth bore witness alike to the massive death throes of suns just like our own. Death begat life at every turn, and people still managed to survive grief, work hard, find humor, love, and—sometimes—a little meaning amid the static. Even as our species faced the all too real possibility of extinction, babies still got themselves born.

You'd think someone like yours truly, who'd been obsessed with the void since before she could speak and who'd funneled her fear into a fascination with science, would be able to maintain some semblance of objectivity about life at the edge of the precipice. But there were more things in heaven and earth, tra la, tra la. I couldn't seem to rid myself of the conviction that a cosmic drama was taking place between darkness and light, that how we maneuvered this odd moment mattered, not only to us and the eight or so million life forms on our planet, but also to the vast web of superclusters, filaments, and voids in which Earth, like one of Indra's mirroring jewels, hung suspended. And that, like each of us, I had my own urgent part to play.

So we begin where any story begins, which is anywhere at all, in this case in a hospital room at a research facility optimistically dubbed City of Hope, where one of my favorite people in the world struggled from her narrow, tube-bedangled bed to articulate her particular take on these themes and a host of other topics to her current visitors. Her brother Stanley H. Fiske sat red-nosed and watery-eyed beside her bedside table, availing himself more frequently than anyone dared mention of the generic box of tissues perched beside a dreary tray of uneaten applesauce, grayish green beans, and pallid fish, each of which seemed to have been Saran-wrapped with greater care than it had been cooked. Every time Stanley removed his eyeglasses to swipe them with a flimsy tissue, Gwennie paused, as if wanting to make sure her brother could actually see her as she spoke, particularly when Mother asked, "Gwen dear, how can I help get the house ready for you tomorrow?"

Gwen brushed aside Mother's offer with a bruised hand that still wore its ghastly bracelet of an IV line and launched, instead, into an itemization of what Stanley could do. I personally doubted Stanley could do anything but weep, but Gwennie had no mercy. "I swear I'll strangle you with my bare hands if I come home to find a bunch of ketchup-smeared McDonald's bags stuffed at the bottom of the trash. You know what Dr. Drew said about that crap and your cholesterol." Stanley looked aside sheepishly as Gwennie proceeded to take considerable care in describing the appropriate disposal methods of the inevitable sunflower seed shells littering the carpet beneath the sofa. Ditto the hoarder's-worth of newspapers and physics journals she just knew Stanley had strewn across every surface of the living room and den during her five day stay at the hospital following her averse reaction to her treatment.

I noticed that Mother took no offense at Gwennie's offhand dismissal of her offer. She'd been a peach ever since Gwennie had gotten her diagnosis, and I knew it would be she, not the brilliant but domestically inept Stanley, who'd take care of the empty McDonald's bags as she made the Fiske home sparkling clean and welcoming for Gwen. Fast food lunches aside, it had been Mother who'd brought Stanley dinner these past few nights, and if she hadn't cooked the meals herself—Dhani had done the honors, of course, perfectly seasoning each dish with mint, cinnamon, saffron, and the *garam masala* she was famous for—Mother had kept my physics mentor company while he fretted over what would become of his sole sibling.

We all understood his dread. His marriage to fellow scientist Doris Abrantes long past, Stanley had shared a household with his sister since shortly before I moved in a decade and a half earlier. In those days, Gwennie still had all of her hearing and Stanley his playful magician's charm, bending astonishingly from his towering height to retrieve a coin from my flip-flop, then froggishly hopping around, glee splashed across his wide forehead and cheeks, his eyes made even bulgier by his thick-lensed glasses. While Stanley mentored me in physics, Gwennie kept house, cooked her nourishing vegetarian dishes, and hennishly fussed over the two of us. No one spoke it aloud, but I knew my physics team shared my observation that the Fiskes behaved like an old married couple, with all the predictable nagging and bickering and profound dependency.

The latter had become particularly pronounced ever since Stanley crossed swords with my then-fiancé Assefa. It's a long story, but Assefa had actually attempted suicide— yes, I know, it's awful—after Stanley stunned everyone, especially himself, by flinging a rotten racial epithet at him. It hadn't exactly been my fellow Nobelist's most shining hour, but Assefa's uncharacteristic sexual aggression toward me hadn't been his, either. We seemed to inhabit an era in which no one could be counted on to act well—or entirely in character.

Assefa was actually in town at this very moment. Thanks to an offer he couldn't refuse to head up Interventional Cardiology at the UCLA Medical Center, he was moving back to SoCal. He'd brought his girlfriend Lemlem Skibba with him to look for apartments. Upon introduction, she'd caught me eyeing the attractive gap between her two front teeth and confessed apologetically, "I know. I'm 'tooth *mingi.'"* Which, seeing my confused expression, she leapt to explain meant she was considered bad luck by her Omo Valley tribe. Which struck me as more than a little nuts, given how she'd turned Assefa's life around.

I don't mind admitting that I felt more than a few pangs of jealousy. Not that I regretted my marriage to Adam. Hardly. But I was currently as wide as a house with our first child, my ridiculously burgeoning breasts supported by my ridiculously protruding belly, and Lemlem, with her slender, piquant curves, flaming cornrows, and thin gold band encircling her delicately flared right nostril, had to be the most captivating woman I'd ever seen.

Not to add to the impression of hopeless narcissism, but the timing of Gwennie's original diagnosis had been crap for me. (It goes without saying it was much crappier for Gwen.) When Gwennie first phoned with her dreadful news, Adam and I were minutes away from boarding an Air Emirates jet to bring Makeda back with us to So Cal, along with her newly adopted daughters Sofiya and Melesse. After the series of horrifying raids on orphanages by Al Shabaab, we'd managed to fast-track the trio's emigration to the States on humanitarian grounds with the promise they could live at least awhile with us. That was before we knew I was carrying our bun in my oven.

We'd been trying for years and had pretty much given up hope. At 27, I was just a hop, skip, and jump away from the age that Richard Bucke had declared most propitious for the attainment of cosmic consciousness. Which would undoubtedly be a great help in my project to facilitate zero-carbon-footprint travel, applying the Principle of Dematerialization for which I'd received the Prize. But alas, I was pretty sure I was condemned to be stalled at the more pedestrian level of self-consciousness that the vast majority of humans would ever attain, one that also seemed to include a penchant for murder, mayhem, and disaster. Which is hardly the most uplifting thought when you're about to have a child.

At this moment, with Gwennie looking like hell and my bun inserting what must be a butt proportionately similar to mine so far up my diaphragm that I feared she might float with my bottom ribs right up to my neck, gloom threatened to overtake me. Would Gwen live to see the face of my little girl? Would this child end up beating the record set by Beulah Hunter's baby Penny Diana by lingering in my womb longer than Penny's whopping 375 days? Would Adam murder me for my crankiness before then?

The appearance at the doorway of Assefa and Lemlem put paid to my reverie. Stanley nervously cleared his throat, and Assefa padded pantherishly toward him with that tweeter-moistening grace of his, reaching up to clap him on the shoulder with a solicitous expression. Except that, being nearly a foot shorter than Stanley, it was Stanley's elbow that Assefa actually patted. It was like this every time they met: Stanley radiating guilt from every pore despite Assefa's assurances that he'd long forgotten what Stanley had called him; Assefa assuming his most Aesculapian posture despite having once pronounced my mentor a monster. So much had changed since their original rupture. Wasn't it Stanley who'd arranged Assefa's transfer from UCLA to New York-Presbyterian University Hospital of Columbia and

Cornell, where Assefa had found quarters with a small group of Ethiopian-Americans that included U.N. staffer Lemlem Skibba? But I'd learned with my own failure to resurrect Grandfather that guilt can be as tenacious as the Green-eyed Monster in wrapping itself around our more rational selves.

Even in her diminished state, it was Gwennie who had the presence of mind to pronounce, "Shift changing time. Nurse Cory will kill me if we load up this room with too many bodies."

I inwardly winced. It was only a few weeks ago that I'd heard Gwen whisper as if in a trance from a bed just like this one, "I never wanted it to be like this." Wringing her hands and making the tubes attached to them tremble, she kept asking me to remove her clothes, then changing her mind, as if she were preparing for a journey, then deciding not to go.

Now Gwen motioned with her head for a kiss from Stanley, who complied with obvious relief, followed by Mother, then me.

The three of us filed out into a hallway shiny enough to broadcast every whorl of previous floor polishers, which I couldn't help but notice had created a pattern of comma-like shapes not unlike the undersides of Polygonia butterfly wings. Mother offered an upbeat, "Well, at least she's in full form. I haven't heard one of her political rants for ages. It's got to be a good sign, don't you think?"

She turned to Stanley, but he was already shuffling down the hall. She pivoted back to me. "How're you doing, love?" Her fingertips were silk against my cheek.

"Elephantine," I replied.

She cupped a hand against my bloated midsection, grinning. "You're nearly there."

A favorite phrase of Sammie's came to mind. "From your lips to God's ears."

"Honey, you know I believe in a higher power, but surely it doesn't have ears."

Thinking of the ticking time bomb of climate change, I whipped back disconsolately, "You're right about that one."

But Mother was determined to inject cheer wherever she could. "This little one will be the answer to all our prayers."

I didn't say what I wondered all the time these days: *But will* we *be the answer to* hers? The earworm I'd acquired of late took advantage of my vulnerable moment. *Hurry up,* it sang in pressured cadence. *We're running out of time!* Lately, I'd taken to talking back to it. "Leave me alone," I muttered under my breath, as I turned toward my section of the parking lot.

I came home to find Adam attacking the pile of dishes in the sink, the scent of spicy *wat* permeating the house like the frankincense I'd first smelled when visiting Makeda and Father Wendimu at Tikil Dingay. How the world turned! Then, I'd been filled with uneasy curiosity to meet the woman who held a prior hold on Assefa's heart. Now, Makeda was doing anything she could to repay us—unnecessarily, I insisted, to no effect—for putting up her little family, including cooking nightly meals of *shiro* and *wat* and *samosas* to die for.

Adam's ungovernable cowlick stood straight up from his sleek chestnut head, and I wanted nothing more than to come up behind him and wrap my arms around him. But the balloon of my belly wouldn't let me. Instead, I awkwardly leaned my head against his damp back, inhaling his pheromonic Campbell's chicken soup B.O.

He turned and kissed me on the lips, making a satisfying smacking sound, and I laughed. He had a dripping plate in one hand and held an equally drippy dishwashing brush like a conductor's baton in the other. I nodded at the brush and, humming Ponchielli's *Dance of the Hours*, proceeded to do a regrettably perfect imitation of one of the dancing hippos in Disney's *Fantasia*.

Defying logic and fairness, my husband had become more fit and handsome with every passing year. I'd privately regretted more than once during this pregnancy that he hadn't succumbed to the Couvade Syndrome—otherwise known as the "hatching phenomenon"—and put on at least a little girth with me. Some fathers-to-be actually got morning sickness along with their partners and even felt cramps when labor came on.

But who could complain as he leaned back against the counter and enthusiastically flourished his wand? As if every other man would be equally thrilled to see his lover stomp the floorboards so lumpishly.

Which was only one of the thousands of reasons I loved him.

I knew Makeda had already left to drop off the girls at the Children's

Center at Caltech, whose director had made a huge exception in admitting them as members of our family. Things were working out well for this new Ethiopian wing of our clan, though it was small wonder Makeda had landed an internship at the Southern California Regional Office of UNICEF, with the carrot of a possible paid position once she completed her degree in global health at UCLA. Hadn't she and Father Wendimu managed to wrangle international adoptions for nearly five hundred children over the years from their hardscrabble orphanage in Tikil Dingay, assiduously keeping AIDS and civil war orphans alive and adored until couples with means whisked their young charges off to more promising opportunities? Makeda knew the underbelly of world health all too well, having been orphaned herself in the revolt against the Derg and subjected almost immediately afterward to a botched genital circumcision in Tigray.

Of course, it hadn't hurt that the renowned Stanley H. Fiske had lobbied for her and that fellow Nobelist Fleur Robins and her husband Adam Manus had purchased a home ample enough to accommodate the three of them. That was, of course, down to Mother. Adam and I could never have afforded the whopping down payment and mortgage on this San Marino home, just a stone's throw from the Huntington Gardens, whose paths Stanley and I had once skipped, debating the nature of dark matter and the validity of multiple universes.

After a lost and lonely childhood spent mostly in Father's voidish Main Line mansion, I swore I'd never live anywhere larger than the Fiskes' cozy Pasadena bungalow. But I had to admit I did love our new home. It had enough bedrooms and bathrooms—five and four—to accommodate Makeda's crew and our own coming bunlet. And it had enough Mission style features—exposed rafters, quatrefoil windows, covered walkways—to remind us that our Hispanic friends' ancestors were the true legitimate residents of SoCal. Unsurprisingly, the house seemed to suit us all. Melesse and Sofiya spent no end of time playing hopscotch in the walkways and running up and down the staircase, their delicate chocolate hands barely touching the scrolled metalwork banister as their deft feet flew. And Buster was particularly fond of sleeping in front of the vibrantly tiled, arched fireplace, snoring like a jungle cat and purring like a house afire. I knew Jillily would have joined him if she could, but she'd been ensconced for more years than I cared to recall in the deepest hole in my heart.

Of course, one of the best things about our Old Mill Road digs was their proximity to Caltech, my home away from home ever since Stanley H. Fiske had whisked me from Mother's post-divorce New York penthouse to mentor me in quantum physics, calling me to a life of the mind that no one had ever imagined for the child who'd flapped and whirled and screamed bloody murder out of sheer emptiness and boredom. At Caltech, I'd met Amir Gupta and Gunther Anderten and Katrina Kelly and Tom Haggis and Bob Ballantine and even that impish erstwhile lab chimp cheekily dubbed Lord Hanuman by Amir. It was there, too, that I'd deepened my connection to Adam, whose tutoring when I was just twelve had led to the whole adventure in the first place.

I hardly ever flapped anymore. It was a last resort of emotional release, to be used only when something exceptionally disastrous occurred, like the loss of someone I loved, Al Shabaab's recruitment of three-year-old orphans to serve as child warriors, pelicans plastered in crude oil, Miley Cyrus' aardvarkian tongue driving another nail into the coffin of contemporary childhood, and the possible election of a dangerous dolt who denied human agency in global warming—yet another roadblock in the way of our project to actually do something about it. I'd learned over the years, mostly thanks to Adam, to say what upset me and to ask for my favorite kind of Mack truckish hugs when things got really bad. But that didn't stop me from worrying whether my bunlet would be as plagued as I'd been by such a pitifully profound set of sensitivities. (I knew I really should stop referring to her as the Bunlet. We had a name for her now. Adam had urged me to pore over passels of baby naming books before he succumbed with more grace than I would have mustered to what I'd wanted to name her all along. Callay Myriadne Manus-Robins she'd be, for surely her incarnating into this world warranted more than a few *callooh callays*.)

But as is often the case, I'm afraid I've digressed. With a noisy clearing of his throat, Adam wiped his hands with a dishtowel and managed to maneuver me into his arms, whispering so strategically in

9

my ear that my tweeter signaled it hadn't forgotten what a mini-explosion felt like. "So what is Her Grace going to get up to today while the rest of us slave away at the lab?" I felt a pang of guilt. Speaking of butt thrusts, it was after a particularly vigorous one by Callay that I'd decided it really was time to hand over the reins of our project to Amir, whose early circumambulations around string theory, the space-time continuum, the relative weakness of gravity, and mini-black holes had been particularly helpful in propelling my mind toward the discovery of C-Voids. We'd been banking ever since that those black holes within human cells would eventually enable us to initiate a process that would obviate most fossil fuel-propelled travel. Tom had more recently coined the term "Dreamization" for our project, putting together the dematerialization and rematerialization we were hoping to use to move people from one place to another. With Amir in charge, the work of Dreamization would go forward while I struggled to deliver some semblance of bleary-eyed competency to caring for an infant. And if you don't think I shuddered at the prospect, you've never grown up in a house with a whole wing devoted to small children your father had saved from the devil abortionists.

I answered Adam with a slight tone of defiance. "Probably see if I can manage one last prenatal yoga class with Siri Sajan before I completely lose the capacity to stretch the toes I can no longer see."

Adam gave a grunt of appreciation before warning, "Don't push it, babe. It's been great that you've kept it up, but it's getting pretty close ...."

I waved a hand. "Oh, don't worry. Siri Sajan watches me like a mama bear." I paused. "Speaking of which, how would you feel about Mother being in the delivery room with us for the birth?"

Adam raised a brow. "Does she *want* to?"

"Oh," I hedged, "I haven't officially asked her. We just spoke loosely about the concept. Well, really, she happened to mention that her friend Dory was there when her daughter Lilia gave birth to Jemima, and I said that sounded nice." I stifled the impulse to pinch.

Adam crossed his arms. "Tell me what you're thinking, Fleur."

"I don't know that it's even a thought. It just occurred to me that she might appreciate ... well, you know. Seeing the baby coming out. The generational thing and all."

"I'm surprised."

My laugh sounded a bit forced. "By my atavistic reversion to the matriarchy?"

"Noooo, I wouldn't exactly put it like that. By you wanting your mother there to comfort you."

I felt my face flushing. "No, it's not that. I just thought it would be sweet for *her.*"

"Fleur, I'm good with it. Really, I am. But I just think you should call it what it is."

"Which is …?"

"You're scared, and you actually feel close enough to your mother now to look to her for comfort."

"Am I?"

"What? Scared? Aren't you?"

"Well, maybe just a bit."

"You wouldn't be human if you weren't a little. Don't get me wrong, I'm sure it'll all go fine."

"Oh my God," I marveled, "*You're* scared."

"Me? Don't be ridiculous." He ran a quick hand through his hair and made a face. "Oh, hell, of course I am. Of course *we* are. Both of us." He shot me a sheepish grin. "It's a relief to say it out loud, isn't it?"

"I guess so. But I'm not sure it helps."

"Maybe we should talk about what we're afraid of?"

I eyed him warily. "What are *you* afraid of?"

"It's not what you think. I think the baby will be fine."

"Well, there *is* that, isn't there?"

"Yes, but I have a good feeling about her. I think she's going to be sturdy as all get out. No rational reason, but I do."

I attempted folding my hands across my belly, then gave up. "Well, then you must be worried about *me.* But honestly, I don't think you have to, because honestly—despite all my moaning, I'm in pretty good shape. Siri Sajan says she's never seen a pregnant woman more …" And then it dawned on me. "Your mother."

His green eyes moistened, and a little groan escaped him.

"Oh, sweetheart." I led him out of the room to the den and motioned to him to sit next to me on what we liked to call "the queen's settee"—a cat-shredded, lumpy old sofa Mother had commissioned after seeing a photo in *Architectural Digest* of a similarly Liberty-patterned one in Elizabeth Regina's private rooms at Buckingham Palace. Three feline lives and hundreds of Krispy Kreme Powdered Blueberry-Filled doughnuts later, it had descended into something more likely to be found in a homeless encampment.

I nuzzled Adam's head, detecting a slight whiff of something lime-ish. "I'm not going anywhere," I said. Dying in the throes of childbirth, Adam's mother had left him with a slightly crippled left leg and a longing for what he would never have.

"I don't think … and I don't want to worry you, but you know I would never be able to live if …"

"I wouldn't be able to live without *you*, either. But I am not going to die on you." And I realized then that I simply couldn't. That was that. I felt a surge of strength that I didn't believe I'd ever felt before, not even when I was convinced I was going to resurrect Grandfather. I'd failed at that, but I could not, *would* not fail at this.

"Well, that's settled then," I pronounced. "I think Mother will do us both good. Even if she did stop pushing me out of her tweeter long enough to give me this pointy head."

"Oh, the head. You really do exaggerate, you know. You've got a perfect oval of a head." He laughed. "A true egghead."

"Well, at least you're right about something." We kissed for a long time, pulled apart, and then we kissed some more—even longer, with him fondling my gigantic breasts and me pressing my hand against his member and then taking it out of its zippered cave and caressing it more and more vigorously. All the while kissing. His ragged breath became my breath. I sensed his heartbeat in sync with my own. I wondered if Callay Myriadne was in tune with us, too. As Adam cried out, I felt momentarily certain that nothing bad was going to happen to this baby, to me, to us, to generations that would surely spill forth from our love.

Well, anyway, that was what I felt right then. Once Adam left for the lab, favoring me with a cheeky smirk before closing the door, it dawned on me that Grandfather would never see my little girl. Pushing aside any thought of Siri Sajan's class, I heaved myself up the stairs to the baby's room. An animal-themed alphabet frieze by Michael Spink cavorted across one cream-colored wall. Opposite it hung a sepia-toned framed photo of Grandfather pushing a gleeful young me on a swing. His walrus mustache was a strawberry blond in those days, the gleam in his eyes an ad for good health. A heavy gloom descended on the room, and I stood awhile, staring. Eventually, I forced myself forward and lifted the picture off its nail, propping it on my knees as I plopped heavily onto the single bed Adam had positioned catty-corner from the crib.

The child's hair was a mass of nearly white ringlets. Would Callay be as fair as this, or would she favor the more robust coloring of Adam's clan? On that swing now, I swept up toward the clouds, aware of my grandfather's adoring eyes, my heart in my throat.

But the sound of a motorcycle spouting noisy smoke farts jarred me back to the present. Below stairs, the grandfather clock in the study sounded eleven chimes. I shifted my position, grateful for the thickness of the plush mattress pad Mother had purchased for an arm and a leg. It occurred to me that I'd be spending a good deal of time on this bed, certainly more than Mother had spent in my pink-painted room when I was young; she'd been too wedded to the bottle—speaking of dematerialization, shrinking into invisibilized form to elude Father's whip-like words, my stricken grandfather's helpless *ugga umph uggas*, and my own frantic screams that only Nana, with her Mack truck grip, could manage to quell.

I lifted a thick corner of the whimsical quilt sewn by Stanley and Gwennie's mother that had once graced my bed in *their* home. I poked it against my cheek. I'd actually coordinated this room's color scheme of robin's egg blue, buttercream, apricot, and deep forest green to go with it. "No insipid pink," I'd proclaimed to Adam, "for our Callay!"

What I hadn't said to him, nor to anyone else, was the thought that kept me up after too many nightly pees: would my having aborted Baby X at the age of thirteen be penalized belatedly by one of the more punitive gods and spirits in the vast panoply of religious traditions, like the Norse goddess Vár, who wreaked vengeance on those who broke vows, the Albanian Perit, turning those who wasted food into hunchbacks, or the Shinto Amaterasu, who rewarded an act of rudeness by bringing an age of darkness upon the world? Or even

Yahweh, who seemed to have quite a predilection for smiting? Of course, even the most benign of gods could be something of a stickler when crossed: Artemis turning Actaeon into a stag, ripped apart by his own dogs, for staring in awe at her bathing body; Zeus punishing Ixion for flirting with his wife by fastening him eternally to a burning wheel.

Whatever my crimes over the years, my own worst punishments seemed to consist of huge dollops of melancholy, regret, and dread. But if my daughter's health were to be compromised by her mother's sins? I swept my hand across the photo sitting rather heavily on my knees, wishing I could again feel Grandfather's gnarled hand wrapped comfortingly around mine.

But now I noticed that my fingers had made tracks on the glass, which was dustier than I'd realized. Looking up, I saw that someone had left the window wide open above the crib. Pushing a fist down into the mattress, I rose gracelessly to return the picture to its perch on the wall, and then shuffled over to pull the window closed, taking care to hear the click of its brass latch.

It still amazed me how quickly things got messy. "Hell in a handbasket," our old housekeeper Fayga—she of the serious aversion to dirt—used to say. She'd frantically ply her powerful, industrial grade vacuum at dust balls and cracker crumbs, sending me fleeing in terror lest I be suctioned in myself. That fear didn't get any better over the years. Once I started studying physics, I learned that the universe was rife with black holes, sucking in vast clouds of gas and whole solar systems like our own. Great debates raged in my field around John von Neumann's theory of entropy and his description of wave-function collapse as an irreversible process. In the course of my work on Dematerialization, I was one of those who'd posed the possibility that physical information might permanently disappear into black holes, effectively dissolving many disparate physical states into the same dead one.

You can see what the presence of a little dirt did to me. Lacking a mother sober enough to see to me or a father who'd cared to, I'd clearly osmosed the household staff into my psyche more than I cared to admit. Rubbing my thumb against my blackened fingers, I felt a distinct sensation of impatience with our current housekeeper,

Lukie. She might be a sweetheart of a human, but she could use a bit of Fayga's fanatical compulsiveness. I made a mental note to make sure she dusted this room thoroughly before the baby came. I wanted everything pure and clean for my child.

But who was I kidding? How could anything be clean and pure for our little girl when everything was going haywire on the planet? I ducked my head as if I could block out the impossible dilemma. We had to live our lives as if we had forever, didn't we? Otherwise, we'd climb under the covers and go paralytic with despair. And that simply wasn't going to be an option. Not for me, anyway. And certainly not now. I headed for my own room and yanked a loose-fitting T-shirt from a cupboard. I'd decided to go to yoga after all.

Sanctus

The Soul of the World was troubled. It wasn't enough that in many places the earth had become fire, that grain crops were declining, that coral reefs were dying, that sea levels were rising and glaciers retreating. The birds she'd counted on to sing her awake each morning were in dangerous decline. She'd already been mourning the losses of the Lord Howe thrush, the Santa Barbara Song Sparrow, the Arabian Ostrich, the Grand Cayman Oriole, the Seychelles Parakeet, the southern starfish; the growing roster of the missing was relentless. It felt as if birdsong itself would soon be gone.

The starlings whose murmurations soared wavelike through the sky were succumbing to the theft of permanent pasture by livestock farming. As the earth heated up, signs of spring were moving forward, and migratory birds were arriving early at their breeding grounds. Those harbingers of new life, the rousingly bill-clattering White Storks, were wintering in Europe, rather than Africa, foraging at rubbish dumps, rather than breezily canopied savannahs; ironically, as humans reduced the number of open landfills to prevent birds from choking to death on plastic and rubber bands, those selfsame storks would be taxed to come up with new solutions or starve.

The World Soul settled uneasily onto her mossy haunches and let the Fates do their reweaving around her. She shot an encouraging glance at Clotho, put a steadying hand on the shoulder of Lachesis, and directed a stern eye at Atropos, lest she go wild with those shears of hers. A soul could absorb only so much grief at a time.

Chapter Two

I LOVED SIRI SAJAN, but within weeks yogic aspirations devolved into the lesser goals of getting out of the bathtub on my own, scratching the bottom of my foot, and picking up anything from the floor. My acid reflux kept insisting that the baby was late, late, late for her very important date. Never mind that it was only day 281 of my pregnancy. On day twelve of my admittedly compulsive marathon of prepping for her, I heaved myself down the hall to repeat the ritual, telling myself that keeping busy would also distract me from the fact that Gwennie's release from the hospital had been delayed, yet again, by a resurgence of her blood infection.

Here are some of the items I'd already washed—some by hand—and folded and refolded and which I now tackled anew, as if practicing for what was soon to become a far more necessary constant drill:

> 1. The hand-dyed, dusty rose gown in which Mother had transported me from Bryn Mawr Hospital to Father's Main Line estate. Despite my overall eschewal of pink for my child and this particular gown's utter impracticality, with its satin lace ruffle at the neck embellished with a floppy chiffon flower affixed with a polished pearl broach, I couldn't possibly bear the

pain in Mother's blue eyes if the daughter of her daughter didn't wear it home. Besides, I was madly in love with its similarly adorned matching headband, which had proclaimed that the decidedly pointy-headed, bald child in the earliest photo of me was, in fact, neither a boy nor the po-faced alien she appeared to be.

2. Eight snap-front, soft-as-cashmere coveralls in a riot of rainbow-hued colors, my favorite of which bore the motto, "Schrödinger's Diaper: isn't full until you check it."

3. An equal number of shirt-and-pant sets appended with enough lambs, calves, and kids to convince any sensible child she'd been born on a farm.

4. Six pairs of the kind of footless Martian pajamas once worn by the babies Father had rescued from the devil abortionists, purveyed to him in bulk by wholesaler Leland DuRay (whose shady dealings had contributed to Father's unceremonious ouster from the Senate and the subsequent—but regrettably temporary—loss of his far-too-rigid mind).

5. Six pairs of socks so small that I was convinced, despite Mother's frequent assurances, couldn't possibly accommodate an actual human foot.

6. Two large hooded towels with floppy bunny ears, whose silliness never failed to make Adam and me spill into each other's arms with unalloyed joy.

7. Eight tie-dyed short-sleeved onesies purchased at an undoubtedly ridiculous cost by Sammie at her favorite Venice craft shop.

8. One precious wool sweater knitted by Nana for me, which I'd worn but once thanks to the itchy rash it induced—I swore to Callay I'd brush it against her little hand first to make sure she'd suffer no such reaction.

9. More cream-colored burp cloths than I'd cared to count, which Mother kept adding to, convincing me I'd been the pukiest child on the planet.

10. Ten receiving blankets, one ordered by Amir from India that bore a vivid scene of a dancing Lord Hanuman balancing the world on his fingertip; speaking of whom, I really did need to call Jane Goodall to see how she'd weathered her recent bout with the flu.

11. Several sweet swimsuits from Mother with unusually wide-brimmed, matching sun hats that came along with her solemn declaration that her grandchild would never have to deal with as many (thankfully basal cell) skin cancers as she had. Which, needless to say, took me as predictably as a slide in Chutes in Ladders to my anxiety about the dangerous world Callay was coming into.

I, who'd persevered past frustration, self-doubt, and the tremendous enmity of my father and his Cacklers, Big Oil, Congress, and Rupert Murdoch, couldn't decide whether to house the short-sleeved onesies in the top or middle shelf of what had once been my own antique baby dresser.

As luck would have it, Makeda arrived home early to save me from my insanity. I nearly laughed when she appeared in the doorway. If she'd intended to look coolly businesslike in her tailored gray jacket, buttoned just so over her Gap business casual black sheath dress, she'd failed miserably. Her spirit was too buoyant, her curves too generous, her eyes too alive to strike the tone she thought she needed to cultivate in her new world.

But at this moment, as she lingered at the threshold to the baby's room, I had to confess she looked rather woebegone. Muttering something about being a fool to think she could fit in, she began to turn away. Without stopping to ask what was wrong, I rushed in with an ill-conceived attempt to cheer her, complimenting her on her outfit, then proceeding to comment that, whether she showed up at work in a Hillary-esque pantsuit or a brilliantly embroidered, traditional Ethiopian *habesha*, her intelligence, experience, and charm would guarantee her success. "Let's face it, you're a natural to realize the American Dream. Oh, I know there are glass ceilings right and left in 'post-feminist America,' and most of us still hate our bodies for being too female, but you can actually be a leader on that front. Besides, the fact that your thesis is on pharaonic circumcision makes you a shoo-in."

Turning to face me with a frown, she asked, "Why?" If I'd taken the time I would have paid more attention to the fact that her coppery face had shifted a bit to the incarnadine end of the spectrum.

"Because I read recently that female genital mutilation is on the rise among African immigrants in the U.S., and somebody's got to do something about it."

Makeda favored me with an impatient stare. "And you think it should be me?" Her eyes flashed. "That's all that I am good for? Forget that I might have dreams beyond my own early circumstances? I can see it now: Makeda Geteye, poster girl for the inferiority of African cultures. See how gracefully she copes with her own deformity."

I clapped my right hand over my left wrist. Flapping was not going to help. I sought out Adam's ancient mantra. *Use your words, Fleur. Let her know what you really mean.* (And if you think that's awfully nursery school-ish for a pregnant woman of 27, then *you* climb inside this body of mine and see what its staticky nervous system does to your perfect aplomb.)

"No, please. Wait. You're confusing what I said." Her sharp intake of breath told me I was still on the wrong track. "No, *I'm* the one who's not being clear." I let Siri Sajan into my current team of inner advisors. *I know I'm breathing in, I know I'm breathing out.* "Look, I wouldn't dream of you being a poster child for anything. I hate it when they used to write about me as the greatest Aspie since Bill Gates—forget that neither of us has trouble with social interactions. Well, not much. Speaking for myself. I have no idea about him."

Was that the faintest hint of a grin playing at her pursed lips?

"Here's the thing. When I was little, the worst thing I could imagine—and I imagined it all the time—was the void. I saw all creatures' behavior as attempts to distract them from a voracious, yawning nothingness. Birds constantly flitting from branch to branch, weeds fighting their way up through cracks in the sidewalk, just about every single thing we humans think and do."

She cocked her head but clearly wasn't inclined to give an inch. I remembered my first visit to Tikil Dingay, how she'd been when I'd confided that Assefa had nearly raped me, stopped only by the intervention of Stanley H. Fiske. Her disbelief. Her rage. And how I'd made it so much worse by telling her that the man she'd pined for was actually her half-brother, her mother having secretly slept with her husband's best friend Achamyalesh (which made a kind of sense to me at the time, since his name translated as *You Are Everything*).

What an idiot I'd been, and definitely not a savant-y one. And if my stupidity hadn't yet occurred to me, her response had made it abundantly clear. It was Newton who'd set the foundation for what would become classical mechanics with his characterization of the inevitable consequences of the exertion of force of one body upon another: "For every action, there is an equal and opposite reaction." I could still recall the burning sensation—and the shock!—of Makeda's hand slapping me sharply across my face. Her fury had left its imprint on my conscience far longer than had the red brand on my skin, reminding me that using one's words is also a choice. Sometimes it's best to say nothing at all.

More nervous than ever now, I reached around to give myself a comforting pinch on the bulge above my bra line, pulling my dress even more tautly against my balloon of a belly.

But no hand scored my face this time. My current instance of idiocy was rewarded instead by Makeda falling into a broad-hipped squat against the door, her skirt hitching itself above her knees in a way that surely threatened the integrity of its seams.

She buried her head in her hands, issuing guttural gasps of words. "On top of everything, I'm going out of my mind not knowing if Father Wendimu is alive or dead." Tears sprung to my own eyes. Rumor had it that the orphanage had been decimated by Al Shabaab just weeks after she'd fled, and—with no means of contacting anyone in Tikil Dingay—we all worried that, like the captain of a ship, Father Wendimu had gone down with the refuge he'd created. "I shouldn't be troubling you with my own worries. You're about to have a baby, for God's sake."

I summoned the sanity to ask her if there were more reasons

why she was in such distress. Shuffling to her side, I assayed a clumsy kneel in order to put my arms around her, but was soon persuaded of my folly. Instead, I brushed what I hoped was a consoling hand across her head until the resemblance of its pleasantly scratchy texture to Assefa's tight coils made me pull back as if it were fire.

"I know it sounds petty, but the students were marching—actually marching! with placards!—because the university has decided that sororities and fraternities be subjected to the same drug and alcohol regulations as on-campus housing. I know I should not apply the values of my native land to my new one, but I can't help but feel that this is nothing. Nothing!" Her eyes raked me with a momentary contempt, and then she succumbed again to her tears. "How can I be here when children at home are being kidnapped, tortured, forced into warfare or into so-called marriages with their abductors? To cook for them? To spread their legs night after night and give birth to those monsters' children?"

What could I say to this, I who was about to bring forth a child conceived in such tenderness?

Wordlessly, I signaled to Makeda to sit beside me on Callay's quilted bed. Together, we hobbled toward it like an awkward four-legged beast and landed on its luxurious loft with a resounding synchronized plop. This time, with Nana's Mack truck grip as my guide and my poof of a belly notwithstanding, I managed to at least partially encircle my friend with my arms until her sobs began to subside.

"You'll do it, you know," I whispered, wiping the wetness from her face with my pale fingertips. "You'll use all that suffering to great good, just as you did back at the orphanage. You'll help even more children because you'll impact the powers that hold them at their mercy. And you and your own beautiful family will thrive. Sofiya and Melesse will have a good life, and you will, too. You matter, too."

I held my breath. Had I screwed it up again? Makeda shook her head, and her face betrayed a sense of wonder. "How did it happen?"

"What?"

"How is it possible that you and I have become sisters?"

I laughed. "Pretty crazy, isn't it? Who'd a thunk it?"

She looked at me as if I were a moron, then, realizing it must be a colloquialism, announced that she had to pee, which made me aware I had had to, as well. We met again in the hallway, and I proposed a bracing walk at the nearby Huntington Gardens.

"Bracing?" she laughed, mischief in her eyes.

"Well, you'll walk, and I'll waddle."

"Only if you promise me we'll turn back if it becomes too much for you."

"Cross my heart." She shot me a confused look. "Oh, never mind. I promise."

What I couldn't have promised, because I couldn't have predicted, was whom we'd bump into at the Huntington's Chinese-themed Garden of Flowing Fragrance. Just as Makeda and I were exiting the Pavilion of the Three Friends, a scallop-roofed architectural wonder, I spied Assefa, hand in hand with Lemlem, with Abeba in unhurried pursuit a few paces behind.

It was hardly a casual encounter of friends. Things were civil enough between Abeba and me—she was the current go-between for Mother with Cesar, the hyperactive adoptee Mother had taken under her wing after Nana had died. But Makeda and Assefa? They hadn't seen each other since Assefa's return to his homeland six years ago to ostensibly search for his missing father, but in truth to reclaim the woman who'd been his first love. He'd broken off our engagement by phone from that faraway land, only to be rebuffed by her in the end.

I'd wondered more than a few times whether, now that they shared a country again, Makeda would be fearful—or eager—to see Assefa, her inseparable childhood friend, her first love, her half-brother? I wanted to turn to look at her, but I couldn't. Instead, my eyes had fastened themselves on Assefa. I saw his expression shift from a relaxed grin to confusion, then shock.

Meeting up with Makeda and me had to be a regular twofer: the women he'd once simultaneously loved, who'd condemned him to the fate of the Hanging Man, suspended between two countries, two women, two Assefas. At least that's how he'd described it to me shortly after he'd tried to hang himself, riddled with confusion, rage, and shame.

But this current life of his was truly a new incarnation. He'd come into his own as a cardiologist, come to terms with his father's indiscretion before that man had died, and found the woman who would sew his heart together again. It occurred to me that, in keeping with his newfound authority, he was just the tiniest bit heavier these days, his high cheekbones even more charming with a bit of flesh on them. He'd shaved off his goatee, the one that used to tickle my inner thighs as he sucked my tweeter till I had my mini-explosions. For a moment, I was overcome with dizziness, and I wondered if I was going into labor, but just as quickly the sensation passed.

It was Lemlem who broke the ice. Or at least induced a melty drip or two. Sensing the tension, she smiled her gap-toothed smile and stepped forward to warmly greet me and introduce herself to Makeda. I knew the two were sizing each other up, despite their generous smiles, their hands that continued to stay clasped during their ritualized series of questions.

"And how are your children?" Lemlem asked. "I hear they are adorable."

"They are, they are, thanks be to God."

"How old are they?"

"Sofiya is the older one. She is five years. Or will be in a short time. Her birthday is coming very soon."

"Ah. She must be a joy to you. And how lucky that she has a sister with whom to share this new life." I sensed in her a repressed sigh. "And how about the other one? How old?"

"Melesse. She is Melesse, and she is nearly four. Just a month away."

Lemlem's eyes twinkled. "I remember when my own sister turned five. Such a party I heard she had."

"You were not there?"

Lemlem pointed to her gapped front teeth. "I am *Mingi*. Considered bad luck, so not allowed to come. But I heard, I heard. The dancing was very good. And the food, of course."

Neither woman spoke of the injustice of it, but it was in their eyes.

"I will give Sofiya a party," Makeda pronounced suddenly. She flicked a quick glance at me. "If it does not inconvenience Fleur and Adam, of course." I shook my head obediently. "I hope you will come."

Oh no! I saw that Assefa and Abeba looked as uncomfortable as

I felt. With any luck, Callay would actually arrive earlier than Penny Diana Hunter, and the presence of a newborn in the home might serve to change Makeda's mind.

Not that I didn't want to celebrate Sofiya—of Makeda's two girls, she was the more easily engaged, ready with a running hug, a silly joke, an exuberant, if slightly out-of-tune song. Melesse was shyer, coping with all the trauma she'd endured as an AIDS orphan by burying her nose in books, tracing her fingers over the pictures and sounding out simple words with her endearing lisp whenever she wasn't playing with her older sibling. I knew it was going to take time to persuade her that I was constant enough to be allowed into her heart. I also wondered whether Melesse hadn't yet figured out how to emerge from under Sofiya's broad shadow. Adam and I had secretly nicknamed the older sister, "the Sparkler," and I imagined her taking great delight in a party thrown on her behalf, possibly with piñatas and party favors and games to play with all her preschool friends.

But now, Lemlem was politely handing Makeda off to Abeba, who deposited a trio of kisses on Makeda's cheeks while managing to completely avoid her eyes. Abeba's upper lip was stretched as thin as Cook's had been in the old days, like a worm fried in the sun on its arduous journey between lawn and parkway.

As for Makeda, well, her voice had deepened so profoundly that if I hadn't been looking at her I'd have thought she was a man. (And believe me, you would *never* mistake Makeda for a man.)

Gruffly, she offered, "I was so sorry to learn of Achamyalesh's passing." Unsaid were the words, *He was my father. How could all of you who knew that hide it from me?*

"Thank you. We were given a long life together." *During which he betrayed me with your mother.*

"We must be grateful for our blessings. The two of you raised a most accomplished son." *Who is my half-brother; it breaks my heart still.*

Now it was Makeda's turn, in an awkward do-se-do, to face Assefa, who'd actually backed away and was huddling by a tall bush like a radiation tech stepping behind a lead shield. He stepped forward, betraying barely a sign of the shame he surely felt, holding out a hand.

But Makeda, defying the difficult pleasantries, proffered her

27

cheek for the traditional trio of kisses, and somehow her courage broke the ice, because soon enough we were all laughing at the irony of this Ethiopian reunion in a Chinese Garden on the grounds of a man who'd made his fortune building SoCal's rail system by ruthlessly exploiting Mexican labor.

I knew their humor would flag if I mentioned that the very same magnate, Henry E. Huntington, had shocked San Francisco society when he married Arabella Huntington, the widow of his uncle Collis P. Huntington, whose own code of conduct was said to have been epitomized by the saying, "Whatever is not nailed down is mine. What I can pry loose is not nailed down."

Makeda and I said little once the Berhanus and Lemlem departed. Our walk back to the parking lot required a deft navigation through clusters of mostly silver-haired women arrayed like fading hydrangeas around invisible beds of very visible David Austin roses, posing and preening under so many attentive, if somewhat rheumy, eyes. I knew what *I* was thinking: mostly variations on the theme of *Well,* that *was awkward.* But I couldn't begin to imagine where it had sent Makeda. And to be honest, I was too self-involved to inquire. We separated into our bedrooms as soon as we returned. But I didn't know what to do with myself.

I removed my clothes, took a drought-defying, long shower—baths were out now for Belly Woman—and stood afterward, all pruney-fingered, in front of my full-length vanity mirror. It wasn't a pretty picture—hardly the body Assefa had licked from head to toe and back again, with such glorious pit stops in between. It was one of those odd ironies of life that, despite my utter adoration of Adam, every once in a while I couldn't resist picking at the scab of Assefa, dwelling self-pityingly on my hurt that he hadn't unreservedly returned my love.

It was just as well that the phone rang. It was the ringtone I'd programmed for Mother's number.

"It occurred to me that we're all going to be ridiculously busy soon. Want to come over to the Fiskes for a cuppa? Cesar's been kind enough to wait here all morning for the delivery of the patient lift I ordered for whenever Gwen gets the green light to come home. It's going to very important for her state of mind to be able to get out of bed and actually sit in a chair for part of the day. Even after losing all that weight, she's still pretty heavy. The lift will be a big help to Stanley when no one else is home to help lift her. But the delivery men haven't arrived yet— surprise, surprise—and Cesar has to go somewhere, so I'll be cooling my heels here all by my lonesome until they arrive."

After shouting to Makeda that I was running out for a bit, I started up the old Prius and drove all of the four and a half minutes it took to reach Stanley and Gwennie's Rose Villa Street home.

I actually had to hold the small banister to haul myself up the two steps to the porch. Cesar startled me by flinging open the front door. He sped past me with a barely audible, "Hey, Fleur, how you doin', dude?"

Mother caught the door before it slammed shut in front of me. Shaking her head, she pursed her perfectly outlined Chanel Infra-rouge lips for a quick couple of *bisous*, muttering, "I worry about that boy."

Her voice had an edge, and I turned around to see Cesar striding quickly, not to his motorcycle, but to Fidel Marquetti's house, disappearing inside.

'What the—?"

"Oh, God. They were right."

"Wait. Did I really just see that?"

Mother fell back against the wall. "I can hardly believe it myself. Gwennie swore she saw him let himself into Fidel's house a few days before she was hospitalized, but I wrote it off to chemo brain. Then the other day when Dhani was here, she phoned and said she'd seen the same thing. Followed by the loudest and cheesiest disco music you can imagine blaring from Fidel's backyard."

I shuddered. The last time I'd actually seen Fidel, he was covered in blood, having just shot our mutual next-door neighbors' dog. "Honestly, I guess I'd assumed Fidel moved after what happened with the Kangs. I don't think I've seen him since."

"Was Cesar even here when that happened?"

"No. He was with you. It was Christmas day."

Mother frowned, then nodded. "You know, I'd forgotten that we used to split the holidays. What's really odd is that I guess I've heard the story so many times, I actually remember it as if I'd been here myself."

I shuddered and stifled the impulse to flap. "I'm glad you weren't." It was the most hideous thing I'd ever witnessed. Fidel running in circles, screaming and holding his hand on his butt where Chin Hwa had bit him. The dog not moving, but blood seeping from underneath him like some creepy life force of its own. And Mrs. Kang with her hands pulling at her cheeks, her dress soaked right through with the water from Fidel's sprinklers so you could see her underwear. She was so skinny and helpless-looking. I didn't think any of us knew what to do until Gwennie had the decency to go over and hold her.

We went in and sat together in a grim silence. On my side, I was trying to figure out how Cesar would have even met Fidel. Finally, I ventured the question aloud, but Mother wasn't looking at me. She strode to the front door and opened it. Gloria Gaynor's I Will Survive blasted into the room. Cesar, or whoever he was with over at Fidel's, must be playing the music at full volume for it to be this loud two doors away.

I joined Mother on the porch. The hairs stood up on my arms. It occurred to me that, of course, Fidel hadn't moved. Any buyer of his Spanish bungalow would have gotten rid of that weird, Martian garden of his as soon as they moved in. "Mother, maybe Fidel's away on vacation and somehow arranged for Cesar to water his yard for him. You know how Fidel feels about his precious plants." We all knew. It was pride (and prejudice against his Korean-American neighbors) that had led to Fidel murdering Chin Hwa after the unfortunate Jindo had taken a giant dump on his pansies.

Mother pulled me back inside and leaned back against the door as if barring it.

"I don't know. But maybe you and I could …"

I tried folding my arms in front of my chest but had to give up. Callay seemed to second that by giving me a sharp jab with what was undoubtedly an elbow.

"Mother."

"What?"

"Don't go all *How to Get Away with Murder* on me. We can't go spying on Cesar."

But that was just what we did.

The last strains of *I Will Survive* were blaring from the backyard as we crept up Fidel's ivy-lined driveway. I was sure I felt something bite me on the arm. I tried not to pay any attention to it, I really did, but gruesome scenarios involving Valley fever and Lyme disease started multiplying in my mind. Would Callay survive at this point if I died of West Nile virus? What if a pack of rats was preparing to attack us from the ivy?

It wasn't until Donna Summer launched into *Hot Stuff* that Mother found a slightly larger gap between two wooden fence posts. I let her lean in to take a look, convinced that my belly would just bounce me back, but the particular shade of pig pink that Mother's face had taken on convinced me to try.

I had to hand it to Fidel. With the same attention to detail with which he'd created a front yard mosaic of thick grasses, beehive ginger, urn plants and monkey paws, he'd constructed his own outdoor disco hall in back, with colored lights mounted on a pair of graceful birch trees and crisscrossing a raised, wooden dance floor bordered by life-sized cardboard cutouts of John Travolta, Michael Jackson, and Donna Summer herself, all of them applauding the dancers, who seemed to be—could they be?—Fidel himself and our Cesar. At least, the former had the same red-faced coloring as our neighborhood dog killer and the latter had on the same black boots Cesar had been wearing when he'd sailed past me a half hour before.

Beyond that, the two were nearly unrecognizable. Fidel was dancing surprisingly well, given the height of his spiky silver heels. He was no longer a spring chicken, so the shiny, black waves that flowed over the shoulders of his white, décolleté gown must surely be a wig. But nothing but nature—or, as I realized later, surgery or hormone treatments—could have fabricated the twin milk-chocolate mounds that seemed about to burst from his heaving chest.

If Fidel was, in his own fashion, a model of glamorous taste, the way Cesar had gotten himself up was another story. Pancake make-up had been applied to his face sufficiently thickly to cover the signature birthmark that sat above the inside corner of his left eyebrow like an off-center *bindi*. Above his calf-hugging boots was as much of an expanse of bare skin as a rather short Guatemalan male could muster, climaxing in a wisp of black lace that exposed an undulating ass whose perfect contours most of female America would have died to have been born with. A mix of metaphors, to be sure, but I was hardly in a state of grammatical sagacity.

I fell away from the fence—Cesar's spiky, platinum blond wig and elaborately painted face fixed in my mind's eye—to land right in Mother's arms. Her body was vibrating.

I stepped back, and we stared at each other like a couple of gapeseeds. Mother squeaked, "What the hell?"

And then, before I could object, Mother had loosened me from her grip and was climbing—climbing!—over the fence, somehow managing to use its thick hinges as purchase for her feet. As she went over, I couldn't help but note the imprint of the pricey *Arche* brand logo on her rippled black soles.

It is no small torture to be standing on one side of a fence with a debilitatingly large belly when your mother has just landed with a great howl of pain on the other side. About the only good news was that the music had stopped and sounds of sympathy soon superseded cries of Cesar and Fidel's own understandable shock.

I screamed, "Let me in!" and the gate began to open out, revealing Mother sitting on the ground, rubbing the top of her head, a redder-than-ever-faced Fidel stooping down with his arms around her shoulders amidst a large, glossy-leafed bush that I would later learn, with some gratitude, was aptly named Soft Touch Holly.

But little was soft about the scene before me. Mother looked dazed, and I saw with some fear that Cesar did, too, particularly as he'd turned back from opening the gate to stand directly above Mother, his jaw slack, his legs curled inward as if to protect his poorly-packaged privates. His garishly made-up eyes looked decidedly wander-y.

I unceremoniously shoved him away, issuing a terse, "Get a grip! Call an ambulance!"

I didn't know whether to be appalled or relieved to hear Mother cry out, "For God's sake, change your clothes before they come!"

Chapter Three

WHY IN THE world were medical facilities inevitably kept at a temperature just barely above freezing when the ailing body cried out for every kind of warmth? After a shivery wait of nearly three hours at the Huntington Hospital ER, Mother had been pronounced "good to go home" by a harried resident with an ominously protruding mole on his chin that brought to mind the proverb from Luke 4:23 that I'd first read at the age of three, "Physician, heal thyself." I nearly ran after the man to make him promise he'd have the worrying knob looked into, but Mother was already grabbing her clothes from the little cubby at the corner of the room and pulling on her lacy, black La Perla panties. Her balance was more than a little wobbly. I quickly stepped forward to support her lest we have another injury to contend with.

Emerging from that dolorous prison, we exchanged grateful glances at the feel of the balmy afternoon air. I held Mother's arm with one hand, while in the other I clutched copies of paperwork confirming that her insurance would pick up the undoubtedly pricey tab for her use of a cot fit for a largish doll and with instructions ending with the caveat that Mother should visit a neurologist if her mild headache turned into something more.

Within the hour, she and I huddled together on the smaller of two smoke-colored, Jean-Michel Frank Bauhaus sofas in her capacious living room, while perched at the edge of its companion was a sullen-faced Cesar Jesus de Maria Santo Domingo Marisco, clad— thank God— in jeans and a T-shirt, with only the faintest hint of glittery blue mascara to remind us of his get-up earlier that day.

I kept an ice pack clapped on Mother's head as she spoke with exquisite tact, her face nonetheless wreathed in worry and pain, for which I'd never forgive Cesar, though it had admittedly been she and not he who'd decided to climb that fence. As if she were a teenager and not a woman about to become grandmother to my own increasingly restive bun. I prayed not to go into labor until Mother recovered from her wallop.

"Cesar, dear," Mother murmured, "You could have told me, you know. We alcoholics have been around a block or two ourselves."

Cesar's face screwed into a mask of contempt as he flung out a defiant, "Don't even go there. Alcoholism is a disease. Cross-dressing isn't."

Mother drew back as if she'd been slapped. Her ice pack landed in my lap and I re-applied it as she adjusted her strategy.

"Of course, you're right. I didn't mean to imply that it is, only that—"

Cesar wasn't having any of it. He stood and leaned in toward us, fists clenched at his sides with visible self-restraint. "Don't you dare patronize me. You know nothing about me. You and Miss Hand-Flapping Queen of the Universe over there. It's been Fleur this and Fleur that ever since I was kidnapped from my family and brought to this damned country."

Mother squeaked out a hapless, "Kidnapped? But no, really— Cesar, you were adopted. Nana and I took you to visit your mother. And, since then … you know I've done everything I could to support your contact with her."

"Yeah, but now she's stopped calling, hasn't she, and I don't even know how to find her. The only people who ever bothered to ask how *I* feel about things have been Nana and Fidel, and now one of them's dead and the other won't want anything to do with me. Did you ever think of that when you decided to come spying on me? Before ruining my life for the millionth time? I've had your number from the very beginning. You're all a bunch of hypocrites, thinking you're doing good when you're so fucking selfish except when it comes to rearranging your lives to accommodate the genius freak. Move to Pasadena? Sure. Never mind that Cesar, who's had a hard enough time with his ADHD, has to change schools when he's finally begun to make a few friends. Nobody needed to drive a car when we lived in Manhattan. Did it ever occur to you that Nana never would have died if we'd just stayed put? But, oh no, we have to go where the freak goes." His upper lip trembled as he fought back tears. Mother grabbed her ice pack from me and fumbled with it before flinging it onto the coffee table.

The irony was that at that moment it was all I could do not to flap. It wasn't the venom in Cesar's voice, or the name-calling. Over the years, I'd been called all sorts of things (admittedly, mostly by Father), from Autistic Weirdo to Odd Duck to Sneaky Little Monster. I was used to it. No, what got to me was the implication that Cesar had been languishing in my shadow. That the boy who'd been abandoned by a crack-addicted mother had also been—not exactly kidnapped, but evidently being adopted had felt the same—subjected to another series of losses, most of them thanks to me. I was mortified. If only I could peel off my own skin.

But before I could begin to summon an apology, he'd fled the house, whose windows quaked with the force of the slamming front door.

Mother and I sat wordlessly together until I rose and wandered blindly out the French doors leading to the side garden. Broad beams of sunlight filtered in through the leaves of the young sycamore Mother had planted when she'd moved here. It had been her way of honoring the robust, mature version that Grandfather and I used to watch together for hours at a time, the one we'd called, "our tree." The one Father had cut down from spite.

The air was quite still. Quiet enough to hear the whirr of a turquoise damselfly as she shot across the lily pond. Quiet enough to hear Mother whisper from behind me, "It's not your fault. It's mine."

I turned around and studied her face. Telltale smoker's vertical lines scored her upper lip more deeply than ever. I saw the weariness in her. The heaviness. She, who'd been so filled with optimism ever since winning sobriety.

"Dear God," she muttered, "I really have my work cut out with that boy, don't I?"

The baby moved, and I took Mother's hand and placed it on my belly. Callay shifted position again, a small temblor inside me, and what must have been a foot poked out visibly. One lone tear ran down Mother's face. I brushed it away with my fingertip and pulled her toward me in a long, clumsy attempt at a hug.

I stared vaguely over her shoulder until the delicate purple and white flowers of a particularly abundant milkweed plant caught my eye. They trembled at a slight gust of wind.

"Oh, look!" I cried out, pointing.

Mother skewed around to see.

Scores of tiny, translucent golden eggs sketched out a diamond design across a long milkweed leaf that gestured gracefully toward us. They sparkled like miniature Christmas lights in the late afternoon sun.

Taking Mother's hand, I tiptoed us closer. Mother squinted. "What—?"

I spoke softly, as if even the vibration of my voice might disturb them. "They're monarch eggs. First stage of a caterpillar's life. A butterfly's life." A little cry of joy escaped me. "As soon as they hatch, they eat the leaf they're born on. Talk about biting the hand that feeds you."

"Oh, I wish I had my glasses." Mother leaned in closer to get a better look.

"The little caterpillars can't move very far, so the mother butterfly needs to lay her eggs on exactly the kind of leaf that will nourish them. Any other plant simply won't do. And once they start feeding, they grow like crazy, but their skin doesn't stretch like ours, so they have to keep shedding their exoskeletons while they grow."

"Like snakes!"

"Sort of. If you like, we can be on the lookout for when they reach the pupa stage. The chrysalis. They'll be hanging from a branch like little pea pods."

Mother snorted. "My scientist daughter is getting carried away now. With any luck, you'll be feeding your own little pea pod by then."

"Oh, my god. You're right. I'd better!" I felt a wave of regret at the thought of missing the evolution of those delicate little droplets, but then a pang of distress overtook me.

"Mother!" I cried.

"Hmm?"

"Do you think Cesar landed on the wrong sort of leaf?"

Frowning, she nearly spat at me, "Don't."

"What?"

"Don't say that. It makes it all sound so final. As if something terrible has happened that can't be undone."

Ah. There it was again.

As a child, I'd had the delusion that watering my dead grandfather's shrunken member would accomplish the feat of resurrection. I'd reasoned that if the part of his anatomy that served conception were revived, he would be, too. I'd come a long way since then, but was our team's end goal all that different? In this case, we sought to stave off our species' extinction by lessening our reliance on fossil-fueled travel. Would we be able to make a difference in time, before the verdict of climate change became final? I felt torn between my impatience to get this baby girl of mine born and a sense of urgency to make the Dreamization project a living reality so that she might actually have a future.

Hurry, intoned that insistent voice, *hurry, hurry!*

Chapter Four

OUR LIVES WERE fast turning into a medical drama. An OB-GYN visit for me—according to my doctor, everything still "on track," with no need to think about inducing yet. Then, just to make sure, a neurology workup for Mother with unenlightening results. Within the same week, heartening news came via group text from Stanley H. Fiske. Gwennie would finally be sprung from the grand and sanitized complex of City of Hope to be delivered the following day via private ambulance to the Fiskes' much humbler digs on Rose Villa Street. I gave a little prayer of thanks that Stanley had gotten home in time on the day that Mother had bonked her head to take delivery of the patient lift.

I called Mother immediately. She sounded as thrilled as I was, but there was a new ingredient in her speech that I found profoundly discomfiting.

I couldn't help but ask, "Why are you laughing?"

At first, she sounded defensive. "Well, it's good news, isn't it? It must be that I'm happy." But then she ended up confiding, "I can't help it. Life seems a lot sillier ever since I landed on my head."

I probably didn't help matters much by commenting that life seemed a lot more nonsensical to *me* ever since I'd seen a nearly naked Cesar on stilt heels doing the bump with Fidel Marquetti, but at least we were able to move on from there, divvying up the work that had to be done before Gwennie came home. A night care nurse needed to be hired, a host of prescriptions to be filled, organic groceries to be fetched from Whole Foods.

But we agreed that there was one thing we couldn't do on our own. The patient lift may have been delivered, but—insanely—it had not been put together; evidently, that should have been arranged ahead of time. I rang off and punched in Ignacio's number. There was no way we could leave it up to Stanley to set up the vertical lift hoist on his own. My fellow Nobelist was the original absent-minded professor, and it was all too easy to imagine him bungling the assembly of the heavy contraption, ending up suspended upside down, one foot caught in a wire loop like the Hanging Man in Sammie's Tarot deck. Which brought back to mind Assefa's attempt to kill himself on an IV pulley at UCLA Medical Center. Which really didn't bear thinking about. I pinched myself a few times on my fleshy upper arm, and that seemed to do the trick.

So here we were, Stanley and Ignacio and Mother and I, trying to figure out how to make the damned thing work, which hadn't been helped by the men's refusal to consult the instruction booklet first.

But once Ignacio applied his gift for sensate reality, the steel beast stood facing the bed like a ready servant, and it was decided that Mother would be Gwen's stand-in (or in this case lie-in) as we sought to make sure Stanley knew what to do with its services once Gwennie arrived.

I insisted that this time we consult the manual.

"Okay," croaked Stanley, reading aloud from the little pamphlet in his most froggish voice, "First, roll over." That was fine, so far as it went. We took it for granted that we, the installers, were not ourselves required to perform any physical maneuvers. Mother obediently turned onto her side. "And now, slide sling under side features of hapless person, then roll over in opposite direction." It dawned on me that the instructions had been written in one of those lousy translations of Chinese. I prayed that Mother's new funny bone would hold still for the rest of the operation.

But it was Stanley who guffawed as he read, "Tuck excess material inside patient."

I broke in quickly, "Under. They must mean under."

But I could tell Stanley was teetering. "Encouraging neck strength, put padded support behind esteemed head of hapless one." He snorted, then continued, "Put sling under two legs of hapless one and tie together for modesty of all." He looked up, his bug eyes twinkling from behind his thick lenses. "Yeah, but what do we do with the other legs?"

Ignoring him, Ignacio struggled to tie together Mother's legs without violating her privacy. Stanley and I kibitzed from the corner of the room. And all the while Mother issued forth a running series of objections. "No. Wait. Pull it down. It's cutting into my thigh. No, now you've got it too low. Okay, that might be a bit better. This is like Goldilocks and the bloody bears." Seeing Stanley grinning, she commented in a slightly injured tone, "I don't know what's so funny. He's got me bound so tightly, I can hardly breathe." I had to admit that she resembled nothing less than a trussed turkey.

Ignacio stepped forward to deftly sort out the ties and then activated the pump that set the whole thing in motion, Mother and all.

Once she'd been airlifted out of bed and onto the chair, Mother burst into high-pitched peals of laughter that went just over the edge. "Whee!" she giggled like a schoolgirl. And then, to make it even worse, "Again!" she cried.

Stanley and I exchanged a look. How in the hell was he going to do this in the coming days all by himself? And what in the world was wrong with Mother?

That night, I woke with a start. With a murmured, "Thirsty," to an awakened Adam, I rolled out of bed and up the hall to the baby's room. I turned on the dimmer just enough to see from the hands of the vintage Cat and Fiddle nursery clock that it was just a few minutes before 3:00 a.m. I'd learned from Siri Sajan that this preternaturally quiet hour had been dubbed by ancient Hindus the *Amrit Vela,* or Time of Deathless Consciousness. Reputedly, the perfect time to meditate. I considered it, but instead went down the staircase as quietly as a lumbering elephant, got my glass of water, switched off the alarm, and wandered out the French doors to the back garden, breathing in the poet's jasmine growing against the quartet of trellised arches against the rear of our house. Another thick, tangled hedge of it sprawled across the redwood fencing at the property line. The air was alive with its perfume. I made my way under a canopy of stars and a full moon, framed by a shimmering corona.

I loved the reciprocity of the moon's magnetism and a woman's cycle, how that pitted orb regularly rolled our earth's liquid envelope, maintaining the stability of our rotational axis, while droplets in our own troposphere framed this satellite nearly 240,000 miles away. No wonder humans had from time immemorial been moved to call the moon sacred names—Selene in ancient Greece; Coyolzuahqui by the Aztecs; Yrikh by the Canaanites; Queen Jiang by the Chinese; and in Ethiopia, Yuk. For me, a sacred chant of *Callooh! Callay!* would do— our child having been conceived under a Milk Moon in an act layered with lust and love.

The crickets were performing a percussive cantata as I shuffled out to inspect the patch of land where we'd yanked out our scraggly ryegrass the previous winter to plant dymondia—our own small contribution to water saving during SoCal's endless drought. The ground cover had failed to take hold almost from the get-go, its leaves turning completely white before withering entirely. We'd tried again, Ignacio muttering under his breath as he'd inserted each little clump into the soil, swearing that he didn't see what the fuss was about, there being many more practical plants to choose from. But I'd fallen in love with dymondia. When thriving, its silvery green carpet looked like something out of a fairy garden. Now, in the moonlight, I saw shiny little islands of it sending emissaries toward other solo clumps, the greener leaves bridging the dirt to make the connection.

There was a barely discernible rustling in the twining hedge of jasmine closest to me. Goosebumps rose up on my arms as a creature emerged from the dark. My hands made little fists as she paused, assessing my threat. I noted the telltale shape of her, her short tail and tall ears, but was mostly mesmerized by her intense greenish-gold eyes. I'd heard that Pasadena was home to bobcats, but I'd never seen one with my own eyes. Despite my anxiety, I nearly laughed aloud. Only days before I'd been afraid of being bitten by a mosquito, and now here I was, eye to eye with a creature that—if sick or rabid—would be more than capable of doing me grievous bodily harm. I knew I should back away slowly, make a ferocious noise. But I stood stock-still and stared. She stared back at me. I'd already taken in her bulging belly. Had she taken in mine?

I recalled Assefa's story of his childhood encounter with a pair of kudus, those odd-eared, delicately striped antelopes of Africa that were given their sweet-sounding name by the Khoikhoi people. The grandfather of Assefa's best friend, Girma—I believe the old man was called Demissie—had insisted on taking the two boys on an initiatory expedition into the forest. After an exhausting hunt, Assefa had ended up cradling the head of a dying kudu calf in his lap. He'd been convinced that the poor creature's spirit had entered his own body at the moment of its death, only to give him strength, many years later, to break the nose of a khat-intoxicated boy who'd slashed Father Wendimu's neck.

I involuntarily shuddered and saw that the bobcat had noted my subtle movement. With a warning flash of her eyes, she darted back into the hedge and was gone.

I was trembling, but not from fear alone. What a gorgeous creature! I prayed that she'd find a place to bear her kittens in peace, that they would all find their way back to the San Rafael Hills, where they might stand a fighting chance of survival.

By the time I walked back toward the house, the clouds had covered the moon, and I nearly tripped on the edge of an uneven paver. There was no way around it: we humans were gifted with great ingenuity, but the low-voltage lights lining the path were a sorry substitute for the lustrous light of Selene.

My lack of sleep that night didn't help much the next morning when I drove to join Mother at Stanley and Gwennie's. If Gwen had looked unwontedly frail at the City of Hope, she seemed even more delicate in her familiar digs. Seeing this thinner, yellower, and balder incarnation of her previously hearty self drove home the truth that she was still a pretty sick puppy.

Despite growing up with a grandfather doing a slow shuffle toward death, it occurred to me now that I knew very little about aging. Then, I'd only been aware of the melty eyes, the grunted *ugga umph uggas*, the mystery map of soft lines engraved on the hands of my very favorite person on the planet. Since Grandfather couldn't speak, he couldn't tell me of his pain, his nostalgia, his dread of the great darkening to come.

But Gwennie could. Once Stanley had managed to move her from bed to chair as we'd all practiced—with only one tense moment when she dangled over-long in the air, with Mother, in the corner, tittering alarmingly—Gwen began to speak quite frankly about her concerns, fretting over the prospect of Stanley being left on his own to fend for himself, worrying that Callay might not have a habitable planet to finish out a decent lifetime, fearing she'd miss seeing the culture-shifting power of my scientific discovery put to use.

"There's one thing I know for sure, Stanley," she said, taking a moment to dab a tissue at the spittle that tended to collect these days at the corners of her lips, "You weren't meant to live alone. A lot of men aren't, but it'd be worse for you." She skewed her body a bit and extended a hand toward the other side of the living room, which was piled nearly to the ceiling with copies of *Living Reviews in Relativity*, *Reviews of Modern Physics*, and *Proceedings of the National Academy of Sciences*.

She pointed a bony finger at her brother. "You've got to get yourself a woman when I go. It's long overdue. You're nearly sixty-years-old. You're not exactly Prince Charming anymore, but you're still a good catch. Time to get over Doris Abrantes. She's not the only fish in the sea and hardly representative of the female of the species. Marrying a Nobelist would be a feather in any woman's cap, and what you lack in grace would be made up for by intelligent conversation."

Mother and I hardly knew where to look, but I did catch Stanley blushing. Honestly, I'd never given Stanley a thought in that department. Even with his slight geriatric stoop, he was still far taller than the average man. His Coke-bottle-lensed glasses magnifying his somewhat buggy eyes, his unusually long neck and tendency to hop when excited, made me forever think of him as the most intelligent, most endearing frog ever. But as I snuck another look, I saw that there was an appealing softness to the little paunch he'd acquired. The still-thick and shiny mane of hair that had turned silver over the years, which he wore a bit long and professor-ish, was actually quite attractive. But he also looked terribly tired. The bags under his eyes were more pronounced than usual, and the lines from his nose to his chin seemed etched more deeply. Gwennie's illness had taken its toll on *him*, too.

I managed to convince him to take a nap in the den. Mother—verifying that I could stay a few more hours—excused herself for her scheduled hair appointment with Kelly Zhang.

I fetched a chair from the kitchen, and Gwen and I sat together side by side, our faces in and out of shade as a column of clouds paraded before the sun. We observed the happenings out the front window much as Grandfather and I would in the old days, watching the patterns made by birds flitting from branch to branch in our tree. But Gwennie was a heck of a lot gabbier than my mute grandfather had been. I listened with eyes as wide as a child's as she spoke of her first love. The young have the hardest time imagining that their elders weren't always—well, not to put too fine a point on it—old.

Gwennie took great pains to impress on me that the boy was the cutest guy she'd ever seen. "His name was Jack Green," she reported, followed by a pregnant pause. Her face had a surprisingly kittenish expression for a woman who'd just barely cheated death. "Oh, just to think of him, Fleur! I get goosebumps to this day. His eyes weren't green, like your Adam's, but the color of starling eggs. He was Black Irish by heritage, with a dimple in his chin, olive skin, and the sleekest, blackest hair—a little like your Buster's fur. He wore it long." I sat without speaking as she sensuously stroked a pillow with her venous hand. "He was something of a hippie. Truth was, I was too. If I ever get my energy back, remind me to tell you about driving up the coast to Santa Barbara during a wildfire, peaking on acid." I think my jaw actually dropped, for she added quickly, "Don't worry. Really, it was lucky it was such a bad trip. It was the first and last time. The whole episode cured me of ever wanting to take psychedelics again."

She took an orange from the bowl of fresh organic fruit Mother had placed on the side table and began to slowly peel it. Gwen was one of those people who have the knack of peeling an orange in one long spiral, and I stared, fascinated, as she muttered, "Where was I? Oh, Jack. And the demonstration. We were marching from UCLA to the Federal Building. The university was a helluva lot smaller in those days, probably about as big as Pasadena CC is now, and it seemed like the whole campus was there. The war was that unpopular. I wish we could whip up that much passion to end our endless wars in the Middle East.

"I was poor as a church mouse. Stanley was studying back in Philly, and our parents were still alive, barely getting by in this house. Thank God they'd paid off the mortgage by then. They knew about Jack, and I knew they had hopes we'd tie the knot. I also knew that Jack wasn't the knot-tying kind. But I would have given anything to have something more with him.

"Anyway, we were about halfway through the march when I realized I had a problem on my hands. Well, not exactly on my hands." She snorted, and then put down her orange to blow her nose. "It was my panties. They were so old that I realized the elastic was giving out. Right there on Wilshire Boulevard.

"I was mortified, but what could I do? I explained what was going on to Jack. God bless him, he didn't bat an eye. Just said, 'Let 'em fall, step out of 'em, and keep walking.' And that's exactly what I did, shouting, "Hey, hey, LBJ, how many kids did you kill today,' even louder as I did a little two-step on the sidewalk. Later, with Jack finally in my dorm bed with me, the two of us sharing a cigarette, we fantasized together about what the cops made of the pair of undies left behind on the street." She sighed. "It was the last time I saw him. I heard he'd fallen for Penny Spheeris, the queen of the film department. She had all the confidence that I didn't and ten times the looks. Curly black gypsy hair halfway down her back. She ended up directing *The Decline of Western Civilization, Part II: The Metal Years*. About heavy metal. Not exactly my cup of tea. But then again, I surely wouldn't have been one of hers."

At that point, Gwennie looked so sad—and so tired—that I convinced her to let me airlift her back to bed. As a little snore escaped her, I found myself wondering what would have happened if pouring water onto my grandfather's shrunken balls had actually achieved my goal of resurrecting him. I might never have even met Adam, who Sammie likes to call "your one-stop shop for everything good in your life." I wasn't sure I liked giving so much credit to one person, even the man I adored, but I had to admit her assignment had some merit. Though we quantum physicists like to speculate that choices not made are played out in an uncountable series of multiple universes, I couldn't imagine what would have happened to me without Adam comforting me at Grandfather's funeral, introducing me to Stanley H. Fiske and quantum physics once Mother had hired him as my tutor because no school would accept me, and traveling all the way to Ethiopia to claim me as his own.

My hands traveled, as they tended to do these days, to my watermelon belly, which still never failed to strike me dumb with the oddness of incarnation on this extraordinary planet, where human creatures were gestated like baby butterflies in a giant wet chrysalis and where the processing of a billion bits of memory, perspective, and sensation simply ceased when the body housing its incarnation wore out.

My cell phone went off and I sped to pick it up before it could wake Gwen. It was Mother, laughing uproariously. "Do you think I should dye my hair blue? It would be a hoot, don't you think?" Whispering, I wrung from her the confession that Kelly Zhang had insisted she call me to discuss it before going ahead with the coloring.

I walked down the hall. "Mother!" I hissed.

"Yes?" she squeaked.

"Get a grip. I've just put Gwen Fiske to bed. She's fighting cancer. I'm going to have a baby. Do you really think blue hair is the statement you want to be making right now?"

Contrite, she seemed to regain her mind. "God, I don't know what I was thinking."

I didn't either. But then I recalled her neurologist mentioning in passing that emotional lability wasn't an infrequent side effect of concussion.

Mother raised her voice. "Are you still there?"

"Yes. Yes, of course."

Her voice was leaden now. "I'm an idiot. You should get home and have a rest. This is a lot to ask of yourself right now."

Actually, she was right. I was exhausted. When Stanley stumbled out of his bedroom, bleary-eyed but insisting he was fine to take over, I took her advice. I went home and slipped under the covers, nestling my shoulders against my favorite down pillow and muzzily pondering aging.

I heard the front door slam and the high-pitched voices of Melesse and Sofiya gaining in volume as they ascended the stairs. Sofiya was speaking in a combination of Amharic and English to her sister. I caught "mustn't mention to *Enat*" and "if he does that again, just tell me," phrases guaranteed to set off alarm bells, but my fatigue was too great. Promising myself to investigate later, I let myself slip off the cliff of consciousness into sleep.

But when I woke the next morning, I recalled nothing but Mother's craziness in wanting to dye her hair blue. It bothered me so much that it became the first item of conversation when Sammie arrived.

I greeted her with a fierce hug, murmuring, "Thank God! I missed you terribly." My best friend—or Belly Sister, as we liked to call each other—had been in England for the past three months on a sabbatical. We had no end of topics to catch up on.

As we plopped onto the queen's settee, I couldn't help but tease her about the British accent she resumed whenever she traveled back home, along with her automatic response of "That's brilliant!" to any good news I had to offer. But her reaction to my recap of my last conversation with Mother was nothing if not gratifying.

"You're joking, right?" Her thick, butterfly brows lifted in appropriate astonishment, and she pursed her lips disapprovingly. "You've got to admit it, Fleur Beurre, we don't exactly have the most conventional of mums."

"Well, to be fair, yes and no." Sammie's mother had settled comfortably into her long-term relationship with Arturo Denardi, but when she'd first started seeing her considerably younger yoga teacher, Mother had called her a cougar. Which was a serious case of the pot calling the kettle black. Nonetheless, both women had been accomplished in their fields, Aadita even contributing to C-Voids and P.D. with her insights into quantum mathematics and her knowledge of Indra's Web, and Mother nearly single-handedly overhauling the priorities of the $155 million budget of the LA Public Library system. Neither woman had been interested in retiring, though the somewhat older Aadita had reduced her teaching load at Caltech to part-time and Mother had traded her role as city librarian for a seat on the library department's board of commissioners.

"I can just see her, sitting down at one of her board meetings looking like an aging Avril Lavigne," I muttered.

Sammie added wryly, "Especially when the rest of them probably have tight perms and pale blue rinses that are about as far away from punk blue as possible. Your mum's already more gorgeous and stylish than any of those old girls, but there's no question, it'd be, well, *off*. I saw a couple of older shopkeepers in Notting Hill sporting a bright turquoise streak or two, but that's London."

We both said, in unison, "Definitely not Pasadena!" and laughed. Sammie murmured under her breath, "The Judds," and we giggled again.

"Speaking of London, how was it?" Sammie had spent most of her sabbatical pursuing a solo walking tour of the Lake District, bookended by a week on each side in her beloved London. I would never have mentioned it, but it had felt like a major deprivation not being able to bend her ear with every detail of my final trimester of pregnancy.

She seemed to hesitate, then replied brightly, "Perfect, if you don't count the fact that they're all still grieving over Brexit. But first things first." She gestured toward my bun. "How are you doing? I feel awful that I didn't call to check in, but ... well, anyway, isn't she supposed to be out of that belly and keeping you up nights by now?"

"Well, she's keeping me up nights, but that's only because she's sitting directly on my bladder. The doc says to give her time. He doesn't like inducing until a woman goes two weeks after her due date, and I've got a week and half before then." I gave a sigh big enough for Sammie to scoot over on the sofa and put her arm around me.

She tilted my face toward her and said, in dead seriousness, "Want a Smartie?"

I screeched, "Where are they?"

She got up and fetched her somewhat battered leather bag and dug into it, retrieving two hexagonal tubes with M&M-looking candies pictured on the package. It was a given between us that Smarties were far superior to their American lookalikes, being somewhat bigger and having thicker, crunchier, and more vibrantly-colored shells. Orange Smarties were filled with famously orange-flavored chocolate, and we each sagaciously saved ours for last.

But they didn't stop us from yakking away, our teeth smeared with chocolate; we were both known for being "high verbal," and we proceeded to re-earn our reputations.

When Sammie asked about the girls, I clapped my hand to my forehead. "Oh shit. I heard Sofiya insisting that Melesse should tell her if he ever did that to her again."

"He who?"

"That's just it. I have no idea. I was falling asleep when she said it."

Sammie frowned. "Sounds ominous."

"Right? Do you think I should just ask her myself? Or tell Makeda and let her handle it?"

"Mmm. Well, she *is* the mum."

"I guess. If it were Callay—whatever it was, I'd want to know." I felt myself edging toward the void and stifled the urge to pinch.

Sammie knew me. "What is it?"

"I don't want anything awful happening to my girl. Ever." Shuddering, I pushed myself up, muttering, "Gotta pee."

When I returned, easing myself down onto the sofa, I said, apropos of nothing, "There's actually a story behind Mother's craziness with the blue hair. She's been a little wacko ever since she got her concussion."

"Concussion? What the fuck! I go away for three months and all hell breaks loose?"

"That's not even the half of it." I explained about Cesar, describing the scene with him and Fidel with as much flourish as possible, only half-aware that I was laying it on thickly to get maximum sympathy.

But Sammie merely sat quietly, and I assumed she needed a moment to let it all in.

"Listen," she said, staring so hard just behind my left ear that I actually turned to see what she was looking at. "Something unusual happened to me, too, while I was away."

My heart fell. "Oh, honey, what is it?"

She flushed. "I met someone."

"But that's a good thing, isn't it?"

She looked up and, with a little flick of her beautiful black locks, said, "*Very* good. Well, I hope so. I think so." She gave me a searching look and added, "Her name's Amira."

It took me a minute to realize that my sense of my friend was about to undergo a paradigm shift. I felt suddenly mortified that I'd been making fun of Cesar, who must surely dance somewhere in the alphabetical direction of LGBTQ. What must she think of me?

What did I think of myself?

"Right," I sighed. "Don't bother about what I said just now about Cesar and Fidel. Put it down to me just being an asshole. Let's try this again. Tell. I want every juicy detail."

Favoring me with a reassured smile, she lay back onto the sofa with her head against its overstuffed arm. "Okay, Frau Jung. And can I tell you how much I love you? I felt the same as you when Amira and I were introduced at a party for a journalist just back from Iraq. Totally shocked. I mean, my heart started beating like a maniac the second I looked into those amazing green eyes."

I cackled. "I know all about green eyes! But wait, who *is* she? What's she like? Did you get much time together?"

"She actually took a fake sick leave from her job and came with me to the Lake District." Sammie's eyes came over all moony. "We were like a couple of gypsies, with just a couple of sleeping bags and some minimal cooking gear." She laughed. "A hell of a far cry from how we met. She's a BBC TV commentator. But don't get me wrong. They didn't choose her for her looks. She's drop-dead-insanely-gorgeous, but she's as smart as you, Fleur, in a history and current affairs sort of way. Knows way more than I do about the Middle East, the history of Judaism, Islam, Buddhism, you name it. And she's witty. You and I are funny in a corny sort of way, but she's got that 'take the piss' British humor that I remember from my school days, except when I was a kid it was typically aimed at *me*." She blanched. "Oh, God, poor Melesse. It could be bullying—or it might even be something creepily sexual. You really are going to have to tell Makeda right away. I couldn't bear the thought of that little angel being tormented."

I frowned guiltily. "God. You're absolutely right, Sam, and I will. But *come on*. I'm dying to hear about this."

"Okay, but I guess I really am a little nervous telling you."

"Sammie, you could have grown a couple of horns and murdered someone and I'd still love you."

"Reminds me of that awful Trump comment that he could shoot somebody in the middle of Fifth Avenue and not lose voters."

"Don't even go there."

She laughed, putting a hand on my arm. "Just kidding." She took a deep breath. "You really are my dearest, darlingest friend. Anyway, you know me. I've never been attracted to girls—at least I never had been—and, honestly, I haven't been attracted to *anyone* since Jacob."

"I can believe that. That asshole could turn anyone off men forever." And then I blushed. "I didn't mean to suggest that was why you—I mean … God, that sounded totally disrespectful. Honestly, I have no idea what I mean."

"I get it. I've been trying to figure it out, too. But I don't think it's anything to do with him. I think it's all about her. I can't really say I'm a lesbian." She laughed. "Sounds pretty ridiculous, doesn't it? Like I'm ashamed. Which I'm not. But I'd never even noticed women before in that way. But Amira? Oh, Fleur, I think I'm in love and we live worlds apart and she's got the kind of job people die for and she's there and I'm here and I know I'm getting way ahead of myself. But what am I going to do?"

"Oh, sweetie. You're reminding me of how it was when Adam left for his post-doc in Boston. And we weren't even lovers then. It took me going all the way to Ethiopia for him to fly out there and finally tell me he wanted to sleep with me." I paused.

"What is it?"

"Was it different? I mean, of course it was, but well, *experientially?*"

She blushed, and I have to tell you that Sammie blushing is not an everyday event.

"Girlfriend, some lines just need to be drawn, but I will tell you this. I never, ever thought I'd want to have anything to do with anyone else's VaJewJew but my own." We giggled. We'd shared a great admiration for Amy Winehouse's music and had laughed ourselves silly when we first heard the name she'd dubbed her tweeter. Of course, the word *tweeter* was a whole other story. I'd used it so long I couldn't recall if it had been passed along by one of the Vestal Virgins of my early life—Sister Flatulencia, Cook, Fayga—or whether it had come to me onomatopoeically when I had my first teenaged mini-explosions to fantasies of Hector Hernandez's bulging member. Which were, by the way, ever so much nicer than the real-life version pushing itself into my unprepared tweeter.

But Sammie was saying quickly, as if to glide past her embarrassment, "If anything, it always struck me as kind of gross to think about it. But I'm here to testify that when you're in love with someone … well, Hope Sandoval really knew what she was singing about."

"Mazzy Star? *Fade into You?*"

She nodded knowingly.

"God, I haven't thought about that one for, what, fifteen years?"

"Probably."

I lumbered over to my cell phone. "I think I have it."

As Hope Sandoval sang in that whispery voice of hers, Sammie asked, "Have you ever…?"

I couldn't believe there was something Sammie and I hadn't talked about, but life was obviously more full of surprises than I'd ever imagined. "Been attracted to a woman? No, not really. I mean, I think Lemlem is the most beautiful person I've ever seen, but I don't think I'd want to be with her. More like *be* her."

"Be her? Why would you want to be her?"

I gestured down to my gargantuan belly.

"But you're absolutely radiant, Fleur!"

"Not that kind of radiant."

She hesitated, and then asked, "It's not about Assefa is it?"

I waved a hand. "Oh, don't be silly. Of course not."

Chapter Five

IT WAS A fine day to have a party. Wonder of wonders, it had actually rained a bit the night before, and the scent of poet's jasmine was everywhere. Most of Sofiya's classmates from her school's "Beaver Group" of four to five-year-olds had already arrived and were already wearing paper hats and tooting mercilessly on their party horns. Mother was here, of course, as were Dhani and her family, as well as my physics team, including Bob. Bob had actually brought a date, an appealingly curvy and incessantly talkative county health inspector he'd met on an anti-Monsanto march. I learned only later that Saffron Melamud was one of the survivors of the terror attack in San Diego, and I marveled at the resilience of the human spirit that this young woman seemed so ebullient, so carefree.

Dhani was in the kitchen, cooking up a storm. Adam and Abeba had just finished hanging across the back of the house a beautiful banner painted by Sammie that bore in exuberant Day-Glo pink the words "Happy Birthday!" and in squiggly Amharic, "*Melkam Lidet!*" Ignacio and No-Longer-a-Baby Angelina were busy blowing up the last of the pink and purple balloons. With a bunch of fat ones tied together on the Lutyens bench next to her and a rather anemic, smaller cluster at her father's side, Angelina was good-naturedly teasing Ignacio that his beer belly was restricting his air supply. I loved watching the sweetness between them, such a far cry from anything

I'd ever experienced with my own father. Angelina would turn seventeen soon and had all the confidence of a daddy's girl.

Cesar, needless to say, was not here. We hadn't seen him since the day of the incident, and both Mother and Abeba were worried sick about him. Mother hadn't been able to bring herself to ask Fidel where he thought Cesar might be, but pregnancy had made me brave and I'd marched up to his front door a few days ago, prepared to be confrontational. But Fidel was meek and redder than ever and confessed that he, too, was concerned about where Cesar might have gone.

Truth be told, I got far more than I'd bargained for in my encounter with Fidel. As I was about to turn away from his door, my ex-neighbor had invited me in for an *Arroz con Leche*, which I could hardly refuse, since rice pudding (cooked Indian style by Dhani) had cinched my reunion with Sammie after our terrible rift when she was twelve and I thirteen. Me being me, I ended up spilling out the story of our rapprochement to Fidel in his cozy, black-and-white, checker-tiled kitchen, trying not to stare at the feminine cleavage making little gaps between the buttons of a burgundy shirt that clashed rather dreadfully with his ever-inflamed skin. When I got to the part of the story where Sammie and I had sought refuge on her front porch from a sudden downpour, she snorting rice pudding out of her nose and me giggling so hard that I'd peed myself, Fidel had thrown his head back in a laughter so broad I could see that each of his molars bore a silver filling. I wondered whether our country had crippled the state of Cuban dentistry with our embargo. And whether the feminization of this Fidel had turned him from a murderer into a more genial sort of man.

As if to confirm the latter, Fidel had contributed to the conversation the information that rice pudding had a place at most of the world's tables, its cultural variations including:

1. A Lebanese dessert called *Moghli*, seasoned with anise, caraway, and ginger.

2. *Slátur*, an Icelandic rice porridge served as a main dish that included cold liver sausage.

3. The Danish Christmas version, *Risengrød*, covered in dark fruit juice.

4. Sutlijash, a Macedonian variant, perked up with black poppy seeds.

It occurred to me that for someone so well versed in such a variety of international cuisines, Fidel had behaved like the worst of bigots toward the Kangs, but I knew I'd get nowhere if I let my mind travel down that particular dark alley. Instead, I exclaimed, "How did you know all this?"

To which Fidel had responded, "Started my cheffing days at an upscale diner in West Texas, didn't I? My boss studied at the Cordon Bleu." (Except that Fidel pronounced it as "Cordonay Bloo-ay" in a combination of southern twang and Spanish lilt, causing me to surreptitiously pinch the flab beneath my armpit to keep from tittering.)

But any hint of hilarity fled the scene as soon as Fidel demonstrated his need to clarify how he and Cesar had met. It had evidently been on the evening of Gwen's last birthday bash, which filled me with melancholy; she'd seemed as healthy as a horse back then. "He was admiring my garden, and well, you know how things go." (I didn't). "We saw we had a lot in common. He speaks Spanish. Plays the guitar. Likes the same music. And dancing." He flushed even more. "Oh, yeah. I guess you know that."

He seemed pressed to convince me that he hadn't had anything to do with Cesar's cross-dressing, the conversation becoming far more graphic than I might have anticipated. "He's no trannie, you know, and I wouldn't be either, probably, if my sum bitch of a father hadn't yanked my *pinga* ever since I was a baby and then that worse sum bitch of an uncle hadn't asked me every night of my life after Papi died how much I'd liked it. It got to the point where I couldn't think of anything but pulling my *pene* and I couldn't have been happier to get rid of the damned thing when Medicare decided to cover the procedure. I can't tell you what a relief it's been."

By that time my face was undoubtedly redder than Fidel's, but he kept talking as if he were Mother's old Chatty Cathy doll, whose string had been pulled one too many times and kept repeating "Let's play house"—whatever *that* meant. While he droned on, I was captive to an unwelcome set of imaginings of young Fidel's nightmarish world, wondering what excuse for a father would do that to his son and what kind of monster of an uncle would have taken pleasure in grinding in the torture.

Before leaving I asked, "Just one thing has me a little confused: if you've made the transition, why do you still dress as a man?"

He looked at me as if I were crazy. "Do I look like a woman?" Considering the strong jut of his chin and his sharp cheekbones, I had to admit that he didn't, not really.

"Well then, why in hell would I want people to think of me as a freak?"

As a physicist, I knew that the world was filled with mystery, but I concluded at that moment that there would never be a fathoming of the odd complexities of the human mind.

I had no answer to Fidel's admittedly rhetorical question, but I felt a wave of empathy for the myriads of dilemmas unfolding from human suffering, like the butterfly effect gone badly. I nearly forgave him his murder of Chin Hwa. But not quite.

And now here I was at this birthday party, about to celebrate a child who'd endured her own horrors. But in her case, a pair of angels named Father Wendimu and Makeda Geteye had come along early enough to— hopefully—make all the difference. Really, there was no accounting for the fickle twists of fate.

Looking down at the ground, I mused mournfully, *Nor for the shifty gods of shoe size.* Thanks not only to the voluminous heft of my belly, but also pregnancy's propensity for loosening the body's ligaments to help with birthing, the bottoms of my feet resembled nothing more than odd-shaped pancakes. The only shoes I'd been able to fit into this morning were my ancient, stretched-out Mahabis, the ones with unavoidably bright yellow soles that I'd bought thinking they looked oh-so-trendy. At this point in their entropic cycle, they looked about as stylish as the muumuu I wore that Adam, anticipating my future engorgement, had picked out for my last birthday; the garment's red and blue chevron design pointed down toward my feet as if to purposely accentuate the color clash. *Never mind,* I told myself. *It's the thought that counts.* And if Adam thought I was the sort of woman who didn't mind looking like Mother Hubbard, so be it. And so much for our future sex life.

As luck would have it, my ruminations were interrupted by Makeda, who joined us just in time to let loose a gasp of what might have been either dismay or delight. Angelina, Ignacio, and I immediately turned to see what had prompted her reaction.

I saw that Assefa had appeared at the edge of the lawn with Lemlem, but what a Lemlem this was! Attired in a turquoise flared dress belted tightly at the waist, her matching beaded cornrows were complemented by a headband made of an intricate design of tiny triangular seashells. Tucked flirtatiously over one ear was a dewily fresh, purplish-pink hydrangea that matched the color of her bee-stung lips. And then the goddess smiled, a little shyly, I thought, the gap between her teeth lending just enough imperfection to make her wildly desirable.

We all felt it. Everyone moved toward her like a magnet, but we were too gobsmacked to actually comment on her appearance—all but Bob, that is, who cried out, "Kitten's paws! *Plicatulidae*! Where'd you get them? Did you make that thingie yourself?"

It occurred to me that it was possible that only I—well, and undoubtedly Saffron Melamud—knew what a collector of shells Bob was; he was crazy about anything to do with the sea. I'd discovered that myself on my one and only visit to his apartment in Palms, when one thing had led to another, culminating in his semen staining the Wookie in his Star Wars bedspread and my discovery that I was embarrassingly capable of having casual sex. But that was in another incarnation entirely, one ushered in by Assefa dumping me for Makeda. Now she and I stared open-mouthed at the woman who'd ultimately won his heart.

Lemlem's exquisite skin took on a slightly burnt sienna glow, as she hastily responded, "No, I'm afraid I'm not nearly so talented. It's the custom with my people to celebrate birthdays with feasts of clay-cooked bread and bananas, mangoes, and homemade coca. There's nothing we love more than to dress festively in objects from nature." She patted her headband. "This was made by an Ethiopian designer who was born, like me, in the Omo Valley. She goes by the name Tizita."

I blinked, and before I could censor myself, turned excitedly to Assefa. "Like the music! Teddy Afro!"

Assefa was slow to respond. So slow that I worried that everyone was watching us. His eyes slitted briefly, as if in warning. "Yes. Yes, of course. It is a common name in our land." He nodded perfunctorily and gave Lemlem's arm a squeeze, mumbling, "Now let's go find Miss Sofiya." He gestured to the small wrapped package Lemlem held. "We have a little gift for her." I saw that he kept his hand solidly on the small of Lemlem's back as he ushered her toward the playing children.

My eyes watered, and I quickly excused myself. In the downstairs guest bathroom, I flipped the lid closed and flopped down heavily onto the toilet seat. I figured it must be hormonal. I adored Adam, loved our life together. But Assefa's voice whispered inside me, "Who are you to think you can escape *tizita?*"

Through my tears, the flame of the Diptique candle on the Malibu-tiled vanity top flared into a great blaze. I felt a sudden urge to pee. I heaved myself up to lift the toilet lid and loosen my gargantuan cotton panties, just in time, as it happened, for a rush of warm water to flood the bowl.

I knew immediately what it was. After clumsily rubbing my vulva with a great wad of toilet paper and hauling up my panties, I burst from the bathroom and rushed to find Adam.

He was standing toward the back corner of the yard with—natch!—Assefa and Lemlem. Mother was there, too. The three of them parted like the Red Sea when they saw me.

I barreled into Adam's arms, bellowing, "My waters have broken! Oh, Adam, it's really happening!"

I turned to my mother and cried, "She's coming!"

Lemlem laughed and ventured, "Well, then, perhaps you should go to the hospital?"

The only one who looked unenthused was Assefa. His tone was neutral as he pronounced, "It is her first. It will take awhile. They have time."

But as Adam made his excuses and began pulling me toward the house, I noticed a telltale twitching at the corner of Assefa's left eyelid and felt glad.

We know that when one ocean wave supersedes another, all visible evidence of the previous one is gone, but in fact, the substance of each wave is formed from its predecessor. But if we accepted that a future measurement can affect an atom's past, as was suggested by the recent work of Australian physicist Andrew Truscott, what if the preceding wave could be altered by the wave to come?

Every one of a woman's eggs is present inside her from birth. The egg of Callay had already been in me when I'd made love with Assefa, who was in me somewhere, too, and whose essence would be in Callay—through the person I'd become during my wonderful, terrible romance with him. Perhaps she, or the possibility of her, had all the while been in him, too.

That particular train of thought was subsumed by something altogether different once Adam and I reached our bedroom. We sat at the edge of the bed and held each other for what felt like many lifetimes. I began to loosen myself from his arms. "I think I forgot to pack a pair of slippers, though these will probably—"

But Adam said, "No, wait." With a kind of ferocity, he stroked my hair, then claimed me in a long, lingering kiss. Pulling back reluctantly, he searched my face. He whispered, "We're about to embark on the adventure of all adventures, but this is the last day you'll be all mine." His green eyes were like saucers. I touched his cheek, which felt almost feverish with anticipation. The earnestness of him stabbed me. While my body clearly had its own imperatives right now, I wished—well, not to be crude, but I wished I could fuck him.

Whatever had I been thinking? Assefa may have swept open the door for desire, but this man, this Adam? *This* man was its home.

Chapter Six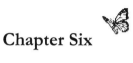

IT HAD TAKEN nearly an hour to get to Cedars-Sinai Hospital, during which time labor began in earnest. More than once on that ride I had cursed my otherwise beloved obstetrician Dr. Abalooni for moving his practice from Pasadena over the hill to West Hollywood. Now, with no little gratitude, I watched the back of my mother in the mirror that was angled over the hospital bed. She was leaning forward to massage the god-awful cramp in my calf. Her body obscured my open-for-all-the-rest-of-the-world-to-see tweeter, which I was quite pleased *not* to see. I knew, though, that she'd have to move out of the way of my sight line soon enough, once my contractions intensified and Callay slid closer to her grand entrance.

Sister Flatulencia, who'd officiated at more births of my father's unwanted babies than she'd cared to enumerate, had once described childbirth as a series of increasingly intense menstrual cramps. Why, oh why had I trusted an ex-nun to be my expert on matters relating to the female body? But I could hardly have gotten my sex education from Nana, whose tweeter had most certainly clamped up sometime after giving birth to the son who would later die serving his country, and Mother had been no help at all, saying she'd been dosed with enough Demerol to keep her nearly comatose during my sojourn down her birth canal. (Alas, it had evidently stopped working at the pushing phase, when her clenched tweeter had decreed, Adam's claims to the contrary, that I'd be born with a bullet-shaped head.)

Cramps? Hah! I could already tell the difference between the belly-clenching aches wrought by Mr. Heavyflow and this wringing vise that gripped my body every few minutes, threatening to annihilate me. I distracted myself by studying one of the banes of Mother's existence, the cowlicky bald spot at the back of her head that Kelly Zhang liked to call her "cat's butt." If I weren't in such pain, I'd have laughed. That was *exactly* what it looked like. But another contraction snaked its way through me, and I shrieked, instead.

"Where was Adam in all of this?" you ask. Down the hall barfing his guts out. I learned about that later. At the moment I knew only that he'd looked queasy enough for the nurse to temporarily banish him from this icy room before she left to fetch another heated blanket to help with the leg cramps.

"You're doing beautifully, my darling," Mother murmured, taking a break from rubbing my leg to move up toward the head of the bed to caress my brow. Even in this torture chamber, I loved the smell of her Chanel No. 5 blended with the sweet cocoa scent of Sherman's and, at this moment anyway, the slightly bitter tang of sweat. But when I faced forward again, the sight of my bared body in the mirror nearly blew me away.

Who *was* this beast, with her twin mountains of thigh and ass bookending a vibrant, visceral cave, furred at the top, with fleshy curtains parting to let pass an ooze of something unidentifiable. I was mortified. Even more so when Adam re-entered the room, looking slightly sheepish but determined to join me at my side just as a particularly powerful wave overtook me. Mother rubbed my upper arm, and Adam kept a tender, but firm hand cupped over my belly. I reached blindly to grip the hand of each of them as my body wanted to arch and I let it.

For a time, we three got into a groove. Me alternately laughing, panting, crying, swearing, breathing into the pain, and writhing like a giant worm. Adam seemed to have vanquished his own bodily bedevilment and was fully present, his emerald eyes beacons of promise that this would turn out okay.

But all bets were off when the pushing phase finally arrived. I was way too exhausted to notice how wiped out my little team was. Cursing had become my primary mode of communicating, and I'd devolved into some ugly, slime-breathing demon that shouted over and again, "What's wrong with you? Get her the fuck OUT."

Dr. Abalooni was the pinnacle of patience. Later, I would use my Nobelist cachet to persuade the International Astronomical Union to dub a newly discovered star in the Andromeda Constellation, *Abalooni*, but for now he was simply the human who helped prevent a triple-knotted Nuchal cord from tightening around Callay's neck, saving her from a dangerous drop in blood pressure and me from the Caesarian chop shop.

He did so with such swift grace that I knew nothing of the danger my child was in. It was just as well. As I struggled with the equivalent of a seven-pound watermelon pushing itself through an opening the size of small sink drain, my body became a conveyor of integrals of information to a self that was beyond spacetime, with a consciousness that somehow contained all that had come before and all that would ever be, down to the minutest detail of what I'd had for breakfast that morning (plain yogurt, walnuts, blueberries, and Kashi GoLean Cereal) and up to the explosion of supernovas trillions of miles away. It was as if all the particularities of "me" existed solely to provide a witnessing lens to the vibrant, pulsing dance of life. And then the shape of a butterfly coalesced from the vastness. It had immense black wings with just the slightest strips of white at their outer margins and a pleasingly furry-looking discal section, which became a kind of throbbing veil or membrane, filled with colors more brilliant and subtle than I'd ever imagined, through which I passed to find Grandfather (!), Nana (!), and Jillily (!), whose black tail flicked into its signature question mark shape and beckoned me back out again.

And then in a flash all this liquidity coagulated into a primitive lump of sensation, and I trembled with the shock of an actual living creature slithering from my tweeter with what Adam later described as "a *Holy Shit* cry" and I thought of as the most compelling sound I'd ever heard. Her first nickname was born with her, as we both saw she was covered with fine, dark, Lanugo hair. For months, she wouldn't be Bunlet or even Callay, but Monkey. Our little hairy

Monkey Girl. And in honor of that initial incarnation, we would agree to ask Jane Goodall and Serena McKenna to be her co-godmothers. God forbid anything happened to us, Gombe Stream National Park would be as good a place as any for a child to be raised.

Later, in the sanctuary of my private hospital room, Callay down the hall in the nursery, and Adam snoring like a steam engine in a bare-bones cot beside me, my mind returned to that numinously liminal state I'd experienced during labor. What stood out were the colors, which I felt hard put to name. I'd heard that butterflies could see many more colors than we do—they and bees, too. Both had a wider ultraviolet range than we humans, while heat-seeking rattlesnakes' vision extends farther into the infrared. What if there were ways beyond the liquescence of childbirth to expand our vision, opening new doorways of perception?

My eye was momentarily caught by the photograph on the opposite wall of an earlier incarnation of this hospital that I'd learned in a previous pregnant families' tour had been originally dubbed Cedars of Lebanon. *Beautiful name*, I'd thought at the time, *for beautiful, earth-surfing trees*. I'd read somewhere they were sometimes called the Trees of God.

But wait. I sat bolt upright in my bed.

My British colleague Stephen Hawking had finally come around to the idea that the blueprint of an object is not destroyed by its disappearance into the vortex of a black hole, but was stored in its event horizon. It was something that the team and I had been banking on. What we hadn't factored in was the possibility that the blueprint might continue to exist but be simultaneously transformed.

And now the hairs on my arms rose up—not unlike how I'd felt at that moment years ago in my bedroom at Stanley and Gwennie's, when it came upon me that human cells were comprised of infinitesimal black holes, continually exchanging dark and light matter.

It occurred to me now that the team and I needed to be prepared for the possibility that harnessing that exchange of energy through the Principle of Dematerialization might produce a singularity—a quantum leap in consciousness for our species!

The image came to me of the fiery dance of energy encircling black holes, its little licks of flame darting into an unknown dimension to retrieve something previously unimagined from the encounter. Could it be that our project would not only make possible fossil-fuel-free transportation, but also set in motion an evolutionary shift in human awareness? Something that would powerfully impact the precious little creature who'd just exited my aching tweeter? If so, we were facilitating something whose outcome was beyond our scope, but one we would nonetheless be held accountable for. How might that impact life on planet earth?

I fell asleep with many more questions than I had answers for, but despite my preoccupation with one little girl and the whole of the cosmos—or perhaps because of it—I dreamed all night of trees.

Sanctus

The Cedars of Lebanon were gasping. Their broad, horizontal branches reached out desperately; their roots, dug into limestone, were thinning. They'd been sacrificed in the past to the gods of Mesopotamia, Phoenicia, ancient Egypt, Greece, Rome, and the early temples of the Jewish people, in whose "Song of Solomon" they were compared to the beauty of the beloved. But now it was Nature herself, harried by her human devils, giving rise to the trees' alarm. The cedars needed the cool temperature of their Middle East environs to thrive, but this devilishly warming climate was leaving them in the lurch. The groves strove to survive by migrating upwards, but the mountains above them just might not be high or cool enough.

These trees were strong and they grew slowly. It took a good century for their striking shapes to manifest, their trunks to thicken, their branches to spread parallel to the ground, sometimes solo and sometimes cross-hatching in groups, creating interesting patterns that scientists could spend a lifetime studying. But all patterning was breaking down now. They were eager to make the adjustment to their new circumstances, but they were running out of time.

Nearly 2,000 miles away, the forests of Swedish Lapland, inside the Arctic Circle, were on fire. The ground and flora weren't anywhere as wet as they'd been. Denmark and Scotland, California and the Pacific Northwest were suffering extraordinary conflagrations, as well. The trees had put out the call to their brethren. Like their sister species across the globe, they were all crying out to the humans, but far too few of that species had the ears to hear them. If the trees but spoke the human languages, they would consider the term "tree hugger" an honorific and give heart to any and all who cared to take note of their plight.

As it was, what could they do but add their voices to the symphony conducted with myriads of variations by the Soul of the World? Hurry up! Wake up! It's time!

Chapter Seven

SIX WEEKS POST-PARTUM. Talk about incarnations. I'd never realized there could be simultaneous ones, not unlike multiple universes, but with each visible to the next. Here I was in a brand new world, smack dab in the midst of the old one. *Everything* mattered: the chill of the morning; the barely discernible shape of the sycamore outside my bedroom window, softly smudged by a grey mist; the faint tick of the bedside clock; the sensation of my breasts filling with milk; the ominous headline of today's *New York Times* that Adam had set on my breakfast tray, "Sixth Crippling Storm to Hit the Northeast: Another Sign of Climate Change?"

Before going downstairs to prepare my Swiss cheese and spinach omelet, Adam had flung the softest of cashmere throws atop our summer duvet. I held it up to my nostrils now, much as I used to thrust the edge of Nana's cave-scented, furry green bathrobe up my nose as a child, seeking refuge in her closet from Mother's mysterious medicinal smell, Father's high-pitched shrieks and ever-pinching hands.

Outside of that discordant headline, there was no shouting here.

But there *was* Mother, freed from the scents of Sauvignon Blanc and Chateau Lafite that had once spilled from her pores. And finally freed of the silly laughter that had initially followed her concussion.

And there was Callay. My little Monkey lay quite still in her bassinet beside the bed, her breath a whisper that announced that the world had been reborn.

I'd fallen asleep after breakfast and had awakened to see Mother staring at me with such tenderness, such *interest*, that my eyes welled up. I fancied I knew what she was feeling. She'd come to claiming the fruits of motherhood slowly. Too distracted by her alcoholism, my father's abuse, and then later the rowdy pull of her Bill W. gang, at last in middle age she'd found her place within that ancient matrilineal covenant. Me, I was luckier. I'd felt the indissoluble bond with Callay as soon as I beheld her wrinkled little face. In an instant, she was the north pole of a magnet, I her smitten south.

From outside, ever so faintly, came the susurrations of a distant leaf blower. Closer, a car crawled past the house.

The baby stirred, and Mother peeked into the bassinet. "She's smiling. Wind."

I wanted to preserve this moment forever, or at least keep it close by so I could draw on it anytime I needed. I'd been needing it a long time.

A seagull plied the air with its plaintive cry. Whatever was it doing so far from the sea?

It occurred to me that if I'd whimsically assumed that Assefa was somewhere in the mix of Callay's soul, then Mother was certainly present in every cell of her. But then it occurred to me that Father had to be in there, too. I was going to have to make an effort to be less of an asshole in order to balance him out.

"Darling, I don't know about you, but I've got an awful thirst. Would you care for some chamomile tea?" She paused. "I read somewhere that it helps with milk production. Not that you need any help in that department." We exchanged a grin.

"Yes, please. It sounds wonderful. I don't know where Adam's gotten to."

Mother reappeared a few minutes later with a tray and a frown.
"What is it?" I asked.
"I don't—you don't want to know."
"What?"
"It smells 'off' downstairs. Especially in the pantry."

"Maybe some food is spoiled. Can you tell Lukie to go over it?"

"Of course. Don't worry. We'll take care of it. I'll just pop back down."

But, as it happens, taking care of it turned out to be a little more complicated. My first clue was when the silence of the nursery was rent by the unmistakable squeaks and rattles of Ignacio's battered old Ford truck. As Callay nursed surprisingly vigorously for one who'd seemed fully sated just an hour and a half before, I pondered why Ignacio had come today. His days were Wednesdays, when he single-handedly tackled our formidable back garden—deadheading the Austins, weeding the dymondia and creeping thyme, and cleverly clipping the jasmine and bougainvillea to keep the yard just this side of wild. These past months, we'd had a ritual of lunching together every Wednesday at the kitchen table, he in his socks, and me heating up whichever amazing curry Dhani had packed up for us that morning in an extra-large, insulated cooler. As soon as I'd dollop out our portions, we'd set to with ravenous hunger, he from having worked his behind off all morning, I from lugging around my ridiculously bulbous breasts and my increasingly heavy bun.

But today was Sunday, which I knew was Ignacio, Dhani, and No-Longer-a-Baby-Angelina's day to spend at the track, treating themselves to *LA Weekly*'s "Brunch at the Races" on the days when Dhani wasn't cooking for the event herself. We'd all been so proud when the cooking school Dhani had founded had earned her pride of place amid the ranks of Brandon Boudet's Little Dom's, the L&E Oyster Bar, and—piggy me's favorite—Poppy + Rose.

Laying Callay back into her bassinette after my delicate little flower issued a gratifyingly rude burp, I took myself down the stairs just in time to see Adam, Ignacio, and Mother whispering just outside the back door. Even with the door wide open, the kitchen reeked with a sickly sweet smell. Clapping a hand against my mouth and nose, I moved toward the trio and saw that Ignacio was covered from salt-and-pepper head to heavy gardening boots in a thick layer of dirt.

"What's going on?" I demanded.

Adam cast me a worried, but somewhat sheepish look. "Ignacio's just tried crawling under the house to find it."

"Find what?" I asked, but of course I knew. Living things didn't smell like this.

"Oh, don't —" Mother started.

But Adam was at my side in an instant. "You should go back on up. We'll deal with it. It's probably a possum. Or a rat."

I had a sudden terror. I felt all wobbly and had to put a hand on his arm to steady myself. "How do you know? How did it get in? It couldn't be a bobcat, could it?" *Please God, no.*

Mother screeched, "A bobcat!"

Ignacio said, "I'm so sorry, Fleuricita. I promise you there's no bobcat under there. Whatever it is was smaller than I could find." He looked mortified. "There was a torn screen behind one of the jasmine bushes. It was a very small opening—much smaller than a big cat could fit through, but if I had kept that bush better trimmed, I would have seen it. It is my fault."

Relief flooded through me, and I said a silent *Thank you* on behalf of my four-legged sister. I turned to my husband, "Adam, how could you have let him?" Ignacio was no spring chicken; I knew he battled arthritis.

The shame that etched itself hotly across Adam's face drove home what a lousy thing it had been to say. He had a hard enough time tugging his left leg when walking. How could he have possibly navigated the narrow crawl space himself?

Mother shot me a look of rebuke. Ignacio stared at the kitchen floor.

I leaned in toward Adam's ear and whispered so quietly that only he could hear, "Sorry, my love. I'm an asshole." *I really was.*

God bless him, he laughed and whispered back, "That, my pretty, you most definitely can be. Thank God you've got a redeeming feature or two."

Ignacio seemed confused, but my ever-practical mother turned away and said over her shoulder, "I'm leaving. I'll call Sister F. as soon as I get home. I think her landlord hired a skinny wildlife rescue guy to go under their building when her neighbor's cat got stuck under there."

As Ignacio, too, departed, accompanied by innumerable shouts of apology from both Adam and me, we two went upstairs and tiptoed into our room to stare at our sleeping daughter.

She was still a bit red-faced under her fine lanugo hairs. Beautiful black lashes curled perfectly over her delicate, slightly purplish eyelids. She scrunched up her little lips and wrinkled her nose as if to register an objection.

"It's creepy, isn't it?" I murmured.

"Huh?" he said, taking a step back.

My hand flew to my mouth. "Oh, no. Never her. Never, *ever* her. You must think I'm crazy. Certifiable. I meant the animal. Whatever it is. It's dead down there. So soon after we've brought home this precious new life." I bent over Callay, captive to the subtle scent of her. "She's so innocent. So vulnerable. Still smelling of vernix caseosa."

Adam looked confused.

"Amniotic fluid. They continue to have invisible bits of it in their hair and creases for six weeks or so." But my voice caught. "That poor animal. You don't think it's some kind of sign, do you? I could never bear it if—"

"Fleur, that sounds dangerously woo-woo."

"Yes, but—"

"No buts. Every millisecond on this planet, millions of creatures are dying and being born. You know that better than anyone. It's a constant exchange of energy." He pretended to knock on the side of my head. "Even in our bodies. Remember C-Voids?"

"I know. It's not rational, but I don't want any hint of death near her."

He encircled me in a tight hug. I still wore an apron of spongy fat across my middle, but at least he could get his arms around me now.

"Of course, you don't," he murmured. "But trust me. You saw that determined chin of your mom's poke itself out. We'll get rid of that thing before you know it."

"I suppose so," I said, "but it's not really a thing, and it's still sad that it died under there. I hate it. I hate how cruel life can be."

Adam had leaned forward and was carefully tucking the end of the swaddling blanket a bit more tightly under our sleeping child.

"Adam?"

He looked up. "Mmm?"

"Why do you think death smells so sweet? Don't you think that's more than a little weird? What purpose could *that* possibly serve?

By now, you probably have some sense of my difficulties with the voidishness of not knowing. Somewhere between the times of Callay's subsequent feed and her nighttime sponge bath, I ended up plowing through most of my pile of *Journals of Medical Entomology* to enquire into the purpose of the particularly cloying odors of a dead carcass. For someone who hadn't wanted to taint the preciousness of her daughter's first days with any hint that there would one day be a last, I went at the material with surprising gusto.

I learned quickly enough that it was all down to the necrophages, those species of insects such as Diptera, Calliphoridae, and Sarcophagidae (otherwise known as true flies, blow flies, and flesh flies), who commence their cycles of creation with others' destruction, laying their eggs and thereby colonizing an enticingly honeyed—and very dead—host. In turn, these sugary larvae were consumed by carnivorous species of ants, wasps, and carrion beetles (but not butterflies, Nature having to ethically draw the line somewhere). It was, of course, as Adam had pointed out, the way of life on this earth: death begetting life, life begetting death. And emblematic as well of the universe itself—our own lives dependent on the illuminating warmth of a dying star and our very atoms composed of the dust of dead ones.

I'd told Adam that I hated the whole show, but of course I didn't. Callay would never have been born without the death of my relationship with Assefa. I'd never have met Assefa without the death of Nana prompting Mother to hire Abeba to care for Cesar. And Cesar himself … well, that was another story entirely, one that as sure as Chutes and Ladders slid me right back down to the cruelty of the cosmos.

My hypocrisy was hardly lost on me. In our application of the Principle of Dematerialization to humans, we'd be purposely propelling members of our own species into near-death via their own cellular black holes, only to (hopefully!) bring them back again in a designated new location. Like all scientific advances, we'd be taking a rather grandiose leap into the unknown, but one predicated on other successful leaps by thousands of fine thinkers before us. (As I'd heard a ballerina respond when an interviewer asked her how she regained her center after one of her famously majestic leaps, "But no, it is the center itself that leaps, taking me with it!")

Our own leap involved slowing or quickening movement from one location to another via the ripples in spacetime first predicted by Einstein's theory of relativity and later confirmed in the detection of gravitational waves by LIGO's twin detectors in Louisiana and Washington state. But it was Hawking who had moved the center along dramatically with his emphasis on the nature of the event horizon, noting that space itself falls into a black hole at a speed greater than the speed of light. Perversely, due to the extreme gravity around a black hole, matter in its gravitational field actually slows down at the horizon, dimming increasingly to the point of invisibility.

Here the literal leap of Dreamization would occur via an analogous, slowed-down cellular passageway through which we hoped to propel people from one place to another. The process would be experienced as quite gradual for them, with their bodies making the necessary sensory adjustments, but the whole thing would in fact take a mere couple of minutes. Hawking was, of course, working on a quite different track and hadn't entered that particular area of speculation in his own thinking. But he *had* suggested that black holes are far from being prisons, but could instead be passageways through which things could move into another universe. Our initial experiments had indicated it was possible to trigger a return to our own.

I woke the next morning to the sounds of Adam's snores and a murder outside the window. Not the bad kind, mind you. It was a convention of crows. I wondered what they were gabbing about. I hoped to God they wouldn't wake Callay. She'd had a rather miserable, comfortless night, and I'd only just gotten her down to sleep a while ago. Everyone in the world had been right: the sleep deprivation was awful. Each day it was a toss-up whether I'd want to bite Adam's head off or swoon at the pleasure of his touch.

Today would evidently be a good day. Sighing with pleasure despite my profound fatigue, I luxuriated in the moist pressure of Adam's back against my own, inhaling his Campbell's chicken soup smell, which had always been pheromonic for me. My hands felt around behind me, and I twisted just enough to find a space between his thighs and trail my fingers across his member. I felt a surge of power as the soft curl of him hardened. He gave a little gasp, and I murmured, "You know that butterflies mate back-to-back, don't you?"

He rubbed his back against mine in a slow undulation. "Like this?"

I laughed. "Well, sort of. The male inserts his wings in between the female's."

He turned around and urged me around, too, planting a sloppy kiss on my lips. His mouth tasted garlicky-gingery from last night's *yetaklitk kilkil*. Makeda was the queen in our kitchen these days.

"I don't have wings, but I do have this. Will it do?"

My opening felt a little tight, but not too tight to stop me from getting wet. "Well, Dr. Abalooni said we should give it a try at six weeks."

"Should or could?"

I laughed. "Well, that was a Freudian slip if there ever was one."

"I was going to say, we must certainly do what the good doctor says we should do."

"We *could* do," I temporized teasingly.

"We shall do," he said, and proceeded to lick his way down to the portal to an alternate universe of the most delightful variety.

But even the sweetest of fruits are vulnerable to spoiling. The day that had started so well took a decided dive shortly after Adam took off for the lab. Soon after Callay's next feed, Makeda showed up rather hesitantly at my doorway.

"Come in, come in," I cried with pleasure, closing the final snap on the baby's elephant and giraffe onesie and laying her on her back in the bassinette. Makeda, who was generally like a pile of mush over Callay, gave the baby a cursory look, then bit her lip. "Out with it, woman," I said.

"I am very rude to bother you with this when I know you are so tired. The bébé takes all that you have and more …"

"Makeda, you are my sister, remember? I won't be able to rest knowing that something is bothering you, so you may as well tell me now."

"It is the boy. At school."

"Ah." It had taken me embarrassingly long to report to Makeda the snatches of conversation I'd heard taking place between Sofiya and Melesse on the stairway. Sammie and I had decided it might spoil Sofiya's party if I raised the topic right before the event, and then the birth of Callay had consumed me. I'd finally remembered it in the middle of a hellishly sleepless night, clapping my hand so hard to my lips that I'd actually wakened the baby all over again.

Afterward, with a little coaching, Makeda had coaxed from Melesse that a boy in her Raccoon Group was making her life hell over her slight lisp. I think we were all relieved that the bullying hadn't been over her chocolate skin; it would have been too distressing if racism had reared its ugly head amidst the young Bunnies and Beavers and Raccoons. But the boy's taunting over her lisp proved to be just as painful, as she hadn't even known she had one until now. She'd retreated to her books and had to be cajoled to join the circle of children for the morning sharing, solemnly looking down into her lap whenever her name was called.

As Makeda filled me in on the latest installment of the miserable drama, I learned that the little monster was now teasing her for her shyness. (And if you're asking yourself how I could call a child of four a monster, then *you* fall in love with a girl like Melesse— AIDS-orphaned at six months, nearly starving to death before that, being separated for a terrible couple of weeks from her one surviving relative while a hospital staff struggled to bring her back to health after a dreadful bout with the flu, then being dragged to a daunting new land and facing a brand new language to learn—only mitigated by the miracle of being claimed for life by the woman who'd saved her and her sister.)

I shuddered at the myriads of ways a child's innocence could be destroyed and prayed I could protect my own girl from every single one of them. "What's the little creep's name?" I asked.

"Hector," replied Makeda. "But don't you think it's cruel to call a child a 'creep?'"

"Don't *you* wish you could wring his neck?" I shot back.

She favored me with a guilty grin.

Hector, I thought. *Of course.* The name of the boy who'd called me *Linda Paloma* before pretty much raping me in middle school. At least I think that's what it's called when someone gets you drunk on your very first taste of beer and then inserts his member in your tweeter before you even know what's happening. The act had had awful consequences, culminating in my father's final disowning of me for the murder of my first bun. I prayed every night that Callay wouldn't be punished for her mother's folly. You never know what the Furies will take it into their heads to do.

Just in case, I decided to call on my better self. "The poor child must be suffering his own set of insecurities to be a bully at so young an age."

"It's true, it's true!" said Makeda, with enough emphasis to reveal she'd been going through her own inner battle.

"Listen," I said, "do you want to invite him over for a playdate?"

She drew back. "What? Why would I? Yes, I can have compassion for him, but I hardly think that Melesse would relish it."

"Yes, I can see that, but if you were there? And maybe I could be, too. But not Sofiya. Her protectiveness might make him more scared, and then he might get nasty."

Makeda rubbed her chin thoughtfully. "But what would they even play? You know Melesse—she'd rather bury her head in a book than play with anyone but her sister, let alone someone who has been cruel to her."

"I get it. But don't you see? It might actually defuse the situation. Help get them on a new footing."

I could tell Makeda wasn't convinced. She promised to think about it, but her voice was flat, her expression worried.

To be honest, I wasn't sure it was a good idea, either, but I did mention it to Sammie on the phone later that day.

"No, you're right. It's brilliant. They could write a little play together, then perform it. I went to this amazing talk at a Jungian confab near Belsize Park the night before I met Amira. A lovely man, I think his name was van Eenwyk, gave a talk about healing children from the traumas of war through art and imagination. They've evidently been doing it for ages at a place called the Butterfly Peace Garden in Sri Lanka. What if I bring over some art supplies and maybe even some costumes and we let Melesse and Hector have a go?"

Personally, I thought the whole thing might end up a disaster, but, as was often the case with Sammie, my friend's enthusiasm proved to be a powerful engine. It was she who finally convinced Makeda, and the following weekend, Mother watched Callay in my room while Sammie and I converted our large-ish den to an improvised little theater.

When Hector's rather harassed-looking mother deposited him with unseemly relief at our front door, Melesse hid behind her mother's skirts. The boy wasn't at all like the miniature Hector from Walter Reed Middle School that I'd imagined. This Hector was a carrot top with Tom Sawyer freckles and drooping blue eyes and a slightly recessed chin. Nor was he the dummy I'd assumed. He explained earnestly that he had exactly three hours and fifteen minutes before his mother came to pick him up.

The boy asked to see the backyard, as he'd heard Sofiya bragging that we had a better swing set than the Children's Center. Makeda was able to persuade Melesse to let go of her long enough to be leveraged into a swing next to her tormentor. The fact that she was comfortable going much higher than Hector seemed to give her sufficient confidence to suggest they play one of her favorite Ethiopian games, *acoocoolu*. I'd played it with the girls myself and knew it was a version of what I'd grown up calling hide-and-go-seek. Nana and Sister Flatulencia would occasionally play the latter with me when the saved babies were napping. In its Ethiopian form the game had rituals that had to be observed before the "chicken"—*acoocoolu* being the operative chicken sound—could be declared free. They had to touch the original wall where the seeker had first shielded her eyes and kiss their own hands for good luck. The seeker, in turn, had to identify the hider, reach the wall before her and kiss her own hand to win the right to hide the next time around. During the hiding phase, the seeker called out, "*Coocoolu,*" and if not yet hidden the hider shouted,

"*Anelgam*" ("it is still not day") and if hidden, "*Nega*" ("the sun rises"). We'd already established that Hector was a bright boy, and he caught on just fine, but for some reason he had a devil of a time pronouncing the unfamiliar *anelgam*. Makeda and I exchanged glances as Melesse took great pains to help him learn to say it properly.

"Again-am," he'd say, and Melesse would repeat, "*Anelgam*," The poor child was nothing if not determined. He tried over and over, making it even worse with permutations of "*Alengum*," "*Agelum*," and even—accidentally, I presumed—"*Alaikum*."

I felt a bit worried that Hector would feel too much shame to absorb the kindness that Melesse was offering him—particularly ironic, since his bullying had focused on her speech impediment—but instead they both began making up preposterous variants of the word, laughing so uproariously that they initially missed seeing Sammie enter the scene in a flowing, sequined purple robe and a star-strewn wizard's hat crowning her auburn head.

Hector saw her first and let fly a loud, "Wow!"

Van Eenwyk proved to be right on target. The children decided to stage a play about "King Chicken," who uttered curses on anyone he didn't like. "*Alengum!*" "Akeedum!" "No-Like-Em!" And when someone did pass muster, Melesse would cry, "*Anelgam!*" and Hector would chime in, "I-Like-'Em!"

The kids made such a racket that Mother marched downstairs on behalf of Callay to demand they quiet down. Later, when she and I relaxed in my bedroom with Sammie while Makeda and Melesse went off to fetch Sofiya from her own play date, I mused, "Isn't it funny that animals figure in different versions of the same essential game?"

Mother raised her head from admiring her granddaughter, "What do you mean?"

"Well, in English it's 'Olly olly *oxen* free.'"

Sammie jumped in, "You know, you're right. It must be an archetype."

I laughed. "With you, everything's an archetype."

She chucked me on the shoulder. "With you it's all black holes."

"Touché," I cried. "Well, if it *is* an archetype, at least it's a tasty one. I've heard it called 'Sardines.'"

"Oh, but that's a different game," chimed in Mother. "I played that one as a girl. There's just one hider, and each consecutive finder crams into their hiding place with them until the last one becomes the loser."

Gesturing towards Sammie, lazing beside me on the bed, I laughed, "Then you'd better get over here quick, Mother." She happily piled in, plumping the pillow between us before laying her head against it with a satisfied, "Ahhh." Then she sat up again. "But no, that makes Callay the loser."

As if on cue, the baby gave a lusty cry and I fetched her up onto the bed with us, the object of three sets of admiring eyes as I unhooked my bra to nurse her.

At that moment, Adam poked his head in the door. "Did I hear a baby crying?"

We three giggled, though I hated it a little when Sammie murmured in my ear, "Should I tell him he's the loser?"

He wasn't, of course. But something had gotten hold of me ever since the hour before I'd gone into labor with Callay, and I confided it in Mother once Sammie went home to call Amira.

It took me a while to get there. We were again cushioned against the mound of plump European pillows while my baby slept. I turned onto my side to face Mother, clapping my hands cozily inside my thighs. "I feel like I'm spending most of my life in bed."

Mother smiled, brushing a lock of hair away from my eye. "The fate of the young mother. Though I must say," she added with a tinge of melancholy, "I drew that phase out way too long, hiding out in my room from your father."

I considered her face, noting that the twin furrows between her perfectly penciled brows seemed to be deepening by the day. It killed me when she was sad. "You hated him, didn't you?"

She bit her lip. "I'm afraid I did. Is that awful?"

"I hope not. I did, too." I paused. "I know you were still a teenager when you met him, but did you love anyone before him?"

"I didn't, Fleur. Not really. He was my first." She gave a cynical laugh. "Though I was hardly his. It wasn't just him being so much older. I found out soon enough that he couldn't keep his hands off other women. And as a senator, he had his pick."

"But, in the beginning, do you think he loved you?"

Mother considered the question. "No. Frank was a narcissist. I don't think he was capable of love. Of any kind. I think I was just another conquest. The trouble was, as soon as we found out I was pregnant, your grandfather wouldn't let him adopt you out, the way he did with his other children."

"All the saved babies," I said.

"All the saved babies," she affirmed dryly. But then her face brightened. "At least Callay is the daughter of her father's true love."

It was a quaint way to put it. It should have cheered me, but instead, I was overcome by a great wave of sadness. What did it mean that I wasn't the daughter of my own father's true love? Or my mother's, for that matter?

"Do you think it's possible to have more than one true love?"

"Darling, what a question. How in the world would I know? I've had such an abnormal life."

"Don't say that."

"Why?"

"Because there's never been anything about *me* that's been normal. And here I am, loving Adam and Callay like crazy, but fantasizing that my daughter will have a little bit of Assefa in her."

Mother raised an eyebrow. "It's like that, is it?" Then she added gently, "It's been disproven, you know."

"What?"

"Telegony. The theory that babies carry genetic material of the men their mothers have been with previously. I think the word is etymologically rooted in the stories surrounding Odysseus's son Telegonus."

I had to hand it to Mother. She was up on her Greek mythology. I supposed it came of having been a librarian all those years.

"But isn't that a butterfly?"

"If it is, I hadn't heard of it."

"With gorgeous turquoise wings."

"Well then. But what's this about Assefa? I thought you were long over him." She gave me a searching look. "Are things okay with Adam?"

I nodded reassuringly. Truthfully. "Way better than okay. He's the sweetest, kindest, most tender man I could ever hope for. I adore him. But I've been thinking about it a lot. Ever since Assefa came back to L.A. I'm not sure it's possible to be 'over' someone you've loved. I mean, have you gotten over the loss of Grandfather? Or Nana?"

Mother gave me the point with a shake of her head.

I was still unsettled. I couldn't leave it alone. An emotional hangnail. But not, I hoped, too much like Assefa's Hanging Man. "Were you the daughter of *your* father's true love?"

She nodded vigorously. "Oh yes. They had a hell of a love affair, your grandparents. It was why he pined so hard when she died."

I shut up then, asked if she'd mind if I took a little nap. I'd tired myself out. Maybe it was the talk of Grandfather or maybe it was my breasts, their nipples sore from constant suckling. I'd been sleep deprived for what felt like forever. But as I fell asleep I curled inside this increasing sense of closeness with Mother. She might be a little taken aback by my words about Assefa, but she wasn't judging me. I could tell.

It meant the world to me.

Chapter Eight

IT WAS ON a bright and (for SoCal) rather freezing day—temperature, sixty degrees Fahrenheit; humidity 35 percent—that the physics team found the time to join me in visiting Gwen.

Gwennie was looking heartier by the minute. That awful yellowish tinge to her skin was giving way to a pinker hue, and her skeletal appearance had been supplanted by increasingly visible amplitude to her upper arms and the welcome hint of a double chin.

Gwen barked a loud laugh when I brought them all in. "Oh my goodness, I had no idea when you asked if I was up for visitors that I'd get the whole kit and caboodle. Except for that monkey, of course." She burst into an off-tune rendition of "The Gang's All Here" from *The Pirates of Penzance*, holding her encircling fingers up to her eye to mime a pirate's patch.

Predictably, Amir interjected, "Not a monkey. A chimp. Lord Hanuman is a chimpanzee."

"Actually," Tom commented dryly, "He's a god. Only *you* would name a lab chimp after a character from the *Ramayana,* bro."

"*Rescued* lab chimp," retorted Amir. "He's hardly a lab chimp these days. At Gombe, he's always on the move. Free. Strong. You'd barely recognize him."

"*Ramayana*? Best spectacle I've ever seen since my *mor* and *far* took me to see *Die Walküre* as a kid," rhapsodized Gunther non-sequitorishly, a faraway look in his mismatched eyes.

Katrina waved a hand sideways. "Oh, Wagner. So depressing." And then she blushed.

The room fell silent. Katrina had violated our unspoken agreement not to mention depression in front of Gunther. He seemed to carry the classic Scandinavian gene for it.

"No," objected Gunther, "it's a good story. The cruelty of the gods. To have control over who will live and who will die. Wotan condemning his favorite daughter to a rocky isolation. I remembered falling speechless when I saw Brünnhilde surrounded by a magical fire onstage."

Katrina shuddered. "It makes me think of cremation."

Gwennie, who was listening to the back and forth with shining eyes, jumped in. "Did you hear how the Vatican 'clarified' their rules about cremation? They condemned the practice of scattering of ashes, along with ideas of death as the definitive annihilation, or as part of a death-rebirth cycle, or even as a reconnection with the universe. I read that and thought, 'Well, goody for them. I'm glad they're so sure what happens we die.' What do *you* think, Stanley?"

We all looked to the corner of the room where Stanley had silently recessed himself. I wondered whether he was troubled by the conversation about dying with a sister who'd barely escaped it.

"What do you think about that, Stanley?" Gwen poked again. "You think the Church is onto something?"

She wasn't the sister of a physicist for nothing. "What do I think?" he croaked, hopping into the fray. "It's all about the molecules, isn't it?"

I turned to Gwen. She'd brought it up. Maybe it was relieving for her to talk about it. "What about you, Gwen? What do *you* think?

"I think this American obsession with staying Perky Polly healthy in the presumption you can fend off death forever is just ludicrous. And frankly, boring. If I can't have a couple of scoops of Ben and Jerry's Chunky Monkey before bedtime, then what's the bloody point of being alive?"

Stanley issued a plaintive, "Does that mean I can eat my McDonald's again?"

Everyone laughed. Gwen had been fiercely vegetarian since long before I'd come to live with them and was a strict enforcer with her junk food junkie brother.

It was Tom who reminded the team that they needed to get over to the lab. I felt a slight pang, wishing I could join them. But Callay was due for a feed, and Mother was still anxious she might not accept the bottle of pumped milk I'd left in the fridge, even though she'd chugged down every ounce the last three times she'd babysat for her.

We were approaching a moment of high drama for Dreamization. We'd made significant progress following the standstill forced upon us by a know-nothing Congress' ban of our research for several years. Somehow slipped into a back-room deal between Democrats and Republicans—over, of all things, drug testing for drug task force officers—was an agreement that we could pursue our research, funded solely by private resources. They'd given us six months before congressional representatives from both parties would review the results for suitability. We were eager to take anything we could get and fortunate enough to obtain full funding from a Silicon Valley entrepreneur, with the caveat that his support would go nameless. An anomaly, we soon learned, as most people of wealth seemed to be interested, these days, in advertising their "brand."

Following up on groundbreaking work by Oriol Omero-Isart and his team at the Max Planck Institute of Quantum Optics, we'd already managed to use two laser beams to create optical cavities where water bears could exist in two places at the same time. Water bears, or moss piglets, are tiny little tardigardes that can curl up into dry husks called "tuns" in a seeming dead state for decades. Ironically, it takes only water to re-animate them. (If only I'd been so lucky with Grandfather.) Employing the insights of cell therapies used in the treatment of various diseases, we found a way to issue instructions to a key "trigger" cell that signaled all a moss piglet's cells to simultaneously exchange its light matter for dark and then reverse the process, effectively throwing the water bear into a cellular black hole where it actually dematerialized from one of its two places and rematerialized into the other. But quantum mechanics was, by definition, most reliable when applied to subatomic particles. Moving a moss piglet from one place to another was a far cry from moving humans.

Unfortunately, given our narrow window of congressional approval and the fact that global warming was proceeding at a dangerous pace, we didn't have the luxury of working our way slowly up the food chain. Moving a much larger animal from one place to another by synchronizing its C-Voids was the logical next step before attempting to apply our work to humans.

And even if we managed that huge (and most would say, impossible) task, we faced ethical considerations. We were all adherents of the Precautionary Principle and were committed to investigating any imaginable negative outcomes lest we inadvertently cause all hell to break loose. So far, gene and cell therapies and medical nanotechnologies had risen or fallen on their viability, with nary a one creating a Frankenstein among us. That was heartening, despite my moment of doubt following giving birth that Dreamization might create a singularity equaling what some techies were predicting as a wedding of man to machine.

But the question of which species to choose for our next set of experiments presented a dilemma. There was definitely some risk involved. Adam and I—and Stanley, too—were pretty cat crazy, Amir was mad about chimps, Bob was a fish and bird guy, and Katrina and Tom were dog people who'd lost two of their own in an unlucky couple of months. Only Gunther was personally untouched, having been raised on a Swedish farm and being well used to sacrificing other creatures for human benefit.

We certainly couldn't start with humans, as much as Gunther swore he'd be happy to volunteer. Given Gunther's habit of depression, none of us fancied our experiment being characterized as assisted suicide. Tom and Katrina had soul searched and finally allowed us to settle on a dog. It would be dreadful to lose one, but, alas, the process of scientific research can be as cruel as nature herself. Tom had his eyes on several candidates at UCLA's Semel Institute. His reasoning was that if we lost a dog that was already being subjected to studies on narcolepsy, it might actually be a blessing for that creature. And if we were successful, we could offer him a new life fit for a canine king.

Today, I was going to miss out on the group's actual selection of that animal and a spare. I drove home feeling sorry for myself, but needless to say when I set my eyes on my little girl, that particular pity party broke up.

"How's she doing?" I asked Mother, unhooking my nursing bra. Mother being keen on organization, the nursery was so sparkling clean that I'd hesitated for a second at laying my coat on the bed. But my body had its own agenda. I loosened one of my milk-engorged breasts.

"I'm so relieved. She finished a bottle just an hour ago."

"Fine for her," I laughed, "but my boobs are bursting." I gently prodded my daughter's delicate lips with a leaking nipple, thanking God that she seemed willing to cooperate.

Mother was already throwing a shawl over her shoulders and reaching for her Hermès bag.

"What? Going so soon?" I cried. "I thought we might order in a pizza from Il Fornaio."

"Since when do they deliver?"

"Not them. Post Mates."

Mother responded dryly, "Families with babies are probably keeping them in business."

"I really don't have the energy to cook." I realized how whiny my voice sounded.

"Darling, I wasn't criticizing. Remember, I'm the woman who kept Robert Mondavi in business while Cook and Dhani kept that ridiculous household fed."

But The Whine was unvanquished. "Why don't you stay? Adam probably won't be back for hours. They're picking out the dogs."

Mother raised her eyebrows. "You must hate not being a part of it."

In response, I gestured with my chin toward Callay, who'd fallen asleep in my arms with a dot of milk between her half-closed lips bubbling with each tiny snore.

Mother smiled. "I wish I could stay, but I've actually promised to meet Cesar for dinner."

"What!"

"I didn't tell you?"

"That he was in touch? No, you didn't," I replied with some asperity.

"Honestly, I didn't want to distress you. After what he said about you—"

"Mother. That doesn't matter at all." *Was that true?* "I know how much you've been worrying about him."

"He contacted me after that awful shooting. He'd actually been at that club the week before." She flushed. "He'd evidently gone off to visit a friend in Florida after we—"

"I thought he didn't have any friends," I interrupted with some bitterness.

"Darling, I know he hurt you."

"I think he was an equal opportunity hurter."

"Yes, well. He's back in town. Staying with Fidel, actually. And I really think he's trying to make peace. He asked how you and the baby are."

I considered my own selfishness. Here I was, Odd Duck Extraordinaire with this gorgeous family and a world constantly singing my praises. Well, minus the flat-earthers and Big Oil and Cacklers and climate change deniers. And there was Cesar, struggling to express his own individuality in a world that would be nearly unanimous in treating him like a freak.

"Tell him I wish him the best."

Mother nodded her approval and gave me a couple of *bisous*. "I will, darling, I certainly will."

I learned later that Cesar hadn't shown up at their designated meeting place. Mother had driven over to Fidel's, who'd confessed he hadn't seen Cesar for several days. (They'd evidently shared their concern over a cup of coffee and what Mother described as the most heavenly flan she'd ever tasted, and Fidel had revealed to her that he'd left a wife and two daughters behind in Cuba that he'd ceased contact with ages ago, which made me feel unaccountably sad.)

Nor had the team found the right dogs. The ones that were about to be retired were just too weak for us to attempt such a significant trial with them. We were all getting nervous. Would we be allowed to continue our work in the coming year? Our climate scientist pals kept sending out the alarm, citing deadly floods in southern Louisiana, wildfires scorching California forests and towns with equal and unprecedented ferocity, melting permafrost releasing anthrax in Siberia, thermometers hitting a record 129 degrees in Kuwait, not to mention forest die-offs on multiple continents. The Republican presidential candidate calling climate change a Chinese hoax didn't exactly augur well for our project if he won. And he seemed to be gaining traction, despite increasing alarm across the globe.

I knew I wasn't the only one to feel sickened by our ailing body politic. With Gwennie, the response was predictable, but even Makeda was nearly half mad at the anti-female sentiment displayed during this electoral season.

"I do not understand it," she cried at the tail end of a dinner so delicious that Adam I were too busy mopping up the last bits of our spicy *tibs* with handfuls of *injera* to respond. "Here you have a woman with more credentials than God who is willing to take on the most difficult job in the world, and they want to lock her up? I could understand this in my own country. We are still very backward when it comes to violence against women and any real equality. But here? Do these people feel no shame?"

It troubled me that she still thought of Ethiopia as home. It took me back to Assefa's descriptions of his own struggle with homesickness, played out in his conflicted attraction to both Makeda and me in a mental state he'd called "the Hanging Man." I didn't want to even consider that my dear friend, nearly as close as Sammie to being a real sister, might be dangling in the limbo of being an eternal outsider. "It's hardly all of us, you know," I finally replied.

Adam shot me a look, as if to say, *Here, let me help.* "It must feel awful to have come here and all of sudden you're exposed to all this racism and sexism and xenophobia. Like it's not safe for you. Or the girls."

Makeda lifted her dark eyes to his and nodded. "Yes. I am worried. Particularly for them."

"How could you not be? I am, too." He rose to gather our plates, streaked like abstract paintings with red remnants of *tibs* gravy. I stifled the impulse to grab them from him and lick them clean.

Instead, like the student I'd once been, I took the hint from the man who'd once been my tutor. "It's very frightening. And given what you and the girls have already suffered, it's got to be hitting a raw nerve." I put a hand on her wrist as she was rising to help Adam.

"We would never allow you to be deported, you know." I paused and offered with no little embarrassment, "It's one perk of being a Nobelist. I've got a little clout."

"Yes, but who says I would want to stay if things got too terrible?"

It felt like a slap in the face, but I instinctively knew she was right. Why would she stay if the US ceased to be a beacon of light for the world? For her and her daughters?

For the very first time, I considered what our team would do if the man Gwennie liked to call Voldemort actually won. Would I be able to bear it if he cut off our funding just as we were on the verge of averting climate catastrophe?

Until now, it had never dawned on me that we could shift our project to another country. I began mentally running through the possibilities. The EU countries would be our team's best bet, but the one major nation that spoke our language had just voted to exit. Would Britain even maintain its commitment to the Paris climate accord?

But just as soon as I began considering worst-case scenario options, I was swept with such a strong surge of grief it was physical. My hand flew to my heart.

To leave this house, Caltech, Mother, Sammie and Aadita, Dhani and her family, the Huntington Gardens, the Pacific Ocean? I might have to leave Buster behind, too. There could always be visits, but still. I'd never been very attached to Manhattan when we'd lived there, and I'd lost all feeling for the Main Line when Father chopped down Grandfather's and my tree. But leaving SoCal? Its ridiculously fine weather and ubiquitous bougainvillea bushes and palm trees, its cacophonous crows and wild parrots, Korean barbecue and Vietnamese pho, the casual air of acceptance and neighborliness, Spanish speakers and the rich influence of Mexican culture and architecture? SoCal was my known, where I could feel comfortable in my own skin.

Suddenly what Makeda and her girls and Assefa and Abeba and Achamyalesh and Lemlem and Dhani and Ignacio and Sammie and Aadita had gone through was no longer a concept. To lose one's roots was like losing a mother. Which didn't bear thinking about.

I was overcome with new respect for all those who'd endured the kinds of suffering that led to the void of voluntary exile. And for the first time, I felt an active hatred for anyone who'd casually consign such sojourners to deportation. As if what they'd already endured wasn't enough.

I said as much to Adam that night, throwing an arm over his chest in our bed, his shoulder my pillow. I sucked in silent breathfuls of his Campbell's chicken soup B.O.

"You know what they say," he responded, nuzzling my ear. "The political is personal." (The moment felt too sweet to point out that he'd gotten the old feminist slogan the wrong way around.) He heaved a great sigh. "We've known that all along with climate change."

I looked up at him and felt oddly comforted. I wasn't alone. He'd been worrying about the prospects of Callay's future on this planet, too.

Chapter Nine

I'D FIRST HEARD about West Hollywood's yearly Gay Pride parade somewhere in my teens, but this particular march was a new phenomenon. The LGBTQ community had organized it on the heels of the election. The organizers were calling it the Gay Survival Parade. And with Mike Pence topping off the toxic gingerbread house with his attempts to divert HIV/AIDS funding to conversion treatment—i.e. electroconvulsive shock therapy—survival might actually be at stake for some of the participants.

I'd promised Sammie I'd go with her. She'd been Skyping daily with Amira and told me she'd feel like a hypocrite if she didn't go. "I don't know what it means to be a lesbian besides loving a woman, but I think I'd better find out."

It felt odd to me when she put it like that. What did it mean not to be a lesbian besides loving men? But I'd promised I'd join her the next day.

When I shared both my question and our plan, Adam burst out, "I don't think you should go." To my raised eyebrow, he responded, "What it means to be a lesbian right now is that you're a sitting duck for psychos, right alongside Muslims, Hispanics, blacks, and Jews. You saw that photo in the LA Times of the sign near the LA art museum: 'No Niggers.' What about people on the Metro Rail tearing off women's hijabs? Swastikas painted on school walls? There was an article just a few days ago in the *New York Times* about nearly a thousand acts of verbal and physical harassment of gays and lesbians since the election."

I replied with equal heat, "Well then Sammie and I will be in good company at this parade."

"Endangered company."

"You mean like Makeda and the girls? Dhani? Ignacio? Sammie on two counts—don't forget her dad was Jewish."

Adam ran a hand through his hair, a sure sign of frustration. "Fleur, this parade isn't like Gay Pride. It's political."

"Weren't you the one who told me the political is personal?"

"Yes, and I'm also the father of your daughter."

"So people who have children shouldn't take a public stand?"

"Not expressly to be provocative. No."

"So the fact that I've had tomatoes thrown at me at press conferences by Father's Cacklers and been insulted by social media stalkers and had our livelihood threatened innumerable times by Congress doesn't suggest that our work is constantly exposing us to crazies? What about that guy who kept sending me letters that I'd soon be roasting in hell?"

"He was locked up in prison."

"For stalking another scientist with a gun in his backpack," I shot back. "Did we stop our research after that?"

Adam took a step away and heaved a great sigh. "You're right. I'm an asshole."

"Ha! I thought that was my job." I came up to him and took hold of his hand. "What is it, love? This isn't like you."

"I'm fucking scared, is what. Scared that I can't protect you or the little Monkey. It's bad enough that a lunatic's going to be running this country now. But you at personal risk? Man, I can't stand it."

"I know," I said. And I did. No one I knew had yet found a way to tolerate the election results. I wasn't the only one who'd complained of feeling gut punched. Engineering the movement of human beings from one place to another through Dreamization sounded like a piece of cake compared to the challenge of weathering four years listening to a man captive to a particularly toxic void. I knew from firsthand experience that a human can tolerate only a certain degree of emptiness before erupting.

There was even a citizen's initiative for our state to secede. People were bandying about the phrase, "The United State of California," despite it having about as much of a chance as the proverbial snowball in hell.

The organizers had changed the title from parade to march to emphasize the seriousness of the situation. They'd suggested that people forgo the gaudy costumes associated with the Pride Parade, along with the disco and trance music, and had urged everyone to exchange any hint of nudity for mourning attire. I'd actually dragged out the black Sacha Drake dress that I'd worn to Nana's funeral, though I could barely pull it over my milk-engorged breasts and still pooched out belly. I knew that vanity should be the last thing I should be thinking about right now, but I hated how I looked in it. Shakespeare may never have actually penned the truism, "Vanity, thy name is woman"—Hamlet's lament actually referring to "frailty"— but it tended to be true, nonetheless. Which was why I was at least partly relieved when Sammie called at 10 p.m. to say she doubted she'd be well enough to get out of bed the next day. "It's either the stomach flu or food poisoning. It's amazing I got far enough from the loo to find my cell to call you."

"Sweetie, I'm so sorry. Sounds pretty bad."

"Can't keep a thing down. And it burns! I actually had prawn *vindaloo* for lunch. Terrible timing."

I could only imagine how that was going down. Or coming up. Ear to cell phone, I'd just entered the kitchen for a late night snack. My appetite vanished.

"Can I do anything?"

"Just kill me."

"Not likely," I replied. "Is Aadita coming over?"

"Already here," she said, then screamed, "Mum!" and hung up abruptly, presumably to hasten to the toilet.

Thank God for mothers, I thought, turning to head back upstairs to tell Adam I wouldn't be going after all. Talk about relief—I knew he'd be thrilled. And truth be told, I relished the thought of a lazy day with him and Callay.

But my cell phone was ringing again. I checked Caller ID. It was Stanley. I tried heading him off at the pass. "Don't worry, I'm not going."

He laughed a little weakly. "Gwennie said I was wrong to try to stop you. She said *somebody's* got to stand up for our rights. Obviously hinting that it should be yours truly."

I hated getting in the middle of their brother-sister spats. "Give her my love, will you? I'll try to make a quick run to your place tomorrow, maybe late afternoon? Dhani baked Gwen the most amazing cinnamon buns."

"She'll kill you. Says she's gone straight from being chemo-induced anorexic to obese."

"Well, that's a lie."

"I know," Stanley replied with a happy chuckle. As much as I adored Gwen, I was well aware that for Stanley she was the sun and the moon, though he'd never tell her that himself. I knew how thrilled he was that she seemed to be beating her disease. We were *all* incredibly grateful. As if in agreement, my milk came down with an insistent, ballooning warmth.

But before I could exit the kitchen, I was stopped in my tracks by the phone sounding off yet again, this time with the custom ringtone I'd set up for Mother: Will.I.Am's "I Got It from My Mama." As I felt the wetness spread across the front of my blouse, I answered impatiently. "Yes, Mother?" Didn't anyone bother these days with the custom of not calling after 10 p.m.?

"Listen, will you do me a favor, love? Could you and Sammie keep your eyes open for Cesar tomorrow? Fidel phoned to say he was intending to come back to town for the march."

I sighed. "I'm not going. Sam's sick."

"Oh." She sounded disconcerted. "Well, do you know anyone else who might be going?" The fact that Mother didn't ask what was wrong with my friend spoke volumes.

"Isn't Fidel going?"

"No. He's afraid he'll get deported."

"For God's sake, isn't he legal?"

"It's not a question you ask." No, I supposed you didn't. Especially not now. "Mother, you've tried with Cesar. You've got to let it be. With any luck, he'll call you at some point. You obviously can't force it."

"I realize that, but I'm afraid I'm a bit of a basket case. It's just that I never had to really worry about *you*, so I have no practice managing this kind of anxiety."

"You're joking, right?"

"Not really."

Speaking of feeling gut punched, I struggled to catch my breath. Adam must have wondered why I'd taken so long downstairs, as he entered the kitchen now, carrying Callay. He was staring at me with concern.

I kept my voice in a purposeful monotone. "When I was flapping and screaming and pinching myself? When you couldn't find a school that would take me? When I got arrested in the middle of the night after the Boy Who Called Me Beautiful talked me into taking off my clothes in a stranger's backyard?" Purposely ignoring Adam's hand signals, I went on, my face feeling unusually hot. "When I had to have an abortion?"

There was a long pause. I saw Adam leave the room, throwing me a worried glance as he clasped Callay tightly to his chest. Mother still sounded unperturbed. "Please don't think I'm stupid, but it's true. I never really worried about you. Not deep down. Not to the point of sleeplessness. You had this lucky innocence, as if nothing could really touch you."

I was so stunned that I sat down, grateful that there was a kitchen chair to catch me.

"What about when I gave that disastrous speech at the Nobel ceremony? Talking about Grandfather's balls in front of the King of Sweden?"

"But that was funny."

"Not for me. The press treated me like a fool. And the Cacklers had a field day with it."

"But you just kept going. You're so resilient."

I stifled the temptation to pinch my inner thigh. I promised myself I'd never do it again after Callay was born. I couldn't bear to set her such an awful example. What could I possibly say now? Mother had clearly perfected a way to protect herself from the kind of worry that had dogged me ever since I'd learned I was pregnant. She'd managed to blind herself to the fact that her young daughter had been perpetually gripped by a terror of the Everlasting Void of Eternal Emptiness.

I managed to get off the phone with the plea that I had to feed Callay, but the fact was, my milk had dried up during our conversation like an old sponge. I fetched a bottle from the fridge. Thank God for pumping.

My daughter was kind enough to sleep through that night, though the beneficial effect on my state of sleep deprivation was blunted by a series of nightmares involving Father, our truculent new president, and a knife-wielding, evil twin of Uncle Bob. I fed my little girl the next morning with great gratitude for her purity, then dozed off again until an unheard of 11:00 a.m.

Listening patiently and (wisely) without commentary to my rant about Mother, Adam offered to scrape me up some breakfast. I lumbered out of bed. Leaning against the marble bathroom sink counter, I stared at my sleep-swollen face in the mirror. Extracting a strand of dental floss, I went at my gums with a little too much force. As I rinsed my bloody mouth, I wondered what made for a good mother, really. Nana had been like a mother to me in my early days. She had a grip like a Mack truck and the vocabulary of a marine, but I knew I was safe with her. Gwennie had a generous heart, but she always held back just a bit, as if she were afraid of intruding; she felt more like an auntie than a mother. So many of us humans had been forced to make do without the intimate claiming that I'd seen between Dhani and Angelina, Aadita and Sam. Adam himself had had no mother at all, yet he was the most tender man on the planet. Next to Grandfather, of course. And then there was Stanley—as odd duckish as could be, but profoundly protective of me. It occurred to me that I'd gotten some of my sweetest love from men. But male and female alike— Grandfather, Nana, Adam, Gwennie, and Stanley: I knew that each of them had at times felt worried sick about me. Unless you had the equanimity of the Buddha himself, wasn't that part of the deal?

As if to corroborate that line of thought, I heard Adam running up the stairs shouting loudly enough to wake the dead. I hurried into the hallway, and Makeda did, too, ordering the girls back to their bedroom.

"Oh Jesus, Fleur!" Adam cried. "Thank God you didn't go!"

I managed to wrest from my distraught husband the news that someone had driven his car straight into the middle of the march. CNN was showing videos of bodies flying everywhere and one particularly nauseating photograph of a baby stroller upended on the sidewalk of Santa Monica Boulevard. Hunkered together in front of the TV, Adam, Makeda, and I learned that at least ten people had died, with many more wounded, and that the driver had been apprehended hiding in the bushes behind an apartment building on Kings Road. A previous mugshot showed an exceptionally pale man with a Swastika tattooed on his neck and a look in his hazel eyes that spelled nothing but trouble. I found myself wondering what kind of a mother *he'd* had.

It would later be reported that Dustin Eagleton had been a follower of a man named Craig Cobb, who'd splintered off from something called the Creativity Movement to establish an enclave in North Dakota he'd dubbed Creativity Trump, two misnomers that fairly took the breath away. Cobb had evidently gained some local media attention for his claims that the word "gay" had been created by Jews to distract white people from the perfidy of homosexuals. Well, maybe the guy was creative after all: he'd managed to defame two birds with one stone.

The phone, needless to say, was ringing off the hook. In a kind of daze, I listened consecutively to a sobbing Sammie, a ranting Gwennie, and an uncharacteristically confused Stanley H. Fiske.

When Adam finally flicked off the TV in disgust, a moist-eyed Makeda sat silently for a moment, as if gathering herself. Muttering that she'd promised the girls a late breakfast of *enqulala tibs* with spiced butter, she made for the stairway. Soon enough, the smells of grilled onions and jalapeños and cardamom wafted up to the second floor. Adam and I stared at each other wordlessly for what felt like eons before the baby monitor signaled that our Monkey was fussing. He went to fetch her as I woke from my trance enough to check on the older girls.

The air felt understandably tense. In the furthest corner of the room, seated with her back against the wall with her legs splayed in front of her, Sofiya wrapped her plump arms around her less robust younger sister. Melesse's *bunna* eyes were as wide as saucers. I managed to coax them toward one of their unmade beds and navigate them both onto my lap—well, as good as—to tell them that something had happened, but not to anyone we knew, and not to worry; everything would be okay. I wondered how many generations of adults had made such hollow promises to their children. Was that one more requirement of motherhood, a mastery of the lie?

As if to prove my point, Makeda appeared at the doorway, an unconvincing smile plastered onto her face. Taking it all in, she said resolutely, "You need to eat first, then we will talk." Her words sounded harsh to my ears, perhaps to theirs, too. Sliding from my lap to the floor, they looked from one of us to the other with questioning expressions.

"Darlings," I found myself saying, "sometimes we grownups get scared, too. Bad things do happen occasionally, and we don't like that, either. But I really can promise you this: I know that your *enat* and Adam and I will do everything in our power to make sure you are safe." Makeda and I locked eyes, and she gave a slight nod. I could sense, if not actually hear, all of us breathing a bit more deeply. Lord knew that in acknowledging that awful things could happen, I wasn't telling these girls anything they didn't already know. But I'd just discovered something myself: it was our commitment to each other that somehow made even the darkest void more bearable. Why hadn't I recognized that before? Wasn't it how I'd first fallen in love with Adam?

As the girls slid down the banister to get their food and my own mouth watered a little, reminding me I hadn't eaten, I sought out my husband. I found him in Callay's room, where he was changing her diaper. "Who's my little *stinka*?" he said cheerily, folding up a diaper containing what had to be the smelliest poo on the planet into a tight ball and sticking it into the bin by the side of the changing table. I made a mental note to empty it very, very soon. We'd both marveled more than once that such a small being could poop so frequently and with a volume and odor that rivaled one of the larger carnivores.

He carefully fit her little limbs inside her lion-patterned onesie and was about to pass her to me when I heard the familiar strains of "I Got It from My Mama."

"Grand fucking central," I muttered, aiming for my phone.

"He's safe!" Mother's voice exulted. "He texted from Guatemala. He's found his mother, and he's staying with her an extra week or so. He wanted to reassure me that he hadn't gone to the march, that he hadn't come back to LA after all. Oh, Fleur, he's okay!"

"Yes, Mother," I replied, my voice less than enthusiastic. I found myself taking some pleasure in adding, "But a lot of people aren't."

Mother sounded embarrassed. "Of course. I'm such an idiot. But, Fleur, you understand, don't you? I'm just so *relieved*. Wasn't it kind of him to call?"

I realized that my voice sounded as dry as dust as I responded, "Mmm. Very kind." I couldn't resist the final jab, "You realize Sammie and I could have been there if she hadn't gotten sick." I didn't even let her reply before I cut the connection.

Adam, who'd been listening, raised an eyebrow. "You know, the Green-eyed Monster comes in many shapes and sizes."

"Don't," I said, putting up a hand. "The last thing I need right now is a lecture on what a jerk I am."

I was so disoriented that I ignored my promise to spend some quality time with Adam. Instead, I began packing up Callay's gear, thrusting a diaper bag and Dhani's cinnamon buns into her stroller, and announced I wanted to take a walk with her to Stanley and Gwennie's. Adam looked hurt, but he let me go without remonstration, only reminding me to take care at intersections, as I was understandably distracted. I assumed he'd return to the TV as soon as he shut the door.

It was a warm day, and I began to sweat after a couple of blocks. I stopped to admire a lavender bush spilling over someone's perfectly painted picket fence. I tugged off a fuzzy, purple-flowered sprig of it and held it my nose, unaccountably reminded, not of my own garden or of Mother's, but of Father's Main Line estate—its vast invisible beds of roses and its lavender bushes tended with loving care by Ignacio in the days he competed with Father for Dhani's affections. It struck me that, if he were still alive, my father would have been one of the people fulminating against the recent successes of the LGBTQ movement. I flung the lavender away and resumed pushing the stroller.

The baby woke just as a flock of wild parrots flew in irregular formation overhead, making their inevitable racket. I knew that the question of how SoCal came to be home to so many species of this non-indigenous bird family was subject to some dispute. SoCal had seen a certain amount of illegal bird importation in the '40s and '50s and then again in the '80s, with smugglers tending to release their contraband when they feared getting caught. But some old timers claimed that the preponderance of wild parrots was either the result of the Bel Air brush fire of 1961, where people released their pet yellow-heads to save them from the conflagration, or the similarly released seven hundred or so birds who'd been kept at Simpson's Garden Town in east Pasadena before their own disastrous fire. Others insisted that they were the collateral damage of the closure of Van Nuys' Busch Gardens Theme Park, where some birds escaped in the transfer to new facilities and others were consciously released.

Whatever their roots, they were a hardy bunch; their transformation from domestication to the urban wild was solid. And brazen. I recalled seeing a particularly beautiful lilac-crowned parrot land on Mother's pool decking to have a nice drink on a sizzling June day while she and I sat within arm's distance, laughing with delight on our chaise lounges. I couldn't wait to talk to Callay about such things, but for now I had to be content with the languages of touch and smell and nonsense syllables.

No one answered when I rang the Fiskes' bell, so I used my key to let us in. Gwennie was just walking toward the front door as I struggled to get the stroller over the threshold. Its back wheels went all hinky on me, wanting to aim straight for the door. I smiled apologetically after a crankily muttered, "Get in there, you fucker," slipped out of my mouth.

Gwen's head was turbaned in a thick white towel. She was grinning broadly, a living testimony to the human body's ability to spring back from near disaster.

"You're walking!" I exclaimed.

"I know. Isn't it a hoot?" But Gwen wasn't wasting any time. She flung the towel from her head, damp strands from the shower she'd obviously just taken forming a pixie parade across her forehead. Eagerly reaching into the stroller's cavern to lift out Callay, her joy was palpable. She'd only seen videos of the little Monkey. Now that she held her in her broad arms, it looked as if she'd never let her go.

It hadn't even occurred to me that, in setting out for this visit, I was going to offer Gwennie such pleasure. Asshole that I was, I'd thought only that she and Stanley might be a comfort to *me*.

As it happens, Stanley had gone off to the lab to distract himself from the awful news, so Gwennie had Callay all to herself. I headed for the kitchen, heated up the oven for the cinnamon buns, and put the kettle on for tea.

Gwennie appeared at the doorway, murmuring, "You know, I think you'd better take her. She's a bit heavier than I might have suspected."

"Oh my God, of course!" I swept over and relieved her, took the baby back to the stroller—where she seemed content to repose with wide-open eyes—and backed it behind me right up to the kitchen door. I wasn't even going to try to navigate the damned thing over that narrower threshold.

I pulled out a chair for Gwennie, who was standing over the stroller with wet eyes. "You're barely up and walking, and I shove a baby into your arms."

Gwennie sat down, panting just a little, replying dryly, "You didn't shove anything except that giant stroller, and I grabbed her myself, so enough with the guilt trip. How are you doing? I can't believe you and Sammie could have—"

"Don't," I said, lifting the kettle to pour boiling water into two orange and white Caltech mugs. "We weren't, thank God."

She raised an eyebrow. "Or goddess."

I grinned. Gwennie was the most spiritual agnostic I knew.

The room was beginning to smell like heaven. I pulled the buns out of the oven and placed them on a serving plate, then set down forks, dishes, and napkins in no little haste. I realized I'd eaten nothing so far. I was ravenous.

Later, the two of us reclined comfortably on the old sofa with Callay at my breast and a down pillow under Gwennie's head. A little hesitantly, I broached the topic of her miraculous rebound.

"Honestly, I didn't think I was going to make it," she confessed.

"I was a little worried, too," I admitted.

"I think it was Robert Frost who wrote about the afternoon knowing what the morning never conceived of. Or something like that, anyway."

"What do you think he meant?"

"That time and age bring surprises you'd never have imagined." She paused, a hard glint in her eye. "Like Herr Drumph."

"Oh no, let's don't. My milk'll dry up." We both laughed, but it took discipline to avoid that dark alley. "I think he was talking about wisdom."

"Oh, I'm not very wise. Not like you guys. Just got the one BA from UCLA all those years ago. Never got further than clerical jobs, really. Glorified ones—working for worthy non-profits and such, but clerical jobs, nonetheless."

"You don't have to have a PhD to have wisdom."

"Well, Miss Scientist, I think Stanley would ask you to explain how wisdom is different from knowledge."

"Wisdom is knowledge of the heart."

Gwen cocked an eyebrow. "Deep." I shrugged. "My heart's pretty rusty, Fleur. Didn't have many boyfriends after Jack Green." She gave a wry grin. "As in one. So I don't know how much wisdom my heart has accrued."

"Romantic love isn't the only path of the heart."

Gwennie's chuckling seemed to delight the baby. Pulling away from my nipple, Callay gave a series of coos. Gwen rubbed a finger against her cheek and then kissed her stockinged foot. Sitting back again, she said, "Fleur, you're too kind. I know that being a spinster might have a certain cachet in literary and scientific circles. Jane Austen, Emily Dickenson, Louisa May Alcott, Rosalind Franklin, Rachel Carson. Even your Jane Goodall fits the bill these days, though she's technically a divorcee. But they each had something fine and precious to recommend her. Me—my biggest claim to fame is serving as caretaker of my brother Stanley's home life and being a kind of mascot to the physics team. As I age, I find it annoying that so many clichés come true. Older women, particularly if we're not accomplished, are pretty much invisible. When I walk down the street, nobody notices me. I'm just a plain woman in a doughy box of a body."

"Oh, Gwennie. Don't be so cruel to yourself."

"It's not cruel. It's true." She added shyly, "But never mind, I've had my Bach and Wagner, Baez and Seeger, all the jazz greats to mirror my joy. And Beethoven, of course. Nothing like a deaf musician to cheer a woman going deaf herself. But here's the thing—another cliché, I fear—an absence in one area really can lead to a gain in another. One door closing and another opening, and all that. I think I've become a pretty astute observer of human nature over the years."

"Well, that's definitely part of wisdom—"

But she interrupted me. "For example, I'd like to know—really—why you paid me this particular visit."

There was no point putting up a fuss. Callay had fallen asleep across my chest, and I rose carefully to place her inside the stroller without waking her, tucking her elephant-patterned blanket around her as the room felt suddenly rather chilly. I grabbed a frayed red throw from the back of Stanley's favorite chair and offered it to Gwen, who shook her head. Instead, I wrapped it around myself like a shawl. Settling back onto the sofa with my knees tucked under me, I confided in her about Cesar. Perhaps because of a reluctance to out him, and perhaps because of our own awkwardness, Mother and I had had an unspoken agreement not to mention what we'd witnessed in Fidel's back yard that day, passing off our incursion as only an idle curiosity about her neighbor's back garden, based on the exoticism of the front, and ascribing Mother's concussion to a trip over a fallen branch in the driveway. I'd told Adam and Sammie, of course, but then I told them pretty much everything.

Gwennie looked gobsmacked. "Oh my. It really does take time to catch up with social change, doesn't it? I feel rather foolish saying it, but he always struck me as a very masculine sort of boy."

"I know. The same for me. Sammie says it doesn't matter. It's how they ... how *we* feel on the inside."

"Well, of course, that's true." She giggled. "Actually, on the inside I'm Twiggy."

"Who's Twiggy?"

Gwennie stared at me for a long while, then shook her head. "I really *am* old, aren't I? She was an English model who tortured all us girls with how adorable and skinny she looked. Like a twig." It took me a minute. Gwen sighed. "I guess you had to be there." And then, "So how *is* Cesar doing?"

"Sounds like he's doing just fine. He evidently tracked down his mother again."

But Gwen was, as she'd said, an astute observer of human nature. Her expression softened. "And you? How are you with all this?"

It was as if pressure had been building in the magma chamber of a volcano. I blurted out, "I don't give a damn what kind of makeup he wears, how sluttishly he dresses, or whether he ends up a he or a she. I don't even care that he blames me for all of it. It's Mother. She obsesses about him. All the time. And then has the nerve to say she never worried like this about *me*." Realizing how emphatically I'd spoken, I slid a guilty glance toward the stroller, but nary a peep from that quarter. I prayed I hadn't given her bad dreams.

"Oh dear." Gwen sat up and leaned over to gather me toward her ample bosom. I let myself collapse into the warmth of her body, in between sobs taking in the richness of what smelled like a combination of peaches, perspiration, and fresh mint. She spoke so softly, I had to ask her to repeat herself. "She's forgotten, you know. "

"Forgotten what?"

"That she used to call Stanley and me all the time. Wanting to know how you were settling in. Whether you were making friends at school." She paused. "Whether you missed her."

I sat up, wiping my snotty nose against my sleeve like a child. "Miss her? I didn't. At least nothing like how I missed Grandfather." I shrugged. "But Mother—I never thought much about it. I guess I was born missing her. Sort of like having blue eyes or dirty blond hair. It was just what was."

Gwennie's eyes filled. "Alcoholism's really the devil, isn't it?"

I spat out reactively, "She wasn't much more available after she got sober. It was all about her Bill W.'s."

"Oh love, alcoholics don't get sober so quickly. Not really. Not so as they can access their feelings very well. It takes time to be able to bear them without smoothing them out with booze, or some substitute for booze."

I went inside and thought about that one, sniffing around the dark crannies and back cupboards of my mind. "Sort of like numbing yourself out in case you're tempted to pinch and whirl?"

A faint smile turned up the corners of Gwennie's lips. "Something like that."

"What a boob I am. I feel like a three-year old."

"No matter. I feel like I'm ninety-nine."

We burst into giggles.

I loved how she gave herself over to her laughter. It spilled messily out of her, punctuated by a doggish snort or two.

"May I ask you something? Would you mind terribly if I called you 'Aunt Gwen?'"

Her voice was matter-of-fact, but her eyes gave her away. They looked all melty, the way Grandfather's did when I'd reach out to hold his hand while we sat watching our tree. "Not at all. I'd quite like that," she replied.

The walk back home felt about twice as long as it took to get to the Fiskes'. By the time I yanked the stroller over the threshold, Callay was screaming and my back ached from having to push the stroller most of way while holding my daughter to my shoulder, a stench stronger than horse shit just inches from my nose. I hurried with her upstairs to change her diaper, calling out, "Adam! We're home!" only to be greeted by Mother, staring at me solemnly from the top of the stairs. A pit forming in my belly, I cried, "What's wrong?"

"Nothing. I just—"

"Where's Adam?"

"He went to play golf with Tom and Amir."

"Golf?" He never played golf. Said it reminded him too much of his father and his cronies from the Senate.

Mother stretched forward to take the baby from me when I reached the landing, but I merely plowed on toward Callay's bedroom with Mother hurrying to keep up with me. "Evidently a couple of wealthy physics alumni offered to take them out to Brookside, and Stanley told them it would be impolitic of them to say no. "

I set the baby down on her changing table, girding myself for the mess and muttering, "They'd better not be associated with the oil lobby, or I'll kill them."

Mother made a face. "Forget that, this little girl's poo just might kill *us*."

I couldn't help but grin. But then I forced myself to focus on the task at hand. The little Monkey had ceased crying, as if relieved that she herself was about to be spared the smell. Mother took the rolled up diaper and soiled wipes from me and left the room. We both knew that no diaper pail could sufficiently contain this intensity of Eau d'Excrément de Callay.

When Mother returned to the room, I'd already snuggled under Gwennie's childhood quilt, and my little Monkey was sucking at my nipple like there was no tomorrow. Mother sat hesitantly at the foot of the bed as if I might kick her off if she settled her whole bum onto it.

"Where're Makeda and the girls?"

"At a birthday party for a boy named Hector." Mother's face flushed as if she'd just realized that was the name of the boy who'd first gotten me pregnant. She hurried to add defensively, "Life goes on even in the midst of disasters."

Looking down at Callay, I replied, "It certainly does."

But Mother clearly mistook my meaning. "I never meant to hurt you. When Adam called me, I—"

"Adam called you?"

"Well, yes, he said that you were very upset, so I—"

I really was going to kill him when he got home. "Listen, Mother, I'm exhausted. Now's not a good time. I really think Callay and I need a nap after she finishes feeding. It's been a long day."

Mother's eyes widened. "Of course. Forgive me." She stooped to plant a quick kiss on the baby's forehead, accidentally brushing her lips across the tip of my nose. I said nothing.

Contrary to what I'd said to Mother, once the baby finished her feed, I was wide awake. I thought of texting Adam to see when he'd be home, but instead tiptoed downstairs and curled up opposite the fireplace. It was too warm to light a fire, but it was soothing to just sit there, admiring the artistry of its Spanish tile work. Buster arose from the outer hearth and leapt onto my lap. His motor thrummed loudly, as it always did, and I stroked his sleek black coat in a kind of ecstasy. Jillily had been a great purrer, too, and her tuxedo markings had been similar to Buster's but for the white dot beneath her nose. But there was a delicacy to her that contrasted sharply with the powerful muscles under Buster's fur. There was no way this animal on my lap was anything but male. What was it, I wondered, that made us humans vulnerable to disconnecting from our birth gender? It was a question, of course, that had no answer. Each species—and each era—seemed to have its own ways of dealing with the void.

I found myself speculating what it would be like for the dog we chose for our experiment to dematerialize and—please God—come back again. Would such a remarkable experience fill its void for the rest of its days?

Buster butted his nose against my cheek. I stroked him more vigorously. He stretched out a paw and plied his nails against my chest, careful to retract them before pulling them back. I knew he loved me. I knew that animals feel love, even for us confused humans who struggle so fruitlessly to be at peace inside our own skins.

I noticed a tiny spider making its way across the nubby fabric of one of the cream colored throw cushions at my elbow. Its skinny legs worked hard to make it over each little hill. I prayed Buster wouldn't notice it and lap it up with one quick flick of his tongue. There it was again. Life eating life. To survive, yes, but also out of boredom. Life playing with life as a kind of practice. Cruelty. I had it in myself, as well.

I lifted the cat and put him down on the sofa, where he instantly commenced an elaborate grooming ritual, beginning with his apron of soft, white fur. I strode over to the landline that reposed beside a rather somber picture of a young Grandfather on a small side table, his walrus mustache still dark and imposing. My mother picked up after the first ring. "I'm sorry," I said. "I was terrible to you. I wanted to make you feel bad. It hurt my feelings when you said you didn't worry about me."

She paused, and I was afraid she'd hung up.

But when she finally spoke it was clear she was fighting tears. "I *did* worry about you. That was a lie."

"So why say it? "

"I wanted you to think that I have confidence in you."

I picked at the dry skin on my lower lip. "Are you telling me that everything you said was untrue?"

"Yes."

I didn't believe her. "What else did you worry about?"

"That your experience with your father would warp your relationship with men. That being with a sick grandfather all the time would give you a grim view of life. That you were lonely, but I couldn't find anyone to play with you. That the boy at the pond had done something worse than you could find the words for. That you would never be socialized. That you got too many colds. That your pelvic pain meant you'd never be able to have children. That you would be victimized. That I'd scarred you. That you'd hate me for the rest of your life."

Hate her? How could she not know? I'd been haunted from the beginning of memory by her tantalizing presence behind her locked bedroom door, behind her wine glass and her eternally uneaten plates of food, by the absence of her graceful, velvet hands—which I'd so longed to feel enclosing my own. I'd idolized to the point of pain her perfectly proportioned body fitting perfectly into her impeccable Chanel suits. Her pearls and her Infra Rouge lipstick and her No. 5 perfume. Her cherished Austin roses in their invisible beds. Her multi-syllabic words; her half-smiles, hinting at something too delicious to be spoken; the quick flash of fire in her eyes when Father spoke rudely about her own father. When he used all those nasty names for me. I'd adored her the way one adores a brilliant sunset. The way we wished upon the first star in the night sky. She'd been my beautiful, unattainable queen.

They say we become our mothers as we age. Following in her footsteps, I merely replied, "Well, I don't. Hate you."

"Really?" she asked, her voice tremulous.

When Adam finally came home, I wanted to berate him for being so late. Instead, I turned off the breast pump and removed the flanges from my nipples, scooping up all the fussy pieces to take downstairs to wash and store. Adam gave my shoulder a squeeze before I left the bedroom.

When I came back up, he was standing naked by the window, absent-mindedly scratching his chest. All anger fled me as I stood at the doorway, rendered speechless by his still taut muscles, the angular flare of his hipbones from his waist, the cleave along his spine that I loved to trace with my hands, his slightly corkscrewed left leg with its calf larger than the right for the harder work it had to do. Despite his limp, he'd stayed as fit as he'd been the first night we'd spent together at Shutters. He'd surprised me back then, insisting we detour to Santa Monica Beach on our way home from Ethiopia, grabbing me tightly to him as we bobbed and screamed in the wild waves. The beauty of him now took me by surprise all over again.

But when he turned around, he said, "We have to talk." I tested his tone, replaying it in my mind. Not angry, but resolute. I tensed. "I'm sorry," he said.

"For being so late?"

"Huh? No. For asking you to not go to the march."

I frowned. This was not what I'd been expecting. "But you were right. I shouldn't have gone. Look what happened."

He shook his head. "Yes, it was bad. Very bad. The fucking worst. But I should have realized it was your call." He walked over to the bed and sat, patting the duvet beside him. I joined him, and he took my hand, gazing searchingly into my eyes. "I've been driving around for a couple of hours, trying to sort this out. I was trying to control you. Wanting you to save me from my own fear. Which—really—is what that loser was doing when he drove into the crowd."

I rolled that one around in my head. It had a certain clarity to it. Something like what you'd expect from a quantum physicist who'd actually made the effort to push his feelings aside for a moment to make room for thought.

I loosened my hand from his and stroked his chest and shoulders, feeling teary. "This is why I love you."

He laughed. "Because I own my shit?"

"Well," I said, letting my hand drift down to his member. "That and a few other things."

"No. Wait. I think you have a part in this, too." I pulled back my hand, aware that my heart was beating a bit faster. "I know it's a cliché for new dads, but I'm feeling a little taken for granted."

"What do you mean?" I asked defensively. You may have noticed that one of us was exhibiting more of a gift for self-reflection than the other.

"Well, take today. You went out without any acknowledgment that we'd planned on hanging out together. Taking Monkey with you as if she belonged to you. I have something to do with her being here, too, you know. I knew you were upset, but you could have turned to me."

I flushed. "Don't pretend you're the victim here. You were just fine. Went golfing, for God's sake. I hope you aren't going to turn into your father."

Adam stood up, his neck muscles working. "Wow. *That* was a low blow. I wouldn't have expected it of you."

I felt mortified, but when you're digging yourself a grave, why not just jump in? "I wouldn't have expected *you* to rat out on me to my mother. To beg her to apologize to me."

He licked his lip and looked a bit red in the face himself. "Maybe I shouldn't have called her, but at least I was trying to help. Your comment about my dad, though … and I didn't *beg* her to do anything. Just told her you were hurt."

We stared at each other. Adam broke eye contact and strode over to the dresser, his foot dragging a bit more than usual. He yanked open the bottom door to retrieve his plaid pajama bottoms, pulling them up as if he didn't want to be naked in front of me. I wanted to jump out of my own skin and had to stifle the impulse to pinch my upper arm.

I knew I should apologize, but I couldn't seem to force the words out of my mouth. Instead, I said, "Did you enjoy yourself golfing? Whom did you go with?"

"That simply won't do, Fleur." His tone reminded me that he'd once been my tutor. And in more than philosophy and physics. How revolutionary it had been at the time to hear him urge me, *Use your words, Fleur.*

As if in response, I said, "I'm embarrassed." I saw he was waiting for more. "I shouldn't have said that. It was a low blow. I *was* angry that you'd tried to tell me what to do the way my father would have done." Still, Adam said nothing. "But you're not him." It was a relief to recognize it. I really had been a bit possessed. "If anything, I've been acting like him myself, judging Cesar for being a freak. As if he's any more of a freak than I am." Adam frowned. "Oh, okay. We're all freaks."

Adam snorted. Thank God. It was as if a demon had squeezed all the love out of us for a while. Well, to be fair: out of me, anyway. As he took me in his arms and I felt the void recede, I murmured into his shoulder, "I guess that was why Father liked to hate me so much. It relieved him of feeling his own freakishness."

"His own humanness," Adam murmured back.

"That, too," I replied.

Chapter Ten

I WAS OUT walking Callay, tracing the synchronized dance of two white butterflies overhead, when my cell phone pinged. It was Adam. His voice was filled with enthusiasm. "Melky's coming," he announced excitedly.

"No way!" I cried.

We hadn't seen Melkamu Berhe since he'd served as our informal Ethiopian tour guide six years ago. As Jane Goodall's mentee, Melky had generously agreed to ferry me to Tikil Dingay from Bole Airport on my fateful trip to meet my rival for Assefa's affections. Actually, it was when he'd arrived weeks later to take Adam and me back to the airport that Melky had first revealed his interest in Makeda as a woman.

We'd barely heard from Melky since. Nor had Makeda. There's nothing like a few acts of terrorism to put paid to the best of plans. But as far as I knew, he was still single. It never failed to amaze me when someone of excellent character struggled to find a partner, though it did occur to me now that perhaps their very excellence militated against finding the right match.

I was thrilled at the prospect of seeing Melky again myself, but my wheels were turning with how I might make sure that he and Makeda got to see each other. Of course, the best way would be to have him stay with us. I hurried downstairs to ask Lukie to prepare the spare bedroom.

The morning that Melky arrived turned out to be less than auspicious. Monkey was running a bit of a fever with her first cold, and I'd quickly discovered that I was the most overprotective mother on the planet. While waiting for our pediatrician to call me back— his delay quite possibly having something to do with the fact that, despite Adam's entreaties, I'd phoned his answering service at 6 a.m. on a Sunday morning—I managed to wake virtually everyone I knew to share my distress. The ridiculous thing was, virtually every person I called had never had children. Except for Mother, who wasn't picking up her phone, possibly because she slept with earplugs now that Cesar was staying with her again; she'd confessed that she didn't have the heart to ban the trance music blaring from his bedroom every night. Stanley merely mumbled that he was sorry. Katrina, whom I'd surely roused from a deep slumber, had groused, "Everybody gets colds, Fleur." Amir had pronounced with great authority, "Turmeric and ginger." Bob made some weird analogy about sea life. Sammie rushed to reassure me that I kept apologizing for my over-the-top anxiety only because I lived in Pasadena and hadn't had enough exposure to Jewish mothers.

I didn't have the heart to call Makeda, who wouldn't arrive back in town until later that morning from a previously planned visit with the girls to the Disneyland Hotel. Sofiya had been suffering the return of old nightmares of people coming to steal her and her sister away from their adoptive mother, and Makeda, Adam, and I had determined that the situation called for the distracting ministrations of Minnie Mouse and her crew.

Thankfully, the considerably calmer Adam took charge. After Googling the appropriate fever medicine for six-months-old babies, he administered baby Tylenol and was suctioning the mucus out of her nose with a tiny rubber bulb when the doorbell rang. I flew down the stairs and found a somewhat balder and, if anything, heftier Melky beaming from the porch and wrapping me in a hug that bested Nana's Mack truck grips by about a hundred pounds.

"Melky!" I squealed.

He held me at arm's length and replied with a giant grin. "Ah, this is what they mean by a sight for sore eyes. Motherhood becomes you, Mrs. Manus."

"Oh my God," I laughed, as he lifted his suitcase as if it were a toothpick and followed me into the hall. "The last time I saw you, Adam and I hadn't even—."

But here was Adam coming down the stairs with Callay against his shoulder. "Adam hadn't what?"

"Swept me off my feet."

"I think the ocean did that."

It came back to me then—that shocking embrace as we were buffeted by the waves of Santa Monica beach, with Adam's giant hard-on pushing against me as he brazenly confessed that he'd reserved a room for us that night at Shutters.

I nearly flapped. As Sammie liked to say, it was "TMEI"—too much emotional information. Here was Melky from what felt like another lifetime, juxtaposed against the memory of my first sexual encounter with Adam, and little Callay here with us, too. I moved toward Adam with the intention of getting a feel for how hot her cheeks were, but he—murmuring, "She's going to be fine, love"— strode past me to shake hands with Melky. Melkanu straightened his wire-rimmed glasses before seamlessly taking the sleeping Callay from my husband and settling her against his own sturdy shoulder as if he held babies everyday. With exquisite tenderness, he stroked the damp wheaten curls on her head, and, giving her an ecstatic sniff, planted a kiss on her crown as if anointing her.

Adam gave him an approving nod. "I like a man who's not afraid of little ones."

"Oldest brother of nine siblings. They're all grown now. They're taking over the world—literally. Four of them spread across Africa. One at Oxford, two in Germany, and one here in the States. Teaching at Yale, at least as long as she can hold onto her visa." We did a group wince. "The boy in Addis is going to be a father himself any day now." He grinned. "I guess that means he's not really a boy."

Adam answered cheekily, "Time to make one of your own, bro?"

As if on cue, we three turned at the sound of a key turning the front door lock. An exuberant Sofiya and Melesse flooded the hallway with sound as they burst inside, their Minnie Mouse ear hats bobbing as they twirled around us.

"We went on the teacup ride and spinned around and around!"

From Makeda on the porch behind them, "The word is 'spun,' *lehb*."

"I went on the Small World!"

"I did, too! The children were dancing!"

Their mother dragged herself inside, pulling a suitcase and wearing her own Mouseketeer hat with a red bow-tied pigtail sticking straight up at the top. Her expression said it all, especially when she saw Melky standing there with a still blessedly sleeping Callay, despite all the noise. Setting the suitcase right down, she swept the silly hat off her hair and tried to tamp down its messiness. "Girls, girls!" she cried. "*Zeni beli*. Be quiet, please. The baby. And can't you see we have a visitor?"

Chastened, Sofiya and Melesse stopped and let their eyes travel up to Melky's broad smile as if staring at the tallest of trees. Melesse, ever the shy one, was the most affected. She put a hand to her mouth and ran up the stairs. Sofiya couldn't help but throw out a loud, "We had so much fun!" before capering after her.

I relieved Melky of my little girl as he leaned down to kiss Makeda once on each cheek and then once more in the Ethiopian way. He murmured, "I am so glad to see you after making such a brief acquaintance at Tikil Dingay. But you are more beautiful than before." He touched his own graying goatee as if to signify how he'd aged. "How is that possible?"

I watched a new sort of light come into Makeda's eyes before turning away to give them some privacy. "Welcome back from Disneyhell," I said over my shoulder, beckoning to Adam. "We should put Monkey into her crib. She's got a bit of a cold."

By the time we came back down with our girl a few hours later, the kitchen was filled with the sharp tang of *Bunna* and raucous laughter.

Her face a bit red and her eyes streaming, Makeda looked up, and—like her daughter earlier—put a hand to her mouth. "The bébé, she is okay?"

Adam patted Monkey's back. He said, "She's fine. It's just a little cold. Fleur's anxious because Callay's never been sick before."

"Of course, she is," Melky said soothingly. He said with obvious sincerity, "She is your most precious person. Your world now."

I saw Makeda eye him with some surprise. But she said nothing. Until, that is, she asked if we'd mind if she left the girls with us for a while, as Melky had expressed a wish to see some of the city's highlights.

"I was thinking," she said, "the Norton Simon, old Pasadena, and, of course, the Huntington."

"You are not too tired after what Fleur called 'Disneyhell?'"

Makeda laughed. "There is no keeping a good woman down."

Go, Makeda!

"It is not only the gardens—although I have to admit they are quite a bit grander than our Gullele Botanic Garden—but there is an exhibit at their museum you might like, since you, too, are a fan of Octavio Butler."

I made a note that they'd gotten to favorite authors already. Always a good sign.

"They have these wonderful hand-lettered placards she made for herself, almost like messages of self-encouragement for one of her infamous writer's blocks, that I think you will particularly like. They are childlike in appearance, printed in slanting lines with bold colored pens and paint, as if Sofiya or Melesse had written them."

"Ironic," Melky mused, "for such a hard-headed woman."

"Even a hard-headed woman can have a soft heart," Makeda lobbed back.

Melky's eyes gleamed. "Very true, indeed. I stand corrected."

I noted to myself that they'd already developed a flirty repartee I'd never observed in either of them, except—I suddenly recalled—when Makeda and Adam had nearly driven me out of my mind with jealousy in our few days together in Tikil Dingay. It occurred to me that my Green-eyed Monster may have given my dormant desire for Adam a little push back then, which might in turn have given him the encouragement he needed to make his bold move at Shutters. Perhaps I should give Makeda some credit for that. Looking at her now from that vantage point—her insouciantly-cut, gauzy modern Habesha top, with its beautiful border of turquoise, yellow, red, and pink complementing her glowing sienna skin—I wondered that I hadn't felt any of my familiar pangs since Makeda had come to live with us. But looking over at Adam, who threw me a frankly adoring look back, I concluded with some surprise that the Green-eyed Monster may have actually been put to some ghostly green bed once and for all.

A lusty cry erupting from the vicinity of Adam's shoulder interrupted my reverie. I rushed to take our little girl from him, and her rooting lips reassured me that she was healthy enough to be hungry. I unbuttoned my blouse and let her begin to suckle as Melky and Makeda prepared to go out.

Chapter Eleven

I WAS SO glad that Mother and I had arrived at our truce over the worrying-about-daughter issue. The following few months were filled with delicious days of communing by three generations of what poet Naomi Ruth Lowinski liked to call "the motherline." This particular day started off especially joyously. For once the stifling humidity of this horrid, yearlong LA heat wave had abated, allowing a brisk wind to riffle our hair and freeing our limbs from their torpor. We'd decided to take advantage of the clemency with a field trip to the Los Angeles County Museum of Art, where an exhibit was being curated of Marc Chagall's "Fantasies for the Stage," comprised of set designs and costumes for, among other things, Ravel's ballet *Daphnis and Chloé*, one of my favorites—with love ultimately prevailing over the Green-eyed Monster.

But there was nothing monstrous about the exhibit, save for a scary bat costume or two. Chagall's affinity for music and his predilection for peopling his paintings with chickens and goats had bequeathed an odd piquancy to his set designs and costumes. Callay had pointed delightedly at some of the more fanciful mannequins, and Mother and I had actually danced around a bit to the operatic accompaniment to this spacious show. Luckily for us, none of the other visitors seemed much bothered that one young woman pushing a baby stroller and one middle-aged matron attired in tasteful pearls and stylish heels were cavorting amid the creatively-clad figures.

It was in that spirit that we exited the museum with Monkey in tow and made for the traffic light that would allow us across the street to the parking lot. As we waited for the light to turn, Mother continued to prance around, her long silver hair with its striking blue stripe—yes, she'd done it—flaring like a rock star's in the wind tunnel of Wilshire Boulevard.

"How can you still look this beautiful?" I cried against the racket.

"Oh, pish. Beautiful," Mother shouted dismissively. "I'm so sick of having to be beautiful, I could spit." She shocked me by doing just that. I gave a silent prayer of thanks that the wind hadn't been aiming in my direction.

"But it's a gift. Beauty makes everything easier," I objected.

Mother leaned in toward me and put her face surprisingly close to mine. "Haven't you learned yet that the obligation to look beautiful shreds a woman's heart? I could never bloody well relax with a man. Always so damned conscious of keeping an appealing expression on my face, carrying my body with poise. It's actually one of the main reasons I took to drinking. Give me enough glasses of wine, and I didn't give a fuck. I could be a slob, or—God forbid—angry-looking, or goofy, or just ordinary and prosaic and boring." She shook her head emphatically. "Beauty? It's vastly overrated. Give a girl a book, a sport, something outside of herself that she can be passionate about. Now *that's* a gift."

It felt like a bizarre conversation to be having at the noisy intersection of Wilshire and Ogden. For some reason, I felt vastly disappointed. I'd always looked up to Mother for her elegance. Yes, her beauty had also felt like a shield that somehow kept me out. But I'd rationalized it like this: who cared about being left out in the cold if your mother was a goddess?

Making a mental note to discuss this with Sammie when she returned from her trip to London, I quickly changed the subject, pointing out to Mother how many of the cars whizzing past us were Priuses, Volts, and (this being LA) Teslas. "It's such a good sign," I emphasized. "Even if we get Dreamization active in the next five

126

years, every bit of reducing humanity's carbon footprint right now helps."

I wasn't sure Mother could hear me. Callay, who'd watched her grandmother twirl with wide and wondering eyes, began fussing a bit, not yet in baby warrior mode, but issuing those fretful sounds young humans make when they're beginning to realize they're uncomfortable. Mother leaned toward the stroller, beginning to sing the Hokey Pokey with full physical demonstration. When she reached the point of turning herself about, she did so with such enthusiasm that she lost her balance and began to fall, arms flailing, over the curb.

They say timing is everything. And as I'd learned, everything and nothing are the closest of kin. Mother struggled to right herself, but just as she seemed about to regain her balance, a bright red Metro Rapid bus hurtled impatiently into the right lane. It clipped her shoulder, making an ominous thwack, and I screamed a panicked "No!" as I saw her fly through the air just slightly ahead of me, close enough that I instinctively yanked away Callay's stroller to avoid impact. Time slowed down. Molecules moved visibly within the shapes of cars, shops, signs, and concerned-looking people in my vista, whose mouths uniformly became ovoid. Across the street, the vertically aspiring SBE building and the squat LA Fitness structure beside it traded places, and the trees that had been planted to soften their concrete insult outstretched anxious branches toward us.

Not again, I thought. Not another concussion! As if to assess the potential damage, the scientist in me sought to estimate the speed of Mother's trajectory before she landed with a heavy thump back onto the sidewalk. The bus that had batted her like an airless ball came to a full stop, its rotund driver descending from its opened door and running toward her. Mother's body was arrayed at an odd angle, and her eyes were wide open with surprise. But not blinking.

Not blinking, not blinking, not blinking. I tried to take it in, but I could not.

Sudden death is indigestible; it simply doesn't want to go down. That's why we frequently greet the sight of it with a resounding "No!" Sometimes, as with Assefa's grandfather Medr, whose wife was raped and murdered before his eyes, we cease to make any sound at all. I sensed movement around me, my baby crying, mouths opening and shutting a few inches from my face, a uniformed stranger grasping my elbow, settling me—my fingers locked desperately around Callay's stroller handle—onto a bus stop bench.

Something inside me stayed locked. I dared not let in what had just happened. How could a life, a vital life, be extinguished in one unfathomable nanosecond?

I cannot begin to describe what happened immediately after that. I recalled—and still recall—nothing of it. Captive to a torpid state, I was walked through the next few days by Adam, Makeda, Melkanu, Stanley, Aadita, Sister Flatulencia, Dhani and her crew, and the whole physics team. I heard their voices as if from underwater. I vaguely recall a familiar hand—it must have been Adam's—at my back, propelling me into a limousine, then later coaxing me out of it toward the place where my mother's body was to be lowered into the ground. In a box. *My mother in a box? How would she ever breathe?* I heard the word "God." It meant nothing to me. Perhaps it never had.

I knew I couldn't manage my life without a mother. Gwen had become a bit more motherly once I started calling her Auntie, and Sammie was the best belly sister ever. But, blood-wise, I had only my little girl and a host of half-sisters Father had saved from the devil abortionists, and we hadn't spoken in years.

You were about to say, "But you have the most amazing husband ever." And I was well aware that I did. But it wasn't quite the same as having a mother. My own. Mother.

After many years of fighting it, I fell fully into the Void of Everlasting Emptiness. I knew it so well. I knew the smell of it from my days in Father's house, when everyone but Grandfather was Otherwise Occupied by their own ways of evading the void. Mother herself was preoccupied in those days with her wine glass with its medicinal smell and her need to keep in close proximity to her bed. Fayga dallied with dirt, Cook kept busy coming up with fresh purees for all the Saved Babies, Sister Flatulencia forged ahead with caring for Mother and coping with her own crazy digestive system, Father crammed his hours with campaigning against the devil abortionists, the Saved Babies were saddled with their hunger and their poops and pees and head lice. I had Jillily, of course, with her question mark tail and her motor. And Grandfather. But then he got so sick he couldn't even say his *ugga umph uggas*. I had the Austins and my diaries of various lists, my books and my favorite weed and my pinching and banging and the tree that Father cut down after Grandfather died. But the void was always there, whistling in my ears and digging out the pit in my stomach, whispering that dust I was and dust I would forever be. Alone.

That old familiar place sucked me in and hugged me close to it, as if it had been longing for me ever since, waiting for the right moment. It claimed me now.

I could not watch the internment of Mother's casket directly, but registered it hazily through lowered lashes, much as I registered my baby's presence in Makeda's arms. I could not look at Callay. Nothing in me wanted to. My eyes were Medusa's. I dare not direct them at my child.

Instead, I headed downward into an inner landscape, assaying the upside-down tree that presented itself, inviting me into what lay below. I navigated painfully between gritty, bistre roots that grabbed my toes and scratched my soles. Jagged branches tore out patches of my hair. I didn't care that the way down was murky and long. It was, after all, the only direction available to me. This tree must be ancient, like the sequoia I'd once seen on a visit to Tulare's Giant Forest with Sammie and Jacob, one side of its impossibly broad trunk seared to blackness by a voracious wildfire. Circling it, we'd found a plaque proclaiming it to be the oldest known living thing in North America.

This particular tree wasn't anything like that, nor like the bulbous baobabs I'd spied on the road from Addis Ababa to Gondar. It bore no resemblance to the mythic Hindu Ashvattha or the Kabbalistic tree rooted in the stars. No, this one had a trunk that was rooted in nothing. I wasn't even sure that it was alive. No bark crab spiders on it, nor green lacewings, nor carpenter ants, nor tree cattle spreading their luminous webs.

I worked myself down without a thought for where I was heading, at times slithering and sliding against an oozy moss that emitted a smell that was vaguely familiar, not unlike the cave scent that clung to Nana's ancient, tattered bathrobe back in the old days. My descent concluded gracelessly, as the tree came to a cabbagy end a few feet from what passed for ground. I landed with a kind of bounce, rump first, brushing my butt as I rose to look around.

I seemed to be surrounded by an impenetrable fog, and I struggled to descry details, close or far, to no avail. I knew there were others down here, sensed shapes nearly touching me as I wandered blindly, but for the life of me I could not make them out. Until, that is, a familiar hand took mine in his. I loosened free and traced the old familiar whorls and callouses with my fingers. "Grandfather!" I cried. Again, his hand. Even here, wherever here was, he was mute. I dared not allow my hands to seek his wrists, elbows, shoulders, and face. I feared that he existed here only as a pair of hands.

And speaking of hands, the next thing I experienced was a familiar Mack truck grip, but when I felt around me there was nothing to touch. Nana here—at least in energy—too? What was this place?

But then I managed to make out a rickety sign, set at an angle into the sponginess underfoot. I dropped to my knees and crawled toward it. It was so withered and its recessed lettering so tiny that the letters looked as if they'd been carved by the tip of a skewer. I forced my way through the thick soup that passed for air and eventually came close enough that I could squint out the words: "Here sits the King of the Crying Babies."

Sure enough, my ears picked up sounds so faint they might have been the birth mews of kittens. The mist began to part a bit, only in patches, but enough to reveal a man seated upon a gilded throne whose base seemed to rest on thin air. He wore a crown that bled onto his forehead from its jeweled tips, and with a tightly set jaw he surveyed what to me was still a vast grayness, his beady eyes looking haunted and lost. And eerily unblinking. I wanted to flee. If only I could again find the tree that I'd managed to climb down. The last person I ever wanted to see again was Father.

I turned back, but there was no tree, no hints of fallen twigs or shriveled leaves in sight. There was nothing for it but to approach the king of this Hades. But the closer I got, the younger he became, until a mere infant lay naked on that high throne. He was squealing and looked utterly bereft and helpless.

What could I do but leap with all my might to grab hold of one of the legs of that throne and assay it arduously, hauling myself up to finally gain purchase on that vast seat, managing to settle my butt on-to it and hold the baby in my arms? I looked into his eyes. They were dark and luminous and conveyed a literally wide-eyed hope and promise.

Everything in me melted. "What happened to you?" I whispered, stroking his smooth forehead. His skin was so soft! But in the next moment, it was a baby girl I held, her skin a deep olive and her round eyes Hector Hernandez's, which also failed to blink. It didn't take a quantum physicist to conclude that this was Baby X, the fetus I'd aborted, the soul whose adventure I'd cut short in order to have my own. What happens to us *all?* I asked. Was life nothing but a nearly interminable dance of dashed innocence?

I caught the sweet odor of faded petals and looked around. Wafting close to my hand, rootless, was Mother's Anne Boleyn rose bush that had succumbed half a lifetime ago to root rot. And then I felt something sleek and familiar caress my ankle; my breath caught in my throat as I looked down to see Jillily's question mark tail. I reached the unavoidable conclusion that I'd fallen into the hole in my heart. But someone was missing. My pulse quickened, and the atmosphere became one of increasing impatience. There was movement all around me.

By the time Mother arrived, I'd been mysteriously persuaded to sit with the others, now fully visible, around a campfire that managed to give off no heat at all. If this was hell, it was one that had frozen over. I was shivering like crazy and felt worried for Mother. She arrived naked, her breasts no longer sagging and her eyes open wide.

"No!" I cried without sound. "I don't want you here! Go up! Go back up! I need you there!"

She gave me a look of infinite compassion. "You can do this. You are strong."

"No! I thought we'd settled it. I need you up there worrying about me!"

"I can't go back. It's against the rules." She looked over at Grandfather, as if for verification. He nodded, a slow tear descending a cheek that I noted was plumper than when I'd last seen him. How was it that he'd grown hardier after death, while Anne Boleyn was again thriving? Could there be healing on the other side?

I crossed my arms in grim defiance. "I won't leave here. I'm staying."

"I'm afraid that's not possible. You can't cut short your destiny. It will be yours, my darling. You will have earned it. As I've earned mine." And there she was, a naked infant now, falling into her father's arms. She radiated a kind of ecstasy, as did he.

How could I deprive them of that?

My eyes strayed over to my own father, now standing nearby. He was a grown man again. He took a hesitant step toward me. Could I even allow it? He seemed to want something from me. I sensed he would suffer forever, in a kind of limbo, unless I responded in some way.

I looked again at Grandfather, cradling his baby daughter. I felt ashamed. I didn't want any of this, but it seemed to be my new reality. Who was I to judge reality, even in this purgatory?

I allowed myself to stand and directly face my father. Our eyes locked for what felt like an eternity, mine blinking from time to time, his not. Something in his expression conveyed gratitude, as if it were a rarity for him to be seen. And then, of all things, he winked. It wasn't a complicit wink or a suggestive one, but the kind a magician might give when he was about to perform one of his more baffling tricks. And sure enough, he bent his knees and jumped. High. Very high. In point of fact, he jumped so far he took flight. But he was Father no more. Instead, he'd transformed into a beautiful black butterfly with bright yellow spots, its hind wings bearing the black swallow tail's signature large orange circles with black spots inside.

It swept in graceful arcs before me in a series of interesting patterns. So interesting that I couldn't help but follow as it flew off, leaving behind Grandfather and Anne Boleyn and Baby X and Nana and even Mother. With each step, my foot was greeted by a stepping stone made of some sort of shimmery, springy sponge. The pathway I followed formed a roundabout design of its own until I stood at the entrance to a cave. I could have sworn that I'd seen the butterfly disappear inside, and yet as I stepped forward to follow it, I heard a voice warning, "Don't come any closer." It wasn't Father's voice. If I hadn't disabused myself of religious belief decades ago, I might have guessed it was the voice of God. It had the energetic force of an invisible giant hand barring access to the cave. And then the butterfly emerged, faltering, its wings becoming increasingly wavery. I'd seen that in butterflies before when they were about to fall to the ground, their wings flattened together in dying as if in prayer. Every time, I'd had to turn away. But this butterfly, this Father-butterfly, dissolved in midair with a bright and startling spark. In the next instant—defying logic—it reappeared off in the distance, winging strongly again. I thought I heard laughter as it flew away. I felt there was a message here, but I had no idea what it might be.

I turned back, but the stepping stones had disappeared, and in their place, rooted this time and right side up, was a tree—but not just any tree. It was the sycamore that Grandfather and I had named, "Our Tree." Well, to be truthful, it was I who'd named it that, as Grandfather had been mute as long as I knew him. The tree now offered me a low hanging branch, actually bent it toward me, and I hopped on like one of the inevitable birds whose patterns I used to observe. Noting that each branch disappeared as I reached above it, I climbed.

***

My sojourn in the hole in my heart hadn't resolved my grief. If anything, it brought it back up with me in liquid form. Dissolved in tears, I sat in a collapsed posture in the folding chair that had been provided me at the gravesite. Most of the rest of the assembled mourners were moving on to their cars, but I brushed Adam away when he came to collect me. I needed more time here, facing the physical evidence of that earthen-housed casket. I could think no thoughts but what Mother would not be able to do now that she had died. Here were but a few of the things she would not do:

1. She would not see me introduce my daughter to the Austins.

2. She would not read to her *I Can't, Said the Ant*; *Go, Dog, Go*; or *Goodnight Moon*.

3. She would not spoon into Callay's little mouth her first bite of applesauce.

4. She would not watch her pedal her first tricycle and bicycle.

5. She would not run to bring a Band-Aid when she fell off and skinned her knee.

Mother had done none of those things for me. But it was all going to be redeemed, made much better when I watched her do them with my little girl.

That's how it was supposed to be. But now she would not discuss with me the progress of my child's potty training, suggest seasonings for pureed food, thrill with me over her first steps, nor comfort me on Monkey's first day of school. She would not babysit when Adam and I were desperate for a night out, would not give me advice when he and I quarreled, would not despair with me over my daughter's choices in clothes. She would not sit at our table for Thanksgiving and Christmas. Would not bend over me and plant a kiss on the top of my head, sweetening the air with her Chanel No. 5. She would not show me what it was like to grow old with grace or even do so with constant complaint. Would not give me a chance to ferry her around in a wheelchair, or spoon feed *her* when it came time for pureed food.

Out of the corner of my eye, I noticed that the crowd heading back toward their cars had stopped, making an interesting, Anthemium-like pattern on the gravestone-dotted lawn. No one had seemed to notice that I'd ascended back to ground level. Or had descended before then, for that matter. What all seemed to see right now, since it was so unusual in Los Angeles, was a murmuration of starlings above Forest Lawn Memorial Park. The birds swept as one organism, making intricate patterns beneath the clouds in a dazzling rush of whirring wings.

I knew something about starlings. Adam's education of me had been thorough in more ways than one. I knew that they maintain their glorious cohesion by each keeping its eyes on seven of its flock. I asked myself now, "Who are your seven?" Did they change from situation to situation, phase of life to phase of life? And is our human number seven, or seventeen, or even more? Mother had most certainly been one of mine. Even in our worst days, her whereabouts served as a kind of fulcrum for my own movements in time. Was that why I felt certain now that nothing would ever again hold meaning— no sense of a magical harmony of the universe, of the soul of the earth and her sky?

As if on cue, I saw one shape break away from the people on the faraway lawn who continued to stand still as statues, staring up at the sky, starling-struck. As he approached me, I wanted to cover myself, let myself be sucked back again into the Stygian murk below. But instead, I watched Assefa navigate gracefully between the headstones until he stood right in front of me. I had to shield my eyes from the brilliance of the sun to look up to him. He wasn't a tall man, but I was seated. Fallen. The fact was, he did seem larger. Just days ago, I'd learned from someone, probably Mother herself, that Lemlem was three months pregnant. Already, Assefa had the posture of a man whose seed had made its mark.

But his whispered voice caused me to straighten myself, too, in order to hear him. "Dukula." It came to me as if from an ancient tunnel.

I sucked in my breath. "Why are you here?"

"To pay my respects."

I barked, "Respects? Who do you respect?"

"Your mother." He paused, then his voice turned painfully tender. "You."

"Me?" I gestured vaguely toward my chest. I knew I was a total mess. I'd barely brushed my hair or teeth before Adam had tugged me out the door.

"Yes, you."

Old feelings stirred within my void, anger leading the charge. "You didn't exactly treat me with respect back … then."

He took a step away from me, as if struck, clearly struggling with the impulse to defend himself. What an asshole I was.

"I may not have treated you with the respect you deserved, but that was not about you. It was about me. You were the purest being I ever knew."

At that, I started to laugh. I laughed and laughed until I realized I was on the verge of hysteria. My anger whipped me back into shape.

"If you respected me, then … did you love me? Was anything that happened between us real?"

His chest heaved visibly. "No. I didn't love you. It is not past tense. I do love you. Will love you."

"Even with Lemlem pregnant with your baby?"

"You know as well as I do that the heart has room for many loves."

"I suppose I do." I looked up. The birds were gone. "I wanted to have your baby."

He said nothing for a moment, but his eye tic gave him away. Finally, "Yes, that child would have been extraordinary. But you have your own little girl."

He lost me then. What he said felt like a concept. I couldn't go near Callay. If I went near her, I would want my mother with us, and that could never be. I no longer felt like a mother. Had no desire for my child. I knew I never would.

Of course, our seven never really disappear from view, though we may blind ourselves to them from time to time. Ultimately, my lostness would be relieved by a woman with a powerful inner compass. Someone who knew that "bébés" were, in the final analysis, the ones who truly mattered.

But that time had not yet come. When we returned home, Adam deposited me on the living room sofa and went upstairs with Makeda and Melky, presumably to tend to Callay. The house felt too quiet, but for the grandfather clock in the den that marked its seconds way too loudly. Nothing was as before. Buster padded over from his bed beside the fireplace and leapt onto my lap, kneading my thighs with racketing purrs, but I felt none of the glow that usually spread across my body at the sound of him, the smell of him, his touch. My mind wandered to that Hades where I'd encountered Grandfather, Father, Nana, Jillily, Anne Boleyn, Baby X. And Mother. I pushed Buster off me and he landed with an offended grunt. I lay down on my side, counting his rhythmic lickings of his backside, until I heard the *ker-klonk ker-klonk* of Adam descending the staircase. His bad leg must be hurting; the variance in sound between the two feet was more marked than usual.

He brushed my hair away from my face and tucked it behind my ear. His breath on my cheek made me feel ticklish, but I couldn't be bothered to wipe away the sensation.

"Fleur, love. I'm sorry, I know this is hard, but Gwen is heartbroken that she doesn't feel strong enough to come over. We really should get over there. It would be such a kindness to her, if you possibly can."

I stared at him blankly, then allowed myself a weary nod.

"Good." He patted my thigh. "I'll just take a tick to have a shower. Callay had a runny poop and I feel like I still smell of it." I labored up the stairs behind him, oddly determined to fetch my purse. I saw him watch expectantly as we passed our child's bedroom, but I didn't stop to look in on her. My purse in my lap, I sat on our bed, registering without emotion the sounds coming from the bathroom, Adam's ugly sobs competing with jets of water hitting the shower floor. After he'd emerged, fully dressed and face flushed, I allowed myself to be pulled along, like a rag doll, out to the car.

I felt a flicker of anxiety when Gwen and Stanley stood at their gaping front door. Gwennie looked way too pale for someone who'd supposedly beat cancer. But her grip on my arm was strong, nearly as intense as Nana's back in the day. "Oh, darling Fleur, it should have been me. It was supposed to be me." I knew she was wrong. There are no such trades in this life, not when the Fates are out for blood.

Adam and I sat on two chairs facing her and Stanley on the sofa. She'd pulled her legs under her, and a decidedly distracted-looking Stanley tucked a blanket around her shoulders.

"It's okay," Gwen said. She shot me an apologetic look. "I'm just getting over the fucking flu that's been making the rounds. Thank God for Tamiflu. My doc promises me I'm no longer contagious. Did you get your shots?"

It felt like she was talking Martian, but Adam nodded and murmured, "I'm so sorry, Gwennie. You needed this like a hole in the head."

No one said a word. It was as if he'd taken a dump in the middle of the room.

As if to smother the faux pas, Stanley blanketed every bit of it with an analysis of the efficacy of this year's flu shot. "The effectiveness of the vaccine is pretty much determined by the influenza strains the CDC guesses will be making the rounds in the coming year. Unfortunately, H-three-N-two's a bugger, and we haven't yet reached more than about a forty-three percent effectiveness against that particular strain. We're much better with influenza B—I believe that one's about seventy-three percent effective—but if we're unlucky enough to have influenza A at the top of the dance card, as it ended up being this year, the flu shot ends up being only about forty-eight percent effective. This"—he swept a hand toward Gwen—"is what that failure looks like."

"Yes, well," said Gwen dryly, "let's hope this is the only statistic I end up being at the wrong end of this year."

Adam shot me a distressed look. I knew what he was thinking. This was the worst possible conversation to have when I'd just lost my mother.

But Stanley hauled out some chamomile tea and McVitie's Wholemeal Digestives—I think all of us but Gwennie would have voted for coffee and Krispy Kremes—and we, or at least the three of them, ended up having a couple of laughs at the latest Trumpisms. I think Adam was so happy that I was actually eating that he let himself go, having what looked like the best time ever shouting out, "Do I look like a president? How handsome am I, right? How handsome?"

It was a spot-on imitation of what Gwennie liked to call our Creep-in-Chief, but I didn't have the heart to point out that, as bits of McVitie's flew from his mouth with each word, Adam didn't exactly look his best himself at that moment. Instead, feeling increasingly uncomfortable somewhere around my heart, I gestured in the direction of the front door and mouthed, "I've got to go."

He tried valiantly to engage me as we drove the few blocks home, remarking that Gwennie looked considerably better by the end of our visit than she did at the beginning, but all I could think was that I might be having a heart attack. The pressure around my chest felt ominous.

When we got home, we heard Makeda call out, "Is it you?"

Adam responded, "Is that a trick question? What would you think if we answered, "No?"

Melky's hearty guffaw beckoned us into the dining room, where he sat next to Makeda, their knees touching under the table. Makeda was pushing the stroller back and forth next to her, as Callay made fretful sounds of distress.

"Okay, *gull*," Makeda said, standing. I couldn't help but note that her accent reminded me of Sammie's. She took my arm with one hand and pushed the stroller with her other one. When we reached the den, she pointed to the queen's settee. "It's time." She plopped down next to me, bringing the scent of frankincense with her, and reached forward to gently unbutton my blouse, and then opened the only kind of bra I had these days, the nursing kind. "Oh, you poor thing," she murmured.

I looked down. No wonder I'd thought I was having a heart attack. My breasts were terribly engorged. Carrying Callay with her, Makeda left the room, whispering, "It's alright, little one, relief is on the way." She returned with a moist, warm washcloth, which she tenderly applied to the fuller of my aching titties as a compress. I said nothing but closed my eyes with the mix of sensations: the searing pain, the tightness, a welcome new warmth. The next thing I felt were my daughter's delicate lips at my nipple. I felt Makeda press down on it tentatively to see if she could help the baby gain purchase. And lo—I felt milk squirt from me into my child's mouth.

If it had been anyone else, I would have felt violated and pushed Makeda away. But for now, her hands were my hands, her will my will.

I opened my eyes. Even as she kept her brown index finger on my pink nipple, Makeda looked at me with an absolute lack of pity. If anything, her expression hinted at something that might have been awe. Which made me want to laugh. But I didn't.

Instead, I looked down at my little Monkey and remembered her. She glowed with the radiance of a new sun. I was afraid *she'd* forgotten *me*, but instead—as forgiving as the planet that continued to carry the terrible weight of us humans—she paused briefly in her sucking to burble laugher and delight, her eyes moist with the joy of recognition. She let her perfect little body nestle, content, safe, at home in my arms. I gave her thickly diapered bum a tender squeeze and she began sucking more vigorously until my breast and nipple began to soften. I felt Makeda take her hand away. I put my own in its place, stroking Callay's cheek with my ring finger. Her skin was as soft as the petal of an Anne Boleyn.

Chapter Twelve

BY THE TIME Sammie returned from her latest rapturous visit with Amira, I was at least somewhat functional. I rose each morning and fed the cat, brushed my teeth, showered and shaved my legs, ate my breakfast of Greek yogurt, walnut halves, organic blueberries, and Kashi cereal that years of living with Gwennie had accustomed me to. But more importantly, I'd reconnected with Callay, my breast milk warm and flowing as I held her compact, but growing, body and marveled at her increasing alertness to her environment. I marveled at the way she burst into a double-dimpled grin when I came to lift her from her crib, laughed with her when she squealed with glee when Buster's tail brushed across her face, stood speechless when she reached her perfect fingers with careful precision for the plush, long-legged chimpanzee that Adam liked to dangle before her eyes.

On the outside, I was a woman moving slowly through her grief. Bursting into tears at odd moments, becoming distracted in the middle of sentences, savoring what small joys she could in the general leadenness of loss.

The inside was another matter, and I was able to articulate its contours only when my best friend returned to town. Having turned off her cell during her month-long camping trip in the south of France with Amira, Sammie had called as soon as she collected Adam's score of frantic messages. "Fleur, I'm booking a flight as soon as we get off the phone. Oh, my darling dear, how utterly ghastly and shocking and bloody unfair."

But I'd sidestepped her empathy and insisted she maximize her time with Amira. I knew her lover would be inaccessible in Afghanistan for however long it took to gather material for the BBC documentary she was producing on the status of Afghani women in the sixteenth year of America's war against the Taliban. "I'm okay, Sam. Or at least through the worst of it, I think. Just take care of yourself and tell Amira to be safe, too." My comment barely hinted at what was going on in my head.

Sammie arrived just in time for our party celebrating the issuance of Melky's Employment Based Immigrant Visa to the U.S. He and Makeda hadn't even told us about the process until his lawyers had confirmed its success, as they hadn't wanted to stress us during Callay's early months and then Mother's death. Given the current climate, we all knew how fortunate he was. The fact that UCLA's Institute of Environmental Studies had provisionally hired him and that Governor Jerry Brown's office had vouched for him had evidently sealed the deal.

Adam and I were out of our minds with happiness for both of them, and I—in particular—felt a surge of a kind of cosmic relief, as I'd been consumed by guilt for years that I'd ruined Makeda's life forever. I'd shared way too much information about Assefa at our first meeting at the orphanage, including the fact that he'd tried to commit suicide after learning that she was actually his half-sister, which, needless to say, was shattering to her, too.

As if she were a mind reader, Makeda had impressed upon me when she told me about Melky's visa that she would never have met him but for my surprise visit to her at the orphanage. That, at least, was true. The fact that the two of them had now fallen in love would have been evident to even the most oblivious. I took a wistful pleasure when I heard the strains of a *tizita* song coming from Makeda's bedroom late at night, especially after she'd shyly shared with me shortly before Mother died that she'd made an appointment with famed Philadelphia reconstructive plastic surgeon Dr. Ivona Percec, who'd had significant success in restoring the clitoris and its orgasmic function in female genital mutilation reversal.

When Sammie rang the bell, the party was already going full blast. A hectic mix of red, white, and blue streamers and miniature Ethiopian green, yellow, and red flags festooned the house. A Teddy Ab Ethiopian reggae song blasted from the speakers, and Buster batted at balloons until he burst one with his claws, sending him racing frantically down the hall. Makeda's girls and their friends spun like little whirlwinds amid the grownups' rocking hips and dancing feet.

Sammie had brought with her a large Fortnum and Mason shopping bag, and out of it she extracted a green and yellow Wallias soccer team T-shirt for Melky ("just so you don't go too far to the other side"), a Jo Malone candle for Makeda, a gift box of fancy French jams for Adam and me, and, to cries of great delight, a set of Rupert Bear miniatures for the girls. Before everyone could finish thanking her, she'd commandeered me up the stairs, ostensibly to see how much Callay had changed in her absence and to present her with a stuffed British bulldog that I swore looked exactly like Churchill. We both know her actual intent was to cuddle with Monkey and me in the bed in the baby's room.

She lay a soft hand on my shoulder. "Okay, then, gull, tell."

Tears streaming down my face, I began to share my experiences of Mother's death and its aftermath, adding, "I hate that she died while dancing. Celebrating Callay. So joyous and carefree. It felt cruel, as if a mean-spirited god is in charge of things."

For some reason, I felt a decided reluctance to speak of my sojourn in Hades, but, gesturing to her to pass me a tissue, I did manage to haltingly confess that I still couldn't wrest from my mind the image of Mother's expressionless face, with its staring, sightless eyes.

"It's become a kind of emotional tic: the first thing I see as I wake up, no matter what dream I might have been having; the last image in my mind before I fall asleep. Any time of day, if I close my eyes, that's what I see."

Sammie squeezed my shoulder, her own eyes moist with sorrow. "Oh, love. It's trauma. The loss of her was bad enough, but the shock of it. It was intolerable. *Is* intolerable."

But I didn't stop there. "Now that you mention it, I worry about Callay. She was right there, Sam. Saw the whole horrifying thing. I'm worried she's living a nightmare of her own, with no way to actually grasp it or speak about what she's suffering."

Sammie swept her eyes over my baby, who'd finished her breast-feeding and was cooing contentedly up at us, repeating her first word, *Moomah,* to our great delight, her dimples deepening in a series of charming grins. Sam directed a pointed look at me. "Right. She's obviously in agony."

Thank God for best friends. I let loose a loud guffaw.

"Baubo," Sammie said.

"Huh?"

"The Greek goddess whose naked hoochie koochie dance was the only thing that could comfort the grieving Demeter."

I shot her a look of pretend consternation. "Well, don't get any ideas."

"That's okay. I'm saving my gorgeous self for Amira."

We both laughed. I'd forgotten how comforting just being with Sammie could be. "Okay, now you. Tell. Are you still every bit as much in love?"

But she wouldn't have it. Her expression sobered. "No, really, back up a bit. What you've been going through is classic PTSD. Have you thought of seeing a therapist? As much as I adore you, I wouldn't share Janet with you, but I'll bet she could offer you some great referrals."

I interrupted hastily. "I know how you've loved Jungian analysis, Sam, and I'm sure it's helped you get over that shithead Jacob enough to make room for the real thing, but, well, I think I need to work this out on my own."

"But that's just it with you. How can someone so brilliant be so bloody dense? It's as if you have to learn over and over again that none of us is on our own. We're not designed to be hermits. How many of us actually live by ourselves in caves?"

"Actually, Sam, Plato had it that we all live in caves, chained to walls that we're stuck facing, with our only intimations of reality being the shadows cast by objects passing behind the campfires behind us. Unless we free ourselves and climb the mountain of transcending ordinary life. Of course, Aristotle was much more into embodied living as a source of understanding and wisdom. I've always thought about quantum physics as a kind of amalgam of those two points of view. Think about Neils Bohr's discovery of the spark that happens when electrons jump from one orbit to the other, each with its own color, linking energy with light. And speaking of light, what happens when we throw Socrates into the mix, with his reverence for the intellect as a kind of divine spark?" Something started stirring in the pit of my belly, then spread across the rest of my body in the form of an unusual alertness.

Finally becoming aware again of Callay nuzzling against my shoulder, I saw that Sammie was giving me the stink eye.

"You're incorrigible, you know. What does any of this have to do with your loss of your mother?"

And then it hit me. "Oh God, Sam, you are the queen!"

Thrusting the baby into my friend's arms without warning, I scrambled out of bed, saying hurriedly, "Listen, I need to get down to the lab and make a few calls. Do you mind watching Callay?"

As I rushed out of the room, I heard her exclaim, "What the hell? The lab? In case you hadn't noticed, there's a party going on downstairs."

Sam probably thought I'd gone over the edge, but I'd have to explain later to her—and to Makeda and Melky and their friends down below. I was sure they'd understand.

Maybe I *was* being a little manic, but I sensed in that scientist's gut of mine that I was on to an important next step in making Dreamization a reality. Father *had* been trying to show me something, and it had everything to do with the disappearance and reappearance of his butterfly avatar. That was the thing about butterflies. They were about transformation. The great crisis and miracle of their lives was all about moving from one whole identity to an entirely different one. From laboriously earthbound to flutteringly soaring. We humans weren't strangers to that experience, but I'd always thought of it as far less concrete.

As Adam had explained to me when I was barely into my teens, there was a reason that the ancient Greek's symbol for the goddess Psyche was the butterfly. I remember the hairs raising on my arms as he'd said—rather casually, I thought, given its significance— "The human soul is always in movement; we change our minds, and what we think about changes us, constantly, just as the molecules comprising our being, along with everything else in the universe, are constantly in flux."

But now I'd been gripped by an intuitive flash that there was a whole world of application of the conversion of chemical energy into motion that we'd barely plumbed. Had Our-Father-in-Hades been hinting, as I now thought he had, that a chemical enzyme present in butterflies might be our engine for Dreamization? Sliding out the front door and pulling my cell phone out of my bag as I headed out toward the Prius, I punched in a number I knew by heart.

"Hall-o?"

"Gunther, it's me. Who do we know in the field of entomology? I need to learn about the chemical states of butterflies."

"You're a physicist." He said it as if it were an accusation.

"Yes, and you—according to Tom—are a Chelsea fan. As an Arsenal fan, I won't hold that against you. I need to know about the chemicals that are active in the transformation process of a butterfly. Didn't you once mention you knew an entomologist in the biological engineering division?"

You might notice that neither of us had bothered to exchange a civil "How are you?" or "How's it going?" Most scientists were as unbothered by the social niceties as one of Adam's favorite singers, Neil Young, who reputedly had the habit of getting up from any number of important dinners without a word to grab a guitar and find a private place when he felt a new song coming on.

"Ja," Gunther said. "Joe Parker. Why?"

"Long story. I think a specialist in butterflies might offer us the final key to Dreamization."

"Call you right back."

He was as good as his word, catching me just as I was turning onto California Boulevard. "Joe said that the person you want isn't at Caltech. She works for the Natural History Museum. I have her office number and cell. Which one do you want?"

"Give me her cell." I'd pulled to the side of the road and was drumming my fingers on the dash.

"It's nine-thirty."

"I know."

We hung up without saying goodbye.

Sally Price was my kind of woman. When I introduced myself and explained what I was looking for, she said, "Come on over. I was getting a little tired of *Sons of Anarchy*, anyway."

Fortunately, she didn't live as far as the area adjacent to USC, where the Natural History Museum was located. Instead, within twenty minutes, I found myself walking up to a sweet Spanish bungalow at the foot of Eagle Rock's Hillside Park. Stars lit up the sky, and the night-blooming jasmine lining the pathway was heavenly. A lanky, striking-looking, forty-something woman in a rather misshapen T-shirt, jeans, and fluffy slippers stood in an open doorway from which music loudly spilled. My spirits soared with the synchronicity of it, as my ears identified Neil Young's straining voice lamenting mother nature being on the run in the 1970s.

Shaking Sally Price's powder-soft hand, I gestured with my head toward the house. "And that was in the 1970s. There's nowhere to run now." I smiled apologetically. "Which is why I'm disturbing your peace and quiet so late on a Sunday night."

"No worries. I've got way too much peace and quiet these days. Boring myself silly." Sally Price ushered me in and hastened to turn off the speakers. The television was still on, but soundless. On the screen, three rough-looking men wearing bandanas rode ominous-looking motorcycles up to the front of a boarded-up warehouse.

"*Sons of Anarchy*?"

Sally Price made a self-deprecating face. "It's not the show, really. Though it *is* a rather clever adaptation of *Hamlet*." She shook her head, her pale brown face flushing a little. Her eyes flicked over to the screen. "No, it's the guy in the middle. He's called Jax Teller in the show. I suppose this is life's little joke for me passing up on a blind date twelve years ago with a new British actor in town named Charlie Hunnam. He ended up marrying someone else a year later."

Staring at the mute screen, I sympathized. The man was ridiculously gorgeous—sensitive and sexy looking at the same time. Shooting a quick look at Sally Price's lithe body and her face like an angel's despite the good-natured laugh lines at the outer corners of her slanted, pitch-black eyes, it occurred to me that she and Charlie Hunnam would have been—at least in the physical beauty department—a perfect pair.

Mistaking my thoughts entirely, she said, "I know. It's nuts. An entomologist and an actor would make an awful couple. Which is why I turned down the date. Well, that and my sociopathic ex-husband having secretly racked up so much debt I'd had to sell at a loss the house my parents had bought for us. It took five years' worth of scrimping just to pay everything off and get him out of my life forever. These days, I'm afraid it's only felines I trust in the male department." She craned her neck until both our eyes lit on a long-haired calico cat sitting atop a tall bookshelf in the corner of the room, a king of his house blinking in self-satisfaction. "And butterflies, of course."

Which was her signal to get down to business. But in the back of my mind, I was already hoping to count on Sally Price becoming a friend. My favorite kinds of women were—like Sammie—super bright people likely to swing from the sublime to the ridiculous and back again in a heartbeat. It didn't hurt that we women had verbal centers on both sides of our brains, as opposed to men's, whose verbal capacities were contained solely in the left hemisphere.

"So here's the scoop," I said, and I actually told her the whole sad saga of my sojourn in Hades, crying a bit when describing Mother's fall, and sobering as I went into detail about my own. Why had I chosen to share with a stranger, rather than a friend like Sammie, what would undoubtedly be described by most people as a momentary slip into psychosis?

Sally Price confirmed the rightness of my instinct by casually commenting, "My mother always said that nothing went better with the deeper truths of life than hot chocolate. I make mine with organic cocoa and sinfully rich whipped cream. Want some?" But she was already up and out of the room, returning five minutes later with a pastel-colored tray appositely depicting Alice's foray into the rabbit hole. Setting it down on a rustic pine coffee table, she plopped herself onto the dusty-rose chenille-covered couch beside me. It dawned on me that no one but a single woman would live with such furnishings and that this had to be the coziest place on the planet to be sharing the oddest secret of my already odd duckish life.

"So," she said, putting down her wide-rimmed floral cup and licking at her chocolate mustache. "Let me make sure I'm following you. You think your father was directing you toward the enzymatic activity that occurs as the caterpillar moves through its stages of metamorphosis?"

I swallowed hard. "Yes, I do."

"Well, let's think about this. On the surface of it, it seems pretty questionable that applying a butterfly enzyme would activate Dreamization." She stopped, and gave me a complicit wink. "But we scientists are all about the questions, aren't we? Forgive me if I repeat a bunch of stuff you learned in high school. As you probably know"— I didn't—"in order to effect its metamorphosis into a butterfly, a caterpillar must release enzymes that literally allow it to digest itself. Inside the chaotic mess that ensues in the pupal transformation, everything turns into goop except for pre-existing discs that have been present inside the holometabolous insect larva, or caterpillar egg, from the very beginning.

"Each of those imaginal discs contains the potential for each butterfly body part. In some species of butterflies, those discs begin to take shape even before the caterpillar enters the chrysalis stage. But," she paused, tapping her nose and then scratching it, "how could that possibly be applicable to humans? We have no such discs that I know of. And if we did, would they enable us to achieve flight? And not just any flight, but a material surge beyond the spacetime continuum? That's a pretty big leap, pardon the pun."

I knew it seemed ridiculous, but something inside me felt increasingly insistent. My heart was flipping and flopping. "I have no idea, but bear with me as I think aloud. I suppose you're familiar with water bears, or moss piglets? Those tiny little tardigrades that can curl up into dry husks called tuns, in a seeming dead state, for decades? Ironically, it takes only water to re-animate them. Several teams before us had already figured out how to create optical cavities by using two laser beams on water bears that allowed them to exist in two places at the same time. Employing the insights of cell therapies used in the treatment of various diseases, we've re-animated the tuns using water, then found a way to issue instructions to a key trigger cell that signaled all a moss piglet's cells to simultaneously exchange its light matter for dark and then reverse the process, effectively throwing the water bear into a cellular black hole where it actually dematerialized from one of its two places and rematerialized into the other. Pretty miraculous in its own right. What if there's something in caterpillars' enzymes that might help hasten that process for humans?"

Sally Price shrugged. "It's an incredible long shot, but who am I to say absolutely not? We humans have harnessed so much of our natural world to completely alter reality. It'd take a lot of experimenting with a team comprised of entomologists, biochemists, and physicists to see if there was actually anything we could use." But then she shook her head, puffing out air loudly. "I'm afraid I feel pretty dubious—I think we'd certainly know about any human counterparts of imaginal discs by now."

"Ye-ssss, maybe. But what about the enzymes of dead butterflies? Has anyone investigated their properties with human application in mind? My father-butterfly took flight again only after he'd folded his wings and seemingly died."

"Well, on a purely practical level, that would be a heck of a lot easier to investigate. Extracting enzymes from living butterflies would be a right pisser. Sorry," she laughed, gesturing toward the TV screen. "I really do need to stop watching that show."

But I was off in my head now, wondering whether the human body actually did have some sort of imaginal discs of its own, embedded somewhere within the black holes in our cells. Had Dreamization always been a potential for us humans, one that had taken millions of years and just this moment of existential crisis to discover? Was that why it was even possible for us to imagine it?

When I came back to the present, Sally Price had drained her cup and was holding it aloft, her eyes fixed on mine. "You know, I like it. I'm a big believer in signs myself. I have no problem with you seeing something most people wouldn't give the time of day to. You phoning me just when I was beginning to weary of Jax Teller for the very first time feels right to me. If I actually stop fantasizing about the one that got away, I'm going to need *something* to obsess about." We both laughed, and she set down her cup with a sharp ting right next to mine. "Whether we accomplish what you're hoping for or not, we're bound to learn some interesting things. If you're looking for a new team member, count me in."

Chapter Thirteen

WITH SALLY PRICE leading the way, and with our corporate sponsor helping us fly under Congress' radar, we spent the following year or so experimenting with the enzymatic action occurring on dead butterflies. My wish had come true: Sally had become a friend. Thank goodness, Sammie and Makeda weren't the fully paid-up members of the Green-eyed Monster Club that I was, so I wasn't forced to carve my heart into pieces to share my limited free time with the three of them. Adam called us collectively "the Force," since our joined energies seemed to multiply exponentially when we occupied the same room. Of course, it was something of a play on words, since "the force" in *Star Wars* refers to the sacred universal energy that connects us all, while *force* is also a scientific term for a vector that has both magnitude and causes movement in the other.

Unsurprisingly, I'd been able to persuade Sister F. to step in with caring for Callay when I returned to work three mornings a week. If I do say so myself, Callay was the most amazing child: her voice had the clear and pleasantly piercing quality of a wood thrush, her apricot-hued cheeks were as chubby as a cherub's, and her scalp gave off an intriguing scent that was slightly minty, with just a hint of something tart, like ripe grapefruit. And best ever in the beauty department, her round, birth-blue eyes grew greener by the day, reminding me of the love shared by myself and Adam that had made her.

She was a bit slow walking—as Nana might have said, "Still unsteady on her pins"—but, unsurprisingly, she was proving to be quite precocious verbally. By a year-and-a-half, she could actually articulate at least some of her needs with rudimentary sentences. She'd come up with her own names for the people closest to her, a few of which became household nicknames employed by us all. I'd begun to make a list of them when she was nine months old, and, needless to say, as more and more people came into her orbit, the longer the list grew. Here are some of them:

1. For me, of course, Moomah.

2. Adam became Dadam.

3. Makeda was Kayka.

4. Sofiya, whom Makeda had already enrolled in AYSO, was tickled to be called Fifa, and her sister Melesse was equally delighted to have become Yes.

5. Melky she aptly dubbed Bear, except she pronounced it *Behw*.

6. Sammy was, to my friend's glee, Mammy.

7. Sally Price became Thrprythe.

8. Sister Flatulencia's moniker was what Adam called "another corker," though Sister F. didn't seem to mind at all hearing those rosebud lips joyously cry out to her when she arrived on her babysitting days, "Thtinky!"

9. Finally, Buster—and don't even think of suggesting a cat is not a person—became for all of us Buthter-do!

I knew Callay was in the most loving hands with Sister Flatulencia, and it filled me with a sweet-and-sour nostalgia when I'd return home in the afternoon to see that woman's familiar slender form standing sentry by my daughter's crib, her posture just a little less erect than in the old days and the pubic-looking tendrils escaping from her signature bandana now white with age.

Speaking of the life cycle, thank goodness we were able to use the natural deaths of butterflies in the butterfly pavilion to make our work possible. I can't tell you how not-so-secretly happy I was when Sally and her entomology team discovered that, at least for our purposes, the usefulness of butterflies purposely killed by common research methods—freezing and heating; submerging in ethyl acetate or KAAD; grabbing the thorax—proved to be nil. Instead, twenty to twenty-five of those who'd died naturally were harvested from the pavilion each morning, driven to Pasadena at what was undoubtedly ticket-worthy speed by Sally Price to ensure we had enough viable yellow and gold and brown and blue cadavers to work with. Coming so soon after Mother's death, I wasn't sure I'd be able to kill the glorious creatures just to move our project along—especially when some species, such as monarchs, were threatened with extinction.

I found it particularly poetic that our project to save our species was being propelled by dead butterflies when all of life on this planet was made up of dead stars. The fact was, thanks to Sally Price's expertise in entomology, I ended up learning more facts about butterflies than I could possibly have imagined, including some features of a surprisingly sexual nature, such as:

1. The female butterfly has a digestive organ right next to her vagina called the *bursa copulatrix*.

2. The male butterfly, like many other insects, delivers his sperm inside a package called a *spermatophore*. This package can contain all kinds of goodies, such as proteins that help sperm swim quickly or—as Amir put it—"the competitive little buggers plug up the female's vagina so other males can't get in."

3. But the female has her own tricks, like disabling those proteins and using them to maintain her own body and her eggs.

155

4. But the male would prefer she restrain herself, giving him better odds of fathering some eggs. So he builds *spermatophores* with tough outer envelopes. A female can't mate again until she's cleared the first *spermatophore* out of her system.

5. Inside the female butterfly, sperm swim to their own storage organ while the rest of the *spermatophore* goes to the *bursa copulatrix* and gets broken down.

The bursa's digestive power is prodigious, its enzymatic activity exceeding what goes on in the caterpillar's gut. But more important for our purposes were the nutrients of the *saprophyte*, or bacterium, that flourished on the dead butterflies—in particular, the *saprophytes* that attached themselves to the *bursa copularix*. After innumerable failed attempts at their distillation, Sally Price and Gunther successfully injected those *saprophytes* into a series of moss piglets. The *saprophytes* acted as a force, exceeding our wildest dreams by increasing the piglets' capacity to dematerialize and then rematerialize farther and farther across their cages.

Our best hunch about why this was working was that the force of the injected *saprophytes* somehow called forth a miniature gravitational wave, or wrinkle in spacetime, allowing the moss piglets to disappear at the lowest part of a wrinkle while being tumbled along the spacetime fabric, reappearing at the next rise of a ripple. The first time we'd retrieved a moss piglet from another corner of his cage, I had a strong hunch that he'd gone through his own version of what I'd experienced during labor and, even before that, on the morning of Zeki's funeral in Tikil Dingay, when I had initially felt as tiny as Uncle Bob in his pocket-sized incarnation, then expanded Alice-in-Wonderlandishly, observing unusually colorful tops of trees outside the orphanage before returning to my normal size again. It would give me no end of satisfaction that sweet Zeki, whose life had been cut much too short by medication-resistant epilepsy, would live on by contributing something significant to the development of Dreamization.

In that first Dreamization of a tardigrade, I'd turned excitedly to Adam and Amir and Katrina and Tom and Gunther and Bob, exclaiming, "We need to work on this. I want to see us find a way to mathematically compute the ratio between the experience of diminution to the point of disappearance and the expansion back into visibility relative to riding gravitational waves at a quantum level. And we need to know how the organism resettles back into its original size and shape." Needless to say, no one had laughed at me. We hadn't come this far, nor had science itself, by ridiculing the seemingly outrageous. Reality had proven itself from the dawn of time to exceed the farthest flights of the human imagination. That was, after all, why the human psyche had sought out such an infinite variety of gods.

Returning home from the lab that night, I'd dug through my closet—still way too crowded with a score of Mother's Chanel suits that I couldn't bring myself to give away—to find the little enamel cask containing some of the gritty Ethiopian dirt that I'd held back from flinging onto Zeki's casket. On an impulse, I poured some of that dark soil into my hand, sniffed its undiminished dank richness, then tucked as much of it as I could into the pink pocket of one of Mother's suits. The incongruity of it felt particularly satisfying and settled my rumbling belly down after all the day's excitement. I'd been passing wind like crazy ever since coming home.

Adam and I had our own private laughs about how central digestive processes were proving to be for Dreamization, given what was going on in our own bodies. We didn't know whether it was the Ethiopian cooking or just getting older, but our farts were becoming increasingly odoriferous, and we joked that we'd soon be giving Sister F. a run for her money. Like her, we'd tried Beano to disappointingly diminishing returns. Speaking of the relationship between digestion and sexuality, we did find that the more frequently we had intercourse, the less we passed gas. As Nana might have said, "Who knew?"

Having more frequent sex wasn't hurt by the fact that Melky had permanently moved in. Now that Makeda had returned and healed from her genital restoration surgery, performed personally by Dr. Percec, the two lovebirds would disappear at odd times of the day and night, coming out of their bedroom laughing and glowy. I took no little secret pride that I'd managed to fund the operation with my Nobel prize money, which I'd finally managed to convince her—and it was true—had been just languishing in a bank all these years.

I believe it was Claire Booth Luce who said that no good deed goes unpunished. Somewhere in the midst of the sexual Renaissance at our Old Mill Road property, Adam developed a rather voracious appetite for porn.

How did I know? Because Adam, being Adam, couldn't bear to keep it from me. One night, when I was feeling particularly haggard from juggling my time between Callay and the lab and eagerly looking forward to falling asleep as soon as my head hit the pillow, he brought over his laptop to my vanity table and pulled up a porn site showing a series of couples copulating, including a very dark-skinned man and an equally pale-skinned woman engaged in an activity that he explained to me was called "*soixante-neuf*."

"The practice has been around forever. In the *Kama Sutra* they call it 'the congress of the crow.'"

Frankly, I couldn't imagine crows in such a posture. How would they possibly avoid pecking each other's genitals to pieces? And I didn't know which embarrassed me more: watching two people engage in something that I would have presumed demanded privacy or having to be schooled all over again by my ex-tutor, this time in an area at the crux of our connection.

I was disgusted. And uncomfortably reminded of my time with Assefa. And aroused.

But when we fell onto the bed, clawing off each other's clothes, it wasn't Assefa I wanted to be touching, but Adam I wanted to try out this new act with, Adam's face I wanted to see when we eventually shifted ourselves back into a more familiar position, Adam's eyes I wanted to be looking into as a massive mini-explosion melted my mind.

Alas, that was far from the last of it. Adam began wanting to turn on the computer before almost all of our encounters, and I began to feel increasingly suspicious when he'd disappear for what felt like ages to the men's room when we were all scribbling away at our blackboards in the lab. But it took something he said on the night of

Sally Price's birthday party to bring it all—no pun intended—to a head.

Just that day, I'd found what felt like just the right gift for her: a dusky-blue-verdigris, heart-locket necklace that was adorned with a brass butterfly. As I busily wrapped its little box on the dining room table, Adam slipped into a chair beside me and said in a voice that sounded suspiciously fake-casual, "Sally's quite a dish, isn't she?"

"A dish?" I replied, filled suddenly with a me, too-ish sort of foreboding.

"Yeah, you know." His bad leg was jitterbugging up and down like a nervy adolescent's. "Sexy." A pause. "Have you ever imagined what it would be like to have a threesome?"

I pushed the package away from me. I heard the ice in my own voice. "No. But evidently you have."

Adam flushed, which was a rarity for him and one that should have signaled that I was veering dangerously close to shaming him.

"Well, I don't know too many guys who wouldn't want ..."

"Wouldn't want what?"

"To try it on with two women."

Moving right past the questions that formed instantly in my mind—*Was that really true? And what did it mean?*—I replied, with no little asperity, "You're not talking about just any two women. You're talking about Sally Price. And me."

Adam literally hung his head. But I didn't care, instead taking an unmistakably sadistic pleasure in seeing it.

"Sorry," Adam said. "I'd better get dressed," he mumbled, exiting the room.

We didn't say a thing to each other on the way to Sally's digs, which were packed to squeezing point by our mutual friends and Sally's from her separate life. Thanks to the ridiculous crowd, which ended up spilling onto the sidewalk in front of the balloon-festooned bungalow, it proved easy to avoid each other for the rest of the evening. Which didn't mean that I wasn't keeping a *Murder She Wrote* eye on Adam as he moved from chatty little group to group, at one point giving Sally what I thought was an excessively tight-looking hug. How was I ever going to be comfortable with my friend again? Could it be that he'd broached the topic to her first? Had she encouraged

159

him? And if she had, how dare she? How could I complete my project with my colleague and my husband carrying on an affair?

You can see where this was heading. The Green-eyed Monster was back in full force, and, as usual, was no respecter of the facts. Nor of emotional restraint. Which was why, when the evening ended, I pinched my belly and banged my head against my headrest and shouted at Adam almost all the way home from Eagle Rock to Pasadena. The fact that I was more than a little inebriated and he, as our designated driver, stone sober didn't help any.

What did help a bit was that about a half mile from home, he pulled over the Prius and stopped the car. "Okay, that's enough." His voice wasn't all loud and shouty like mine, but instead exerted its effect via a steely authority. "I get it. It was stupid and insensitive to suggest it. What you and I have is precious, and I let my fantasies run away with me into territory they didn't belong in."

That shut me up for about a minute. "Where do they belong? Why are they there in the first place?"

Okay, that was dumb. But I was drunk. And hurt. And afraid.

"Listen, Fleur." He tried to take my hand, but I pulled it away. He stared out the windscreen, muttering loudly enough for me to hear, "I probably didn't fool around enough as a teenager. Too damned insecure. And then there's the baby thing."

"The baby thing?"

"Well, you know. I love her more than life itself, but dirty diapers and breast pumps and our attention pretty much focused on the Monkey twenty-four seven when we're home. I guess I've been feeling like an afterthought." He paused. "And honestly, a little bored."

Bored. The word chilled me. I knew about this. Mother had warned me of it when she was alive. How I wished I could run to her and collapse against her shoulder. I began to cry, as much now for missing Mother as for what felt like Adam's betrayal. That was something I was learning about the loss of a mother. It keeps happening over and over again as if for the first time. At every moment when a mother's love and interest would come in more than a little handy, the void presented itself in all its gaping nothingness. I waved Adam away when he leaned over to comfort me. I couldn't speak.

Oddly, I thought, he took that as an invitation to keep talking. "It's not like we're really connecting when we're together at the lab. The project's like a second child for you. Sometimes, I feel like I'm last on your list there, too, with whoever has the best ideas jumping to the head of the line."

I dug a tissue out of my purse and honked into it. I wasn't able to think very clearly, but the latter rang true. I felt awful. I told him so.

"Me, too," he said. "Do you think we can do something about it?"

"I don't know. But you've got to stop watching porn all the time. I don't know much about all this, but I know it isn't helping."

He stiffened. "I think that's my private business, don't you?"

I lashed out, "Well actually, I'm sorry, but you've made it mine, as well."

"We need to talk about this when you're sober."

"We need to talk about this when you're not so hot for Sally Price."

The conversation hadn't gone so well, after all.

We tried again the next day. We walked Callay in her stroller to the Huntington Gardens, where we could let her toddle and fall and toddle again on a long stretch of thick grass bounded by camellias and eighteenth century Italian limestone statues that led to a grand Baroque fountain. As we watched her squeal with the sheer freedom of it, Adam turned to me and ventured a tentative, "I'm sorry."

"For what?"

"God, you're going to make me spell it all out, aren't you? You must be very angry."

For once, the student had surpassed the teacher. "Not so much angry as hurt. And jealous. And hurt. And afraid." I paused. "And hurt."

We both laughed. It helped.

I said in a rush, "To be fair, it's not like I've never been attracted to anyone else."

At the very same time, he was saying, "No one's as beautiful to me as you."

We laughed again.

But I sobered quickly enough. "But maybe not so sexy. You said you were bored with me."

"Not bored with *you*. Bored with myself. And insecure. That's why I went on that site in the first place. I thought if I upped my game ... I thought *you* were bored with *me*. I really have been feeling like I'm last on your list."

I studied him, his green eyes round and earnest. "Adam, you're my sun and moon and stars. I mean it. If I've made you feel taken for granted, it's my fault."

He turned to check on Callay, who'd arrived at one of the statues and was staring up at it as if it were God.

"Listen, Fleur. I know some of this is unavoidable. That little one's both of our sun and moon and stars."

"And a great deal of why I feel so fiercely connected to her is that she's the product of the two of us. Of our love." I added shyly, "Of our sex."

Adam pulled me to him. We kissed, and I felt his hardness against me.

"We don't get enough of this, do we?" I whispered into his ear.

"No," he replied. "Not like this. I know we've been fucking more, but we're always in a rush, or tired, or keeping quiet in case we wake the baby."

I responded slyly, "Makeda and Melky don't let that stop them from yelling 'Hallelujah!'"

Adam laughed. "They don't have to end up with a little girl between them if they wake her."

As if on cue, Callay seemed to realize that we weren't next to her. She began screaming that high-pitched scream that is capable of shattering eardrums and champagne glasses (the latter of which I can personally attest to). We parted without a word, both of us running toward her and exchanging a look of infinite sweetness as we ran.

Which didn't necessarily solve what I'd come to think of as the Porn Predicament. I ended up confiding in Sammie and Makeda (but needless to say, not Sally Price) the following week.

Unsurprisingly, Callay was there for this conversation, too. A young child is the living embodiment of ubiquity. Adam and Melky had gone off to the soccer league they'd joined following an after-dinner comparison of their newly-blossoming beer bellies. They'd taken their informal cheering section, Sofiya and Melesse, with them. I'd called Sammie to see if she could come over since I'd lose her again soon for her upcoming visit to Amira, who'd just returned—safe, sound, and triumphant—to London from her latest working trip to Afghanistan. Makeda joined us enthusiastically at the kitchen table.

The three of us dunked our McVitie's Digestives in our PG Tips tea as Callay sat on the floor with Buster, who'd endeared himself to me even more this past year by patiently submitting to my child's rather rough petting style.

"So I've got this little dilemma," I ventured.

"Look out," Sammie snorted, turning to Makeda. "We both know from how she put it that she's got a major problem on her hands."

"No, really," I said. "It's not funny. It's Adam." I slid a guilty glance toward Callay, then shrugged. She wasn't *that* precocious. Still, I lowered my voice to a near whisper. "He's gotten addicted to porn."

"Oh really?" asked a surprised-looking Makeda.

"Oh shit," said Sammie.

"What do you know about it?" I asked her.

"Only that it was the final straw between Jacob and me."

"Oh shit," said Makeda.

I led them both through the sequence of events, leaving out, of course, the impact of Makeda's sex life on us.

That dear woman was actually little help at all. "I can't imagine what is more exciting than having the one you love with you in the flesh. Who cares how other people express their desires?"

Which was exactly how I felt. So I turned to Sam. "What bothered *you* about it?"

She hesitated. "No offense to Adam, or to guys in general, but it's all so bloody crude. Soulless. And compulsive. Sort of Trumpish, if you don't mind my saying."

I winced. "Adam would die of mortification if I said that to him."

"Look, it's not just a men versus women thing. There's a world of lesbian porn out there, or so I've heard," Sammie said, lifting Callay onto her lap when it looked as though Buster had had his fill of her clumsy handling. Sammie proceeded to sing "Eensy weensy spider" to my daughter's great delight, then repeated it three times to Callay's insistent, "Again!" before setting her down next to the little train set she'd brought her. Callay instantly put Thomas the Tank Engine into her drooling mouth.

Sammie continued, "People have been enjoying erotica from the beginning of time. In one of my early art history courses, we studied everything from Paleolithic cave paintings to early Roman depictions of threesomes to Indian statues of every position possible from the first century on. Something to cater to every taste. As my prof put it, 'One person's *ew* is another person's *wow*.'"

"You're joking aren't you?" I responded. "He didn't really say that."

"Yes, *she* did. And she wasn't a dummy. It helped relieve the tension." She watched me mull that one over. "The thing is, though, for me, it's not so much what's depicted as how. What's the spirit of it? I once saw a billboard in Manhattan that said, 'Porn kills love.' Is erotic material consistent with love or is it degrading? It's like the difference between a Nobel-winning novel and a comic book. That's what drove me nuts about Jacob. He was a bright man, but for him, the cheesier the porn, the more arousing. Some of the stuff made me want to laugh, and some of it scared me with its brutality."

I shook my head. "God, this feels like too much information. I have to admit that I myself got pretty excited after watching a *soixante-neuf* scene."

"Yeah, but did you enjoy doing it?"

I blushed. "Actually, no. I kept worrying about giving him pleasure whenever I started getting carried away by what he was doing to me."

"Sort of like talking and chewing gum at the same time, right?"

We laughed, then had to explain the image to Makeda, who laughed then with us. But soon enough, she sobered. "What is this brutality you speak of, Sammie? In my country—what *was* my country—the unspoken purpose of genital mutilation is to provide greater organ sensation for the man. I believe that any kind of sexual activity that hurts the partner or demeans them is very, very bad."

Sammie nodded emphatically. "I totally agree. God, you name it, Makeda. There's a fair amount of porn around this days that involves rape, simulated or," she shuddered, "otherwise. BDSM—sorry, bondage/domination/sadism/masochism—can cross that line for sure. And worse: pedophilia. Not that we watched any of *that*." She shook her head. "With Jacob, it felt like the most intangible, but creepiest part was that our sex started to feel dehumanized. Not just animalistic, but thingy." She grew pensive. "I've never really thought about this before, but the destructiveness of modern porn is that, besides objectification of women, it treats sex so concretely. It's so literal. It crushes the beauty of the human imagination." She directed a scrutinizing eye at me suddenly, as if sensing that I was on the brink of pinching and flapping. It felt comforting to let her warm hand encircle and tightly squeeze mine.

In our silence, we became more aware of Callay, now pushing her Thomas the Tank Engine along the tile floor and doing her best to sing one of her favorite songs. "I ee wookeen onna wailwode."

I loosened my hand from Sammie's and went over and scooped up my child. "I ee wookeen, too, my love."

Nothing was resolved, but over the course of a few weeks, I could sense something in me working away at the problem. I began to feel like an exaggerated version of the modern woman, trying to keep way too many balls in the air. I had my project at the lab, my commitment to Callay, and now, in a kind of seismic shift, my relationship with Adam was beginning to feel like work, too. And not just in how I spoke with him, but how I thought and felt about him. It wasn't just the emotional equivalent of seeing him with spinach between his teeth. His vulnerability, his humanness hadn't bothered me before. His bad leg, and how matter-of-factly he managed it, had been part of what had endeared him to me in the first place. I'd been touched when he'd voiced his fear that he'd lose me, as he'd lost his mother, in childbirth. I'd been aware for years that he, too, was capable of falling victim to the Green-eyed Monster. As he'd later confessed, learning that I'd slept with Bob Ballantine—yuck! I still couldn't bear thinking about it—had emboldened him to seduce me at Santa Monica Beach for the first time. Nor had I always experienced him as adoring only of me. How I'd anguished over his relationship with Stephanie Seidenfeld. And how many times had I driven myself nuts by stalking the Facebook page of his ex-fiancée Elissa Trooly?

No, this Porn Predicament was a different kettle of fish. For the first time, I struggled with a kind of revulsion against my beloved. I was used to feeling disgusted and ashamed of *myself*. But Adam? Not ever. Even his Campbell's chicken soup B.O. wasn't smelling so appealing these days. If anything, it seemed interspersed with faint hints of Father's bitter underarm odor that I smelled when I inspected his suits as a child, looking for the dough Nana claimed he'd raked in as kickbacks from Leland DuRay.

It was at around this time that I had the Episode with My Brain. I'd experienced infirmities of the body before: ringworm, your garden variety colds and flus, trapped and untrapped gas, and even that bout of fierce tweeter pain that led to my fiasco with Assefa. Giving birth wasn't an illness, but it had sure felt like it. And having my breasts get engorged hadn't been a party, either.

But having my head cease to function the way it was supposed to was in another class entirely. It happened like this: I was holding Callay in my lap as I stretched out on one of our navy blue lounge chairs by the pool. It was one of those unseasonably hot days that climate change had wrought, and though I bemoaned its cause, I rejoiced in bathing my skin in such warmth. The heat of the blue cushion under my body was heavenly. Even though she'd weaned herself months before, Monkey kept trying to reach into my bathing suit to pull out a breast, and I was playfully pushing her chubby little hand away when my cell phone rang, startling us both. I turned my head quickly to reach for it, and the next thing I knew, my visual field had altered in a profoundly disconcerting way. My baby's face and the luxuriant jasmine bush behind it began scrolling upwards like the credits to a film. Callay seemed to sense that something was amiss, as she stopped fussing at my suit and simply stared at me. I stared back, but less at her, actually, than the spectacle of her rolling image.

Murmuring, "Hang on a minute, love," in a surprisingly calm-sounding voice, I clutched her more tightly. My heart was beating a mile a minute, my only thoughts being, *Do not drop this child!* and, *How will I manage to live if the world never keeps still?* As if in response, the scrolling stopped, as did the vertigo that had accompanied it. But my terror hardly did.

I'm ashamed to confess that I used that episode to push my anti-porn agenda at Adam. One Huntington Hospital ophthalmologist, one Beverly Hills ENT, two MRI radiologists, and one neuro-ophthalmologist at UCLA's Jules Stein Eye Institute ended up concurring that there was nothing amiss with my eyes or my inner ear, but at least three had speculated that a combination of stress and the speed of my turning head sending a quicker neurological signal to my eyes than my ear had caused the momentary brain blip. It was the stress part that I attempted to use to my advantage.

Adam and I were sitting not so far from the scene of the mini-disaster, with Callay napping inside and a baby monitor on the small teak table between us, when I took the call from the last consultant.

"Well?" Adam asked as I set down the phone.

"The same. Brain fart." I paused meaningfully. "And stress."

Adam stared at me. I knew he'd been worried sick about me. "Sweetheart. What are you so stressed about?"

"Well, I suppose it could be the combo of work and Callay and the crazy man in the White House."

He was no dummy. "And?"

"Well ... you and I haven't been having the easiest time of it."

"No, we haven't. Is it really that bad?"

I shrugged. "It's not good."

"Is it ... sex?"

My words came out in a rush. "It was never about sex. I love sex with you. I always have." I fiddled with my blouse button. "Well, I did until—"

"Is it that creepy for you?"

"It really is. What if we find ... other ways? You mentioned the *Kama Sutra*. I'll bet there are plenty of beautiful depictions of ... interesting stuff." I knew I was blushing, and not just because of the subject matter. I felt as though Sammie and Makeda were sitting there with us. As if our whole conversation had intruded on my connection with Adam as much as those porn site strangers had sidled into my sex life.

Adam shot me a strained smile. "Can you say more?"

"I can't help it. I want to make you happy. Really, I do. But ever since you started watching that stuff, it's become like an addiction, as if it's more important than me. Maybe I deserved it. Maybe I was putting everything and everyone else first. Or at least acting like it. But these days it feels like other people are in our bed with us. And I'm always wondering if you're imagining I'm Sally Price when you close your eyes. And if you're looking at my body as if it's an object, rather than just an extension of me. And if you're just pretending to be attracted to me. And if you're tired of me and want to divorce me."

"Whoa. That's quite a mouthful. Is that really what you're thinking?"

"Yes, and I'm also thinking that I don't know you anymore. That the you who watches that junk isn't anyone I want to know." Finally, the ugly truth had slithered out.

Adam looked as though he'd been slapped. I felt horrible, but what I'd said was at least partially true.

"That didn't come out right. It's not exactly what I mean. I just find that stuff gross. And I'm sad that you don't."

Adam pushed his fingers through his hair in frustration. "Fleur, I'm a man."

"What does that have to do with it?"

"I'm lusty. I like to look. Really, I always have. We never talked about it because it was less of a thing for me. But, like every man I know, I've looked at porn from time to time." He paused before adding slyly, "Porn is to masturbation what fine wine is to a great meal."

"You're joking."

"I am, but you get the point. I assume you masturbate? I can't believe we've never talked about this."

I flushed. "I do. But not much. I'm too tired."

"I'm tired, too, but that doesn't seem to stop me."

His smile bothered me. I hated to think he was taking this lightly. "We've never had this problem before."

"We've never had a child before. The project hadn't been so close to fruition before. We didn't have a world going crazy like this before. Look." He reached for my hand. "I just feel the need for a little variety."

"Why? Haven't you enjoyed how we are together?"

"Fleur, as a physicist, would you be content to have the same thought over and over again? Would you want Callay to keep playing the same games all through her childhood?"

I paused. But something about his metaphor bothered me. "No, but I'd expect that her goodnight kisses would continue to be her goodnight kisses and her hugs be her hugs. Some things are so wonderful they simply can't be improved upon."

I sensed our stalemate. I didn't feel the need for anything more in my sex life with Adam. It felt complete for me. But for him? Well, obviously, he did need to inject more variety and imagination into our intimate life together. I should probably count myself lucky that he wanted to do it with me. And that Sally Price had somehow managed to move to the background of our conversation.

I looked up at him. "It's as if all those spermatozoa in your *spermatophore* have different ideas of what they want to do with my egg, while all she wants to do is keep up her stability and well-being."

Thank God Adam was a scientist. Laughing, he grabbed me and whispered in my ear, "Oh, man, do I ever love it when you talk dirty like that."

Chapter Fourteen

IF I'D HAD any delusions that my sex education was now complete, they would have been disabused a few weeks later when I bumped into Cesar at Trader Joe's. Actually, it was in that store's infamous parking lot. The grocery chain was known for how poorly their lots were designed. This one wasn't any different, and when I say I bumped into Cesar, it was nearly literally, with my back bumper and his front one doing a kind of do-se-do before stopping on the brink of a bonk.

We both managed to park more or less parallel to each other, with the front right of the Prius jutting ever so slightly toward the left front tire of his sputtering old Honda, which probably was once a bright red, but now sported a shade of dusty rust. I saw that he took care not to bang his door against mine when he came out of his car. I also saw that he had a passenger, who exited his car with the alacrity of a child. And, indeed, she was pretty pint-sized for a young woman, maybe about four feet, ten inches.

She joined Cesar at his side until a man in a top-down silver Jaguar honked aggressively and made all three of us jump and make haste toward the market.

We came to a stop at the shopping cart stand. Cesar nodded toward his companion, saying, almost grudgingly, "This is Gladys Morales." Then he added, as if I'd asked how they'd met (which I hadn't), "She helped me find my mother. She was finishing up her social work internship for the University of San Carlos when we met." The girl's smile was friendly and curious. Though her skin was as pale as mine and her hair nearly as blond, she had the signature Guatemalan flat face with almost slanted Asian eyes. She raised an eyebrow at him.

Inelegantly, he took her cue. "This is Fleur. Is it Manus?"

"Actually, I go by Robins."

"Of course you do. Fleur Robins." He looked away from me to shrug at Gladys. "She's my adopted sister. Well, I'm the adopted one. You know, the daughter of the woman who died."

I flinched. The statement was bald, impersonal.

"You know, then," I commented, a slight edge in my voice betraying my irritation.

"Yeah. Fidel told me."

Cesar bringing up Fidel made me marvel even more at the incongruity of it all. The last time I'd seen the two of them together, Fidel was swirling on stiletto heels to Gloria Gaynor's "I Will Survive," and Cesar had worn a thong that left virtually nothing to the imagination. Now he was fully clothed in relaxed jeans and a conventional button-down shirt. The biceps under his short-sleeved shirt were visibly cut. He looked very handsome. And masculine. And he held the young woman close to him like a prized possession.

"Did you just get back in town?"

"No, I ... we came about six months ago."

Neither one of us commented that he hadn't come back for the funeral.

We parted awkwardly, with a nearly dismissive hand wave from Cesar, and Gladys and I exchanging a set of polite nice to meet yous.

As I wheeled my cart into the store, I had to stop and catch my breath at a table stacked with watermelons. I sensed more than saw that the store was quite busy, with people's carts pushing determinedly past me, bells ringing from the service counter, and Jackson Browne singing—what else?—"Linda Paloma" on the loudspeaker. I recovered myself by recalling that I really did need to get home and relieve Sister F. from babysitting duty.

It was in the frozen food section, where I was reaching for Callay's favorite veggie "meatballs," when I sensed Gladys at my side. I turned and held out the package as if offering it to her and then laughed, flinging it into my cart.

"You should come and have dinner with us," she said. Only now did I notice Cesar standing further down the aisle with their cart, not even bothering to disguise his frown.

"Oh, I wouldn't want to bother ..."

"No," she insisted, "we don't have many friends. And I have no family here except for Cesar. Please." She put a hand on my arm. It was beautiful, with long pianist's fingers and a light dusting of freckles that suggested she was no stranger to the sun. I noted that she had a faint female mustache over her attractively upturned lip. Somewhere along the line, I'd picked up the information that many Guatemalans were Mestizo, a blend of native and European ancestry. It made for an intriguing mix in Gladys. She said warmly, "Let me text you with some times."

Oh dear. This wasn't one of those "let's get together sometime" pleasantries. She was getting specific. I gave her my number, and she deftly inputted it into her phone. She smiled widely, and I realized that she had a slight gap between her two front teeth. I nearly said, "Oh, you're 'tooth *mingi*,'" but caught myself in time.

Have you ever noticed how synchronicities tend to appear in groups? I ended up feeling like it was Old Home Week, what with my encounters over the course of a few days with Cesar, "Linda Paloma," Gladys Morales, and just a few days later, Assefa, along with the "tooth *mingi*" queen herself, Lemlem, and their baby Ife, whom I'd not yet seen.

That particular morning was worth celebrating. SoCal had been sodden in the kind of horribly humid heat wave that only climate change could wreak on our once Mediterranean-like habitat. Today was still pretty warm, yes, but breezy enough to preclude the full-body itchies that tended to come over me when I perspired too much. The bees and butterflies and mockingbirds seemed to savor the shift, too, and were buzzing and swirling as I pushed Callay along in her "UPPAbaby" stroller toward the Huntington Gardens. It was only when I passed the ticket kiosk, flashing my Member badge, that

I saw Assefa and Lemlem pushing their own stroller towards me, but it was Assefa's baby who grabbed my attention.

When they told me her name, I of course had to ask what it meant. It was Lemlem who said it proudly, "It is love. Ife means love." I found I couldn't look at Assefa right then. But I *could* look at his wife. Needless to say, Lemlem looked gorgeous, back to her ridiculously perfect slender body in what must be less than six months post-delivery, while I was still battling the baby bulge after nearly twelve more.

The two of them exclaimed over how big Callay was. My daughter, bless her, actually held out a pudgy hand to shake each of theirs when I told her their names. She solemnly pronounced, "How ee do, Atheffa? How ee do, Lellem?" before looking up at me for approval.

"My goodness, Assefa, isn't she precocious?"

He smiled affirmingly, his eye tic going like crazy.

I patted Monkey on the head while responding, "She's the light of my life. But I wish I could just freeze her in time. Actually, I feel like that at every stage. But a baby— oh, do I ever miss having a little baby to hold."

As if on cue, Lemlem lifted Ife out of the stroller and held her out to me. She beamed, but it was Assefa's eyes I was aware of, as if he didn't know what to make of me holding his child against my shoulder. I tried not to visibly sniff her, but I didn't have to. I'd know that cinnamon and Roquefort cheese scent anywhere. But did it emanate from the child's own pores or was it just the residue of her father having recently held her? Either way, I found it incredibly hard to let her go.

After we parted, my own darling singing "It-thee Bit-thee Thpider" beneath me, I wondered how long it would for me to feel less haunted by my memories of Assefa. On a quantum level, once objects have interacted with each other or come into being in a similar way, they become linked or entangled forever. Was there something about the emotional entanglement of humans that echoed that? Might feelings operate like fractals of physical memories?

On the other hand, if we were butterflies, Adam and I wouldn't even have been able to mate without Assefa's *spermatophores* having been cleared from my system. But it seemed more than apparent than ever that humans aren't butterflies, and I was still more than vulnerable to feeling uncomfortably stirred-up by having my ex-lover around.

And speaking of feeling haunted, I had the uncanny sensation of smelling Mother's signature Chanel No.5 perfume as I knocked on Cesar and Gladys's paint-chipped front door a few weeks later. It didn't help my mood much that I was on my own, Adam having been felled by a lousy cold. The doorbell button was missing, and the stucco walls were covered in cobwebs. The earthy-toned Mexican tiles at my feet were breaking apart, the cracks making rather interesting zig-zag patterns, and a bare light bulb above my head looked dangerously askew from its socket. I knew that the rents in SoCal had gone through the roof, right along with our shamefully overpriced house prices, but I couldn't help but wonder how it felt to Cesar to live in this rather rundown place after all those years in Mother's posh digs.

As a grinning Gladys ushered me over the threshold, I felt shame over where I lived. These two were crammed into a living room not much bigger than a postage stamp, their "dining table" actually a narrow glass coffee table with one wrought iron leg wrapped in duct tape. Opposite a slumping gold sofa that shouted Goodwill stood a brown Naugahyde chair currently occupied by one of the fattest and furriest cats I'd ever seen. Dark gray all over except for a nearly white ruff around his neck, it summoned a couple of plump forelegs from under its body, stretched them out in front, and blinked contentedly.

"May I?" I asked, squeezing around the coffee table to offer it a well-received stroke under the chin. "Cat crazy, I am," I said unnecessarily. "What's its name?"

To Cesar's obvious dismay, Gladys offered, "His name is Fidelissimo, but we call him Fidel most of the time. We're so lucky. He's a Maine Coon. We named him after Cesar's friend Fidel, who rescued him from under his house and gave him to us because he's allergic to animals."

Well, I thought, the blood-soaked Chin-Hwa coming to mind, that was one way of putting it.

I tried to shoot Cesar a look intended to reassure him, but he'd disappeared into the kitchen.

Gladys took my purse from me, along with the small vase of flowers I'd purchased for them at my favorite florist's, Jacob Maarse. "*Que bellas flores!*" she exclaimed, setting them down on a rather rickety looking end table that I had visions of the feline Fidel overturning as soon as he had the chance. I was glad I'd thought to bring the white and apricot roses already arranged in a vase, as I doubted the young couple possessed one.

Before I knew it, Cesar was sailing into the room bearing a steaming platter of what Gladys proudly told me was called Chicken *Pepián*.

"Oh my God," I exclaimed. "It smells heavenly!" Once he set it down on a colorful Mexican tile trivet on the coffee table, I leaned down and put my nose up close to it. "What's in it?"

Gladys ticked off the ingredients on her fingers. "Pear, squash, carrot, potato, tomato, corn." She laughed. "Well, and chicken, of course."

My eyes veered toward Cesar, but he'd fled the room again.

Gladys confided, "He cooks better than a woman. His friend Fidel taught him a lot. Gave him a love for it. We're going to open a restaurant one day. We're saving the money from his mother." She hesitated, then went on shyly, "Well, I mean … I'm afraid his biological mother has disappeared again. I meant *your* mother. I hope you don't mind that she—"

"Are you kidding? She had enough dough from my dad to feed a couple of armies." I mentally berated myself. Not the greatest image to use to a Guatemalan, whose people were still struggling to recover from a 36-year civil war prompted in part by our own CIA's support of the military overthrow of their democratically elected government; everything I'd read suggested that the country was still traumatized by the military's massacres and civil rights abuses and forced evictions from their homes.

I tried to save myself. "A restaurant! You should talk to our family friend Dhani. Cesar knows her. She used to cook for us. Then she started a cooking school. She could give you all kinds of tips. Maybe provide you with some staff."

Cesar had slipped back into the room again. He set dishes and silverware down on the coffee table and pulled some gaily decorated floor pillows from a corner. He gestured with his head for us to sit down. I wriggled my bum around until it found its place in the middle of my pillow.

Spooning food onto the plates, he commented curtly, "Yeah, well, I don't want to rely on that old gang."

He said it with such contempt that the words came out in spite of me, "You evidently don't mind taking some of that old gang's money." Immediately, I clapped a hand to my mouth. Gladys looked more confused than anything else by my astonishing rudeness.

Mortified, I quickly added, "I'm so sorry. Foot in mouth disease." Which, needless to say, confused her even more. "No, really." I reached a hand across the table toward Cesar. When he didn't bridge his own toward me, I hurriedly took a bite of my Chicken *Pepián*. Gladys had been right. Cesar was on his way to becoming a master chef. I detected a hint of cinnamon, a bit of coriander, cloves, pumpkin seeds, sesame seeds, chilies, of course, and garlic and onion. I would have thought it might have tasted too sweet, but the bitterness of the roasted vegetables conveyed just the right amount of edge.

"Wow. This is food for the gods." I paused with another forkful midway to my mouth. "Listen, Cesar, that was downright offensive of me. Especially when you've gone to such trouble to cook me such a heavenly meal." I waited to see if he would accept my apology.

But Gladys jumped in for him. "No. Cesar should not have said that."

Surprised, I saw that he actually looked ashamed. He must really love this young woman if he was letting her tame his habitual resentment.

I hastened to take my opening. "No. I get it." I stared into Cesar's deep, nearly black eyes. "You want to do this your own way. Put your stamp on it. A restaurant is a creative enterprise for anyone who can cook like this." And I meant it.

He studied me for a moment, then seemed to relax a bit. "Yeah. That's a good way to put it. I'm totally psyched." He added warmly, "And not just for me. This is going to be a real partnership. Gladys will be right with me every step of the way, from designing menus to working out prices to hiring and managing staff. She's a real people person." I nodded. He was right on that score. His hand reached down to give Gladys' bum a possessive squeeze, "It'll be our baby until we have a real one."

Gladys blushed. I think I did, too. I'd heard a lot lately about gender fluidity, but something must have gotten positively sodden in Cesar that he'd transformed from Miss Hot Little Mama to this convincing young paterfamilias. He'd shed his previous incarnation as dramatically as a doughty monarch butterfly, some of whom have been spotted flying past the Empire State Building at a height of a thousand feet. I had a hunch that, with Gladys by his side, Cesar was about to soar.

As for me, it was more than clear that I knew next to nothing outside of my own little physics bubble and was an absolute dunderhead about human nature. I kept wanting to vanquish the uncertainties of my void by typecasting people, and they simply wouldn't cooperate.

Chapter Fifteen

IT WAS ONE of those rare moments when I actually had a minute to myself. Sister Flatulencia had arrived a little early, traffic from Mar Vista having been particularly light that morning, and I decided to take a walk in the neighborhood before heading out for Caltech. I smiled as I closed the front door, as much at the image of Sister F. sitting on the carpet with Callay, reading her *I Can't, Said the Ant* in a high-pitched voice, as at the gorgeous day that awaited me. It was still warm, but not too warm, windy, but not too windy. The breeze fluffed my hair as I noted a glorious gold and black butterfly flitting above the milkweed I'd planted in the front yard to do my part in increasing the dangerously dwindling monarch population. Forcing myself to bypass my inevitable rage at Monsanto for their monarch-murdering herbicide, my eyes strove to follow the butterfly until a crow bisected my sight line. The corvid careened past the sycamore next door and flapped and fluttered there, as if hesitant to land. When it finally did, a few doors down on a lawn far lusher than ours, it walked with a lopsided gait. I approached cautiously, my heart beginning to beat in dread over what I might find as I got closer. Sure enough, it looked bad. One of the crow's feet was covered by what looked to be a colony of painful-looking bulbous growths.

"Oh, shit," I said, startling a neighbor out watering her yarrow-festooned parkway.

She raised an eyebrow.

"That crow," I clarified, pointing.

She clamped off her hose and approached me. "I know," she sighed. "It's getting worse."

"I didn't ... Has this been going on for some time?"

"It has," she replied, her eyes moist. "The Heislers across the street tried contacting crow rescue associations, several of us have called our vets, and my husband had a long conversation with a wild-life specialist at UCLA. We're in a catch twenty-two. Because he's still able to fly, none of us can get hold of him to take him somewhere to find out what it really is. It could be avian pox; it could be cancer; it could be a fungal condition." She paused, and we both watched him charily hop around. "The damned thing is, he can do the thing we most envy birds for, which is fly, but he can't do the thing we tend to be oblivious to: birds also need to land."

She was right, of course. That was one of the many things trees were for. I thrust out a hand. "Fleur Robins. I can't imagine why we haven't met—and why I didn't even know of this neighborhood tragedy—except that I have a toddler and I also work."

Her sea-blue eyes crinkled in a warm smile. "I'm Halley Smith-Robinson. Fleur Robins? I know about you. My husband's at Caltech. Maxfield Robinson. You've probably never met." She made a wry face. "He teaches English. As he likes to say, he rounds the geniuses out."

I laughed. "Well, I don't know about geniuses, but most of us scientists could definitely use some rounding. Good to meet you, Halley. And no, I haven't had the pleasure of meeting your husband." I refrained from asking whether she worked, too. So many San Marino matrons lived a more conventional lifestyle: supported by their husbands, keeping themselves attractive and fit, volunteering for worthy, if mainstream, charities. The sort of life Mother could have lived but had avoided like the plague.

But Halley momentarily put paid to my wretched bent for stereotyping. "Max and I met at the Iowa Writer's Workshop. He went in the academic direction, and I found my calling in children's books. I'm sure psychologists would have a field day with a childless woman specializing in kiddie lit. I write under the pseudonym Sarah Stevens. How old is your toddler?"

"Oh my God! Sarah Stevens? Callay—she's twenty-three months—is crazy about *Who's Got My Tail?* And *One Cat, Two Cat.* And we've just checked out *Cody's Kittens and Then Some* from the library." I paused. "How many do you have?"

Only later did it occur to me that my question might have been misconstrued, but Halley was right there with me. She laughed. "It's pretty transparent, isn't it? Right now, we've got four." She ticked them off on her fingers, "Catastrophe, Courageous, Clementine—we usually call them by their nicknames, Cat, Corie, and Clemmie, (otherwise known as 'the girls')—and Gerald, named after our favorite Durrell. But don't tell anyone we've got so many, please. Max is embarrassed enough to be married to the Cat Lady of Children's Literature."

"Oh, I'm sure he's not," I said, quite certain of that. If Halley was as clever as her books were and as kind as her concern for the crow suggested, any man would feel lucky to be with her.

Just then, a flutter above us stole our attention. The crow had taken off and soared beyond the sycamore as exquisitely as any of his healthy brethren. "He'll die, won't he," I commented gravely, "unless he has a spontaneous recovery?"

"Yes. That's pretty much what all the experts have said. They even insisted we desist from feeding him if he collapses. If it's avian pox, it's contagious, and he could infect all the other birds in the neighborhood."

I sighed heavily. "Well, I should probably think about getting to work."

Halley put a hand on my shoulder. "Oh, I'm so sorry. I've spoilt your walk."

"No. You didn't. Mr. Crow didn't either. This is nature's balance. These days I tend to think of us humans as the only source of misery in the world, but the dark clouds of death and disaster have been around long before we came along. Besides," I threw her a genuinely grateful smile, "this time there really is a silver lining. I got to meet you."

I realized on my way back to the house that I hadn't asked her why she'd chosen a pseudonym. It would be a good reason to pay her a call, which I knew—for Callay's sake, as well as my own—I was going to want to do. My daughter needed to learn that actual people write books, that they weren't churned out by some sort of invisible magic or computer algorithm, that people could make amazing things by working at them.

I thought about the neighbors who'd come together to try to save Mr. Crow. They might not achieve that worthy goal, but they'd created community. I realized with a pang that—up until today—I knew none of them. My street was filled with undoubtedly interesting people, each of them a whole universe unto themselves, and I'd been entirely oblivious, as if my house were an island. I felt ashamed.

But I had to laugh when I went inside. There was a track of books leading from the front hallway to the living room. Recently, Callay had discovered something else to do with her favorite books: making trains that, to her great consternation, Buster loved to sit on, changing his "train car" each time my daughter cried out, "No, no! Buthter-do! You go! Not for you!" But when I followed this particular winding path, I found my little Monkey sprawled across the track, petting the white belly of a loudly-purring Buster, who lay on his back atop—what else?—*Cody's Kittens and Then Some*. Carl Jung and Wolfgang Pauli would have loved it.

Sister F., undoubtedly alerted by the sound of the front door blown noisily shut by the wind, came in wearing a Physicists are Spacier apron, with its "a" crossed out and replaced by an "i," wiping one of Callay's Curious George cups with a checkered dishcloth. "How was your walk?" she asked brightly.

"*Une salade mixte*," I replied, describing my introduction to Halley Smith-Robinson and the sad circumstances of the ailing crow.

"What's going to happen to him?" she asked.

"What do you think?"

"You never know, my dear. All we can see is the past and the present. Miracles do occur."

Once a nun, always a nun. I wished I had more trust myself in miracles. But then I heard my miracle of a daughter burst into her own mangled version of a song that Adam had recently taught her. I prayed that the synchronicity of Callay singing "High Hopes" would prove to be prophetic for Mr. Crow.

As for prophecy, who would have predicted that Gwennie would recover from her own health crisis with such hardihood? I took Callay to see her right after our arranged visit a few days later to Halley Smith-Robinson, the interior of whose home pretty much seemed like what you'd expect from a couple that keeps four cats. Aside from the lack of the telltale smell. The Robinson home was happily devoid of Eau de Chat and redolent, instead, of what I learned from Halley was called Aromatique Summer Sorbet. The scent was so similar to what they used at Shutters, where Adam and I had first made love, that I nearly swooned in the front hall.

Bending down to shake Callay's hand and tell her how happy she was to meet her, my new favorite author led the two of us into a living room with a pair of facing sofas with loose burgundy and sage slipcovers thrown over them. Placed seemingly haphazardly on the surrounding rustic gray wood floor was an array of Persian-carpet-covered floor cushions. Upon four of these perched a quartet of lazily blinking cats, like feline potentates calmly surveying their shared realm. But as soon as Halley bade Callay to plop down onto her own cushion, Gerald and "the girls" leapt in near unison to come and sniff the new specimen in their midst. My muscles tensed in preparation for quick movement as it dawned on me that these four might think my daughter a potential usurper and get a bit hissy and bitey, but no—they were like kittens with their mama, vying to get in closest to lick the milk-white limbs of this small, giggling creature, who had to be admonished not to lick them back. The cats' shared motoring made quite a racket. And Callay? Well, of course, Callay was in heaven.

It was a heaven that deepened in pleasure once Halley Smith-Robinson excused herself to dance down the stairs several minutes later to bestow on my child her full library of cat-themed books, each inscribed personally to my daughter in a rather unique handwriting with the kinds of inked-in tail curls and flourishes that set Callay whirling in delighted circles at the foot of the stairs. I had one moment of panic—my own whirling at her age had been accompanied by screaming and banging and pinching and, in general, personally causing myself pain—but no Adam would be needed to help socialize *this* little girl. Callay ran to her new friend and wrapped her pudgy little arms around her knees, exclaiming, "I wuv you, Haowie!" Given the meltiness of Halley's expression, the feeling was clearly mutual.

It took awhile to actually get Callay and myself and the two Gelson's cloth grocery bags bearing Halley Smith-Robinson's entire oeuvre out the door and into the Prius in front of our own home. In the end, I only managed to budge Monkey by telling her that if we didn't hurry we were going to be late for our lunch with Granny Gwennie. (Somehow Gwennie had metamorphosed into a Granny from an Auntie in Callay's clever mind after Mother died, and not one of us sought to stop it.)

When we arrived at the Fiskes', Gwennie was just saying goodbye to her physical therapist. He was young, of course, and unusually handsome: his skin like alabaster; his black hair slicked back to frame his perfectly proportioned features; his body, as Sammie liked to say, "ridiculously ripped." As usual, Gwen was flirting with him, telling him that he made her want to lose ten pounds and thirty years, and it looked like he was enjoying it. He flashed me a heart-stopping grin as he passed me. I managed to turn my eyes away from his particularly beguiling butt to say to my friend. "Gwen you're shameless. And p.s., you'd better *not* lose any more weight."

Though she'd widened in the early days of her recovery, Gwennie had ultimately settled into a much thinner body than she'd begun with. Her hair had grown back a brilliant, shimmering silver, and a teasing new dimple had appeared in her smile, as if she'd been to hell and back and had retrieved from that scorched landscape a life-giving balm. She beamed at Callay and bent down as if to lift her up before she caught herself. "Jarod would kill me," she apologized to my oblivious daughter. "'He's not the smartest tack in the drawer, but he's pretty wise about the body. 'One step at a time, Gwen,' he likes to say." Instead, she grabbed Callay's chubby little hand and said, "Come and see what Granny Gwennie's made for you, pet."

I followed the two of them into the kitchen, where a round, blue and green cake was cooling on a rack on the white tile counter. Gwen slid over a short stepladder for Callay, who dutifully climbed up to see it with a little help from Gwen to keep her from falling backward, and I came closer myself to get a better look.

My Monkey clapped her hands. "It's Earth! You made Earth!"

And indeed, Gwennie had swirled icing to create a gorgeous representation of our oceans, separated by glistening green continents. She turned toward me and shrugged haplessly. "I've broken all my rules about sugar and white flour and food coloring spray and gel, but when I saw its prototype on the internet, I just couldn't resist." Gwennie admired her own handiwork, adding as an aside, "The woman who came up with the recipe calls herself OC Mom. She describes how she lost her mother at nineteen to cancer. I felt like I was supporting her somehow. I even sent a picture of this version to her blog."

"And so you should," I said, reaching out a finger to taste one of the shiny green swirls, but Gwennie was fast, playfully slapping my hand. "Oh no, you don't, missy." Callay looked up at me, a little worried, and Gwennie hastened to reassure her. "Granny Gwennie's just playing with Moomah, but we do have to eat our lunch first. I'm going to grill us some lovely cheese sandwiches, and we'll toast our planet." She slid me an ironic shrug. "No pun intended." And to Callay: "Did you know it's Earth Day?"

"'Wha' Earth Day?" asked my daughter.

"It's the day we celebrate our Mother Earth!"

Callay chimed in, "Earth Day, Mother Earth birthday!" And then she threw us both a sly smile. "Caycay made a rhyme." (Except it came out *wyme*.)

"Oh, you clever girl," Gwennie cried, ignoring Jarod's admonition and scooping my daughter up into her arms, attempting a twirl before remembering herself and setting her down. "And yes, it's just like that. Let's make a little party for our Earth." She fetched a package of paper-wrapped Cheddar from the fridge and unwrapped it, then turned her attention to melting a giant daub of butter on her stovetop grill. I suggested to Callay that we change her diaper before our party. She might be a budding genius, but my little girl still regularly peed in her pants when we were out and about. Mother had burned it into my brain not to push her in that department, and I was hanging onto any bits of wisdom she'd imparted before she'd died.

Having deposited a sodden diaper in the black bin in back, the two of us returned to the tantalizing aroma of melting butter and cheese in the kitchen. Gwennie had set up Callay's booster seat at the table and had programmed her iPad to play the latest episode of Peppa Pig. It was just about the only cartoon series we allowed her. I think we all fantasized she'd learn a British accent from it and become one of those adorable children with impeccable manners, one of whom I once overheard in a London tube asking with a pleasing soprano lilt, "Mummy, won't you please buy me a teddy?" But all I got today was, "Moomah, Caycay want blueberries after sammich," with "please" added as an afterthought once both Gwennie and I favored her with a stern eye.

My daughter's own eyes were riveted to the screen now, and Gwen and I knew that there would be no way to regain her attention without shutting the bloody thing off. I very much wanted to talk with Gwen, but I knew we each felt a bit guilty distracting Callay with screen time.

"I'm feeling better than I ever would have imagined," Gwen insisted. "Actually, pretty full of p. and v." She rose up to fetch a printed flyer from the kitchen counter that bore a bold, black headline: Families Belong Together. "Wanna come? You could bring Callay."

I winced. "Gwennie, I admire you so much for—what do you call it? Walking the walk? But any marching genes I may have had disappeared after what happened at the Survival march. Which turned out to be anything but that for some." I paused, not wanting to be insulting. "And even if I were ever tempted again, I'd *never* take Callay."

I found myself reflecting on the few times—all post-2016— when I'd taken my disgruntlement to the streets. I'd actually marched next to Mother in the first Women's March after the election, the two of us giggling self-consciously as we posed for selfies in the pussy hats hand-knitted for us by Sister Flatulencia. Unsurprisingly, the whole physics team had turned out for the March for Science, with Bob bearing a hand-lettered placard declaiming, "The Oceans Are Rising, So Are We," and Katrina wearing the best T-shirt ever, emblazoned with the words, "I Can't Believe I Have to March for Facts."

Both experiences had been a bit surreal. Attempting to vanquish my void in large, claustrophobic crowds felt counter-intuitive. I'd never seen myself as a marching sort of person. Not even a rallier. And we all know what happened when I addressed the huge audience at the Nobel ceremony.

The truth was, in the past, I wasn't convinced that marches did much good, save for filling the anxious voids of their attendees. Instead, I'd put my money on science. But what if science itself was under attack? For years we'd been stymied in our research thanks to a series of know-nothing congresses. The fact that we were able to continue now struck me as nothing short of a miracle.

I knew that ours certainly wasn't the first time in history that the verity of science was threatened. Besides a disheartening tendency on the part of the established scientific hierarchy to shun newcomers' groundbreaking and innovative work, ever since the scientific revolution there had been those who'd called science itself into question. Even fine thinkers such as Hobbes, Rousseau, William Blake, and Nietzsche were distrustful of science's claims to universal applicability. I wish they'd been present for the first moon landing, which pretty much put paid to critiques of science's capacity to deliver on a practical level. But the real naysayers had been various organized religions and their attachment to keeping the unknown, unknown. Ironically, we quantum physicists were also fascinated with the unknown. We approached it, not as a never-to-be-breached secret, but as a vast field for the play of the mind, as sacred and exhilarating to us as religion is to a believer, sports to a player, sex to a lover. The enthusiasm generated by the Higgs field, many worlds theories, and the relationship between dark and light matter often approached transcendence.

But Gwennie? It struck me that activism was her transcendence. She'd been ranting about Big Oil and Father and his Cacklers ever since I'd discovered C-Voids, and the group she'd founded, C the Big Picture, was still going strong. Especially since she seemed sturdier on her feet these days, the fact that she was again prepared to put those feet to the pavement for one of her causes struck me as a very good sign. I said as much to her.

She replied with predictable passion. "Going easy was never my forté, but hell, in this day and age—well, you know even better than I how dire it's become. You and the gang are doing much more than marching on the climate catastrophe front, but Pighead has given us so much more to worry about. And what he's doing now to the children?" Her voice had crept higher and higher to the point that it competed with the squeaks and snorts of Peppa Pig and her porcine family. Callay looked up, alarmed. "No, no, darling, it's okay. Granny Gwennie keeps getting overexcited today. What's Peppa doing? Baby George lost his dinosaur?"

Callay was seduced back to her screen again. Gwen spoke this time in a forced whisper. "I know it's been a daily shit show, but this one? Babies ripped from their mother's breasts? Children in cages? He's gone beyond the beyond. Whenever I think of those kiddies, some of them younger than our Monkey here, my blood boils. If I were a religious woman I'd pray that these monsters would experience a hundredfold the agony they're foisting upon these children and their families. That they know shame. And terror. And rue the day they were born."

I responded dryly, "You might not be a religious woman, but that sounds a little like some sort of ancient curse." I didn't disagree with Gwennie's sentiments, but I simply couldn't bear taking in the whole of what she was describing. It was too awful. "Gwen, I admire you, I really do. But I'm a scientist. Which means I have to do a certain amount of dissociation to do what I have to do."

She blinked. "What are you talking about?"

"Have you heard of James Fallon?" She shook her head. "He's a neuroscientist who studied the brains of serial killers. Sociopaths. He discovered that his own brain had most of the genetic markers that they and their families had. Then he found out that serial killing was spookily frequent in his own family line."

Gwennie stepped back. "God. Can you imagine?"

"I suppose in an odd way, I can. What really fascinated me was that he started to speculate that the lack of empathy that can produce serial killers might actually be valuable in the right proportions."

"Whatever do you mean?"

"I mean, do you want your surgeon to be too anxious about cutting into you to get out that cancer? Or your military generals to be worried about casualties when defending your soil?"

"When was the last time we had to worry about defending our soil?" she muttered.

"But you get the point, right? I think I've experienced it myself. I had a sociopath for a father; how much of it is in my genes? I nearly lost Sammie as a friend by caring more about coming up with the theory of C-Voids than I did our friendship. We scientists can be that way."

But then Gwennie suddenly made a gesture behind Monkey's back as if she was about to bat my child's head.

I jumped forward, screaming, "Gwennie!"

Callay looked up, alarmed for the third time that morning. Gwen gave her a giant kiss on her little blond head, and then leaned forward to plant one on my own cheek. "I don't think Fallon's got *this* scientist all worked out," she said drily. "That wasn't the response of a sociopath, Fleur."

As my heart tried to calm itself, I realized she'd relieved me of at least a bit of the concern I'd been harboring about myself ever since hearing Fallon's story.

"Enough of sociopaths," Gwen declared. She announced heartily, "Who's for cake?"

"Caycay!" cried my daughter.

Laughing as much in relief as anything else, I chimed in, "Moomah!"

"Well, let's do it," Gwennie said.

We dove into that yummy round Earth, as Nana used to say, "like starving Europe." It tasted as good as it looked. Needless to say, it took longer than usual to get a sugar-high toddler tucked into my old bed.

As Callay slept, Gwen and I sat opposite each other on the facing living room sofas and sipped the tangy mint tea she'd brewed "for digestion." Unerringly, Gwennie steered us back to our earlier conversation.

I found myself literally throwing up my hands. "Let's face it, Gwen. You're our resident conscience. You keep us honest when we try to turn a blind eye along with most of the rest of the world to the dangers facing all the buns in the oven. I should have known, when you and Stanley first took me under your wings, that you were a particularly ethical person by your insistence on no meat in your home. Or chemically laced food, for that matter." I grinned. "Not even Krispy Kremes."

And then she covered her face in shame. "What a hypocrite I am, making a cake for Mother Earth that contained all the crap you're talking about."

I reached over to put a hand on her arm, then scooted over to her sofa. "Gwennie. It's not good for any of us to think we have to be squeaky clean. That one'll kill us as fast as any cancer. The earth itself isn't clean. It's made of dirt."

Gwen snorted. "Hell, that is just so damned true." She reached out to shake my hand. "Thank you, girl, for challenging something that's gotten a little too rigid in this old head of mine."

Little did I know that I would soon face my own set of challenges when Sammie's lover finally came to LA. She'd be winging across the Atlantic Ocean in just a few days.

Sanctus

The ocean was aggrieved. What humans had come to call the Great Pacific Garbage Patch was but the latest insult to her dignity. In the past, she'd been respected and revered, the names she'd been given myriad: from Neptune to Poseidon to Tiamat to Enbilulu to Triton to Ikatere. Liquid breath of the earth; rhythmic moon dancer; salty lubricant of wisdom, travel, and adventure—her vast depths were a realm of secret delight, home to the most outrageously colorful creatures on the planet. Poets had praised her; scientists had studied her; surfers, swimmers, and ships had ridden her; and more than a few had succumbed to her steely storms.

But now, she herself was struggling, her ceaseless striving to provide food, oxygen, and weather mediation to the earth's inhabitants increasingly impeded. She was working overtime to absorb atmospheric toxins released by the ceaseless burning of fossil fuels; she could barely contain their greenhouse gases, and her ecosystems were collapsing. Even her sweet seagrass meadows were drowning as sea levels rose, disrupting the lives of the fish, ducks, geese, and swans that were nourished by them.

With her coral reefs subject to mass bleaching and infectious disease, clams and oysters, conches and sea urchins were fumbling at building and maintaining their protective skeletons. In the future, would there be no shells left to hold to an ear to "hear the sounds of the sea?" The most charming of her creatures were at great risk. Polar bears and walruses, seals and sea lions, penguins and sea turtles were flagging.

The sea of love was heading toward becoming a sea of death, and the nations of the world were much too slow to sound and respond to the alarm. Who would rise to the call of that wet and wonderful wild? Who would come to their senses and save their very own home?

The Soul of the World was all too aware of the oceans' plight. She rode with them on waves of worry, their unending motion the rhythmic refrain to her sorrowful song.

Chapter Sixteen

I COULDN'T WAIT to meet Amira. She'd assumed the proportions of a goddess in my mind. I had to force myself not to suggest going with Sammie to greet her at LAX, reminding myself that they needed that moment of reunion to themselves.

The good news was that Sammie drove her straight to our house from the airport, eager, as she said when they arrived, "to bring together my two favorite women in the world." Then, after a beat, "Except for my mum."

Amira, who was even more glamorously gorgeous in person than in the photos my friend had shared, shot Sammie a sly look. "That's what I love about you. Hopelessly sentimental."

I wasn't sure I appreciated the edge in her voice, but extended a hand, then gave up politeness to offer her a welcoming hug, which she treated as an excuse to give me a peck on each cheek, which felt, somehow, off-putting.

Oh dear, you might think, they're off to a rocky start. And from my perspective, you'd probably be right. Not that Sammie noticed. She beamed from ear to ear as Amira announced, "And now you must show me this fab house of yours that Sammie's been boasting about."

I was a little taken aback, but followed orders, leading her (with Sammie right behind) through:

1. the capacious living room that offered an awe-inspiring dramatic flair with its quatrefoil windows and exposed rafters.

2. the den, its dark wooden floors covered with abandoned book trains and milk jugs full of flowers delivered weekly from the gifted florists of Jacob Maarse, and our ridiculously gigantic television concealed behind a sliding wall with a vibrantly-colored Ethiopian hanging.

3. the library, with children's books gradually encroaching on shelves once solely devoted to philosophy, fiction, history, and physics journals.

4. the rarely used dining room, decorated by Mother with an exquisite Baltic dining table resting on baluster legs surrounded by ten fully upholstered host chairs with grey cashmere, button-tufted seats and backs, overlooked by a Hollywood sign lithograph by Ed Ruscha, a "Made in California" piece by Bruce Naumann, and one prized Chagall with an ethereal couple floating over pigs and chickens.

5. the kitchen, gleaming with stainless steel appliances and home to the rustic French country table our increasingly extended family preferred to crowd around, legs brushing against each other in companionable intimacy.

6. the two downstairs bathrooms—one styled around the motif of the giant Chat Noir poster hanging over the tub, the other's walls dotted with illustrations from the original *Winnie the Pooh*.

7. then up the spiral staircase and through all five spacious bedrooms except for Callay's, as Monkey was napping.

I knocked before we peeked in on the girls, who threw us gleaming grins as they looked up from their chessboard on the shag-carpeted floor, and then Makeda and Melky, who were reading in matching chintz-slipcovered armchairs, swiveled to face each other, their bare feet intertwined. I decided to skip the upstairs bathrooms, except for the one that Buster ambled out of curiously. He wound his way in and out of Amira's ankles as she pronounced with a kind of cynical glee that, what with the stylishly modern black litter box providing entry from an oval opening at the top, black and turquoise fish-shaped food and water dishes, and pet toys crowding the tub, our cat had his very own luxury bathroom. I couldn't disagree and fell close to the edge of a whirling pit of upper-class white girl guilt.

It was only when I purposely turned the conversation to Amira's documentary that I could see a bit of what had attracted Sam to her—besides looks, that is. I couldn't help but note that her eyes were, indeed, as green as Adam's, but more almond-shaped than round, as befitting her part-Iraqi heritage.

We three ended up having a light breakfast of toast and fresh fruit salad in the kitchen, a wakened Callay making one of her book trains around our chairs when Amira nodded down toward my daughter. "Well, for one thing, one can't separate the status of women in any part of the world from the relative well-being of their children. We'd hardly be able to take for granted that a bright little girl like Callay would be able to attend school if she were Afghani. The Taliban were notorious for forbidding girls to go to school, and it's touch and go whether a girl can get any schooling now, depending in part on where they live. In some areas, like Kandahar, Zabul, and Wardak, where I managed to do some interviewing, only about fifteen percent of girls are attending school. It's due to a variety of factors: the physical destruction of schools by war, ongoing conflict making it too dangerous to even attempt to attend, a shortage of female teachers—girls cannot be taught, or medically treated for that matter, by men. Not to mention the ubiquity of child marriages, longstanding poverty, and the consequent cultural devaluation of female education.

"But remember, the country is still very much at war, and women and children are casualties of violence in every way imaginable.

The ICC—the International Criminal Court—has been investigating war crimes there for years, and, believe me, there's no reason to stop. Innocent civilians have been at the absolute mercy of the Taliban, the National Security Forces, the US military, and your CIA ever since this damned thing began, which, of course, actually dates back to the British invasion in eighteen thirty-eight and was worsened immeasurably by the USSR's brutal takeover in the late nineteen seventies. Generations have known nothing but poverty and war. And on top of that, tribal cultures are notorious for violence against women. Afghanistan has been no exception. Rape, acid attacks, forced prostitution: you name it, it takes place every day."

This was brutal on multiple levels—not only thanks to the horrifying content but also to the confidence of Amira's delivery. I felt like a humdrum talk show interviewer, with her being the sparkling guest. Reminding myself that this was her job, I tried shoving the Green-eyed Monster out of the room and nodded frequently as she drove home her points. Out of the corner of my eye, I couldn't help but note the admiring glow in Sammie's eyes.

"The moving thing is that Afghani women, like women the world over, lobby strongly for human rights for themselves and their children. I was there to witness a demonstration of one of the civil society organizations that gave me chills, knowing as I did that those women might be arrested, murdered by their families, or subjected to any sort of brutal torture for taking part. People are really trying. Even in the midst of absolute insanity, just like in the US right now, organizations are working heroically to make a sane, safe, and free society. In and out of the country, I had the privilege of meeting representatives of Women for Women, International; Amnesty, International; Womankind, Worldwide; and Women for Afghan Women. And then there are the individuals—women like the brilliant Zainab Fayez, the only female prosecutor in Kandahar, who's successfully spearheaded scores of cases of violence against women."

Amira turned to Sammie, who looked as wide-eyed as I felt, and said, "I want you to meet her, darling. She's funny, warm, absolutely stunning. I pray she manages to stay alive for the premiere of the film at Sundance. I told you, didn't I, that they're co-producing?"

Unusually tongue-tied, Sammie mumbled her congratulations, and I tried to save her with a genuine, "You're doing extraordinary work, Amira."

She smiled then, and the smile actually seemed genuine. "As are you, my dear. I haven't even mentioned what three decades of conflict and chaos have done to the country's natural resources. From what I gather, your work is crucial for all the little girls—*and* boys—of our world. If peace ever comes to that region, they'll still have to contend, as we all will, with climate change."

I flushed, but all I could think was hurry, hurry, hurry!

Chapter Seventeen

I MAY HAVE mentioned that butterflies see differently than we do. They have less visual sharpness, but they make up for it by their capacity to see in the ultraviolet wavelength. What my favorite entomologist Sally Price added to the picture is that it's often the females' ultraviolent coloring that attracts the male of the species, rather than the sorts of olfactory stimuli nature uses to compel other creatures to mate.

When Sally shared that piece of information with me—the two of us slathering on sunscreen before commencing a brainstorming walk around Caltech's grassy Beckman Mall—I found myself wondering anew about the incandescent quality of light that I experienced during those two extraordinary moments of my life that I'd been sure were some sort of previews to Dreamization: my Alice-in-Wonderlandish moment at Zeki's funeral; and again, years later, giving birth to Callay. Death and life. One of the larger debates in the scientific community revolves around the question of whether the universe is infinite or finite. It the latter were true, we could travel through the universe and eventually arrive back at where we started. Sometimes I wondered if my own experiences hadn't contained a hint of that.

But right now, my recollection raised a more pressing question. I knew that when matter is sucked into a black hole, it emits—among other things—ultraviolet light. As Sally continued her description of the butterfly dance, I felt a little frisson of anxiety. What if humans would be at risk of absorbing damaging levels of UV rays during the process of activating their cellular black holes? That would certainly raise alarms in the Precautionary Principle department and might require that we find ways to protect our PD travelers before sending them in and out of the void.

I searched my mind for who might help us out with this. I knew that Jeff Steinhauer was doing some amazing work these days with acoustic black holes in his lab at Haifa's Institute of Technology and that Mike Dunne's team was using the Linac Coherent Light Source to fashion a laser to create an atomic black hole. But none of those lines of inquiry were immediately applicable to our own project and would offer little guidance in this potential dilemma. What if Dreamization proved to be even more destructive than climate change?

I decided to speak to Adam about it that night. Lately, I was inclined to raise a new idea or concern with him before mentioning it to the rest of the team. It felt important to assuage his feelings about being taken for granted (and also, if I was honest, to make him more likely to enjoy our sex minus the porn).

Did it all come down to sex for everyone, or was it just me? I had a fantasy of Herr Freud knowingly twiddling his thumbs.

But to be fair, other types of twiddlers (and wrigglers and twirlers) were putting up a heck of a good fight for my attention these days. Mostly young ones. Callay, of course, even more so now that the word *why* had entered her vocabulary. Being scientists didn't hurt Adam and me in that area, but there were still plenty of questions we couldn't begin to answer. We could manage "Why sun not make Caycay brown like Fifa and Yes?" with a brief description of the cooling and—speaking of UV radiation—anti-UV effects of melanin in hot climates. But "Where Caycay before Moomah belly?" stumped us both. Hadn't I wondered about that one a million times myself?

As for Callay's browner "sisters," their latest attention-grabbing devices were the instruments they'd been assigned at the Children's Center: Sofiya's half-sized violin and Melesse's—God help us—drums. All Makeda could say when they'd first brought them home was, "What were they thinking?" I'd tried to be more sanguine myself, suggesting we install the instruments in the attic room that ran nearly the full length of the house, but it's amazing how far squeaky, discordant, and clangy sounds liked to travel.

But those were hardly the most pressing issues children posed to us these days: there were also those 2,000 plus minors at our borders who'd been taken hostage in a policy darkly dubbed "Zero Tolerance."

Although I found the plight of those little ones unbearable to think about, it was pretty hard to avoid just that in this heaving, hot mess that our country had become. The children fleeing violence and crippling poverty in Mexico, El Salvador, and Guatemala had rightly captured the headlines and continued to take center stage in Gwennie's political rants, which had gotten increasingly operatic in volume and dramatic fervor. One recent political aria, performed for the team prior to a Sunday morning brainstorming session at the Fiskes', had been accompanied by sweeping hands that each held a piece of toast slathered with melting butter that literally flung itself into yellow Rorschachs on the floor as she cried out, "Those mother fuckers! They're a real-life version of Swift's rich Englishmen. This administration might as well barbecue the darlings on skewers for what they're doing to their developing brains with this fucking traumatic separation from their families. You do know, don't you, that the stress hormones being released in these poor kids can do lifelong damage?" The fact that we all shook our heads in assent didn't stop her. "Too much cortisol completely fucks with the immune system, and the kind of fear and anxiety those children are enduring will screw them up forever. Do you know that Australian aboriginal kids ripped away from their families actually showed less white and gray matter in their brains, indicating decreased ability to process information?"

Now *that* was news to me, and I found it particularly alarming. I'd known about Dr. Jonathan Swift's *A Modest Proposal*—officially titled *A Modest Proposal for Preventing the Children of Poor People from Being a Burthen to Their Parents or Country, and for Making them Beneficial to the Publick*—ever since Adam had assigned it to me as a lesson in satire when I was thirteen.

"Wait, Gwen. What are you saying about those Aboriginal kids?"

Gwen flushed. I'd caught her mid-rant, and it was as if she had to pour herself back into her body, head last, in order to consider my question. "I'm sorry, guys, it's just that I can't stand it." She collapsed into the nearest chair and grabbed a napkin to wipe buttery spit from her lips. "I read about it recently in an op-ed. The Australian government tried to 'improve' aboriginal children's lives right up to the nineteen seventies in a policy they called 'Assimilation.' They were actually aiming to eradicate what they thought was an inferior race and culture. Many of those kids ended up being raised in institutional care when they had perfectly loving parents desperate to have them back."

I felt my eyes tearing up. It wasn't all that different from what was taking place right now, but having the information delivered in calm tones made it seem all the worse. I shook my head. "God. Mother lived in the same house with me, but before she got sober, she'd lock herself in her room for hours at a time, completely inaccessible. Even those small separations were torture. I'd bang at her door for what felt like forever until Nana would drag me off to try and distract me. But if strangers had come and stolen me away from her over some impersonal agenda? I can't imagine it. At least I knew she was alive and breathing in that bedroom of hers—especially since she snored like an elephant when she was drunk." Nervous laughter rippled the room. I saw Adam eye me with alarm.

Gunther chimed in, "*Ja.* I'm proud to come from a country where the government actually cares about kids." We all looked up in acknowledgment of this unusual burst of patriotic pride. "Sweden was the first to ban corporal punishment of children. I know it was in nineteen seventy-nine, since my teacher had to inform my father of that fact when I showed up at my preschool with a black eye and welts on my legs and arms." None of us knew quite where to look, including Gunther, who seemed to have shocked himself at his outburst. His wandering eye was working overtime. It took one of the non-scientists in our midst to have the good sense to voice aloud what we were collectively feeling.

"How terrible for you, Gunther," offered Gwen, her voice lowered in tenderness. Only then did the rest of us offer our own commiseration, resulting in Gunther blushing bright red to the roots of his white-blond hair. I'm sure I wasn't the only one who recognized that herein might lie at least some of the cause of our colleague's moodiness, which sometimes descended into crippling depression.

At that moment I was swirling down a pretty deep pit of it myself. You'd think that, after Father, I would have been an old hand at acknowledging the dark capabilities of our species, but there seemed to be no end to my ingenuity in bypassing the most ominous aspects of the void.

Which was how I ended up attempting to deflect Adam's decidedly disconcerting comment while we lay in bed that night. "That was a hell of a doozy you shared this morning," he said. "I'd forgotten how bad it'd been for you as a kid. I'm so glad you two had a chance for a little re-do these past few years." He paused. "You must be missing her."

Without a beat, I responded non-sequiturishly, "I wonder if they've advanced Callay to the front of the waiting list for the Children's Center yet. Gunther reminded me this morning that they've had free, universal preschool in Sweden for nearly ever. The whole preschool situation in the US is ridiculous. Particularly in cities like ours. To start with, they're so bloody expensive. I don't know how people without means manage it. And then having to go on a waiting list almost as soon as a baby is born—"

Adam, however, was quite used to my capacities for obfuscating diversions. Throwing a somewhat sweaty leg across my thigh, he cupped my cheek with his hand before repeating a slight variation of his initial query. "You've seemed a little distressed lately, love. Is it your mom? Are you missing her badly?"

Reflecting that it was rather selfish of me to be suffering the absence of my mother when my own dendrites were already well-developed, I responded in some surprise, "Well, actually, I suppose I am. Her absence is like a nagging, background ache. It's irrational, really. It wasn't as if we were *that* close when she was alive, though it really was getting better. A lot better. I'm so grateful for that. But even at our best times, we never quite achieved the kind of easy relationship that some women have with their mothers. The kind that Sammie and Aadita have. Or Dhani and Angelina." *The kind that I hoped to create with Callay.* "But there's still something about having someone on the planet who's known you forever. Someone who'd die for you."

Adam pulled back a bit and stared at me, his green eyes big and round. He said huskily, "I would die for you."

"Would you?" I stared back at him, then looked away. "I guess you would."

I knew I was blushing. How insensitive of me to complain about missing my mother when Adam had lost his own at birth. A wave of compassion washed over me that was almost physical. "I would die for *you*, too."

He regarded me soberly, as if trying to discern whether or not to believe me. He looked tired. I noted for the first time that dark semicircles had begun to form beneath his beautiful eyes. There were faint lines beginning to etch into his skin from his nose to the corners of his mouth. It hit me like a burning coal. He would grow old. Whether I felt that I'd die for him or not, he *would* die.

I grabbed his hand and put it to my mouth, held it there in a near-bite, as Buster occasionally did to me, presumably to ensure I knew he'd claimed me.

I was hardly prepared for Adam's whispered, "Do you still love me, Fleur?"

I sat up. "Adam. How can you even ask me that?"

His eyes shifted away and back again. "The porn. I worry that I killed it. Killed your love for me."

In a weird mental association, the image of Cesar, dancing in his thong, flashed before me. "No. Well, no. But ..." I paused. "Something did change for a while."

"It felt like a weakness to you, didn't it?"

His line of questioning was too earnest for me to give him anything but the most honest response. "If needing is a weakness, then I guess it did. And it did start to feel like an addiction, like a need with a life of its own. But, really, I worried that I wasn't enough for you. It made me feel so sad. And rejected."

"Fleur, you will always be enough for me. But, let's be fair: I did try to explain. I didn't always feel that I *had* you."

"You have me." I laughed nervously. "You're stuck with me."

"No, really, Fleur. This isn't funny."

It wasn't. I looked at him, saw his naked devotion and, yes, his naked need.

"Really," I said. "You *are* stuck with me forever. If you want me." I knew it was true as I said it. My love for Adam had initially been sparked by his beautiful maleness. It was an intelligent maleness, shot through with tenderness, patience, and persistence. But over time he'd become something close to what Grandfather had been to me. And Mother, in her own way. To the bone and bowel and breath of me, he was my family.

And I knew that I needed *him*. Desperately.

Afterward, I realized what a precarious place we'd been in. The love that Adam and I made that night put all those porn videos to shame. There was no mad scrambling to penetrate or be penetrated, but rather a protean dance of two bloodstreams, two rivers burbling and surging toward confluence. He was in me, and I in him, and between us there was a nearly unending vista of discovery and deepening, as well as the certainty of eventual loss to remind us that every single moment of it mattered.

Time, as Einstein would have us believe, is relative, but death, for those of us who love, is not.

Chapter Eighteen

I MAY HAVE gotten to a whole new place in my lovemaking with Adam, but I'd completely forgotten to discuss with him the challenge that ultraviolet rays might pose to our project. That question came back to me as soon as I saw Sally Price at the lab. We were the first ones there that morning, and I helped her carry in the second batch of boxes of dead butterflies.

"I mean, it would be tragic if we enabled people to dematerialize only to have them develop melanoma years afterward."

"Crikey," she commented, setting down her own burden. "I'm out of my depth on that one, but I don't know how you can predict something like that ahead of time."

"Right?" I slid my box next to hers, then walked toward the lab sink. Even though I hadn't personally handled the deceased lepidopterans, I felt the need to cleanse myself after carrying them. I spoke to Sally over my shoulder. "I don't know if we can, but I'm going to raise it with Adam. I meant to do it last night, but we got ... busy with other things. If anyone might have an insight on how to exercise the Precautionary Principle on this one, he will."

Sally met my comment with silence, then said, "You're lucky to have someone at home to talk to. Now that Cat's gone, I've taken to talking out loud to myself." I knew that her beautiful calico had died fairly recently of old age, but she hadn't spoken much about her loss.

Now, scooting a rolling wooden chair toward me—we'd convinced Caltech to dispose of the fossil-fuel-based polypropylene ones—she grinned painfully. "And what's worse is that I'm answering back. Sometimes I have whole conversations." She made a face. "Pretty weird, huh?"

I plonked myself next to her, hooking my toes under the foot ring. "Not really. I've managed to be odd even while living with others all my life, so lord knows how weird I'd be if I lived alone." She looked dubious. "I mean it. It sounds painful. Actually, what *is* it like to be on your own, day in, day out?"

"Do you really want to know?"

"Cross my heart."

And then Sally proceeded to open a window into her mind and beckoned me inside. As Adam had informed me early on, "The way to feel closest to someone is to know what they're struggling with." Sally amplified her experience in such detail that I ended up quoting her verbatim in a new list I composed that very night, titled, "Ways in Which Other People Vanquish Their Voids, Subset Sally Price." And in case you're curious, here it is:

1. "You're so full of unshared thoughts that you tend to yack the head off of anyone who'll listen to you.

2. "Any odd habit you've ever had will now dig in and become something of an old friend. Me, I like to tear off little bits of napkins and twirl them into long strands to relieve what I guess must be my anxiety. It must be a holdover from the Greek side of my heritage, sort of like worry beads. Or, now that I think of it, Buddhist *malas*. I find the damned things in pajama pockets, unconsciously tucked into books as book marks, wriggling like little white worms on the floor. Cat used to love to steal them and swallow them whole; I'd find them spiraled inside his dried poops in the litter box.

3. "I really do talk to myself. Actual conversations. And tell myself jokes. And laugh at them.

4. "I think about earthquakes too much. I can't fall asleep until I've put slippers and my robe right next to my bed, along with a flashlight and house and car keys and ID information on a necklace I can quickly fling over my head. Back when Cat was alive, I kept a cat carrier with food in it right by the front door.

5. "I walk around in my jammies most of the time. Can't stand bras, and there's no one here to make my titties de-sag for. And I find myself sort of slumping on the sofa like an old lady, as if the gravity in my home is heavier than outside.

6. "I don't brush my teeth, or my hair, for that matter, as often as I would if I were breathing on someone and they could see me. I worry that that means that I'm either a primitive at heart or that I don't matter as much to myself when I don't matter to someone else.

7. "Which leads to the worst of it. And this one gets reserved for late at night. After I've pummeled myself to exhaustion with some obsession like *Sons of Anarchy* or the enzymes in dead butterflies, I think about death. A lot. How I'm going to die. When I'm going to die. If it'll be quick and relatively painless, which would have the downside of preventing me from saying goodbye to the people I love, or if I'll suffer the long, drawn-out death of some incurable cancer or Parkinson's or Alzheimer's, which always struck me as like living in a torture chamber. I try to remind myself to keep some pills in stock so I can save myself from such misery, but when the morning comes I forget all about it.

8. "And sometimes, and this is the most embarrassing, and you mustn't mention any of this to anyone, I imagine that I do die and wonder who will feel terrible about it and who will say a quick, 'Oh, that's too bad,' before going merrily on their way. Maybe it's

because I have no living family that I assume there'll be more of those than the former. I know it sounds masochistic and maybe a little martyr-y, but it illustrates the kinds of weirdness that can take over when it's just me, myself, and I."

It was the last one that nearly killed me. Sally and I stared at each other. She'd stood up at some point, and I'd unconsciously gotten up to join her, facing her awkwardly with my hands clasped in front of me like a movie usher. I knew that some soppy reassurance that I loved her and would miss her terribly would hardly do justice to the depth of loneliness she'd just described. I felt spoiled, all my life having been surrounded by people who cared about me, including at Father's house, where even at the height of my odd-duckishness, I sensed that Grandfather and Jillily and Nana and Sister Flatulencia and Fayga and Cook and Ignacio and Dhani were my tribe, if a fairly cockamamie one. And now, of course, I had someone who'd run into a burning house to save me, who'd die for me.

Disciplining the impulse to pinch, I allowed one long python of a sigh to wind its way out of me. The "word" that finally emerged was not unlike Grandfather's *ugga umph ugga.*

I finally mustered the focus to say, "You might feel like it's weird, but it's not." I thought about sharing with her all my own preoccupations with the void and the Green-eyed Monster and how much time our species had left on the planet. But instead, I added, "Actually, that's just the point. None of it is. Weird, I mean. I'll bet if we did a statistical analysis of what people think about when they're living alone, it would look a lot like what you've described." (What I didn't tell her was that I'd be recording an informal study of it now in my list.)

"Ya think?" Sally laughed. "Nah. I'm more of a mind that it shows that I'm ca-razy!" She did an odd little whirl, capped by making illustrative circles with her index finger by the side of her head.

Now, and only now, did it feel right and safe to hug her. I wrapped my arms around her, marveling at the lack of bulges in her lean frame as I whispered in her ear, "Thank you so much for telling me this. Don't think for a minute that I don't take it seriously."

Suddenly, I had an idea and pushed her away to arm's length. "Would you like to move in with us?" As I could see the automatic objection begin to rise up from her throat, I put up a hand. "Please don't go knee-jerk on me. You know we've already got an extended household. And we love it. It's how I grew up, and Adam was so lonely in that big house of his childhood without a mother and with his father in Washington most of the time that he loves it, too. We've actually got two more extra bedrooms, one with a full bath. And we adore you. We could talk butterflies twenty-four/seven. And you could even teach me how to twirl paper. Think about it. Please." By the end, I felt I was asking as much for my own benefit as for hers. I wasn't sure I'd be able to sleep at night knowing Sally was going through all that torture by herself.

I saw her struggling with what I'd said and counted it as a good sign that she was speechless.

When I said goodbye at the end of the day, I forestalled her teary "Thank you for what you said earlier—"

"Just think about it," I insisted.

***

I have to admit that I was rather busy congratulating myself on the morning that Sally moved in. Adam and I didn't want to embarrass her by hiring a moving company, but we were worried about how she was going to manage the hefty moving fees until Melky and Tom and Amir saved the day by offering to do the heavy lifting. Actually, Melky alone probably could have handled the job, but none of us wanted to say so. It wasn't that she was bringing tons of stuff with her. Most of it was going into storage with the unspoken assumption that she'd make a household for herself again at some point, presumably with a man. (You've probably gathered by now that Sally Price, with her intriguing blend of Greek and Japanese heritage, was unusually attractive.) But still, what she brought with her was heavy: her bed was a beautiful and gigantic pine four-poster; it had a nearly-matching armoire, and a scientist's collection of books was nothing to sneeze at but for the dust accumulated behind older tomes. So Tom and Amir and Melky groaned and sneezed their way up our staircase to Sally's bedroom, with beams of light and the smell of jasmine streaming in through the opened windows, and Lukie prepared to dust each book before putting it away into the wall-to-ceiling bookcases. We all knew that Sally would rearrange them to her tastes as soon as Lukie was out of sight, but no one had the heart to stop her.

The whole household was excited about the new member of our family. Callay couldn't stop tugging at everyone's pant legs and announcing that "Thrpryce" had come to stay, and Melesse and Sofiya had made a banner for her bedroom door bejeweled with sequins and Day-Glo hearts and flouncy lettering announcing brightly, "Welcome Home, Sally!" Sofiya couldn't stand still, running up and down the staircase as each piece of furniture was delivered. She was all elbows and knees these days, having shot up nearly half a foot in half a year. Makeda liked to affectionately say to her, "How did I know that my daughter was going to become a tree?" As for Buster, he'd offered Sally perhaps the sweetest greeting ever, jumping onto her queen bed as soon as Melky and Tom set it down and kneading the bare mattress like a conqueror, purring loudly all the while.

"I think someone might have a bedmate if she wants one," I commented. Sally flashed me a questioning look until I added, "You'd be doing us a huge favor. Buster likes to get in between us when we're sleeping, and it drives Adam nuts."

It hadn't escaped my attention that I'd actually invited the woman Adam had fantasized having a threesome with into our home. I'd raised the fact that I'd invited her as soon as I'd returned home that night, realizing with a thudding heart that it was terribly bad form to fail to consult with him before asking her. It was his home every bit as much as mine, never mind that Mother had paid for it. He raised an eyebrow when I broached it, his hands still covered in suds from Callay's bath. I myself was holding our child at that moment, as if I were unconsciously protecting myself from any possible objection.

"You really should have asked me first, but of course we should have her here. The truth is, I love you even more for your generosity." He paused and ventured cautiously, "Are you sure you'll be okay with it?"

I shot back quickly, "Is there any reason I shouldn't be?"

He rubbed his bottom lip between his thumb and forefinger, a "tell" that he was struggling with how to say something. Finally, he muttered, "Talk about beating around the bush." Then he flushed. "No pun intended."

But I didn't laugh. He said, "Here, let's get this little girl to bed first."

Of course, that took another hour. We had a whole ritual with Callay. "Good night," I'd say, to which she'd append, "*Thleep* tight." And then Adam's, "Don't let the bedbugs bite." Actually, we'd had a whole go 'round on that one the first time, explaining that it was just an expression, which, needless to say, we struggled to explain, finally calling it a joke. She liked jokes. Especially those of the knock-knock variety. My favorite, which she must have learned from Sister Flatulencia, since we certainly hadn't taught it to her, went like this:

"Knock knock."

"Who's there?"

"Olive."

"Olive who?"

"Olive you," in the sweetest voice ever. And then we'd all melt into a puddle together.

She *was* an unusually sweet child. At least *we* thought so. But then, we thought she was unusually everything.

But this night, we collapsed onto our bed fully clothed after tucking her in and turning out her overhead lights (but leaving on the duck-billed nightlight from my own childhood, the one with the chipped beak). I felt a bit dazed with exhaustion, and I found myself starting to drop off until Adam broke in. "I'm over it, you know."

I sat up. "Over what?"

"The three-way thing. Actually, Sally, too. Don't get me wrong. I like her and everything. And she's pretty. Very pretty. But ..." He shrugged. "The truth is, the only one I've ever really wanted was you, Fleur. And now that you've come back to me"—that one made me so sad—"I can't get enough of the way it feels to be with you." He came closer, licking my ear. "Not just with you. Inside you. Inside the folds and twists of you."

A bit shocked, I blushed. I'd never heard Adam—or any man, for that matter—describe what it felt like to insert his member into a tweeter. But why shouldn't a penis have a whole host of sensations when it was inside a vagina? I certainly had a full share of my own discrete physical experiences when he was inside *me*. I searched his face for whether he really was over Sally and it really did seem that he spoke the truth. Relieved, I said, "I *thought* something had changed. You've seemed a bit more ... intense. Honestly, we should probably both thank Sally." I laughed nervously. "But not literally." Shyly, I shared with him as if it were a secret, "It changed for me, too."

He kissed me then, long and slow the way I liked it. The way we both did. He rolled fully to his side and pulled me close, his member poking my belly.

"I think we should take our clothes off," I murmured.

"You're not too tired?"

"For you?" I said, pulling my T-shirt over my head, then un-hooking my bra. I saw him staring at my erect nipples. I knew he still loved my breasts, though they hung a few inches lower these days. I took his hand and put it against me. I felt myself dissolve as he stroked me and moistened me with his lips. I caught myself whisper-ing soundlessly as if from the outermost edge of an event horizon, "Have to tell Sam. Mazzy Star."

Chapter Nineteen

THE FIRST MONTH of Sally staying with us proved to be what Adam had dubbed "a regular cackle fest." It was true. Put three women together in one household, and if they were deeply fond of each other, it wasn't just their menses that synced up.

Sometimes Sammie joined us, but all too often she brought Amira with her. The latter had decided to edit her film here in SoCal, which meant that I was being subjected rather regularly to the tone of condescension she seemed to reserve solely for me.

On a night when Makeda and Melky had gone out and Adam had joined Tom and Amir and Gunther for a night of billiards, I confided my discomfort to Sally, who merely laughed and said, "Sweet Fleur. You do realize she's jealous, don't you?"

Dummkopf! The thought had never occurred to me. Did other people suffer as badly from the Green-eyed Monster as I did? Even people like Amira, with her wit and her winged eyebrows and her olive skin like silk? I really needed to learn to do what Adam often urged on me: "Give it a rest."

Which was why I agreed to go with Sammie and Amira to The Move, West Hollywood's historic gay dance club, before its planned demolition to make way for a megalithic hotel and retail complex. They couldn't wait to dress up for Flamenco Night, and I had to confess that, despite my ongoing discomfort with Amira, I relished the prospect of finding a fun costume for a night out on the town. It would be a far cry from the sweatshirts and Birkenstocks that were pretty much *de rigueur* at Caltech. The flamenco number I managed to dig up at Shelly's Dance and Costume ("Where Every Body Fits In") was a long, black, crepe V-necked dress, a bit more formfitting than I would have preferred, but the diagonal, vibrant red ruffles at the calves and wrists took the attention away from the amplitude of my hips and breasts. I decided to accessorize with a beautiful black silk shawl with embroidered red flowers that Mother had brought back from Spain. I could have sworn it still bore a hint of her Chanel No. 5 when I swirled it over my shoulders.

When Sam arrived to fetch me, wearing a gorgeous turquoise and black dress with a matching vest, she looked absolutely stunning. I gasped, then directed a long, pitiful look at Adam before I followed her out the door.

I'd told him earlier, while he was watching me get dressed with great curiosity, that I was dreading the evening just a little.

"Why?" he'd asked. "Is it because you'll miss me?"

I minced over, the dress still around my knees before being coaxed over my hips, and batted his chest playfully. "It's not all about you, you know."

Laughing, he helped me inch the garment over my hips, giving me gooseflesh with little chicken-peck kisses of various parts of my body along the way. He studied me with appreciative appraisal once I managed to do a twirl for him

"Okay, I'll bite." Then he snorted. "That was a Freudian slip if there ever was one. Well, what *is* it about?"

"Oh, I don't know. Me at a gay club. Or LGBTQ, or whatever I'm supposed to call it."

"Hmm. That sounds hostile and maybe even a little homophobic. Is this the same woman who fought with me over going to the Gay Survival Parade?"

"Yes, but this is more ... I mean, what if someone makes a pass at me?"

He looked me up and down, murmuring, "Which they'd be crazy not to do."

"No, Adam. Don't be silly. I'm not fishing for compliments."

"What are you fishing for? Permission not to go?"

"No, I'm not. Actually, it's not that at all. It's Amira. I think she hates me. And honestly, I'm not so sure I like *her*."

Adam raised a familiar eyebrow. "Well, that *is* a problem. She's your best friend's girlfriend."

"I know, and I wouldn't dream of telling Sam. But what am I ever going to do?"

He frowned and rubbed his chin. "I think it's good that you're going. Maybe if you're able to be with each other in a more let-loose kind of environment, some of that tension will fall away. I've heard that people go wild at The Move."

"I don't want to go wild," I wailed. "I just don't want to feel strained when I'm with Sam." I spread my hands haplessly. "Amira seems to be part of the package these days."

"Ah. Jealousy. It does seem to kick up from time to time."

"That's what Sally thought. But I think it's more than that. I don't get to have my best friend as my own anymore. Do all the things we used to do together."

"Jealousy," Adam pronounced solemnly. "We were both only children. We have a hard time sharing."

"*We?* Do you, too?"

"Isn't that part of what we've been struggling with? And not just in a way that impacted our sex life. I lost a lot of your special attention when Callay came along. And then there's been Makeda and the girls. And Melky. And Sally."

When I looked at it that way, I felt awful. "Oh dear. Do you resent them?"

"No, but I've had to stretch. And I do believe the stretching has been good for me."

I felt flooded with gratitude. "You're a good man, Adam. I hope you don't still think you're too nice."

He laughed. "Did I say that?"

"You did. At Shutter's. When we first—"

But he interrupted me. "Nice? *Moi?*" He grabbed me, pretend roughly, and slid a hand under my skirt.

I giggled but moved away. "Sammie will be here any minute. We can't." I unconsciously plucked at my wrist ruffle.

"What is it?"

Do you think that's why Makeda and Melky are looking for their own place? That it's too 'stretchy' living with so many people?"

"It might certainly play a part." He paused. "They're trying to get pregnant, you know."

"Are they?" I marveled. And then I felt a pang that even I recognized as jealousy. "How did you find out?"

Adam bopped me gently on the head with a bed cushion. "Because Melky's my mate, that's how."

My jealousy wasn't so intense that it could stop me from breaking into a broad grin. "Oh, Adam, and to think that she'd almost given up sex forever."

"I know," he said. "You've been a miracle in her life."

"Not just me. You. Modern science. That surgery she had was a godsend." I let myself soak it in. "But I'm going to miss her and the girls. And Melky."

"I know, love. Me, too."

"But I doubt that I'd miss Amira if she left tomorrow."

Given all that, you can imagine how I felt as—Sammie having gotten into the car behind the Lyft driver—I had no choice but to slide into the back seat next to Amira, who was in the middle. In the light of the still-open car door, I could see that my nemesis wore a simple, sophisticated black sheath and pointed flat-heeled shoes, a floral Spanish comb in her wavy hair her sole concession to tonight's theme. Suddenly, my dress felt way too gaudy, like a kid's Halloween costume, and my skin began to prickle with shame.

But Amira paid no attention to what I wore, just smiled one of her mysterious smiles, granted me a quick, "Hello, Fleur," then turned to Sam and initiated what became a rather lingering kiss. Our Lyft driver was an older man, seemingly of Arabic descent. In the rearview mirror, I spied his darkly disapproving expression. I vowed then to be a better person, starting with commenting brightly to Amira as she finally turned to face forward, "I can't wait to see what everyone's wearing! Thanks so much for including me." Which was received with an imperious nod of her head.

As it happens, The Move was aptly named. Once Sam and I managed to extricate our long dresses from the Ford Fusion, and after Amira rose onto the sidewalk like water pouring backward, we passed under a high red arch to join a pulsing phenomenon composed of individual parts that coalesced—thanks to rousingly hypnotic fandango clapping, myriads of mirrored disco balls, and lustrous light shows displayed on large, suspended screens—into a viscously oozing organism. We fumbled for a table, and a waiter instantly materialized like magic from the crowd.

Taking a sip of my sangría, I let my eyes close halfway and wasn't sure if it was a trick of my vision or something more objectively real, but the upraised arms and undulating torsos of the dancers made fractal-like patterns on the walls. Had Busby Berkeley had some similar experience to prompt his dazzling choreography? Sammie and I used to love to watch his films on the small telly in her bedroom, cuddled side by side under the covers with our matching hot chocolate mustaches. I felt a voidish pang rip through me as I realized we'd undoubtedly never do that again. As if to emphasize that conclusion, Sammie and Amira rose up simultaneously to dance. I followed them with my eyes and then stopped. For there were Cesar and Fidel doing pretty much what they'd been doing—and wearing pretty much what they'd been wearing, with a few flamenco accompaniments, including a floral fan for Fidel and gypsy bells on Cesar's ankles—the day Mother climbed Fidel's fence and suffered her concussion.

I hadn't realized until then how much I'd blamed Cesar for Mother's untimely death, convinced that she'd lost her balance—and her judgment—thanks to that awful blow to her head. As Cesar did a grind with his hips and executed a 360-degree turn with swift precision, I felt the gorge rise in my throat. On top of everything else, how would Gladys feel if she knew she'd come all the way to this country to have her supposed sweetheart dressing up on the sly like a cheesy porn star?

Nearly knocking over my chair, I pushed past dancing couples of every description and sexual persuasion to feel my way to the ubiquitous line in front of the ladies' room, breathing as deeply as I could to forestall the retching I knew was to come. I had progressed to third place when a diminutive and very prettily handsome man emerged from the restroom, making me look up to the ladies' room sign to make sure I was in the right line. The young man wore slicked back blond hair with sexily twirled sideburns, striking spots of coral rouge on his pale cheeks, a beautifully embroidered bolero jacket, and flared black trousers that revealed ridiculously high stiletto heels. He was like a very handsome, but tiny, conquistador. As he was about to pass me, his slightly slanted eyes slid over and locked onto mine. Before I knew it, he'd grabbed me and was giving me such a close embrace that I could smell the sweet orange on his breath. "Fleur! How wonderful to see you! Did you see Cesar and Fidel? They're somewhere over this way. Come and have a drink with us!"

The next thing I knew, the Conquistador Who Was Gladys had grabbed her two companions from the dance floor and seated the three of us with her around a small table so cramped that my right knee, its skin exposed by my ruched up ruffles, touched hers. I was sure I'd get a rash, as her pants were surely made of wool. Rubbing against my still-covered left knee was Cesar's bare one. Fidel was slightly sloshed and smiled at me fondly, as if recalling our intimate conversation at his kitchen table. I don't know what we talked about as we four sat there, but I must have managed to keep up my end of the conversation, as Sammie told me on the way back home that I'd seemed very engrossed. But frankly, our departure couldn't come soon enough for me.

Our driver this time turned out to be one of Sammie's old art school friends. She and Sam were chattering away with reminiscences in the front seat of a Prius. Seated with Amira in the rear, I felt Sammie's lover scrutinizing me as I described who Cesar, Gladys, and Fidel were. I took care to omit mention of Fidel as the murderer of Chin Hwa and of Cesar turning on me the day Mother had taken her tumble over Fidel's gate. Nor did I speak of Fidel's confidences regarding his father pulling his *pene* when he was little and his uncle viciously rubbing in the memory of it.

Speaking of self-censorship, I dared not say a word to either Sammie or her girlfriend about the upheaval the evening had stirred inside me. The sexual revolution had begotten a fluidity that allowed a seemingly simple girl like Gladys to play with her persona and a man like Cesar to find his heart's desires with her. I desperately wanted to be in tune with the progress of the times, but this all felt so strange to me.

But then I reminded myself of all my years as the odd duck in whatever community I inhabited. The fact was, I was the one who was trying to literally abracadabra people in and out of material reality. You couldn't get much more fluid than that.

Chapter Twenty

IT WAS STANLEY I ended up confiding in about my own version of gender confusion. "Meaning," I said to him, "my confusion about what to think and feel about all this. I find myself wondering if it's accidental that our species can no longer rely on either our traditions or our instincts at a time when we're facing the very real possibility of extinction. Whether this existential threat to our biosphere is affecting the balance of our politics, our morality, our sexuality, our level of aggression. What if sex is becoming increasingly divorced from tenderness and the categories of male and female are blurring because procreation is about to become obsolete?"

"Rats crowded in a cage, eh? It's a hell of a leap, and maybe even a possibility—"

I interrupted him in my agitation. "Not everyone I know would think so."

"The thing is, Fleur, you're a quantum physicist, which means you also have a philosophical bent of mind. We physicists are always looking for something to wrap up the whole show with some nice, elegant bow: how many iterations have there been of supposed theories of everything? The great TOE. You know as well as I do that the damned thing continues to elude us. Maybe because it doesn't actually exist. And if we can't find it in the physical world, it's pretty damned unlikely we'll discover it in human nature. Maybe there's no one reason things have gotten so complicated for our species. Maybe what you're fretting over is pretty much down to the old saw, 'What's one man's meat is another man's poison.'"

"You're telling me that the revulsion I feel over porn or my discomfort over the cheesy cross-dressing of someone like Cesar is just my personal biases putting me on the wrong side of history? That maybe I'm just a prude?"

Stanley raised an eyebrow. "Did you hear me say that?"

I sighed. "No. But I've wondered about it myself."

Stanley stopped to study my face. We were on our way to the Huntington's rose garden and, though we hadn't exactly been skipping—both of us having pretty much aged out of that ritual—we'd been making our way at a good pace, as per Dr. Drew's instructions to, as Stanley put it, "keep this old ticker going until I at least get to see Dreamization put into action and the orange-haired asshole put behind bars." I seriously doubted that his doctor had put it that way and that Stanley would actually get to see the latter—I think many of us feared it might actually trigger a civil war. But I prayed he'd celebrate the former with us and then, along with Gwen, live on as close to forever as was possible. I couldn't bear the thought of being orphaned for yet another time.

"You have a habit of being too hard on yourself, my girl. I'd let go of the prude bit. If you don't like pornography, you don't like pornography. Frankly, I think most women, at least, would agree with you." I gave Stanley a sharp look. He grinned and shrugged his shoulders. "Let's just leave it at that." Then he took a deep breath. "But you might consider that you *have* gotten a little taste of something we all end up confronting in ourselves."

"What's that?"

"Intolerance. Your own version of what spewed from my lips at Assefa. Except I presume you've been smart enough to keep your own yap shut, at least with Cesar. It sounds like he's had a pretty rough time of it."

I nodded, feeling rather miserable. When Stanley put it like that, I felt nothing but shame. Perhaps as a distraction, I found myself replaying in my mind my most recent encounter with Assefa, which had occurred just a week ago: me sitting in my car to hear the last of

Sting's melancholy lyrics about human fragility before sprinting across campus for a meeting on quantum entanglement at UCLA's Department of Physics; Assefa synchronistically wheeling Ife's stroller with one hand past Ackerman Student Union while he held out his iPhone with the other. As we got closer, I nearly laughed aloud at the song playing on his phone. Maybe you guessed it. "Fragile," of course. *Snap!*

Einstein hadn't been whistling Dixie when he'd reversed his earlier dismissal of non-locality as "spooky action at a distance." My experiences with Assefa over the years continued to affirm that not only two particles, but two people and maybe even any number of people, once connected in properties—and no matter how far apart—continued to act in concert.

As always, my ex-lover seemed taken aback when he saw me and was rather reserved in his greeting: a quick peck on each cheek and then the obligatory Ethiopian third to conclude the process. He turned off the music. I explained what I was up to.

"Ah. Always the physicist."

"Not always," I objected defensively, bending down to plant a smooch on Ife's sun-warmed head. "That's like saying you're always the doctor. I'm also a parent. Just like you."

"Yes," he granted. "I didn't mean anything by it."

"Never mind," I said, erasing with my hand the stilted air between us. "How can this little girl be so adorable? Where's Lemlem?"

"Actually,"—he seemed to grin despite himself—"speaking of parenthood, she's waiting for her first ultrasound. It's a great department, but Ife was getting restless in the waiting room. We decided that I should give her a little break before we rejoin her mama. They take forever at the OBGYN clinic." He pronounced it "ob gyne."

"Oh my," I said, "You two didn't waste any time." Then, realizing that might sound a little judgmental, I amended, "What I should say is, you must be more energetic than I am. When Callay was this one's age, I couldn't dream of handling another sleep stealer."

For the first time, he let down his guard. "I know exactly what you mean, but we've bought a new home here in Westwood, and there's room enough for *Enat* to join us. Grandmothers are a strange breed. She can't wait to stay up all night with the new baby." Then he seemed to realize what he'd said. "Oh, I am so sorry …."

"Please, Assefa. No worries. It's true, and you're right, I'd give anything to have her back, but there it is. Like the man says, life is fragile." Assefa cocked his head curiously, and I explained about the synchronicity.

"Ah." Assefa allowed himself to look at me then. *Really* look at me, rather than that sideways thing he tended to do these days. "Yes," he said. "I see." And then he added, "That song, it is so beautiful, and yet he sings of the pain of war."

At that moment, perhaps because I, too, had my limits when it came to really connecting with the man who'd meant the world to me, I became aware that Ife was looking up at us expectantly. I knelt and took her hand in mine. Already, her little fingers were finely molded and slender. Like her father's. I stifled a sigh. "I'll bet you want to get back to your mommy."

She howled with glee. "Enat!"

Assefa and I didn't even say goodbye. We didn't need to. I watched him push the stroller away, his back and buttocks looking as strong and supple as I remembered. I found myself hoping such chance encounters would continue to occur over my lifetime, not because I wanted to be with him anymore—I really didn't—but because, if I were a starling, he would surely be one of my seven. I needed his presence in the world to keep me rooted enough in my past to proceed with my future. We'd been through a war or two of our own, but despite our awkwardness with each other, our bond felt anything but fragile.

Stanley's croaky voice brought me back to the present. He was waving a hand in front of my eyes. "Hello. Earth to Fleur. Anybody home?"

I snorted. Professor Stanley H. Fiske calling out anyone else on their absent-mindedness was a joke. "I'm here." And then I paused. "The thing is, Stanley, Assefa was as much a sinner in that awful moment as you were. He behaved abominably."

Stanley groaned. "He did, but I'm used to other people behaving badly. Hell, it would be naïve to underestimate humanity's capacity for nasty primitivity. Nations have been formed and untold millions have been killed because of it. But to find myself falling into the same damned stupidity?"

I felt for him. "As Sammie likes to say, we all have our shadows. Jung evidently thought that the brightest lights of our species cast the deepest ones." He picked up a rose petal that had wafted over from her host's invisible bed. I leaned over for a sniff and commented, "It might be from a Bathsheba. She's got both the apricot hue and the slightly honeyed scent."

Stanley stared at me uncomprehendingly for a moment, then went on, "If Sammie and her Jung are right about those shadows, then maybe we both need to forgive ourselves."

"Maybe. At least you've performed an act of redemption. It's got to be a lot easier to forgive yourself after going the extra mile for Assefa afterward. He would never have met Lemlem but for your arranging his transfer to New York."

He shot me an appraising look. "Nor for you, my dear. The whole thing wouldn't have played out the way it did without you."

That one stopped me in my tracks. God, it was true! How much did we need those miserable moments of failing each other and being failed to move where we were meant to go? And how far back would we have to unwind our fates to discern the trajectory of our unfolding?" I reached a hand into the air and let it lead me into a couple of twirls, aware of the sun shining down on my body as I danced, and amazed that I still had a few pirouettes left in me.

I had to admit that Stanley was right. The butterfly effect was real. We had no idea whether our best efforts would lead to catastrophe or if our lapses and flaws might catalyze something wonderful. I said as much to him, adding, "But if it takes the deaths of precious butterflies to facilitate Dreamization and, possibly, prolong the human experiment on this planet, I doubt that would console the individual butterfly that's lost its own life."

As I spoke, a Red Admiral miraculously landed on my still outstretched wrist as if it wanted to take a whirl with me. It preened its black velvet wings with their bright red circles, thickly salted with white spots. I'd never had a butterfly land on me before, and this one seemed content to hang out awhile, tickling my skin just a little. Did it have any idea the impression it was making? I dared not move.

227

Stanley and I locked eyes, barely able to breathe. I saw a tear sneak down his cheek from beneath his Coke-bottle lenses. A slight whisper of wind stirred, and the butterfly took flight as suddenly as it had landed.

"Goodbye, you beauty!" I called after it. "And thank you!"

Stanley shook his head. "Only with you, Fleur. Only with you. You'll have me believing in God yet."

I nearly laughed, but I stopped myself. Who was I to dismiss the mysterious inter-relation of all things as anything but what people liked to call God? Most times, I tended to forget about that miraculous web of life that the Hindus ascribed to the god Indra. And then something like this occurred, and I realized that some other part of me knew it down to my bones.

When Stanley and I returned to the house at Rose Villa, Gwen was waiting for us with fresh mint tea, homemade shortbread cookies, and one of her riper rants. Stanley had prepared me for the latter as he huffed and puffed rather alarmingly on our way back. "She's started getting anxiety attacks. Pretty much a first for her. You know Gwen. Salty as hell, but solid as a rock. Her oncologist suggested an SSRI, but she's not convinced her distress should get medicated away. Says if she's not a little anxious after surviving cancer, a violent attack on a local gay rights parade, the death of a good friend, and a sociopath in the White House, there'd be something wrong with her. I can't say I disagree with her."

I couldn't disagree with Stanley. Hearing his labored breathing after a walk that used to be a vigorous skip not so many years ago, I was feeling pretty anxious myself.

It didn't exactly help when Gwen let it rip, waving the front page of *Science Times* in front of our faces. "No wonder I got sick. We're a fucking cancer on the face of this planet. How can we even look ourselves in the mirror? What other species shits on its own food source, commits matricide without a backward glance, knows it's making a beautiful planet uninhabitable, and distracts itself with an ignoramus tweeting his ignorance, thinking he's Tolstoy?"

Stanley sighed and put a hand on his sister's shoulder. "What is it this time, Gwen? You really do need to calm down a little. You know what the doctor said. This kind of agitation tends to build on itself."

I could see Gwen struggling to contain her rage. For a moment, she won, a torrent of tears washing her face. "It's the puffins. They're going down. I've adored them since I was a little girl."

I knew what she meant. For most of us, it was the eponymous publisher of children's books that had introduced us to the comical creatures with sad-looking eyes, sleek black caps, and matching bright orange webbed feet and outsized, curved bills.

"The books," I said, and Gwennie shot me a grateful look.

Stanley helped her to one of the living room sofas, where she continued. "Exactly. Every girl I knew was a Puffin reader. *Make Way for Ducklings. Madeline.*"

"*The Wind in the Willows,*" I threw in.

And from Stanley, "*Black Beauty!*" Gwen and I stared at him. "What? You think only girls read those books? My other reading at the time was *The Physical Review.*"

Gwennie and I avoided each other's eyes. Actually, she seemed to have settled down a little, perhaps feeling less alone. "I don't know how I can take it, guys. How many of my friends had to have a plush puffin beside her to get to sleep at night?" She looked across the room to Stanley, who sat in his favorite chair. "Do you remember that trip the folks took us on to Yorkshire? We actually got to see a flock of them at that freezing wildlife reserve."

"A circus," I interjected.

Disconcerted, Gwennie said, "No, they were wild."

Embarrassed, I responded hastily, "Don't mind me, Gwen. It's just that a flock of puffins are called a circus. Or an improbability. Or a puffinry."

Stanley nodded in acknowledgment, but didn't allow himself to get distracted. "I do remember," he said, sitting forward now. "Bempton Cliffs. You nearly fell off that wooden pier in your enthusiasm. I had to grab you before you went down."

"That's right!" she exclaimed. "How could I have forgotten? It was at that moment that I decided you were the best brother ever. And you have been."

Stanley flushed, muttering, "I don't know about that." He sighed. "It's not all gloom and doom, you know. Our Fleur is going to turn things around. I don't know if it'll save the puffins, but it should make a hell of a difference for a lot of species. Definitely our own."

Gwen turned her reddened child eyes towards me. No pressure, I thought. But that voice in my head seemed to take great delight in piggybacking on Stanley's sentiments.

Hurry, hurry, hurry.

Sanctus

The children of the world didn't even know what was hitting them. Tender of heart and organ, immune system and skin, they were the most vulnerable of their species to diseases made worse by toxins in the air, water, and soil. The little ones were increasingly suffering from allergies and asthma, mosquito-borne illnesses, extreme heat stress, poor nutrition, dehydration, childhood cancers, autism, hyper-activity, social anxiety and isolation. They were the least able to weather the impact of more and more wars, persecution, and conflict emanating from scarcity of resources and weather disasters.

Their parents, teachers, doctors, and governments claimed to love them more than themselves, but how many of those adults were actually demonstrating that love in ways that would make a difference? Would the children have a viable future? For how long? Would they live long enough to give birth to their own babies, to nourish their bodies and brains and hearts and make them safe to continue on?

The ennui of this world was impacting them powerfully. Resorting to the seductions of disembodied technologies; sarcasm; cynicism; and precocious, impersonal sex. Distracting themselves in screens and hyperactivity; avoiding emotional intimacy; cutting themselves; bullying and shooting each other; slamming their nervous systems with music full of hard rhythms and harsher lyrics; resorting to opiates and marijuana, alcohol and vapes; dulling themselves—as their grownups did—in dread of what was to come.

The World Soul cried out like the Mama Lion she was to whoever would actually listen: Hurry up now! You really must hurry! For the sake of the children, there's so little time!

Chapter Twenty-one

LITTLE DID I know that my sense of pressure was going to increase exponentially in the coming months, but not in the way I might have imagined. Talk about good things coming of something seemingly bad via the butterfly effect, I marked it all down to porn—or at least the way that grappling with it turned my love with Adam into a fire-tried stone.

The timing was crazy. Dreamization had reached the all-hands-on-deck stage.

Richard Feynman had emphasized that the central mystery of quantum mechanics was that everything in the universe had the nature of both a particle and a wave. Or, as philosophers have put it since Parmenides, life was made up of both being and becoming. The formidable task of Dreamization was to subject a particle to disappearance into a wave and reappearance from it, not just in the same place, but somewhere else via a wave activation mechanism we were working on and what I'd come to call the fractalized activation of C-Voids by spraying a light but potent mist made up of dead butterfly enzymes into a living creature's nose.

The process, as might have been anticipated, had taken much longer than we'd wished. As we prepared for our first test with a live mammal, we kept butting up against Heisenberg's Uncertainty Principle, which summarized the impossibility of simultaneously knowing the exact position and speed of an object, precisely because of Feynman's Central Mystery. Since waves are disturbances in space, how could we assign a wavelength's specific position? But we were closing in on our goal. Thanks to the mathematical brilliance of both Tom and Amir, we'd worked out some provisional formulas using what we'd been able to observe with our tardigrades, but it was quite possible that the dog we'd selected for our first trial, and even the one we'd chosen for its follow up, would be sacrificed on the altar of science. I didn't like to think about it and had, in fact, spent many a sleepless night over it, but I knew I had to be prepared. There was a ruthlessness to science that mimicked that of Mother Nature herself.

It didn't help that the dogs were hopelessly adorable. Dog number one was a three-year-old beagle we'd obtained from UCLA's Semel Institute after they'd finished their narcolepsy studies on him. Given what humans had already put him through, he was a surprisingly resilient and happy guy, wagging his tail at the approach of anyone willing to scratch his ears or give him a full out hug. Katrina conjectured that he was so delighted to be able to stay awake, he'd developed a degree of gratitude unusual even for a canine. We nicknamed him Good Time Charlie, as he kept breaking out of his confines and roaming our lab rooms until we'd find him blissed out beside a trash can, Krispy Kreme wrappers at his feet. The wrappers themselves looked half-eaten, as if the sugar buzz was so good, he'd be happy to chow down on wax paper if it afforded yet another taste of glazed cruller crumbs. I knew the feeling well.

Number two was initially a bit more reserved, but ultimately a very enthusiastic, red-haired terrier with the most plaintive eyes on the planet. He'd take awhile to warm up to you, but once he did, his rump would get going with a zeal that rivaled Miley Cyrus at the VMA Awards. It was Tom's idea to call him Hot Sauce.

Two things helped me in summoning my resolve.

The first was a conversation I had with Gwen in her backyard about her intention to attend an upcoming demonstration by local members of C the Big Picture against plans to build the West Coast's largest oil refinery in Carson. I think we were all amazed by the strength and determination Gwennie had regained since her illness, but it worried me awfully that she'd be trampled if counter-demonstrating Cacklers created trouble, especially since she'd recently suffered a serious bout of arthritis, perhaps as a belated side effect from her treatment, and would have to march with a cane.

"Oh, pish. These marches are pretty mellow. It's not like the old days when the LAPD just loved to bash demonstrators on the head. Even white ones," she added, presumably for emphasis.

I felt annoyed. "Yes, but it can't be good for you. How long is the walk?"

"Stop fussing. It's really not that far, and all I've got is a little garden variety arthritis. Frankly, my dear, I'd much rather creak than croak."

I had a hunch that it was important to her to prove to herself her hardiness after this latest physical insult, but I found myself saying anyway, "Why not let the young people do the demonstrating?"

"Listen, love. I learned something when I thought my death was imminent. I know it sounds counterintuitive, but I think the threat of climate extinction is actually worse in a way for the old. It shouldn't be. We're not the ones who'll suffer the worst of it. Not by a long shot. But our awareness of our own mortality makes the possible loss of all this simply intolerable." She swept the hand not leaning on her cane past the espaliered pomegranate hedge at our side, its orange-red blossoms posing sensuously in the light of the midday sun. "When your time is up, you need to know that this miracle will continue on. To think of our fellow humans never again experiencing the sheer lushness of life, the wild inventiveness of nature? There's no way to bear it. So this creaky old lady has no choice. I'm marching. Or at least hobbling."

Marching wasn't exactly what I was doing when I entered CVS a few days later, hesitantly sidling like a shamed teenager toward the bottommost shelf along the "Feminine Products" aisle. I hadn't said a thing to anyone and had barely been able to admit it to myself, but my period was late. I'd tried convincing myself that it was the stress over our upcoming Dreamization trial, but after multiple sleepless nights I knew I had to put my wondering to rest.

That night, I felt a pang while putting Callay to bed. She was on-ly twenty-three-months-old and was already having to suffer the irritabilities and absences of a working mother with a passion for something else besides her adorable little girl.

When I came out of her room, I could hear Adam and Makeda and Melky and Sally laughing uproariously downstairs. My heart beat quickly as I descended the staircase, the chandelier overhead casting spooky shadows before me with each step. Arriving at the kitchen, I saw Makeda standing at the counter, a glass of imported Mirinda orange soda in her hand. Now that she'd succeeded in getting pregnant, she was going by the book; I knew she'd be devastated if she lost this baby. The rest of the crew was drinking Cabernet Sauvignon; I could tell what it was by the purplish stain on Adam's lips, which only that one particular wine seemed to leave. He broke into a broad grin when he saw me and stood up. "Let me pour you a glass, hon."

Without thinking, I put up a hand. "No, I can't!"

"Why not?"

I sensed everyone staring at me. This wasn't going at all how I'd planned it. And still, they all stared. Sensing that any attempt at obfuscation would be doomed, I blurted out like a kindergartner, "Because I've got a bun in the oven."

Makeda and Melky looked confused, presumably unfamiliar with the idiom.

But Sally knew it quite well. She squealed with delight and rose to wrap her arms around me. "Congratulations!" She translated for our Ethiopian contingent, "Callay's going to have a baby brother or sister!"

Makeda clapped her hands together with glee. "Oh goody!" She turned to Melky. "Our baby already has his first best friend."

Adam, needless to say, was speechless. I was mortified.

Somehow we managed to get through the next half hour without a major argument. But as soon as we closed the bedroom door behind us, Adam spat through thinned lips, "How could you?"

"I didn't get pregnant on purpose."

He brushed my words aside. "Of course, you didn't. But that's no way to tell a man he's going to have a child."

I burst into tears.

But Adam didn't budge. "That won't do, Fleur. I need to know: what were you thinking?"

236

I shrugged haplessly. "I obviously wasn't. Thinking, I mean. I really don't know … oh, Adam, I'm so sorry. Everyone was looking at me, and I'd just found out, and the timing is wretched, and I feel so irresponsible. We'd never even discussed whether we wanted more children. And I couldn't possibly have another abortion. But how will we ever manage? And what if there's no viable planet for any child, let alone ours?" I paused, flushing. "It must have been that night. Remember? I was right in the middle of changing from Yasmin to Junel."

Despite his anger, a slight grin teased at the corners of Adam's lips. We'd had many a laugh over the years at the nutty names that pharmaceutical companies gave their drugs, including the newer class of contraceptive pills. But he clearly wasn't going to let me off the hook so easily. "Look, you hardly created this kid by yourself, but I still can't believe you didn't take the trouble to tell me in private."

I came across to him, unbearably humbled. "I can't either, my love. I won't blame it on my hormones. I'm an asshole."

He grabbed me then and pulled me to him, muttering into my ear. "Yes, you are. But my God, this has to be the best news ever."

I looked up at him through wet eyes. "It is?" Then, like an idiot, "Do you really mean it?"

"I do," he said, his chin bonking into my head as he spoke. He pulled me onto the bed with him and faced me, looking sweetly comical with his wine lipstick. "Our family is growing, Fleur. The fact that Callay won't be alone in the world when we're gone makes me happier than you can imagine." The thought of us being gone wasn't exactly what I wanted to be thinking about, but of course he was right.

It was a great relief that Adam slid so easily into the upending of our lives, since the baby was going to come much sooner than he might have expected. I'd been in such denial that we ended up at our OB's office the following week for our first ultrasound.

Thank God, everything looked good so far. The baby—and I was well aware that some people I knew would still choose to call it a fetus—was a tiny thing. Dr. Abalooni intoned, as if it had never occurred to him before, "I've never quite gotten over the fact that the smallest cell in a human body manages to create life with the largest cell in another one." Adam and I stared at him. He actually flushed. "The sperm and the egg."

"Ah," replied Adam kindly. "I don't think I knew that."

As Dr. Abalooni gently pressed his magic wand, AKA transducer, across my gelled-up belly, Adam exclaimed in awe, as if he'd never been through this ritual before, "Imagine. That little Sweet Pea already has fully developed fingers and toes. And ears where they should be."

I threw him a smile from my exposed position. "Sweet Pea. What a wonderful nickname. I like it."

Adam asked the doctor when we could determine our baby's gender. Told it might be as soon as four weeks from now, he murmured, "What if this kiddo turns out to be a Popeye, rather than a Sweet Pea?" I felt a frisson of anxiety and couldn't wait for the doctor to leave the room.

I let Adam help me up down from the examining table, and I accepted my bra and panties from him. Hooking up the bra strap beneath my somewhat saggy breasts, I frowned. "Do you have a preference? I know some men really want a son. But it could be another girl, you know."

He paused and seemed to consider my question seriously. "I'm not that guy, Fleur. I can see pluses either way, especially for Callay; having a little sister would allow her to share"—he laughed—"or fight over, her girly stuff. Whereas a little brother could be a real treat to boss around. Can't you just see our feisty little Monkey glorying over that?" I had to admit that I could. "I would have loved to have a sister to look up to. But I'd imagine that same-sex siblings experience a completely different level of bonding. What about you? Do you secretly hanker for a boy? Or another girl?"

I realized at that moment that I didn't care if this budding little human would be athletic or brainy, ugly or beautiful, tall or short, fair-haired or dark, male or female. It was the soul of our child I was already listening for and imagining. The rest was incidental. I just wanted our child to be healthy enough to have a good life and a thriving planet to flourish on.

We never know how—or if— we will ever resolve our internal conflicts. Sometimes we end up resigned to living with them until, as

Nana used to say, the cows came home. But sometimes something out of the blue flicks the cows' tangled tails in just the right way to make the seemingly immovable bovines budge. I stifled the temptation to phone Cesar right there and then to offer him an apology. Who cared if he liked sliding from male to female and back again?

Instead, as soon as Adam and I arrived home from the ultrasound, we called out to whoever might be home to come and see the first shiny photo of our Sweet Pea, with the little darling's proportionally outsized head resembling nearly every movie alien and its diminutive feet flung upward as if on a swing. As it happens, all but Makeda and Callay were out, though Makeda did a pretty good imitation of a crowd when she came running, Callay in tow, marveling at our baby's ultrasound image with a hand on her own slightly pooched belly. We all settled in the kitchen, where she oohed and ahhed and Callay fiddled on the floor with a nursery rhyme puzzle that actually played the appropriate songs when you pulled the illustrated pieces off the wooden board. Adam stood at the counter composing a list for a Whole Foods run. We tried showing our Monkey the admittedly blurry photo of our family's new baby, but she seemed unable to get the concept, commenting briefly on her new sibling's contours, "That what Caycay wear for Hoween?"

While Adam did his duty at the market, Makeda and I took Monkey outside to play on her swing. We spoke a bit about the three-bedroom townhouse that she and Melky had found less than a mile away on Los Robles Avenue. I think we both felt that the invisible umbilicus between us didn't want to stretch too far. I was truly excited for them, but couldn't deny my sadness that we wouldn't have many more easy moments like this one; they would have to be planned.

I said as much to her. "I know," she replied, putting a hand on my shoulder and pulling me closer to her on the Lutyens bench where we sat. We both heard a rustling in the jasmine hedge behind us and turned as one. I was half expecting to see a bobcat emerge, but that wild friend would never make such a mistake in the light of day.

"I hope it wasn't a possum," Makeda said.

"Or a rat!" I shivered.

Instead, we saw a twitch of gray ears, and Bobby the Bunny emerged, hopping tentatively toward us. The rabbit, possibly an escapee from some family's home after one of those impulsively dumb acts of Easter gift giving, had been appearing here for about a month, undoubtedly drawn by the baby carrots and parsley that Sister F. insisted on leaving out for him, along with a small stainless steel bowl of water. Bobby had fattened over that period to the point when I didn't panic for him when Callay ran towards him, which of course she liked to do. Makeda rose up to fetch some parsley from the house and handed the bunch to my girl. Callay set it down on the dymondia, and Bobby hastened toward it, stopping to make sure the coast was clear, then grabbed some in his mouth and ran toward the bush. Callay clapped her hands. "He yikes it, Moomah!"

"He certainly does, my love. If he is a he. We don't actually know if Bobby is a boy or a girl." She looked puzzled, but for once didn't favor us with one of her eternal "whys." Instead, she stood, arms akimbo, and watched, fascinated, as he chomped away at his parsley.

Makeda laughed. "Perhaps little Bobby is actually Babette!" Callay *did* respond to that one. "Babbit the Wabbit." We chuckled. Shel Silverstein would be proud.

I turned to Makeda. "I hope the party doesn't scare the hell out of Bobby."

She considered the possibility and then ventured the opinion that he'd be smart enough to stay clear once the crowd began to arrive. I was planning a full-out birthday bash for Callay, and Makeda was already one of my biggest helpers. She'd insisted on contributing to the menu some of her own favorite childhood dishes, including *shiro wat* (chickpea flour stew), *gomen* (collard greens), and, of course, the ubiquitous *injera* at the bottom of the plate to scoop up the rest of the food. Dhani had already offered to bring both a beef and a vegetarian curry, spiced mildly because of the children, along with her signature rice pudding, the one that had reunited Sammie and me when we'd had our awful rift after the death of my father. And Gwen had committed to baking some of her amazing vegan chocolate chip cookies, partly as an act of defiance against the inevitable Krispy Kremes that my team would show up with. The rest of the menu would be filled out by Gelson's Market, whose cold salads and Victor Benes carrot birthday cakes were my sole contributions whenever I contributed to a potluck. Have I mentioned what a lousy cook I am?

I plucked at the piping on my floral seat cushion, hoping Callay's party would feel special for her. I couldn't remember having had one of my own as a child and realized that Father's hatred of actual children and Mother's alcoholism probably precluded whatever normalcy might have been offered to the kind of exceptionally odd child I'd been. And then, one thing leading to another as they do, tears filled my eyes.

Makeda, as if by magic, but undoubtedly more by the sensitivity of one who'd mothered orphans, said softly, "*Ihite.*" Sister. That word still had the power to move me deeply. What would it be like to have Callay move through life with a biological one of those?

"Yes?"

She put a hand on my own as if to calm its restlessness. "It is hard, I know. I, too, would give anything to have my mother see my child grow and blossom. But we must be mothers to each other now."

Like a child, I added, "And sisters."

She nodded sagely. "And sisters. And dearly beloved friends."

I grabbed her into as tight a hug as I could, feeling the beginnings of my own bump butt up against hers.

Eventually, she loosened herself. "I saw that Adam was annoyed when you told us of your bun, but I was actually happy that you announced your baby to all of us. It reminded me of how it was back in Ethiopia. The family, the tribe, it is everything. There are no secrets from those who care about you."

Which brought me back to those awful secrets about Assefa that I'd shared with her in Tikil Dingay. Could they have actually become part of the powerful bond between us, much as dark matter served as the glue of the universe?

"But," I replied, "why did you wait so long to tell me about your own decision to get pregnant, and then when it happened ...?"

"I wanted to make sure it would last."

That one stopped me in my tracks. "It's terrifying, isn't it?"

"It is. It matters too much."

"Maybe it matters just right. Maybe that's what's wrong with our world. We don't allow ourselves to know how much everything matters."

But then she laughed.

"What?"

"Matter or not, have you considered the irony?"

I cocked my head. "What do you mean?"

"Assefa's women—you, me, Lemlem— we are all with child at the very same time."

Chapter Twenty-two

PLANNING A PARTY for a two-year-old is something of an oxymoron, for what can be planned about the behavior of a tenacity of toddlers, a katzenjammer of kids, a lollygag of little ones? Knowing that we'd be working against unpredictable moods, incomplete potty training, and diverse nap times, I made sure to invite plenty of grownups to balance things out—at least theoretically, since most of the adults I knew were nearly as odd duckish as yours truly.

Besides, I wanted everyone who'd so far impacted her destiny to be here for Callay. I'd recently read of a practice amongst some indigenous tribes of naming circles that would spontaneously sing to the newborn its tribal name, which might later be sung to that soul should the person fall afoul of his or her true nature. I wanted Callay to have a full circle, one that would know her at every step of her way.

And selfishly, I wanted one for me. With any luck, we were about to take a step in our progress toward Dreamization that would make me the target of renewed hatred on the part of Big Oil, Cacklers, and all-around Science Haters, the latter of which there were way too many these days. I wanted my people on my side.

Here was our guest list (besides, of course, Makeda and Melky and Sofiya and Melesse and Sally and Lukie, all of whom proved to be absolute bricks on the big day—especially Lukie, who'd put up with cleaning up after this growing, eclectic household without an ounce of complaint or resentment and was the living embodiment of why the anti-immigrant crowd was simply dead wrong). I'm happy to report that virtually everyone said yes:

1. The small gaggle of children who Callay played with at Grant Park; Sister F. regularly took her there to help socialize her as a prelude to preschool, though that was never going to be a problem with this girl. Their parents were invited, too, of course, and most of them seemed to spend half their time in our bathrooms helping their kiddles go potty and the other half bending our ears about how gorgeous those bathrooms were and asking for the name of our contractor.

2. The physics team, plus Saffron Malamud, who, bless her, was about to become Saffron Ballantine.

3. Stanley and Gwennie, bursting with pride.

4. Sister Flatulencia, bursting with effluvium.

5. Halley Smith-Robinson and Maxfield Robinson, carrying half a library of children's books, including Halley's newest, *My Name is Bobby the Bunny*.

6. Sammie and Amira, the latter of whom managed to put me off all over again by dubiously eyeing my belly as if something distasteful lurked inside.

7. Aadita and Arturo, whose tight jeans and equally tight-fit burgundy T-shirt announced that he'd managed to keep up his remarkable six pack over the years; thank God he was good to Aadita, as his getup was just this side of male calendar-ish.

8. Ignacio and Dhani, but we had to make do without Really-and-Truly-No-Longer-a-Baby-Angelina, who was in Texas, volunteering with RAICES, helping to reunite asylum-seeking parents with their babies who'd been

kidnapped by ICE; that our country held children captive in for-profit warehouses that were barely a step above concentration camps was too painful to think about; that Angelina not only thought about it but actually did something filled us all with gratitude and admiration.

9. Siri Sajan, resplendent in her flowing white *kurti* and turban.

10. Assefa and Lemlem and a now-crawling Ife, constantly fussed over by an overprotective Abeba.

11. And finally, Cesar and Gladys, who I'd prayed would show up dressed respectively as male and female, though I had promised myself not to pinch or bang if they didn't; in matter of fact, they arrived looking like the classic young couple, so I didn't have to test my resolve.

Tom and Katrina shocked me by showing up with Good Time Charlie and Hot Sauce, though they had the good sense to bring them straight to the backyard via our back gate lest they give Buster a heart attack. They nearly gave me one, as I was terrified of killing the canines in our upcoming trial run and tried my best to keep an emotional distance from them. Undoubtedly for his own reasons, Bobby the Bunny kept his own distance, too; the rabbit wisely stayed out of sight until the next day. Nonetheless, the dogs had a ball, both literally and figuratively, and I could at least comfort myself by including them in my later conclusion that a good time was had by all.

Not that there weren't a few hitches along the way, but they were mostly in my head and of my own making.

We'd decided to start the party at 3:00 to ensure that most of the kids would have napped by then. The sun was still strong, and the parents slathered sunscreen on their children as soon as they arrived. The little ones played Go Fish and *acoocoolu*, led of course by Sofiya and Melesse. We'd made the exception of allowing the girls to invite their friend Hector at the last minute, and I noticed that this time he pronounced *anelgam* like a pro.

I was glad of the size of our backyard, which easily accommodated the assembled crowd of nearly fifty. Ignacio had done himself proud, artfully arranging twinkly colored lights amidst the jasmine, leveling the dymondia so no one would trip, dead-heading the Austins and the lavender inflorescences, and trimming the creeping thyme to trail just so across the peach-colored pavers so that people kicked up the sweet scent as they trod on them. From my perch on one of the Luytens benches, I saw Ignacio eyeing the luscious blue Endless Summer hydrangeas we'd planted just last year. He looked like he was itching to pull out his pruning shears. I strolled over and told him to stop it.

He threw back his head, compressing his double chin into the single version I'd once known, and laughed heartily, reminding me what a handsome man he still was. "*Ai*, Fleuricita, you know me too well."

"Have you heard from Angelina?"

"Yes. She is very busy, working way into the night. What the government is doing to these children—"

"I know," I sighed. "I can't bear thinking about it. But we have to force ourselves to. And your girl? Well, she's my hero." I gestured at the children making wide circles nearby, laughing, shouting. "*This* is what *all* kids should be doing."

"Yes, but we know that life is not always this kind."

It was true. But sometimes, we humans had a choice in the matter. I looked at Sofiya and Melesse, on the edge of despair when Makeda adopted them and nearly in the clutches of Al Shabaab before she brought them to America. I said a silent prayer that they would obtain their citizenship before the sociopaths took possession of our country and held it hostage to xenophobia.

Just then, Dhani hurried over, asking Ignacio to help her move one of the long food tables out of the sun. Her manner was harried, her thick salt-and-pepper-hair rebelliously straying from a loosening bun. Her dimpled cheeks shone with perspiration, and the lips I'd seen Father chew at were stained the color of blood. I had to bat back the temptation to pinch myself. Some scenes we can never fully banish from our minds.

I stayed where I was, watching Makeda's girls ushering a crawling Ife across the thyme, Callay tripping after them. I wanted to run and giggle with them, but I was a grown woman now, wasn't I? It wasn't just that my body was heavier these days, my spirit had taken the hit of these dark times.

And besides, there was a corn as sharp as a pebble on the side of my left little toe. I bent over and pulled off my Tory Burch ballet flat—berating myself that I could probably free a couple of captive children for the price of it—and tried to readjust it so that the bump didn't meet the seam of my nylon ankle sock. I became suddenly aware that the offending strip of leather was once part of a cow. Sammie and Aadita, both vegans, never failed to remind me that gassy ruminants contributed nearly twenty percent to greenhouse gas emissions. I really did need to stop eating meat. But it tasted so good.

Before I knew it, Adam was by my side. "What is it?"

"Cows."

"Huh?" I tried explaining my melancholy thought process.

"At your daughter's birthday party? Come on, Fleur." He paused, looking down. "I thought there was something going on with your foot." How was it that he'd sensed my pain from hundreds of yards away?

"There was. A corn."

"Not fun."

I smiled. "No, it's not. But look." I gestured toward the children. Sofiya and Melesse and Callay and Ife and Hector now had a train of toddlers behind them.

Adam and I stood silently, like a pair of mature trees surveying new seedlings sprouting up around them.

He put a hand on my belly. "Any movement?"

"Not yet. Believe me, you'll be the first to know." I felt a slight breeze against my cheek. "But it should be soon." I gestured toward our girl, running, falling down, picking herself up, running again. "I wonder how she'll handle not being the only show in town."

But now Callay fell victim to a dramatic bout of hiccups, the inevitable price she paid when she laughed a little too hard, sometimes to the point of vomiting. We looked at each other. Adam shrugged, then went over and scooped her into his arms, bringing her to me—still giggling and hiccupping. Holding her tightly (and glad I could still carry her), I found her sippy cup in the kitchen and held it to her perfect, Cupid's bow lips. It helped calm the spasms, and she nuzzled my neck before asking to be set down. I did so reluctantly. She smelled of thyme. Or more accurately, she smelled of heaven.

Following her out the kitchen door, I made the rounds of the little groups of chatting grownups. Some conversations looked so earnest—Gwen and Abeba in a shady corner, Gwennie leaning on her cane; Dhani in what seemed like deep communion with a flashing-eyed mommy wearing a *hijab*. But then I saw Siri Sajan and Aadita slip into the latters' conversation, so I decided it was safe to join them. They were talking about Pema Chodron. The stranger warmly introduced herself to me as Parveen Barelvi, mother of Umar, then replied to something Siri Sajan had just said about Chodron's contention that we can learn important things even from people we detest the most.

"So what can I learn from Trump?" Dhani replied with some asperity. And then she flushed and put a hand on Siri Sajan's arm. "I'm sorry, but I ..."

Siri Sajan was turning a rather beet red color herself. "No, you're right. I didn't mean to sound so sanctimonious."

But something stirred in me, and I interjected, "No. I think Pema Chodron's right. I have to be honest. I think something in me just loves to hate Trump. Gets off on it. As if I finally have an excuse to be out and out disgusted by someone. To make fun of him. Focus on things like his beady eyes and small hands."

I hadn't realized that Sammie and Amira had joined us, drawn perhaps by the increasing heat of my tone. Sister Flatulencia had found her way here, too.

Sister F. commented, unusually forcefully, "How much we love to hate the other. It's why I left the Church, you know. 'Hate the sin, but love the sinner?' In real life, there was an awful lot more hatred of the sinner than I could stand."

"That's right," Sam chimed in. "That's exactly what Jung meant about the shadow. Offloading our own darkness onto someone else.

He thought we could contribute to the healing of the world by withdrawing our own pieces of the collective mess."

"Yes," Amira put in dubiously. "But isn't it one thing to think something and another to put others through torture over the horrid things we think?"

I laughed. "I guess you're not of the Jimmy Carter school?"

She gave me a blank look.

"Equating having sinful thoughts with being a sinner."

"Hardly," she shot back. "If you'd seen the misery I witnessed firsthand in Afghanistan, with the Muslim attitudes to women…"

At that point, it became clear that I wasn't the only one becoming uncomfortable. All eyes traveled to Parveen Barelvi, whose jaw had tightened perceptibly. We'd wandered into a landmine without even realizing it, and no one felt safe taking a further step.

I nearly laughed aloud at what came next. Cesar and Gladys shyly joined our growing circle. "Did I hear you mention Jimmy Carter?" Cesar asked. "Gladys and I volunteered last weekend at one of Habitat for Humanity's Restores in LaVerne."

As the rest of the group peppered the pair with questions and praise, I had a chance to meditate on my history of guilt, resentment, and contempt toward Cesar, who had to be one of the most full-of-surprises people I'd ever known. No question about it: Pema Chodron was right. My adoptive sibling was certainly becoming something of a tutor to me.

But at that moment a gaggle of children commandeered our serious conversation by snaking right through us. Laughing, we made way for them, then began to join in at the end of the snake, joined now by the rest of the party winding sinuously across the garden, paper cups of wine and Perrier in hand. Someone—I think it was Hector's mom—had the idea of turning it into a mass Hokey Pokey, at which point I fled the yard and ended up in one of the upstairs bathrooms, sobbing my eyes out over all those now absent from this world: Mother, to begin with, but then Nana and Grandfather and even Father. They all became markers of the tenuousness of our hold on life. I found myself on my knees, the white shag rug thrown across the turquoise-tiled floor my prayer rug as I put the plaintive wish to whatever god or goddess or web or butterfly who ruled the universe that my children would live long and fruitful lives, knowing at least as much love as I had, once I'd learned to open my heart to the voidishness of loss.

Some cries are not good cries. It wasn't a good cry that I had when Grandfather died. Nor was it cleansing to sob after Mother's death. It certainly didn't feel good to fall apart after listening to Makeda describe her genital mutilation. And the snotty mess I made of my face after seeing photos of oil-drowned pelicans following the gulf oil spill felt anything but soothing. But now, at his moment, standing at the sink and pressing a cold washcloth against my reddened eyes, I felt calmer than I had in weeks. Who knew how long it would last, but what I felt was something that resembled peace. I removed my painful shoes, placed them neatly side-by-side in front of the bathtub, descended the stairs, and walked across the soft carpet of creeping thyme in bare feet. I saw Makeda and Melky laughing with Assefa and Lemlem and felt compassion for Abeba, who stood slightly away from the four of them, holding Ife and screwing up her lips so tightly that they resembled a prune. Life was hard on us humans.

But not so much for dogs. At least not for now, anyway. Good Time Charlie and Hot Sauce were busily hurtling themselves around to catch sticks thrown by Tom and Katrina and a very enthusiastic Bob Ballantine, Saffron trailing behind him like a worshipping puppy herself.

After Callay had consumed in its entirety the full first slice of her birthday carrot cake; after she actually laughed when Hector appended to the "Happy Birthday" song the words, "You look like a monkey, and you smell like one, too;" after the children had battered to smithereens a piñata shaped like the devil, wicked black horns and all; after I'd hugged and shaken the hands of more mommies and daddies than I could imagine, whose names I'd never remember; after we'd put our exhausted but happy daughter to bed without even bothering to bathe her; after Assefa rang the bell shortly afterwards and I opened the door to his desperation to find his lost cellphone; and after he departed a second time, having found it embedded in a jasmine bush, right next to one of the devil's horns; after he'd surprised us both out in the garden by telling me he'd cried to see our daughters play together, planting a goodbye kiss that aimed for my cheek but made contact instead with my lips; Adam and I found our way to each other and collapsed on the queen's settee, surrounded by people we loved. The original gang was pretty much all here, and then some:

1. Amir and Tom and Katrina and Gunther, minus Bob (and Saffron—I wondered if she'd get lucky tonight on his Wookie).

2. Stanley and a very sleepy Gwen, who kept nodding off whenever the conversation turned to our big moment tomorrow (and yes, I'd foolishly promised our Silicone Valley funder that we'd test Dreamization on the dogs the very day after my daughter's party).

3. Sammie (solo at long last, as Amira had to fly off at an ungodly hour the next morning to convince her boss at the BBC that she needed another month to complete her editing).

4. A disheveled Dhani, who couldn't be persuaded to sit down with us until she'd finished cleaning up nearly all the dirty dishes with Lukie.

5. Ignacio, still slightly sweaty from deadheading and pruning the hydrangeas, which he couldn't keep his hands off once the backyard was vacant and bathed in moonlight.

6. Sister Flatulencia, who sat pretty quietly in the corner with her rosary beads, reminding us of her presence every now and then with a particularly potent silent but deadly.

7. Makeda, Melky, and Sally, the latter lying prone across the carpet with her head in Makeda's lap while Melky stroked her dark, silken hair, prompting me to wonder idly, and certainly not seriously, if she'd get that three-way after all.

Needless to say, I was pretty pooped and more than a little anxious about the next day, but the timing felt somehow right. With any luck, the beginning of my daughter's third year on the planet would coincide with the beginnings of a human history independent of fossil fuels.

At one point, Adam hauled a duvet downstairs from our bedroom, and Sammie and I lay together under it. He even persuaded Lukie to brew some hot chocolate for everyone, and I had the joy of turning my head to see my belly sister's ecstatic smile accented by a whipped cream and chocolate mustache. Oh, how well that husband of mine knew me. I had to control myself lest I ask Sammie to spend the night, but she left soon afterward "to help Amira pack," giving me one of the warmest hugs she'd given me in ages. My body relaxed into the certainty that the world had been set right again.

The team took off shortly afterward, insisting they needed at least some semblance of sleep to clear their minds for the big day. It was more than a little poignant to see Katrina wake the dogs, who'd earned their sleep this time by running and jumping, rather than having it foisted upon them by induced narcolepsy.

Adam and I walked Stanley and Gwennie out to their car. A heavy fog had appeared out of nowhere, and Stanley guided his sister carefully across the wet grass. Even with her cane, she was visibly limping. Especially with this fog, I knew her flagging eyesight wasn't helping her physical balance any. Once she'd been safely stowed inside, Stanley affixed her seatbelt solicitously. She'd been right. He was the best brother ever. If Adam and I had a son, would he be this solicitous with Callay? I insisted that the Fiskes roll down their windows so I could plant kisses on each of their foreheads.

By that time, the fog had coalesced into a moderate mist. My lashes grew heavy with damp. Adam took me by the arm as we walked back toward the house, where fairy lights illuminated a purple sign above the front door that read: "Callou Callay! Happy Frabjous Birthday!" Adam left me for a moment to flick off the battery switch on the side of the house. Everything in front of us went dark, save for the craftsman-style porch light. And yet the world still glowed.

As one, we looked up. Fingers of cloud stretched across the largest moon I'd ever seen. The cloud cover failed to dim its luminous presence, which dominated nearly half the nighttime sky. How was it that humans had actually found a way to walk on that distant orb? Not for the first time, I felt breathless at the miracle of human science stabbing in the dark with such remarkable precision. No matter how tomorrow turned out, it would be a beginning. One way or another, between Amir and Tom and Gunther's brilliant number crunching, Katrina and Stanley and Adam's devil's advocate logic, Sally's etymological expertise, my own crazy hunches, and the implausible hope in all our hearts, we'd find a way to harness dark matter to facilitate human movement at will and need across the globe. And perhaps someday, I might actually be freed from this building sense of pressure, this metronomic command: *hurry, hurry, hurry!*

Chapter Twenty-three

WHEN I DASHED out the door the next day, I wondered if Sister Flatulencia had picked up my own nerves. The house nearly levitated from her effluvium. Yet she was playing so sweetly with my daughter, I dared not say a thing. Callay was in especially bright spirits, calling out to me, "Have a good day, Moomah!" I knew it hadn't hurt that I'd taken extra cozy time with her in bed that morning, singing all her favorite songs, since I knew Adam, Sally, and I would probably come home much later than usual, quite possibly after her bedtime. "Eensy Weensy Spider" played in my mind pretty much all the way to Caltech.

Adam and Sally had already driven to the lab in Sally's Jeep, and they were speaking intently with Stanley and Bob when I entered. I could sense the same blend of excitement and tension in their voices that I was feeling myself. As usual, a ray of sunlight poured through the one crooked blind covering the long bank of windows. It aimed itself straight for a curled up Good Time Charlie, who snored loudly as Katrina kneeled rather awkwardly at his side, somberly petting him. I knew she was terribly anxious over whether he and Hot Sauce would survive our experiment today. For some reason, I found myself recalling my misreading of Fidel's hand-lettered yard sign just days before he'd murdered Chin Hwa, thinking at the time that it had said "Curb Your God" rather than "Curb Your Dog." Neither one of our rescued lab dogs deserved any more curbing than they'd already suffered at Semel.

Katrina finally looked up at me. We exchanged rather ghastly smiles. She rose and approached me for a hug.

"Hey, don't I rate a hug, too?" objected Tom, only now emerging from beneath a lab table where Hot Sauce snuggled on a blanket. Tom bonked his head on one of the table's angled legs as he rose up, and we all laughed nervously until, rubbing where he'd hit it, he reassured us that it probably wasn't fatal.

The room fell silent. "Oh, Christ," Tom murmured, hurrying over and clasping me with extra strength as he claimed his hug.

"No worries," I said. "In a way, it reminds me that she's somehow with us today."

Stanley, the inveterate atheist, blinked a few times, but wisely said nothing.

As Tom let go, I felt Adam grab me from behind. I knew it was he because of his Campbell's chicken soup B.O. He whispered in my ear, "Of course, she is, my love. They're all here, cheering us on." I felt certain he was right. And they weren't the only ones. I sensed ancestors all the way back to the Mitochondrial Eve wishing us well on our attempt to keep the human gene pool going.

I began checking and rechecking our equipment, making sure everything was properly set up. Sally fussed over her carton of butterfly enzymes, ensuring they were at just the right temperature and ready to be inserted into their spray bottles, fresh and potent. Proper preparation was everything at a moment like this.

The dogs both woke up, barking, when Amir and Gunther burst noisily into the room, Amir full of apologies that he'd initially forgotten the dog treats when Gunther had picked him up, Gunther explaining that he'd actually had a flat tire on their way back to get them.

Muttering, "Thank God, he had a spare," Amir waved the dogs' favorite peanut butter jerky treats over their heads, and they leapt up to snatch them, their teeth rather alarmingly sharp and snappy. Amir gave us all a sly grin, saying to the pups, "Enjoy it, guys. It might just be your last supper."

Katrina flung out a curt, "Don't," and Amir apologized, but their little contretemps couldn't compete with Gunther's manic enthusiasm. He leapt over to what we'd informally dubbed our Magic Machine (but had already been formally patented as the Caltech Spacetime Staging Center, Series 1, Model 1), a complicated gizmo that Gwennie might well decry, except for its intended purpose. It was purposely a round-edged, rather than industrially angular-looking contraption, but nonetheless a bulky stand-in for the nanoparticle lapel pin that I hoped would one day replace its launching function. From the outside, it looked unlike any fictional time travel machine I'd read about or seen in a film, especially since—in honor of the generations of children we hoped to save with it—I'd had it painted in the shades of robin's egg blue, buttercream, apricot, and deep forest green that decorated Callay's bedroom. Not only that, Katrina, our resident artist, had drawn the mock-up for its logo according to my own specifications. Right above the machine's full title appeared an image of a monarch butterfly alighting on a Carding Mill rose. The board of Caltech had initially objected, but I'd discovered that one's negotiating position is vastly improved by having been the youngest recipient of the Prize. After all, we were potentially offering our school a vast reservoir of future income and prestige.

No doubt about it, this was big, as was the machine itself. We'd purposely had it constructed to be much larger than the dogs, the main section, which I'd designated as "the womb," was a full seven feet by seven feet, and we'd had the windowed inner capsule insulated with industrial-grade, transparent cushion wrap in case its vibration as it sent its traveler off for a black hole's event horizon jiggled its passenger. The machine wasn't a vehicle, but instead, as its title suggested, would serve as a containing launching pad for the prospective spacetime traveler.

But as much as we'd tried to anticipate at least some of the potential hazards, the implications and consequences of what we were about to attempt were as unfathomable as landing humans on the moon had been in a previous era. There were some questions I stayed quiet about. They kept me awake at night precisely because they had no conceivable answer. I'd worried earlier on about the UV exposure issue, which neither Adam nor the rest of our team could

find any way to address until we were able to study some living subjects who'd actually returned. But if our subjects survived their transit
with no ill effects on their physical health, how would human life—
not just here on earth, but in our relationship with the cosmos—be
altered? What might come of purposely approaching the mystery of
what couldn't be seen directly by any object of measurement, certainly not by the human eye? Might the mystery itself be changed by the
encounter?

But now was hardly the moment for such preoccupations. It was
crunch time, where practicality was king. Our process included two
primary components. The first was the most complicated, based on
my conclusion that cellular black holes were actually fractals of their
cosmic counterparts. Thanks to a continued reflection on my experiences of Zeki's death and Callay's birth, it had dawned on me that it
was in the event horizons of C-Voids that the constant energetic exchange of dark and light matter that constituted life occurred. Our
water bears had pretty much supported my hypothesis that activating
a living creature's C-Voids and then aiming that subject through
spacetime to just the very edge of a black hole's gravitational pull actually bounces them back to earth like a boomerang, much as our
dark moods often bounce back to a greater serenity after we've hit
our true depths.

The aiming process itself had been arrived at through a most
rigorous series of computations utilizing arithmetic fractals of the
Fibonacci sequence. Our preliminary success with the moss piglets
left us wowed by the exquisite symmetry and stunning reliability of
the physical universe. We needed those moments of transcendence.
Much has been said—quite accurately, I'm afraid—about the banality
of evil, but the dullness of much scientific research is less widely
known. I'd said to the team more than once that I could get down on
my knees for the patience with which they pursued their efforts, for
truly nothing would have been achieved without it.

I said it again now, but Gunther would have none of it. He
sought out the first of the small nasal sprayers that Sally had prepared. "Come on!" he cried, his bad eye making strabismic circuits
like the earth circling its sun. "Let's make history!"

Part two of our operation: those nasal sprayers, actually more like misters, containing the activating enzymes of dead butterflies, which allowed an animate body—in the coming case, Good Time Charlie—to essentially liquefy like a caterpillar enough to endure the decomposition and recomposition of Dreamization. The Magic Machine had its own misters that would hopefully boost the more direct blast of the nasal spray with a more diffuse absorption by the subject's skin. If we succeeded, we could all thank Mother for initiating me into the underworld and Father for his elegant demonstration of the heretofore missing piece of the puzzle. Life is nothing if not replete with irony.

Saying a silent prayer to both my parents, I asked Amir to take Hot Sauce into the next room so he didn't get unduly spooked, told Katrina to put a leash on Good Time Charlie, instructed Bob to turn on the machine to warm it up, and suggested we put it to a vote who would actually trigger the timer once Katrina had administered the mist and Tom had coaxed an unleashed Good Time Charlie into place inside.

I took a deep breath when the team responded unanimously with a loud and emphatic, "You! You do it!"

And so we began.

After all these years of work, the whole process, from setting the timer to the automatic unlocking of the Magic Machine, would take a whole of 3.14159265359 minutes. We'd discovered that, not unlike the Fibonacci sequence, pi was transcendental in more ways than one, and it felt particularly meaningful to all of us that we were employing a mathematical constant whose value had been affirmed and reaffirmed from the ancient Egyptians and Babylonians all the way up to Heisenberg and, now, ourselves.

The room was as still as a church from the time our sweet little dog disappeared—Yes! He actually did!—to the moment when three melodious pings (copied, I might add, from the audio signals of our clothes dryer back at home) went off. And lo, right on schedule, Good Time Charlie reappeared! A collective gasp of relief and joy went up, and Katrina leapt forward to gently slide our subject out.

As he emerged, tail wagging, Tom obviously couldn't resist. He asked, "Did you have a good time, Charlie?"

But none of us laughed, and Tom himself fell silent. We looked around at one another, eyes like saucers. For once, this group of highly verbal scientists had been rendered speechless. It was as if we'd been collectively holding our breaths ever since our work had first been validated by the Prize.

Stanley, our team's primogenitor, had removed his glasses and was wiping the wetness from them with the bottom of his cotton shirt. Katrina and Tom hugged each other like there was no tomorrow, even though what we'd just accomplished might actually signify quite the opposite. Moving around Good Time Charlie and squinting at him from various angles as if he'd never seen him before, Amir kept rubbing his love-patched chin, his bright brown eyes ablaze with wonder. Gunther's angular body hovered over the lectern a few feet away; perspiration dripped from his forehead, and his pale skin glowed, his energy vibrating as if he was about to take off like a helium balloon. Leaning against the front of the lectern, Bob looked all of a gee whiz twelve-years-old as he repeatedly blinked. I saw that Sally stood back a few paces from the rest of the group, as if uncertain that she belonged here, but of course we couldn't have done this without her. Adam, who I now knew I'd definitely run into a burning building to save, stood by my side and stared at me with such love and admiration I could hardly bear it.

And then there was a burst of vigorous movement. Charlie started contorting himself to scratch his rump with his hind leg.

Gunther commented drily, "Oh hell, do you think there are fleas on the other side?"

That one did get a laugh. Actually, Bob's response was more of a snort. I looked at him and had a private chuckle of my own. He really was just a Wookie.

Seemingly enlivened by the laughter, Good Time Charlie shook his whole body luxuriantly, as if he'd just had a bath. Then—just as suddenly—he settled down, his chin on Katrina's shoe, and fell fast asleep.

With a quick flick of an eye, I noted on the face of the Magic Machine that it was 1:07:31 p.m. Tom had taken great care to design the machine's clock, set to time each second of the experiment so that it could be replicated with exactitude.

It occurred to me that it was Callay's naptime. I pictured her wrapped in her soft flannel pajamas, her lips pursed as if pondering a profound question, her long lashes fluttering against her soft cheeks like butterfly wings. The fate of all of the children of our world rested on what could be done to mitigate the full blast of climate change. Was it too late? Dared we hold out hope that what we'd just done might help turn back the dreadful tide?

At that very moment, I saw something flit past the gap in the window blinds. Was it a butterfly? I couldn't be sure, but if so, I was convinced it was Father. A vision came to me of Jung and Pauli slapping their knees like farmers and throwing back their heads in laughter, as if I'd been given the only possible answer to a supremely ridiculous question.

I turned back to my team. They were waiting for me to comment on our victory and seemed to have all moved closer to me. I noticed that Bob had a whole dusting of dandruff on one shoulder of his dark green shirt. Why just the one? I still couldn't believe I'd actually slept with him. Life was a great mystery. How many seemingly inconsequential moments and experiences added up to something amazing, something transformational?

And still, our little group waited. Stanley, needless to say, was hopping around like an impatient frog, if a somewhat arthritic one. Katrina twirled her long braid, and Tom was squeezing her shoulder. These people were as beautiful to me as a school of dolphins, overflowing with intelligence, curiosity, compassion.

Finally, with a broad grin, I obliged them. "Well, what are you waiting for? Somebody, go and get Hot Sauce and see if he can do what Good Time Charlie did."

I'd barely finished my sentence when I heard a loud sniff and saw Gunther leap into the machine after setting off the timer, slamming the machine shut behind him. He disappeared in a flash.

I cried out, "Gunther! No!" But he was gone.

Our faces fell. No one said a thing. No one *could* say a thing. We'd just witnessed a catastrophe. I struggled for what felt like an eternity to take in the insanity of what had just occurred, only gradually becoming aware of a pounding at the lab's locked door. When the nature of the sound finally registered, I managed to eke out an anguished, "Won't somebody deal with that?"

Amir, who'd been leaning against a lab table with his head in his hands, dragged his feet across the room and began to shout, "Go the fuck away!" until a voice expostulated loudly in a familiar Swedish accent. Amir flung open the door, and Gunther bounded into the room, beaming despite the fact that his face and arms bore long red scrapes and he seemed to have lost the hair on the right side of his head.

His excitement had spun his wandering eye into full locomotion "I guess we'll have to make a few adjustments for size."

What the hell? I couldn't believe what I was seeing. The rest of the team was obviously just as dumbfounded as I was. Amir was scratching his head like his favorite chimpanzee, and Katrina's jaw looked like it was about to drop all the way to the floor. "Gunther, I could kill you," I cried. Then—as I saw his terrible hurt—I hastened to add, "I could kill you ... and I love you!" He grinned broadly and seemed to be trembling with excitement and who knew what else?

"Man," exclaimed Amir, as he stepped over to high five Gunther. "What was it like, bro?"

Gunther furrowed his brow. "It was like what people describe when they nearly die. Except it wasn't as if just my own life was passing in front of me, but lives of people who'd lived before, all the way back to the beginning and then right back up to the present."

"The event horizon," Stanley murmured. "Hawking was right, but the objects don't have to actually pass inside the black hole to have their information stored. Near contact must accomplish the same thing."

"But then," Gunther went on as if he were straining to recall a receding dream, "it was as if I had some kind of choice to make." He shook his head. "I don't know what it was, but the next thing I knew I was in the hall and desperate to be let inside."

I put up a hand. "No more, guys. We're going to need to give Gunther here—and Good Time Charlie, too—a thorough physical, and then we'll debrief Gunther fully. And objectively. I'm as thrilled as you are, but let's not contaminate his recollections."

I looked over at Adam. He nodded at me, his eyes and nose reddening with tears. I could almost see his wheels turning, remembering the raw, clueless young girl that he'd first tutored in physics over fifteen years ago. He stepped forward and whispered in my ear, "You've done it, Fleur. You and your fear of the void and your meticulous mind have driven this baby every step of the way."

Despite my words about objectivity, that mind of mine was whirling, my nervous system on fire. Unable to contain myself, I did a little two-step and spun around a few times for good measure. "I love you, Gunther, and I love you, Adam, and—well, frankly— I love you all!" For a moment I was filled with such strong emotion I could hardly bear it. I thought of little Sweet Pea percolating inside my belly, of Callay fast asleep in her crib, dreaming her very own dreams. The features of Sofiya, Melesse, and Ifa filed before my mind's eye.

"But we haven't got a moment to waste. Gunther, if there's a God, I hope He, She, or It grants you eternal life. You've just moved us a couple of years ahead of where we thought we were." I turned back to our Magic Machine, which—since Gunther had returned outside its confines— had most likely just been made obsolete. Now that we knew we could actually propel a human being through the void and bring him back again—and at a new location!—I felt an even greater sense of urgency. The sooner we managed to replicate this marvel, the sooner we could submit it for peer review and the sooner scientists across the globe could contribute their own insights and ingenuity to a project that would no longer be ours alone.

But at this moment, the responsibility still rested on our shoulders.

"Let's get to work, people," I cried. "We've got a Titanic to turn around, and who knows how many future generations are riding on it?"

Katrina piped up, "Do you really think there's hope, Fleur?"

I blinked. An existential question if I ever heard one.

"Yeah," echoed Amir. "It's still a long way from what we've just witnessed to people traveling exactly where they want to go by pressing a lapel button."

They had every right to ask. Hadn't I myself been up to my ears in doubt nearly every step of the way? They'd sacrificed so much of their time and energy, foregone lucrative pay from the private sector, and exposed their reputations to vicious public attack, shaming, and disbelief.

How did any of us dare to hope? That elusive ingredient at the very bottom of all the evils piled into Pandora's *pithos*, or jar, was the very item that all those other evils seemed hell-bent on destroying, not unlike the Cacklers and their hollow-souled political enablers attacking anyone working in service to the survival of our species.

Certainly, our little miracle today seemed a pretty solid indication that we were on the right track. But the magic of our machine would have been nothing more than the wisp of an idea in an odd duck's mind without the dedicated group of souls who currently occupied this room. These amazing humans had given me their loyalty and trust. They'd supported my direction in life. They were the equivalent of my seven. Gunther, with his literally wandering eye and his bouts of depression and that wild impulsivity of his that had not only catalyzed this day's astonishing leap forward but had once led him to stand on a lab table to heretically declare in Swedish, "We are God!" The tenderness of Katrina and Tom that overflowed from their love for each other to spill toward animals of all sorts, including a couple of rejected lab mutts whom they worried about desperately, even as they gritted their teeth to include them in our trial run. Amir, math whiz extraordinaire, handsome as a movie star, but smitten with a rescued chimp with a predilection for flinging poop balls. Sally, with her paradoxical attractions to the bad boys of *Sons of Anarchy* and the delicately fluid royalty of the insect world. Bob the Wookie, collector of exotic shells and *Star Wars* memorabilia, a champion of sea life who had the courage to look darkness in the face and decry it. Stanley, with his great mind, his moral lapses, contrition, and wisdom, his goofy humor, and his generosity in turning around the destiny of a strange and lonely child. My very own Adam, my tutor in almost everything, the kindest of fathers and most devoted of friends, honest to a fault, whose openness about not being such a nice guy and willingness to continually hear my own embarrassingly not-so-nice perspectives only added to the depth of our bond and the erotic ecstasy of our life together.

All these companions that the Fates had assigned me, and those outside this room but forever in my heart, had given me something that, in my many years of struggling against the void, I'd never begun to imagine. They'd managed to convince this terribly slow learner that caring about life—and throwing all the dark and light of me into that caring—actually mattered. That if dark matter was truly the glue of the universe, then our own fragility and folly and clumsy fealty to one another and our own natures might actually bring about some salvation to our world. I nearly laughed. Wasn't it Sammie's abusive ex-boyfriend, Jacob, who'd offered me the key years ago in his description of *tikkun olam*? Wasn't that what all of us here had been up to with our clunky Magic Machine? We should have named it Repair of the World, Series 1, Model 1. I couldn't wait to come up with Series 2.

I looked at my team, my pals, my companions through the thick and thin of it, and answered from the very bottom of my own *pithos*, "Is there hope? I have to be honest with you. I have no idea. But with you glorious souls alive in this world, there is gratitude. Perhaps at this moment in time, it's actually gratitude we've been given to go on with. A gift from dying stars. Maybe—just maybe—that will be enough to give us the strength and courage to do what we need to do."

Silence. I became aware of the team staring at me. *Maybe? Did I really just say, "Maybe?"* Something pressing inside me simply wasn't satisfied. "Actually, guys—no maybes about it. This matters more than anything, and I think we all know it."

Then I grinned broadly, my heart at one with the task at hand. "And now, my darling odd ducks of this world, let's get cracking."

Sanctus

The new life stirred from sleep and shifted positions to amuse himself. There was just enough room to stretch his lengthening limbs over the venous cord, her covenant with him in his weightless world. He swayed to the liquid lilt of her voice, dipped a toe, just so, over here, thrust his elbow at an angle over there. Her body's rhythms were his rhapsody. She was his ocean, and she rocked him. Her heartbeat was his drum.

Again asleep, he dreamed miracles he'd not yet seen: hummingbirds and finches, hawks and mockingbirds and cardinals; they flew above him, tracing the sky's invisible web with their muscular wings. Trees and bushes offered leaves and berries to caterpillars and koalas, deer and squirrels and foxes. Down below, worms worked their fat bellies through the roots' slick soil. Their wavery patterns pleased him, and he smiled.

The Soul of the World laid her green hands on the soft blades of his shoulders and claimed him. "Let's keep it going, then, little one, long enough to redeem the stars' sacrifice. When the time comes, and I pray it will, may you and your generation assume the care of this earth, for there is no other like her. If you must have your tools, wield them as custodians, not conquerors. Bring the gift for witnessing that I planted in your species to the waiting cosmos, so that the vastness may know itself in the mirror of your eyes. Enjoy the blessings of your ancestors, who wish to see you find your very own fullness. Sanctus, Sanctus, Shekinah Sanctus. May it be so," said the Soul of the World.

May it be so.

Acknowledgements

No writer lives on words alone. My work on this book has been sustained by an Indra's Web's worth of love and support from Chris Heath; Claire, Tray, Tahlia, and Braden Noble; the many streams of my Karson clan and the British wing of my family; Constance Crosby; Janet Muff; Judy Altman; Nancy Mozur; Robin Wynslow; Alison Crowley; Jeanine Roose; Suzanne Ecker; Pamela Kirst; Carol Blake; the late Judie Harte and Fred Erwin; Frances Hatfield; Leah Shelleda; Deborah Howell and Neil Baylis; Cydny Rothe and Roy Kushel; Molly Jordan; Kathie Clarke; Wendy Wyman-McGinty; Christophe Le Mouël; Robin Palmer; Harriet Friedman; Jane Reynolds; JoAnn Culbert-Koehn; Daniel House; Patty Micciche; Sadie Mestman; Sofia Borges; Elizabeth Trupin-Pulli; the Kickass Kindness Council comprised of Carolyn Raffensperger, Alison Rose Levy, Gary Anderson, and David Eisenberg; Yvette Cantu Schneider; Susan Rodgers Hammond; Marcella and Jay Kerwin; and those Krazy Katzenjammers, Clothilde and Finn.

I'm profoundly touched by the generosity of artist Sylvia Fein in granting me permission to use her exquisite painting, "Bound Together," on this book's cover.

A big thank you to Smoky Zeidel and the rest of my Thomas-Jacob tribe, and especially to the marvelous Melinda Clayton—what a blessing it is to have a publisher who gets my voice and advocates for it so intelligently and wholeheartedly.

My mother Ethel Karson was an inspiring embodiment of the generosity of the world soul; I owe my love of this glorious planet, the earthiness of my humor, my trust in my calling to write, and my commitment to future generations to her, to my father Charles Karson, and to my bubbie and zayda Bessie and Chaim Wodlinger.

I'm deeply grateful to the friends and readers of Fleur, who've kept their ears close enough to the ground and their spirits close enough to the stars to hear her and appreciate her story. It's no small thing in this life to be heard.

And finally, I bow to that skipping spirit who beckoned to me over a decade ago, Fleur herself, who's been my joy and my teacher, driving home to me the values of failure, contrition, curiosity, transparency, and surrender to the great mystery of love. With Pandora's devils making hay on land, sea, and air, is there really any doubt whether we should pry open her *pithos* and attempt to earn its last ingredient by committing ourselves to the flourishing of future generations? The butterflies and the babies have already voted and continue to do so. Can we ourselves afford not to?

Also by Sharon Heath

The History of My Body, The Fleur Trilogy, Book 1
Tizita, The Fleur Trilogy, Book 2

About the Author

Sharon Heath writes fiction and non-fiction exploring the interplay of science and spirit, politics and pop culture. A certified Jungian Analyst in private practice and faculty member of the C.G. Jung Institute of Los Angeles, she served as guest editor of the special issue of *Psychological Perspectives*, "The Child Within/The Child Without." Her chapter, "The Church of Her Body," appears in the anthology *Marked by Fire: Stories of the Jungian Way*, and her chapter, "A Jungian Alice in Social Media Land: Some Reflections on Solastalgia, Kinship Libido, and Tribes Formed on Facebook," is included in *Depth Psychology and the Digital Age*. She has blogged for *The Huffington Post* and *TerraSpheres* and has given talks in the United States and Canada on topics ranging from the place of soul in social media to gossip, envy, secrecy, and belonging. She maintains her own blog at www.sharonheath.com.